STAGED
AND
SCRIPTED

STAGED AND SCRIPTED

DEMONIC MAGICIAN
BOOK TWO

Kleggt

Podium

Cover design by Dalia and Sam

ISBN: 978-1-0394-9555-5

Published in 2025 by Podium Publishing
www.podiumentertainment.com

Podium

STAGED
AND
SCRIPTED

CHAPTER ONE

Dressed for the Part

We had swept up the broken shards of the first area and only slightly bloodied our hands on the sharp points. Tore out parts of ourselves so the rougher edges could jell together. More surface area so we could be the perfect Party. Still early days, and things hadn't properly set before sinister shadows had already started to cling to us and try to break us apart. It was a good thing we lived in the limelight so that we could scour the darkness away.

With a deep breath, I adjusted my purple suit as I approached the village ahead. Took the top hat down to smooth back my brown hair. It was getting unkempt, but I didn't quite trust my troupe to smarten me up just yet. Hat back on and I looked the part. Or at least as good as it got. The dried handprint of blood across my forehead was itchy, and I was keen to get that washed off as soon as possible.

Hardly two steps into the second area of the continent and already the Crimson Shadow cast a dark gloom across our existence. I couldn't deny the name of the gang had some gravitas even if it was a little cliché. That said, if their leader—Lady in Red—was indeed a blood mage or vampire, then it made even more sense.

Did our Party need a name too? Perhaps I would float the idea with the other two when our tempers and imminent amount of violence were closer to base level. If there was one thing to rile us up, it was the sight of another area taken over by the Players that had fallen under the insidious banner of the ever-avoidant woman.

Now I was strolling up to the small village on my own. Fist clenched. Anger overrode any worry or trepidation about what could actually be lurking within. The signpost with three severed heads atop it was reasonably clear about what might be awaiting me. Still, if you knew the stakes, it was easier to tip the odds in your favor. Or so I told myself.

The cobblestone path led toward a group of small single-floor houses. White and dark brown, with thatched roofs. I could see System-created Villagers standing around . . . but there was something wrong. They were immobile, the closest ones looking dazed or spaced out. Frozen in place.

In the middle of the huddle of buildings was an open space—a circular staging area where a fountain sat. Broken wood and refuse had been piled in and around it, and it now flickered with a low flame. Around this campfire was a number of chairs and tables, figures sitting around and murmuring to one another. Players, I was sure of it.

I didn't feel much like putting on an act, even as my show smile spread across my face. It's what I did though—a compulsion. Center of attention to dazzle and wow. Cold-blooded murder on occasion, but show business could be pretty cutthroat. My magic card deck weighed heavily on my inside breast pocket. I no longer needed to physically paw at it to bring forth my summons, but knowing it was close by was comforting. The rest of the scene was anything but.

Now that I had passed the first few houses and groups of zombielike System-created, it was unnerving. It was as if someone had flicked a switch and they became paused in time, doing whatever they were before the Shadow took over the village. Not even really breathing but wavering slightly as if to mimic the process. It was no surprise that my movement drew the attention of the seated figures. That and my almost sparkling suit, no doubt.

"Oi," a man shouted. Long beard and shaved head. Looked like he hadn't even heard of a bath and avoided the rain by instinct. Crimson handprint on his forehead—just like the others. "Who the fuck ordered a clown?" He grinned with more malice than humor.

Three other figures turned and leered at me. Movements up to my left signaled they had a Ranger on the nearest roof. I didn't turn to check—eyes remained forward at the crowd. They needed a little finessing.

A whistle came from the first to stand. Easily seven feet tall, the woman had short ruddy hair and a tongue that spent more time outside her mouth than in. Her muscled figure was bound in leather straps, most of them studded to an extent that seemed conventionally uncomfortable. "I don't know. He's kinda cute. Maybe I can keep him?"

"Boss said to kill all trespassing Players. No trophies . . . or toys." The third of them was a man with long black hair and a slim mustache. He seemed to be concentrating on a book sat upon his blue robes more than my presence.

The fourth of them said nothing but glared at me with yellow eyes. A crocodile person. I was at somewhat of a loss at seeing the stocky figure in chain mail, twin axes at his sides. Sure, I knew the System could bring all sorts of oddities through the portals, but . . . Hmm. *Focus on the act, Max.*

I continued to ignore the Ranger on the roof. Their part had already been cast. I just had to start the show.

"You seem lost, little chicken. Can you not read?" The bald man stood up and took a couple of steps toward me. Still plenty of distance between us, but he was making a show of being the decision-maker. Mouth of the Party. His eyes narrowed in on the handprint partially obscured by my hat. Seeds of doubt were sown. I just had to nourish them.

A wry smile curled up at the side of my mouth. "I see communication here has been as bad as she said."

He narrowed his eyes at me and shot a glance back at the woman. After she shrugged in response, he returned his ire in my direction. "The fuck you on about?"

"The Lady said there hadn't been anything from Jokkar lately. Sent me to investigate."

"Bullshit." He spat on the floor. There was a wavering in his eyes, close to buying the ruse, but not quite.

The Wizard spoke up, still focused on his book. "It's true, Cran. Is it not? Jokkar hasn't sent a missive through for a couple of days. He usually isn't so quiet."

"So what?" The man shrugged as if he was trying to shirk off the truth. "Bastard is probably dicking around playing king in Fort Asshole."

My turn. "That's why the Lady sent me. To see who is at . . . *fault*."

They didn't like that word, and all but the crocodile winced. My silver tongue shone brightly in the daylight, and I twisted the nails further. A slight risk, as I was terrible at coming up with names on the spot. Sometimes these things just clicked into place, however.

"You may call me Man in Purple."

The woman snorted. "We haven't heard of you before. Where's your proof? You don't even have a Party." That was a good point for her side, and their disbelief wound up a little tighter. A shadow over the sproutlings that were desperate for sunlight. Seemed as though the Lady required her converts to gather in groups of five. Pragmatic.

Faux confidence carried my impassive head tilt, as if their questions were so beneath me. "I'm her cleanup guy." I grinned. "For example, your defenses here are atrocious. I was able to walk right up near you and wasn't spotted, despite my garish garb."

Cran narrowed his eyes up at the Ranger behind me, a scowl across his face for my valid point. Even if I wasn't who I purported to be, I *was* right. I continued before they had a chance to poke holes in my ruse.

"As you should all know, the Lady has a dim view on those that fail her. Perhaps this will be enough of a show of my position." I rose a hand into the air, making sure to assure them it was empty.

I clicked my fingers together.

There was a brief zip in the air, and with a groan, their Ranger collapsed. The body clattered down from the roof and then thudded against the ground. I raised a lazy eyebrow toward them. Their neck bleeding from two puncture wounds. The arrow that had done the deed was invisible as soon as I had glanced at it.

I clapped my hands to draw their attention. The invisibility only lasted ten seconds, so we'd need to move on from the short trick. Internally, I smiled at the Dazzle icons over their heads. They *had* been tricked, after all. Each icon improving my damage toward them, I would need to build as many stacks as possible before the polite discourse ran out of steam.

"Alright, alright." Cran waved his hand. "You made your point. *Fuck.* Nex was a good Ranger."

"Clearly not." I rolled my eyes. "May I come closer to discuss, or do you need further proof?"

He didn't seem too pleased about it, but he gestured me over. The woman looked as though she couldn't wait to throw me on the fire and cook me up, whereas the croc seemed fine with me being raw. The spellcaster was still more interested in that book. So . . . now *I* wanted it.

I took my top hat off and put it atop one of the System-created Villagers. Portly man with a vacant look toward the horizon. There was no reason for me to feel bad for them, as they weren't . . . real in the same sense that Players were. Still, they looked close enough to be the real thing, and I was annoyed that this village had been ruined by the gang.

A few steps closer, and I was within smelling distance of their leader. Somehow, it managed to overbear the burning wood of the fountain. I rolled out my shoulders and made a show of withdrawing my ledger and a quill. Slowly, so they didn't catch my other key ability—being able to manipulate my Inventory items by whim. "Let's start from the top, just so I have the full picture." I raised my eyebrows at him as if I were asking his permission.

"Yeah, sure." He pulled a face, but with the ire of the Lady looming behind my words, he didn't have much of a choice. I also didn't have all day while certain plates were spinning.

"Was it just the five of you here?" I held the inked quill to the page in anticipation. The process was set now. It was easier for him to fall into the rut I had created.

"Yeah." He crossed his arms, which sent a cloud of odor my way. An offense I wasn't soon to forget. They should have used the fountain to bathe in rather than turn it into a pyre.

"Some of the System limitations aren't ideal, are they?" I mused, mostly just thinking out loud as I pretended to make notes. Parties were usually limited to five for some reason. We made do with three, at present, but it seemed pragmatic for those possibly weaker than us to have strength in numbers.

The Wizard turned another page. "Yes, that is why the Lady intends to unclasp the clutches of the System and send us back to where we belong."

"May that day draw ever closer." I smiled at him, even though he didn't look my way, before I returned my gaze to Cran. This was somewhat newer information. We had heard that she was looking to take over the throne, but that might just be part of the greater plot. Returning to our real worlds didn't sound like the worst thing . . . The way she was going about it was the issue.

I wanted to press them more on the motivations and actual workings of the Crimson Shadow—why they felt the need to kill or recruit all Players in their path, or why they drank Lady in Red's blood—but if I was the man I was pretending to be, then I should know already.

Instead, I pulled a face. "Last time you saw a group of unaffiliated Players?"

Cran rubbed his chin. "Nobody from the bridge since the Lady came over. The fort probably helped with that, although the place looked like a fuckin' death trap."

I nodded slowly and glanced over in the direction of the now-destroyed ramshackle defenses. Between the village itself, the surrounding hill, and the tree cover, they couldn't see down to the bridge. They must have been pretty stuck in place to have not made note of the fight where we had burned the fort to the ground.

"But there was a small group who poked their nose in two days ago. Not new to the area but hoping we would abandon our duties." The Wizard turned another page. "I assume you met the three of them on the way in?"

"Indeed." Little else I could say to that, not without losing my temper. I had done well to remain calm, so close to these killers—and their stench—but what show face I had been able to keep was slowly waning. About time that we wrapped this up.

I cleared my throat, coughing a little. It wasn't just the stench, but it was part of it. "Ah, also, any complaints you'd like to bring up to the Lady?"

Cran opened and closed his mouth a few times before shaking his head. "No, sir."

She commanded an amount of fear and respect in them then.

A thunderous noise came from one of the houses to our left.

"What was that?" He turned away just as, with a second heavy blast, the front of the cottage burst open. Shards of wood and broken plaster were sent across the village center. The dark shape of a large grizzly bear careened out of the wreckage, drawing all their eyes. Not least because he sported a rather dapper waistcoat and bowler hat.

"That's my cue to leave," I said with a wide grin, giving the Wizard a wink as he looked back down to find his book missing.

And with that, I vanished.

CHAPTER TWO

Overachiever

On reflection, as I look back at the different passages of text within my diary . . . or memoirs? I haven't decided on that. Everything has such a sour slant to it. I let the good days stay as memories but allowed the bad times to paint these pages as if they were somehow more important. More painful and more plentiful, sure, but my heart wasn't driven by that. It kept them away from my day-to-day, I supposed. Left me to relish what good times I truly had amid the struggles.

I reappeared under my hat, and I spun away from the inert System-created that had been wearing it. <Demonic Transposition> put the hell bird I had hidden beneath the purple headwear where I had been standing by the gathered Shadow, and immediately the bird flew into the face of the Wizard. Distraction was a powerful tool, not just for a magician, but for anyone looking to keep their brain in their skull for as long as possible.

The new main attraction on stage was Wolf—a grizzly bear who was a brawler beyond comparison. Even with his newly acquired padded waistcoat and bowler hat, there could be no denying he was a fearful sight to behold. Easily towering above any humanoid when on his back feet, the System had decided making him a Player with offensive and defensive abilities was a good idea—turning a powerhouse into a walking whirlwind of destruction.

More importantly, he was also my biggest fan.

Less impressed were the Crimson Shadow members, now somewhat caught off guard by the large creature blazing toward them, while I had taken a bow and was waiting in the wings. Not idle, however, as a purple card of magical energy blazed in my hand.

The Wizard cast a shield that flickered red, and my dove was suddenly immolated from touching it. As he jerked away from the resulting flash, my aim faltered. Swerving through the statuesque Villagers, I missed the mark of his neck and instead struck him in the side of the face with the thrown card, slicing open his cheek and severing his tongue. I wasn't about to wait and find out if he could still cast spells, so I moved back through the small forest of passive System-created to get more cover.

With a roar, the giantess strode toward Wolf, her weapons blazing a deep orange as they went to clash. The crocodile-like man had slipped back and was trying to gain some positional advantage rather than face the large bear head-on.

Cran turned to face me, anger painting his face deeper than the layer of filth he embodied. "What manner of trick is this?" he growled as he moved to hunt me down, weapons moving into his hands.

"This is just the opening performance," I said with a grin, moving farther away through the Villagers and toward one of the cottages. "For me anyway. This is *your* final act."

"Bastard!" He jumped forward, stalking me as fury blazed through his eyes. Slashing through the inert System-created with his curved blades, their limp bodies falling to the floor as he killed them without care.

Somewhat callous, even if they weren't real in some sense. I was using them as human shields, of course, so I couldn't exactly take the high ground. The sight of it irked me though, and speaking of which . . .

I clapped my hands together, and a cloud of thick fog suddenly enveloped the area around me. My wand of fog cloud attached to the inside of my sleeve in the specially created holster activating at my command. A purple card left my hand and circled out, illuminating a trail through the dense gray shielding me from his intense search. The aim wasn't really to strike him, even if I had a pretty good idea where he was due to the angered grunting he persisted with.

From my Inventory, a mace popped into the grip of my right hand. Judging based on memory, I lobbed it out into the fog. It did not clatter to the ground, which just made me grin wider. The sound of breaking wood from near the fire was accompanied by the sound of Wolf roaring. The large woman must be quite sturdy to still be holding up against him. Perhaps I should take a peek.

My hands clapped together again, and the fog instantly vanished. The ability canceled with a thought, but I added the physical actions to make it more of a show. Cran immediately locked eyes with me from a dozen feet away, my magic card having misled him to where I was not. The true trick was when I had dropped my <Demonic Pact> card, just as we had been obscured.

The demon struck the man a split second after the fog cleared, the spiked mace crushing into his skull. Cran convulsed as he dropped to the ground, and Roger struck him once again to make sure the deed was done. He turned to me as he did so, a wide smile on the body of the slain Villager that he was possessing. The eyes replaced with pits of bright purple, while two similarly colored rabbit ears had burst from the top of the puppet's skull.

"Hey, boss! This fucker didn't see me coming, huh? *Dumb shit.*"

I gave him a nod, my focus more on the battlefield in its entirety at this point than on engaging with him in conversation. The Wizard had a hand over his mouth, blood still seeping through his fingers, while his other hand was casting a buff on the tall woman. Keeping her in the fight—if only barely.

The crocodile person lay against a table, his vacant eyes staring up at the sky as three arrows protruded from his body. Shoulder, lungs, heart. My eyes went up to the top of one of the buildings to see her. My protégé and the last to round out our trio. Three point five, if you counted Roger.

The elf was dressed in a blue waistcoat over a white blouse. Her deep-blue top hat was wider and shorter than mine and hid her radiant blonde hair. Even at this distance, I could see the glare of her bright-blue eyes scour the village center as she drew another arrow to her bow. While not as proficient in trickery as I was, she made up for it by being able to kill things from a distance and healing me up when I eventually split my head open on something.

It was worrying how common an occurrence that was.

I empowered a card and sent it out in an arc, controlling it through the air around the Villagers still standing. Before it reached its target, I split it. One magic and one a demon summon. Blood ran down my hand, but I wasn't quite overexerting myself. Yet. The System didn't like me using <Pick a Card> this way, but a little bloodletting wouldn't dissuade me from persisting.

The purple card struck the renewed magic shield of the Wizard, the bright red flickering but not failing. His eyes turned toward me to see where I was attacking from—and that was my plan. The second card passed behind him as he turned, hitting the nearby table. A Hellhound+ burst out from a magic circle of hellish runes and leaped atop the robed man, crashing through his shield and gnashing at the extended casting arm.

Wolf swiped and struck the woman, breaking whatever enchantment was keeping her up. A wide gash of crimson spread across her torso from his claws, and she stumbled backward. Her weapon blurred as she readied a counter, then an arrow pierced through her shoulder. With her arm now weakened and falling limp, the giant bear crashed atop her and wrapped his jaws around her head. *Crunch*, like a watermelon.

Mentally, I told the hound to keep the Wizard alive. Walking over, I dusted off the dried blood from my head. Down to two vials of the Lady's blood, but we hadn't found another use for them aside from taunting the Crimson Shadow. Good thing they only had an effect when drunk, not just used as face paint. Otherwise, that would have been a short-lived mistake.

Ren dropped down from the house and walked over to join me while Wolf continued to chew through the corpse of the fallen woman. Her scowl was the default look her face usually held, but there was an additional hint of annoyance to it. I had become somewhat proficient in gauging her actual mood but waited for the coming admonishment to be sure.

"You saved the only one unable to talk?" She stood and crossed her arms across her chest.

I raised my eyebrow at the remnants of the gang holding the village hostage. "In fairness, I haven't *personally* killed anyone."

She rolled her eyes, but knew I was right.

Technically anyway. Cran would have been the best to save for questioning, and I had summoned Roger to take care of him. Wizard was second best, and I had done a number on his mouth. Perhaps it wasn't so bad that we couldn't heal him?

"Hey, boss?" Roger awkwardly stumbled his puppet body over to me. "Glad you're still kickin' after the trouble in that death trap. I knew you'd fuck up that metal shit can."

"Hardly broke a sweat," I lied. Broke plenty of things in that fight against Jokkar in the fort, and it was only luck and my persistent practice with my craft that got me the small opportunity to win.

He handed over his weapon. "You can have the mace back. It's fuckin' fun, but I'm eager to expand my . . . repertoire."

"Of course." I nodded and furrowed my brow. "What were you thinking?"

"Let me have a think, yeah? Looks like you got the rest of these fucks already, so I'll go for now? Barbs promised me a foot massage, and we both know where that kinda shit leads." He turned toward Ren and gave the elf a half wink with the awkwardly controlled body.

"Thanks . . . Roger." I gave him a brief bow, and the purple energy blew away in an unfelt breeze, the inert body dropping back to the ground. Letting the breath out of my nose slowly, I allowed most of that conversation to sink out of my head.

Turning back to the problem at hand, Ren also seemed eager for me to focus on the maimed man currently being pinned by the upgraded canine rather than address anything my demon had said. "Good boy." I gestured for him to drop the Wizard, and he did so. He panted at me, his tongue lolling out from a blood-soaked mouth, before he trotted over to the elf for pets.

I stepped over to the man. He wasn't in very good shape, and although I wasn't a fan of torture, I also had no mercy for those who killed other Players under the name of the Lady. The three heads decorating the warning sign outside the village were enough for me to condemn them to death . . . but then again, that wasn't exactly the magician side of me making that decision.

Two different versions of me had somehow wandered into the portal taking us to this world at the same time. The first a workaholic magician tired of the grind but unable to stop craving the adoration and praise. The second a demon hunter from a world where hell was a literal thing. He was also a magician, which is where the System blended the two realities to make my current Class. We had become fully merged after I suffered a near-fatal blow from a . . . Well, best not dwell on those sorts of things.

The point I was trying to get at was he was a lot more used to death and brought the callous attitude to the mix. While I certainly had a lot of . . . care for those around me, I thought as my eyes drifted back to the elf, my enemies saw none of it. The Wizard being no exception.

Other than the Wizard's split mouth and tongue, the Hellhound+ had shredded most of his right arm and some of his leg, his robes dark and soaked with blood. I crouched down beside him.

"Don't even think about trying to cast a spell. Your fate depends on how far your common sense can take you." In truth, he might be able to get something out before I could react. He was somewhat outnumbered, however, and unless he planned on coring my head, I would probably survive whatever attempt he made—especially with Ren's Oathwarden abilities tuned to keeping me on my feet.

"Is it even worth saving him?" Ren stood behind me now, her arms still crossed. "Does he have any answers that will be useful to us?"

Internally, I grinned. I was 90 percent sure she had gotten the ball rolling on the good-cop, bad-cop act. Although, usually I preferred to be the bad cop—as it was endearing to see the Oathwarden have to play nice when it was so opposite to the constant scowl she gave the world. Most of the world.

"He looked like the smartest of the bunch. He probably *would* share information, right?" I raised my eyebrows toward him and gave the slightest of nods.

He gurgled and stared at me with a pained expression across panicked eyes.

"See? Useless. Put a knife on him and let's get going." Ren shuffled her feet in the dirt to sell the idea.

I shrugged and removed my Knife of the Trickster.

Wolf came over, putting his gore-covered muzzle close to the panicked Wizard and sniffing at him with his nose. "Can I have him if you're done?"

In hearing the bear talk, the Shadow squirmed in shock, apparently at his limits of how wide-eyed and out of his element he could be. Wolf was smart for a bear, but his desires were simple and mostly involved filling his stomach.

"Well . . ." I pulled a face and wiggled the blade in my hand. "If he isn't going to give any answers . . ."

The man removed his shaking hands from his split mouth and tried to mime a shape with his fingers. Some manner of rectangle. He looked pale, like he was close to passing out from shock, if not blood loss.

"Hmm, the book?" I brought up my Inventory in the side of my vision. "Answers are in the book?"

He nodded eagerly, bloodied hands going back to cover his shorn mouth.

"Oh," I said, giving Wolf the nod before grinning at the spellcaster. "I suppose we don't need you then, huh?"

CHAPTER THREE

Cursed to Act

Despite the System giving me a spellcaster-adjacent Class, I didn't care for reading that often. Not to sound like a dullard—but I was much more passionate about engaging with learning through practice. Words just got in the way when I could dissemble a mystery by observing it. While most of the enemies we came across weren't the sharpest of tools, they did enjoy writing down important things. Currently, I am staring at this page as I write it, wondering if I appreciated the irony. Perhaps I did.

Ren pulled a chair from her Inventory and sat down on it. "Anything good in the book?"

I wrinkled my nose up, glancing at her briefly before looking back at the tome I had stolen from the spellcaster. Wolf was asleep, having had his fill of the corpses. "You want the abridged version, or we have time for a tale?"

"We've already established you're a shitty storyteller," she said, then gave me a glum smile. "Just a summary, please. I left the Wizard's remains for you to loot. Then I want to be far away from this place."

That was fair. I was somewhat numb to the smell of death and burning wood here, but it was still eerie with all the frozen-in-place Villagers still standing around. "Okay. It's both this chap's spell book and diary—so most of it is useless . . . but some of it paints a useful picture."

I stood, my chair vanishing into my Inventory, as I started to pace while holding the book open in my hands. "They were originally two groups of adventurers that hung around just north of here. When the Lady came through, she offered them a way out of the System. He even wrote down her terms and all—but his diction has a remarkable drop-off at what looks like the point after they took the blood."

Ren slowly nodded. "So our thoughts on it possibly lowering Stats might hold water?"

"Indeed." That was why he was trying to intently stare at the pages. He probably had an issue understanding his earlier work. I stopped and tilted my head at her. "It's almost like a doomsday cult from reading between the lines. Everyone can only be free if everyone is on the same page."

"So that's why it's a join-us-or-we'll-kill-you kind of deal?" The elf rolled her eyes and sighed.

It was pretty basic on the surface of it. Have an in group and an out group and pit them against each other. I snapped the book shut. "This is mostly only gathering speed due to her blood—once she has persuaded them to join, it brings out their hatred for the System and their inability to abide by living within it." Even if joining up was their own choice at the outset, I wondered if they had the option of changing their minds once they had drunk down the red stuff.

"Plus, we don't exactly know her abilities," Ren agreed. "There could be even more going on there."

I put the book into my Inventory and brought up the Map. There could be no way—even if the Lady had broken abilities—that she could have gone across the whole area already, or even twisted everyone present here to do her bidding. Unless she could infect the System itself . . . but then maybe that was her end goal after dethroning the current occupants of the palace. More powerful and broken than me, it was almost unfair.

"Hey, trickster?" The elf brought me out of my thoughts. "Do you think it is ironic that while she is erasing people's ability to suspend their disbelief, you are defeating them by tricking them?"

"No." I shook my head impassively. "I usually defeat them with demons or cutting their throats open."

She narrowed her glare to try to gauge if I was intentionally being dense. *I was.*

"Let me loot this unfortunate disbeliever then, and we'll be on our way." While the grin I shot her was genuine, my joy in having to interface with looting something was not. Despite my aptitude for filling my Inventory with junk for potential tricks, the rest of what the System wanted from me I felt was beyond the pale.

Something I was soon to change my tune on, I could feel, as I opened up the window to see what he had.

[3,452 Gold]
[Health Potions (8)]
[Smart Bindings: +3 INT, +1 WIS]
[Smart Leggings: +3 INT, +1 WIS]
[Shoulders of the Trickster: +3 INT, +2 DEX]
[Arcane Ring: +15% Mana, +5% magic Damage]

"Alright, you can both be witnesses . . ." I stood and saw that Wolf was still sleeping. "Well, *one* of you can be a witness to my character growth. I now *enjoy* the looting process." It wasn't lost on me that the best Stat distribution for my Class seemed to be items *of the trickster.*

Ren blinked, but her expression otherwise remained unchanged.

A hard sell, perhaps. Internally I rolled my eyes that it was easier to convince these hardened murderers that I was an assassin called Man in Purple for Lady in Red than me to have suddenly become an avid loot goblin. That's what they called that sort of thing, I was sure.

"What did he have on him?" she asked, clearly seeing through my announcement to the core reason behind the change of heart.

"Mostly Intelligence equipment, but the Stat bonuses are higher than the first area." I grinned. "I suppose I'm more contented that killing other spellcasters seems to be the most efficient way of increasing my own power."

Ren stood and put her chair away in her Inventory—a slower process than what I was capable of—before turning back to me. "You're not wrong, but you need to be careful about how you approach that line of thinking."

I gave her a bow. "Of course. Crimson Shadow only, and only if we are already intending on combating them." *Or* if I could find a good reason to fight them, *or* if they'd be easy pickings . . . Maybe she was right.

She went over to wake Wolf up. While they both had the outfits to match whatever mania I had dragged them both into, we still hadn't gotten a proper show organized. For me, it was easy to weave in the performance as my combat Skills had been flavored by my previous profession by the System. Magic and trickery were my bread and butter. For the other two, it was something they'd need to grow into.

Ren was an Oathwarden—some mix between Ranger and Paladin. Although she was vague on the details, her main Class function was to assist and keep alive those she had sworn an oath to. At some point this had become *me*, although any attempt to dig through my memories and remember when or how was just blinded by her radiant hair and piercing blue eyes.

Wolf was . . . Well, *gullible* wasn't a fair label to put on him. He had emotional intelligence and some smarts about him. He didn't care much for most of the System but was content enough with the life he now had. While he had agreed to kill and protect us in return for eating his fill at the start, it was hard to not see him as the backbone of the team. He saw us as family now and had more than earned his place by being an unequaled mass of Strength and Damage absorption.

They were both happy enough to play their roles as the System had doled them out. It wouldn't be fair to expect them to do the sort of things I was capable of or approach a problem with the thought processes that I did. But likewise, I couldn't do the things that they could. The fact that they had agreed to be part of my big charade was a show of their strength of trust in me, more so than my capabilities as a leader.

"Everything fine, Max?" Ren came up to me and pressed her hand on my shoulder.

"I'm . . ." My brain halted before it could say *fine.* "I'm apprehensive about what this area will bring." The truth was hard to get out of me sometimes, and I had needed to be humbled before I stopped putting on such a good front when I was crumbling within.

"Same." She looked back at the flickering fire. "Sometimes it feels like we stumbled into some kind of apocalypse, and we're the only sane ones." With an eyebrow raised, she looked back up at me. "For certain definitions of *sane.*"

[Available Quests: 1]
[Save the Villagers]

"Huh?" I could see her eyes unfocused, and we had both received the same message. "So it wasn't the Crimson Shadow that did this?"

We turned and looked at the small forest of statuesque figures. Perhaps it had been, and now the System wanted us to set things back to normal. Was it able to make procedural Quests like that? We had only completed a relative handful after the starter island, mostly settling for the challenging Town Board ones or simple pop-up tasks like this one.

"You think it's worth our time?" I asked them both.

"Is the reward more meat?" Wolf huffed, looking like he would prefer to be napping still.

Ren tilted her head and sighed. "It's *experience,* and we're already here. No meat though, Wolf. Haven't you eaten enough?"

"Yeah," he said and returned a glum expression.

"Let's get this done then." I nodded my agreement. It would be nice to leave the village in a better state than how we found it. Not only to correct the trouble the Crimson Shadow had caused, but also for the newer Players—it'd be nice for them to come to find a normal world when they eventually got here.

"Initial thoughts?" Ren asked, crossing her arms.

I took off my top hat and rubbed my forehead with the back of my forearm. "Magic, probably, for it to be this persistent. Close by, like an aura given off by either an artifact or a person hiding."

She nodded. "And what do you think, Wolf?"

"Wasn't in the house I destroyed." His amber eyes looked back at the wreckage off to the side. "Can't smell anything else over the smoke and death."

"That's becoming standard fare for us, huh?" I grimaced and eyed up the remaining buildings. Even if the spell was local area only, it could be just outside of the village in the sparse trees and hills. As much as we needed the experience to catch up to level ten, I didn't fancy rooting around in the undergrowth when we weren't certain of how hostile the area was.

I rubbed my chin. "Usually I'd suggest splitting up, but that might not be a great idea at present."

"Agreed." Ren nodded as she began to walk off. "You're likely to find something to crack your skull open on otherwise."

As she turned away, I caught the slip of a smile at the corner of her mouth. A rarity, and always a delight. Slightly more common these days, where we were . . . Oh, were we dating? It had all been so casual and natural that it hadn't occurred to me there might be a more official label for our close companionship. Not that I had anyone else to tell that I may have a sort-of-princess elfin girlfriend. Ah, even just thinking about it made me cringe. Probably better I table that train of thought for—

"You think it's in that building, Max?" The bear nudged into me. "You are staring at it."

"Call it a hunch," I said as I quickly rolled with the play, "but that's where I'd like to start."

Ren stopped and turned from where she was headed to look at the cottage that had been the focal point of my absent mind. "Want to make a bet on who can pick the right house?"

"I'm not a gambling man," I lied, knowing full well how often I put simple things such as my life at risk on the regular. "Plus, you already owe me a something, if you recall."

Her mouth opened and closed a few times as the memories came to the forefront. "You ass, trickster." She sighed. "Double or nothing?"

"On one condition." I raised up a single finger. "I get to change my first choice."

She narrowed her eyes but shrugged. Wolf just looked confused as to why I'd change my mind after staring at the other cottage for so long. That'd stay my little secret—probably even from myself if I could help it.

Turning around to glance at the small alcove filled with stout cottages, I tried to imagine which would be the most cliché place the System might have stuck the offending item or person. My knowledge of the tropes was pretty thin, but if I viewed it as a show, then I considered where I may put it for the reveal with the most flair. And then I'd dial it down a couple of notches because the System was not as sharp as me.

I felt that I would probably live to regret that inner monologue.

There was no well in sight, nor a cottage that looked like it might belong to a morally ambiguous—yet still mustache-twirling—spellcaster. I settled for the next best thing and leveled my finger at what might be the village hall, on account of it being slightly bigger than the other buildings. The sign saying "Hall" out the front helped with my deduction too.

"A bit cliché," Ren smirked, "but we'll see, I suppose. After, I'm saying it's that house." She pointed toward one of the cottages. The only defining point that made it differ from the others was that it had more flowers out front. A *suspicious* amount of flowers, almost.

"Okay," I said, narrowing my eyes at it. She returned the same expression, and I stared at her blazing blue eyes.

Wolf cleared his throat. "I pick the one over . . ." He turned and raised a paw to what looked like either a bakery or butcher's shop. "There."

I smiled and gave him a nod before leading them toward the hall. As to what favors I would ply from them, should I win . . . Well, once we found a safe haven, I had a few tricks in mind that I would like us to learn as a team. I hadn't pushed them in the aftermath of the fort battle—I hardly cared to perform magic in those almost three days of rest. Now though, back where the stakes mattered . . .

It was time to become greater, truly reach for the pinnacle of what we were capable of.

My grin furthered as I put my hand on my magic card deck in my breast pocket. I had a good feeling about this area.

CHAPTER FOUR

What Lies Beneath

I don't often write in here before going into battle, as many of our conflicts are ambushes or unexpected. The ones that aren't are usually too stressful to think of anything but the looming battles. Tomorrow will be . . . tough. I will do what I can for all of us. Nothing more could be asked. If you are reading this diary and this is the last entry, well . . . I'm sure you can read between the lines. I left enough space.

I pushed the door of the hall open with a small amount of flair, hoping the reveal would have the cursed artifact or whatever appear before us and I'd have the win instantly. As my luck would have it, that didn't occur.

Instead, we were greeted by a large, softly lit room. Tables and chairs were stacked in the closer corners, while a few short benches sat in rows near the front facing a slightly raised stage. I shivered, salivating a little. A small venue—nice and comfortable for the comeback tour. A side door that we could put a curtained area across, bring through all the props from the back rooms. Maybe get some extra lanterns up across these awnings and—

"Max?" Ren pushed me into the actual building a bit more. "I swear to whatever gods the System has, if you're just standing there imagining putting on a show here, then—"

"Just checking for traps," I said with a certainly convincing smile. She saw right through it, naturally.

"I've come to terms with the fact that we'll have to do a show at some point." She sighed, crossing her arms as she looked around the hall. "That's just part of being with . . . of being in a Party with you. Hence the costumes." Her blue eyes glared at me as if daring me to make a point about anything she had said.

I had mostly tuned out everything after she had insinuated we were together. Perhaps a rather empty-headed and immature response, but for someone who had been starved of any sort of close relationship in my adult life, I was savoring every second of it. It made for a nice contrast to the cold-blooded murder and threats on our lives.

"What do you think, Wolf?" I turned to the bear, who had stuck his head through the door but had not committed to breaking the frame off with his wide shoulders to follow us in.

"A larger venue would suit me better."

I grinned widely. A remarkably on-point observation and agreement, as if it was directly targeted for my ears. Maybe he had said something else and I'd imagined what I wanted to hear.

He wrinkled up his nose and sniffed the air. "Do you usually eat the audience after a show?"

There it was. I deflated and shook my head as Ren started to walk around the room. It was unlikely that what we sought would just be atop the stage or the center of a room. If I wanted to hide something cursed, it'd either be in the back room or perhaps underneath the building with a trapdoor blocking our progress.

I circled the other side of the room. "Keep an eye out on the village for us, Wolf? Just in case our battle attracted some vultures." He gave me a nod and turned around, placing his large rump in the doorway instead. As I passed the left side of the room, I vacuumed up a handful of chairs. Could never have too many. Well, that was a lie, but a few spares at the back of my Inventory wouldn't hurt.

My eyes fell to Ren as she reached the end of the room and stepped up onto the stage. She took a few steps, looking around the floor and walls for anything that looked untoward, before she caught me watching her.

She crossed her arms and glared at me. "Quit gawking and let's get this Quest over with." Her eyes went over to the distracted bear before coming back to me. She did a little twirl on the stage and flourished her hands.

If it were possible to receive my own Dazzle icons, I'd be overflowing with them. Maybe I was hallucinating. I didn't think I could be any further enamored. With Ren, sure, but with the idea of putting on a show—there was brimming passion for the great performance that was slowly blooming.

"*This never happened,*" she hissed. She reset into a more relaxed expression and stepped down from the stage. "Now move your ass, trickster."

"I'll check the back room." My face muscles ached from smiling. How easily the bloodied death from the past hour had just washed away to be replaced by the fantasy of showmanship. The hard part was actually finding an audience. The System-created wouldn't really get the nuance of it, and Players were either the Crimson Shadow or beneath their boots.

I hummed to myself as I walked to the end of the room and pressed a hand against the door. It's not like I had any special sense that could determine if something was awry just beyond it, but I had once seen a magician set themselves alight. Prop malfunction has caused a fire, and as they opened the . . . box or room—it was unclear in my mind—the added oxygen had caused the flames to flare out. Some outfits were pretty flammable too. I shuddered and gripped the handle.

Twisted and opened it up into darkness. I furrowed my brow at the furnishings inside before a lantern came out of my Inventory and into my hand. Surprisingly, it was mostly barren. A few empty shelves and cupboards that looked as if they had been stripped of all contents. Odd, and rather unrewarding. Down on the floor was a trapdoor.

"There's a trapdoor," I announced.

Ren appeared at the doorway behind me as I stepped toward it. "If you fall down the ladder and crack your head open, I *am* leaving you here."

"You wouldn't." I turned my head to raise an eyebrow at her. She tried to maintain her glare—but I could see the cracks, just at the edges of her eyes. Looking back at the simple square in the floorboards with a small metal ring inset, I ran my tongue across my teeth. "You never know, I might knock a third soul awake within me."

"Hopefully that one will be good at . . ." The rest of her sentence drifted off.

"Good at *what*, Ren?" I gripped at the ring and put the lantern down on the floor. "*Good at what?*"

"Landing on their feet?"

That sounded like something made up on the spot. I wasn't sure whether to take it as a compliment as she realized that I was pretty well-rounded, as far as people were here, or be suspicious that there was something she wanted me to improve on but wasn't able to vocalize.

I lifted the hatch, and cool air wafted over me, alongside the smell of . . . something strange? Like damp, but with a hint of something acidic to it. "I sense danger, or perhaps a larder that has spoiled."

Reaching atop my head, I brought my hat down and placed it at the side of the opening. Hand inside, I brought out a dove and had him perch on the brim. After giving it a little pat, I turned to the concerned-looking elf.

"If it's bad, I'll teleport back up here, okay? You stay there and keep eyes on Wolf. Maintain a chain of visuals." Wolf, Ren, bird, me. She nodded at me and calmed. I wasn't naturally a group leader, but she always appreciated it when I took this sort of thing into consideration. We met halfway with our personalities and ideals, and Wolf was just happy to scrap and eat our enemies.

I held the lantern down, and it illuminated rough stonework. Bricks that were uneven and oddly shaped, but it didn't cast light on anything worthy of note at this angle. Instead, I narrowed my eyes at the wooden ladder. It looked sturdy enough, yet could easily be my toughest opponent yet. My ability to suffer traumatic skull injuries was nigh legendary, but I wasn't keen to continue the trend.

"You want a rope?" Ren asked from the doorway.

As I turned to put my feet on the rungs, I narrowed my eyes. Her expression was actually genuine, which was more sad than comforting. It was nice to know she thought the insides of my skull were actually worth saving though. Perhaps I should focus more on my movements than whatever *this* was.

Clasped the lantern to my belt for the journey down and made it down the handful of wooden rungs to stand on the solid ground below. I looked up at the hatch to see the dove silhouetted before it hopped onto the top rung to get a better angle on me and the elf at the same time.

I turned and held up the lantern, casting elongated shadows off of dusty furniture that had long been abandoned down here. The smell was even worse but couldn't just be from the aged wood and mildew. A few steps forward and light hit the back walls. Slowly, I rotated to illuminate the rest of the objects down here, half expecting a ghost or strange Monster to hop out of the shadows at me.

Turns out, I was half right.

The amber light washed over a seated figure. Black cloak obscuring most of their body, only their pale gray face visible. Wide, pitch-black eyes with small circles of white in the center glared back at me from a near-featureless face. A small mouth slowly widened to smile at me, sharp teeth protruding along the way.

"Are you the Monster who has frozen the Villagers?" My question came out remarkably level, given the situation. My eyes shot to the side. Bird was just in view at the top of the ladder still.

"Anssswer my riddle, and I will ssset them free," the thing hissed at me.

Preferably, just killing the Monster would have the same effect. Why it thought I could be swayed into engaging in word games in a musky cellar was beyond me. Unfair of me to judge, perhaps, but their physical appearance didn't fill me with a lot of confidence that this wasn't some kind of trick. And I *knew* tricks.

"Unfortunately, I am allergic to riddles. Do you have a second option?" I was apprehensive about going full tilt into an attack, given that the System should anticipate such action and had done something to make that not a win condition for the Quest. Not like I could ask for a second opinion right now.

"No. Anssswer incorrectly and I will curssse you too."

I moved the lantern to my right hand and held it up. With a grimace, I nodded for the creature to continue.

"Sssssssssssssssssssssssssssssssss."

"Uh." I blinked slowly. "Could you repeat that?"

"That issss incorrect!" Their eyes widened, and the white circles turned crimson and started to spin, distorting as if they were going down a drain. A gray hand with long fingers reached out from their cloak.

System, I rolled my eyes. Switched places with my dove, who ate the curse and dropped to the floor. Landing surprisingly deftly back on the ladder, I sent a card out into the darkness. One toward the creature and one toward the lantern that I had dropped beside some of the dry furniture.

With no hesitation, I hopped up the ladder to the ground floor and flipped the hatch shut, then pulled a nearby cupboard over it—only struggling slightly.

"Should I ask?" Ren asked, clearly asking without asking.

"Just . . ." I turned to her and frowned. "Let me process it for a while first."

"I can smell burning."

"Good." Perhaps a self-fulfilling prophecy. Now the doors to the hall would have a dangerous fire behind them, eager to burst out at the next person who stumbled across them.

The elf tilted her head, trying to read my odd mania. "Did you find the source of the curse and deal with it? Or are you adding pyromania alongside your kleptomania?"

"Yes?" I replied, picking my hat up off the floor. *Poor dove*, I thought. They always got the short end of the stick.

She sighed. "Fuck's sake, Max. Shall we go?"

"Uh, someone is approaching." The bear's deep voice came echoing through the hall.

Whatever odd conversation we were trying to force each other through ended just like that, our faces resolute again, and we headed back into the hall with hardly a nod. Ren drew her bow as we strode through to the doorway as Wolf moved to the side and allowed us to exit.

The outside air was refreshing and somehow helped put the odd creature far behind me. I had dodged the cast curse, right? No System messages had popped up to tell me I had anything wrong with me, and other than being a little disjointed from reality—this reality—I felt perfectly fine.

Of course, as I thought that, my stomach immediately sank at seeing five figures walking down the path toward the village.

"What can you see?" I relented to Ren's better eyesight.

She worked her jaw as her eyes narrowed. A couple of seconds and then she slowly responded, as if unsure whether she trusted what she could see. "No crimson handprints, for starters."

Odd, but too early to start getting excited.

"They don't smell the same as the bad meat," Wolf added, sniffing into the air. "Just normal bad. Unwashed, stressed, and bloodied."

I shivered, almost ready to accept we had met some normal Players.

"Two in armor, two in robes, one in leathers," Ren filtered potential Class information to us.

My fingers tapped against the side of my leg. It was enough for me, so now I had to fill my role. They weren't being overtly aggressive toward us—although we needed to be wary that could turn on a dime. I had already placed a Hellhound+ out of view beside one of the cottages closer to them and was charging up a magic card in my obscured left hand.

Whether Ren had seen, or just anticipated, that was my course of action, she nodded to me and held her bow at the ready.

"Play it cool," I told them. "See what they're all about. If they attack, then we'll need to give it everything. You know the drill." They grunted their acknowledgments.

I walked forward and hailed the approaching group, one of their fighters returning the action. Now that we were almost in parley distance, I could make them out better.

At their front was a fighter in full armor, silver and worn. Based on the shape of the breastplate, probably female—but their helmet obscured their face. Shield on their back and sword still away in their scabbard. Which meant either they were overconfident or weren't looking for a fight. Body language told me she was most likely their leader.

To her right side, a much shorter figure. A female goblin in robes of blue and silver. Long staff in her hand that rose to a loop where a silver bell hung. Her eyes were a bright yellow and pierced me even from this distance. No points for guessing some kind of spellcaster, although the potential theme intrigued me.

The other spellcaster standing behind them was much taller, possibly elfin if I were to guess, from his sharp features. A rather plain robe of beige that was colored more by the stains of battle than anything else. As he turned his head to say something to the larger figure in the middle, his long brunet ponytail flopped over his shoulder.

Said larger member of their ensemble was a giant of a man—or rather a lion? While their wide body was humanoid, the head definitely resembled that of a golden-maned lion. Mostly chain mail armor, with large shoulder plates that radiated energy as if they were heated. Across his back was a large two-handed battle-ax.

The last member was a rather average-looking man with short brown hair, wearing simple leather armor. In fact, how *ordinary* he looked was almost jarring. It made me uncomfortable just to look at him, especially compared to the rest of his group.

They stopped a good twenty feet away from us, and the goblin whistled.

"Rolo was right. Someone did fuck up the Crimson here." She grinned up at the armored woman.

Their leader lifted up her plated hands to remove her helmet. Short black hair, shaved almost bald, and bright amber eyes. Two deep scars ran across her dark skin down her whole face with the hint that the damage continued down her chest. Either something brought here from her previous world or a testament to such a terrifying attack that even the System couldn't fully mend it.

One of her eyebrows raised as she looked over our Party, sizing us up perhaps. Her glare stopped at the elf, and her expression changed.

"Ren?" she asked, surprise on her face.

CHAPTER FIVE

Peer to Peer

A brief moment of silence passed between the two groups. Ren's dour expression turned into one of surprise as she realized who we were faced with. "*Fiona?*"

So this was the fighter that she had mentioned back on the island. With the vague information provided, it sounded as though they had been briefly cordial before one wanted to move on to the wider world. Ren, of course, wanted to stay and enact her revenge—which I helped facilitate. Agreeing to murder seemed more palatable than trying to learn about the world alone.

It had worked out well for me, all things considered.

"Never thought I'd see that scowl again." Fiona shook her head. "Honestly, it's a relief to see that you're not dead or part of this cult shit." She spat atop one of the bodies—I couldn't tell which after Wolf had given most of them a good chew.

"We've had our fair share of run-ins with them," Ren said with a returned sour expression on her face. Left out the part where we had pushed the Lady into the wider world, which I appreciated. "This is Max, and Wolf."

"Wolf." The fighter nodded, repeating the name as if trying to taste the validity. "And *Max.*"

I gave her a low bow, as was tradition. While I wasn't in much mood to start performing tricks, I still had my manners about me. "It's a pleasure to meet you." I straightened back up and clapped my hands twice.

All the Villagers unfroze and started wandering about toward their homes as if nothing had happened.

Fiona, Ren, and the plain-looking man at the back didn't receive Dazzle icons, but the rest did. I also received a very warranted glare from the elf. Sometimes, timing was everything. How long did it take a Monster to bleed, burn, or suffocate to death? Not even the demon hunter part of me knew the answer *exactly.*

The showman inside me could see the thread of eventuality though—as if I received subtle help from the System to ensure I could pull off the tricks and not look like a total ass in front of present company. Perhaps that *was* how it worked.

"Interesting." Fiona's facial expression didn't sell the remark. "You must come from a world where clowns are revered?"

I returned a blank expression, not really sure how far I wanted to dig into that question. Pretty sure there was a smirk on Ren's face in my peripheral, but that could just be my mind filling in the gaps with what I expected. Instead of replying directly, I risked a pointed question of my own. My verbal swordplay was rusty, but the stakes were low.

"Forgive my rudeness, but I don't suppose you've had a run-in with a chap with chainswords previously?" If this was a miss, I might just swap places with my patient canine and make a run for the horizon.

Her face clouded, and any humor she had held drained away. "Yes, I have."

"I hope it brings you some comfort to learn that I have killed him."

She worked her jaw, and her eyes went over to the elf, who nodded briefly. The glare returned to me, but some of the iciness had melted away. "Doesn't surprise me that Ren has kept competent company at least. There's only two of you?"

"Three," Wolf interjected.

The goblin jumped backward. "*Oh fuck!* It talks!"

"Wolf is a Player," Ren explained. "Has all the things we do, just packaged into a half ton or so of grizzly bear."

Fiona whistled. "That makes your survival make a lick more sense then. Look at us yapping on though. We have a camp a little way away from here. We can walk and talk?"

Ren looked at me to see my thoughts. I gave her a nod and smiled toward the Party. "Certainly, a place to rest and have people that don't want to cave our heads in sounds nice."

I handed the Quest in as we set off, our trio walking beside their Party. Only experience. That was rather anticlimactic. Hopefully the Villagers would clear up the mess that the Crimson had made and things would be normal by the time new Players rolled through this area.

"We have a scout around this location," the fighter began. "We've been keeping an eye this way since the fort burned down."

"That was also us," Ren said with a nod.

"Excellent. When nothing immediately happened, we assumed they just fell apart because they're thick as pig shit."

"Or bear shit," Wolf added helpfully.

"So with Rolo telling us three figures had come across the bridge, we anticipated either it was some poor sods about to get killed by the Crimson—or perhaps new cult members ready to join this area."

I rubbed the back of my neck. "We took a few days of rest. It turned out that cleansing the first area of the Shadow was moderately traumatic."

"Cleanse?" the goblin piped up. "You killed *all* of them?"

Ren shrugged as I raised an eyebrow at her. "We . . . hope so." I rubbed my chin as I answered the goblin. Although she had the same pointed nose and ears as the scores I'd massacred my way through on the starter island, there was a life in her that set her apart from the System-created versions. "I think in total we must have removed almost forty of them?"

"Including the ones on the island, perhaps." Ren tilted her head but ultimately was in agreement.

I tried to avoid counting them out too hard—lest I become aware of being a mass murderer. *Damn*—there it was. Their Party exchanged glances, and I wondered if we'd committed a faux pas by being Player killers.

"Not to sound like we have been slacking . . ." Fiona began, her brow furrowed, "but we have killed maybe . . . four."

"Today? That's not so bad." I wrinkled up my face. It was high stakes and could wear on your soul—and the Shadow didn't always fight fair.

"No." The fighter grimaced and rubbed the back of her neck. "In total."

I stared at her blankly before looking at Ren. For a change, I couldn't really read her expression. It was like some odd reveal where we found out *we* were the bad guys. Either that or things here were much different from the first area. Unlike me, I wasn't really sure what to say—without making us sound like monsters or painting them as weaklings.

"We ate more than that just in this first village," Wolf snuffed from behind us.

"Yes, well . . ." Fiona exhaled through her nose. "We have plenty of problems of our own."

She must have fought the chainsword man in the first area, I considered. But the Lady had only converted people to her cult in the last week—Fiona should have been in this area for longer than that. Timeline didn't really add up, so I made a mental note to think more about it later.

Ren moved across, and we switched places so that she was next to the fighter. "Tyler? Katie? Rektar?"

Fiona grimaced. "Katie's dead. Rektar is in a different Party farther north. Tyler is . . ."

"One of your current problems?" Ren nodded.

I leaned my head forward and raised an eyebrow, hoping to be included in the loop. Perhaps a little too energetically, as a wave of vertigo made my vision blur.

The elf raised an eyebrow toward me. "Remember that I said I had seen summoners before? Tyler is one, a certain kind of summoner."

"Are you going to leave me in suspense or tell me what kind?"

"Not so funny when it's the other way around, huh?" Her eyes narrowed, and a crack of a smile illuminated the corners of her eyes. "Necromancer."

"Ah." That was a puzzle I could put together. If he had fallen to the Crimson Shadow, then the Party here had probably been too busy fighting off groups of undead to properly focus on getting rid of the root cause themselves. Or I was being overly generous with my assumption.

"He has been hiding away and sending groups of undead toward our camp every so often. It makes it hard to sleep and rest. Hard to move forward when we could be attacked at any moment." The fighter shrugged apologetically.

"The undead fucking suck," the goblin added.

"My apologies." I gave the short greenskin a soft smile. "I do not believe we've been properly introduced."

"Shit, sorry." Fiona waved a plated hand. "I get so caught up in things I forget my manners. This is Ruby. Then behind we have Larius, Magnus, and Clive."

The very average man being called Clive seemed to fit, as did Magnus for the large lion man. They nodded their greetings as politely as they were able, but they didn't seem to much like socializing. In fact, they had spent a lot of time looking at our surroundings when not giving us odd glares. I had considered the possibility that there might be a trap here awaiting a reveal, but I trusted Fiona—as much as Ren seemed to anyway.

"Pleasure." I grinned with my show smile. Unlikely we'd be acquaintances for too long, but it paid to be on good terms with potential allies in such a conflict-driven world. "Your scout, Rolo, hasn't been able to pinpoint the necromancer?"

"Too dangerous. He tried, don't get me wrong, but Tyler has other Party members assisting him that make it difficult to get close without being spotted." Fiona shrugged.

Not something we couldn't accomplish. Unfair, given I didn't know the whole situation and was just riding the high of having survived the village. Another wave of vertigo made me shudder. I looked out at the scenery as we continued down the road, the village sinking away behind us. Hills, fields, and sparse groups of trees. There were some Monsters out to our right, but I couldn't focus my eyes without them hurting. Terrible timing for a migraine.

"If you have space for us, we'd love to help you out," Ren offered. A very strong statement from the elf, but I had no disagreements. Fixing the wrongs of the Shadow seemed to be our bread and butter now. Winning some applause from an actual audience was starting to warm me on the inside. Or was that nausea?

Wolf nudged me from behind. "You okay, Max?"

I turned my sweaty face to him and nodded. "Better than ever." I maintained eye contact, then corrected course. "Actually, I'm feeling a little under the weather."

He looked up toward the sky and then nodded back to me.

Ren and Fiona had walked slightly ahead during my mania with the bear, so I don't think she'd heard. Ruby certainly did and prodded me in the side with her staff, causing the bell to clink a little.

"What's your Status say, purple man?"

I grimaced, hating to interact with the reports to find out what current malady was ruining my day.

[Health Report]
[Cursed]

"It says I'm cured?" My eyes blurred the text as I struggled to focus. The statement came out as a question, but she didn't catch the nuance of it—so possibly my comprehension was correct. Cured of what? I sighed as I realized this was something I was meant to be better at now.

[Curse: SSSS sssSS ssSSSs]

So I couldn't read most of that, but it certainly didn't say "Cured" anymore. Unless I was cured of the curse? The looming inevitability that I may have mistakenly assumed I got away with the misdirection and my dove caught the curse started to weigh on me, and I—

I walked into the elf, not noticing that they had stopped just ahead of us. "*Ack*, sorry!"

She grabbed me, partially so that we didn't end up on the ground, but also I could see her bright eyes burning into me. "Max, you look like shit—what's wrong?"

"Cursed, I think." I grimaced. As much as I wanted to put up a front while we had company, I couldn't bring myself to lie straight to her face. Couldn't even bend the truth most of the time. We had agreed to honesty and openness, to grow as a Party, and although it took me a few mistakes, we were there.

"What kind?"

She didn't let go of me yet, which either meant I looked a lot worse than I felt, or she was worried and not trying to put a front up while in present company either. It would have been a moment to reflect on, perhaps, if I didn't feel like turning my stomach inside out onto the ground.

"Let me try to read it again," I offered. "My vision is a little blurry."

"Any of you have curse removal?" She turned her head to glare at them. Warmth came up behind me, and she gently pushed me back to lean against the side of Wolf.

I slowly sank down to sit on the road. The comfort the bear provided was better than many medicines, and over our time together, it had become a bonding point for the three of us. He might not talk as much or engage in the System bullshit to as great a degree, but he was family to us all the same. "Thanks, Wolf," I murmured and narrowed my eyes at the text boxes again.

"Depends on the type of curse." The goblin hopped over to me and put her hand on my head. "He is *very* warm."

Ren plucked my hat off and put it on my lap, the slight breeze cooling my hair. It was messy, needed cutting at this point. Couldn't be seen—no, *focus*, Max. "Yeah, it's from the village-hall Monster. Apparently, killing it also gives you a curse, which is why I had to answer the riddle."

The elf crouched down beside me and put her hand on my shoulder. If anything, it just made me feel warmer. Now that she showed me care and compassion on occasion, it made me feel worse for getting into these situations. Shouldn't be putting that burden on her.

"What was the riddle, Max?" she asked me, eyes soft despite her concern.

"It was bugged or something. It just hissed at me." I pouted, as if given a bad deal. Not that I would have tried to answer it, unless it was easy. Perhaps a lesson that killing my way through things wasn't always the best problem solver. *No*, I didn't like that lesson.

The goblin still had her hand on my forehead, which seemed unnecessary. The large lion head of the other Party member loomed into my vision. Why people felt they needed to be in my personal space all the time was beyond me.

"What did the creature look like, *man*?" His voice was deep and just as how I imagined he would speak.

"Dark robes, pale face, large back eyes with white pupils. No other real features, I guess."

He stood back away, his shadow passing and allowing the dim light of day to wash over me again. I felt relatively stable considering, wobbly and sick, yes, but it wasn't getting worse yet. Magnus murmured something to the goblin, which I didn't catch, as I was distracted by Ren. What an odd life I now led.

She leaned forward, her lips near my ear. "I fucking hate people. I can't do this without you."

I shivered, the words almost chilling me enough to break the fever.

A pulse of energy flooded through me as she moved away, coming from the goblin spellcaster rather than something born from how my heartbeat had skipped. Some of the odd feeling washed away, and I regained my composure.

"Thank you." I smiled, placing my hat back on my head but instead missing by several inches. It dropped to the ground, and I pouted again.

"It's not a cure." Ruby shrugged. "Some curses are super fucked, but it'll keep you lucid until we can get you back to the camp."

"Lucid?" Ren tilted her head and helped put my hat back on properly. "That'll be a first for Max."

"Listen," I said, allowing her to help me to my feet. "I haven't even—" One last wave of vertigo threatened to tip my head directly into the cobblestone road, to crack my head open just as I was about to say it. Probably my tight lips were the only thing saving it from becoming destiny. That and the tight grip Ren had on me.

"Fuck's sake, trickster," she murmured, wanting to release the near hug she had on me but also not wanting me to break across the ground.

I leaned forward to her ear. "Show must go on. Can't do this without you, Ren," I whispered.

CHAPTER SIX

Chewing Through It

The rest of the walk went by rather quickly, which might have been due to the fact my head still felt like it was full of bubbles. Whatever the goblin had cast on me, it allowed me to walk along at a normal pace and keep my thoughts on the right page. The page being the inside of my skull. I traveled alongside Wolf, partially for stability if a wave of vertigo came up by surprise, as Ren walked and talked with Fiona.

As much as I hated being out of the loop, I doubted I was in the right mind to fully participate or keep hold of whatever details they were discussing. It might be important things about the Crimson, or perhaps just gossip as they caught up on whatever had happened since they'd last seen each other. Ren might feel uncomfortable being around all these people, but she was able to feign that she was fine with it quite well.

Wolf growled at me in reflex as I pulled at his fur while trying not to tip over. "Sorry, Wolf," I apologized, a sheepish smile across my face.

"It is more the surprise than the pain. I am not angry." He looked up at me as his expression softened again.

"What do you make of our new pals?" I murmured to him as their attention moved back away from the bear's growl.

"Not particularly keen." He raised an eyebrow. "Especially the goat one."

I gave him a pat on the flank. The assumption was that he meant Magnus but hadn't any knowledge of lions in his previous life—which made perfect sense to me. Still, I narrowed my eyes in contemplation, wondering if any of them might secretly be goats and he could see something that I couldn't.

My intense look apparently drew the attention of one of them, and Clive slowed down to walk beside us.

"Hello. Max and Wolf, correct?"

I nodded. "Clive. It's a pleasure."

"Sure," he replied. "I find your outfit very interesting. Both of yours, actually."

While I could definitely agree that my very purple suit was, in fact, *spectacular* . . . coming from a man that looked like he was the living equivalent of stale bread, I was a little suspicious. Perhaps unfair for me to judge based on appearances too, I reminded myself. There was definitely a benefit to blending in that I was too stubborn to internalize.

"Thank you," I managed. "I find it suits my both my Class and personality quite well."

"I find it garish and unbecoming," Wolf murmured, "but I'm a team player."

Clive smiled and scratched at his short brown hair. "System is funny like that, right? Seems to know what you like, how you should progress based on your current goals."

I nodded at him but didn't feel keen to blurt out my thoughts on the matter. Not while the curse was making mashed potatoes of my brain. He did have a point though. Even our level-up abilities had drawn closer together to becoming influenced by one another as if it was intended all along.

Maybe something to encourage people to work together? That just made me wonder what happened to the Lady and her ever-increasing cult. While the first area was just Shadow or the dead, this second at least had pockets of resistance. Even if they were ineffective at removing the blight from this world. I shouldn't be eager for the conflict, *but I was.*

"Camp is just up on the left here," Clive noted, raising his hand to a figure sitting atop a rock at the split in the road. "That's Rolo."

He wore a cloak that made him blend in near seamlessly to the moss-covered stone. I might not have noticed him if he wasn't pointed out. Clothing a similar color—drab grays and greens. His face was shadowed by the garment covering his head, but a singular eye of pure white sat in the middle, reminding me of a cyclops. An awkward shiver ran through me, but I wasn't sure if that was due to being watched by the odd figure or if my brain had finally given up the ghost. Strange.

We circled around the large stone, following the road down to our left, and the camp was immediately visible. Down at the bottom of a valley, hastily constructed wooden walls blocked some of the view of the pale tents and dark browns of crates and the like dotted beyond.

As much as it looked like safety, something within me told me it was anything but. The showman side of me was practically salivating at the potential non-violent audience now before me, but the part of me that killed demons paled at the thought of being around so many unknowns.

Ren slowed to walk beside me. "How you feeling, trickster?"

"Been better." I shrugged. "But have been a lot worse."

She nodded. It didn't need to be said that the time my head was cracked open was probably my worst day. Either of the times that it had happened, I supposed. She leaned in a little closer.

"This place makes me nervous."

"Same." If she was able to readily admit that in the cold light of day, then things had definitely gotten her danger senses up. As much as that made me happier about my own dislike of current proceedings, it did also further worry me.

Ruby turned around and waved to me. "If you come with me to the med tent, Max, I'll get you fixed up."

"Just the curse, or can you do other things?" Ren asked, nudging me with her elbow.

I rolled my eyes, which somehow helped me counterbalance my inner ear, and I didn't stumble into the bear from her jostling.

"Magnus will find you some tents if you plan to stay," Fiona offered. "We have vacancies as of yesterday."

We could read between the lines. Well, Wolf might not be able to, but he was currently preoccupied with staring at the lion man.

I looked at Ren, and she gave me the briefest of nods. The question didn't need to be asked. Shared tent with Wolf on our doorstep. Together and safe. Even in the middle of potential allies, we didn't want to take a risk. If it weren't for the elf knowing the fighter previously, I doubted we'd even be in this position, and we'd be off grinding Quests and looking for our own place to sleep.

It was no tavern, but perhaps we could allow ourselves a little creature comfort before the show truly started.

"How many stay here?" I asked, seeing a couple of figures moving around within as we closed in on the gate.

Fiona wrinkled up her face. "Just . . . slightly over a dozen now. Fourteen? Sixteen?"

"Three groups and Rolo," Magnus confirmed. "Sixteen, plus you three, man."

I didn't like that. The number of people here, at least. Referring to me as *man* didn't really move the dial—it was expected when you had talking animals and people from worlds more fantastical than my own.

The gates opened wide as we reached them, a stout dwarf who was more snow-white beard than anything else apparently on guard duty.

"This way, purple guy!" The goblin hopped up and down to get my attention as the sight of so many tents and potential Players briefly overwhelmed me.

I turned and started off in her direction as Magnus led Ren and Wolf to the right, the elf catching my eye before our line of sight was obscured. She looked uncomfortable, to say the least. Despite being raised to inherit the responsibilities of watching over her community in her previous world, she was perhaps the least of a people person I had ever met.

Being in conflict with nearly every person you met on arriving here certainly hadn't helped—and even as a natural and insufferable performer, I had my reservations about the campground. Just the one night, maybe, and then we'd forge our own path.

Ruby led me through a few rows of tents before arriving at one with a red cross painted on the side. Some things appeared to be universal. Lifting the flap hardly near high enough, she gestured for me to enter—which I did, stooping so that I could push the canvas doorway over myself.

Inside, a simple space with two beds and several cabinets and containers in different shapes and sizes. Drab grays and off-whites, which were reassuringly clinical. I took a seat on one of the beds, mostly just thankful my legs didn't have to strain to keep the rest of me from toppling over like a tower of cards anymore.

"Now then." She entered behind me and pulled out a stool to stand on before walking over to a cabinet. "This isn't related to your cure, but I always ask my patients how they are doing—like with the System 'n' shit."

"It . . . definitely took some getting used to." I frowned, unsure what my actual thoughts were. It was horrifying and restrictive at times, and the good part was . . . I had met Ren?

"I'll say." She snorted as she withdrew a bottle of something green and slimy. "This icky crap helps me diagnose which other icky crap I can use to remove your curse." She gave me an apologetic grin.

"It's all icky crap?"

"'Fraid so, bud. System determined my years of medical research and training was just good for slapping different kinds of goo on people." She grinned widely and hopped up on the stool in front of me.

"You didn't use *goo* in your previous life?" I removed my hat and placed it beside me.

She popped the corked lid and tilted her head. "Oh, I did, but there was more . . . nuance and shit, you know?"

I nodded. Same with how my tricks were now just born from magic and manipulating the tools the System labored us with, rather than manually having to do all the hard work. Energy slowly drained from me as she stuck a finger into the jar and withdrew the sickly looking paste onto her finger.

She rubbed it across my forehead, and while it was cold and soothing, it *was* also pretty gross.

"Takes a minute before I can read it." She rolled her eyes, clearly not a fan of how the System viewed how her work should be done. "Wanna tell me more about the first area? Fiona fucking hated the chainsword guy. Had a weird name . . . Valpor . . . Velorp . . . or some shit."

"Hmm. He was with the Crimson," I worked my jaw as my fevered brain felt a little calmer. "In the fort, which we went and destroyed."

Ruby whistled. "Fiona thought you looked like a right nob, but killing that douche won you some favor with her."

"Being a leader involves a lot of tough calls." Like, calling me names was a hard sell—at least in my opinion.

"So does taking a life." Her eyes observed me for a moment, as if there was more to that sentence, before she changed course. "If you can break the neck of that gangly necromancer, Fiona would be your number one fan."

I did need more fans, that was true. Another reason to defeat the group keeping these people stuck here. With almost three Parties, however, I wondered why they hadn't made a play for it.

Ruby licked her finger and then placed it against the muck on my forehead. Her eyes looked off to the peaked ceiling of the tent as she considered . . . whatever it was that she was doing. A handful of seconds passed before she removed the offending digit. While I was usually put off by people invading my personal space, there was something about the goblin—or perhaps just the medical setting— that didn't bother me.

"Got some good news and some bad news."

"How long have I got to live?" I gave her a grim smile.

"In this world . . . ?" She rolled her eyes. "System allowing, you're fine. It's not a curse that I can cure—but the good news is that it goes away after a nice sleep."

I deflated slightly, unsure whether I was happy about that or not. "Are we talking about a duration of sleep, or it resets after a certain time of the day, or . . . ?"

"Fuck if I know." She shrugged. "It's a *curse*. But hey, I've got something that's *not* slop that can help take the edge off until you can snooze."

The goblin hopped down off of the stool and went to a different cabinet to slide out a drawer. After some inaudible grumblings, she returned and held up what looked to be some kind of bark or root from something.

"I realize this looks like I'm bullshitting you." She wagged it at me. "You just have to trust I take my job very seriously."

"It's to chew?" I gingerly received it in my hand. To her credit, it wasn't slimy at all.

"Won't lie and say it doesn't taste like shit, but it'll keep the symptoms from getting any worse. You'll just have a little fever and lightheadedness until the morn."

"Thanks, Ruby." I managed a smile but hesitated to put the root into my mouth. After a few seconds of her patiently staring at me to complete the act, I started to slowly move it toward my opening maw. Sure, I could dazzle my way out of this . . . but I shouldn't turn down health-care advice. Ren would disapprove.

As if hearing my panicked woes, a shadow passed over the tent entrance before a figure started to enter. Not my protégé, unfortunately, but Fiona.

"How's the patient, Rubes?"

The goblin shrugged. "Be back to normal tomorrow." She shot me a grin, apparently finding amusement in the *normal* that included dressing as I did. "He just has to chew that root, and there will be no further complications."

Now, with both of them staring me down, I had no choice. It crunched as part split off into my mouth resigned to its fate. The shards then became somewhat chewy, like gum. It didn't actually taste that bad, which was potentially concerning. It was like caramel almost.

"Excellent. If you could give us a few minutes alone?" Fiona smiled warmly toward the short greenskin, who nodded and left with a brief curtsey toward me.

I nodded my thanks to her as she departed before clocking that the expression on the fighter had cooled dramatically.

"So got a magic dick on you, huh?"

The helpful root betrayed me, and I coughed, almost choking on my surprise. "Huh?"

"Ren." The woman crossed her arms across her breastplate. "Even got her dressing up in a similar clown outfit."

"Magician," I corrected her. "Sorry, I'm lost on what the question was?" My brow furrowed, and I picked my hat back up to place upon my head.

"The Ren I knew was very aloof, cold, and reluctant to spend time with *anyone* else. I just wanted to find out what you have going on that could change her so much."

Her scowl was probably intended to intimidate me, but it had no effect. "Perhaps I just didn't abandon her."

"You *fuck*." She stepped toward me and leveled a plated fist as a threat. "You don't know what it was like. What she was so hell-bent on doing."

"Murdering a gang to seek her revenge?"

Fiona worked her jaw. "It was foolish. There was nothing to be gained and everything to lose."

A smile ran up my face as I chewed the root. It shouldn't be a humorous situation, but the fever was warming up my brain something fierce. "Then isn't it obvious what we did? What I did?"

She deflated slightly, not really relaxing, but just unable to hold that spark of anger within her any longer. "I'm . . . still struggling to parse that you are both admitting to being mass murderers. You killed all the people on the island, and then in the first area too? No bullshit?"

"No bullshit," I confirmed. "I'm sure you aren't blind to the join-us-or-die attitude the Lady and Crimson Shadow have. We just chose the third option."

Now she relaxed, but I could see there was a fuller picture I wasn't privy to. How long they had known each other, what they had been through, and what had caused their split. Clearly Fiona cared for Ren, in some manner, but it was also clear that she wasn't able to offer the elf the vengeance she sought. Interesting that they had such strong views to differentiate killing Players to killing Monsters. We did one and the same without such holdups. Potentially a bad look.

Eventually, she shook whatever thoughts were clouding her mind away. "Fine. Perhaps what we need is people like you three to get us out of this fucking hole. But . . ." Her eyes bored into mine. "You better never let her down. Or we'll see how magic that dick is when I cut it off."

She barely gave me a second to acknowledge before she turned and exited the tent.

I chewed for a few seconds, in silence, wondering why my unmentionables had become a necessary part of that conversation. In an attempt to avoid letting my mind wander down adjacent paths, I stepped down and left the tent.

The daylight burned at my eyes, and I wavered for a few seconds before getting my bearings. Ren and Wolf should be roughly straight ahead, maybe to the right a little?

Over on the left, however, was a small grouping of trees just outside of the main camp. Shaded and lush with grass and vegetation. Perhaps I could have a brief nap and shake this curse? Or at least get out of this damnable sunshine.

I stumbled over, stepping out of the camp proper into the edge of the wilderness. They'd be able to find me easily enough with this suit on, and I must have caught some eyes on my journey.

Slowly, I sank myself down between a couple of trees, hoping that the coolness of the shade would seep into my head and solidify my brain. I chewed like crazy. Nope, still too uncomfortable to nap—it would be better to find Ren and lay in the tent. Maybe she could hold the pieces of my skull together and comfort me.

Smiling at the possibilities, I went to stand—before I was plunged into darkness.

Before I had a chance to fight against the head covering, something weighty struck me in the side of the head, forcibly giving me the desired nap.

CHAPTER SEVEN

Lock and Key

I groaned as my eyes opened. Blurry at first, before dim light tried to paint me a picture. As I attempted to lift my hands to rub some clarity into my tired orbs, I found I could not, for they were bound behind me.

Gray stone walls filtered into view. I was seated, and . . . I looked down and blinked. In nothing but my underwear and undershirt. My ankles were bound to the legs of the plain wooden chair, while my wrists were to the back supports, as well as to each other. Something else heavy and metallic sat on my right forearm. A manacle? It had an odd feel to it.

I looked around with an eyebrow raised. Mostly a plain, albeit rather grubby, room. A dozen or so feet square, with me somewhat near the back wall. Directly ahead of me was the doorway, made of a dark metal with a closed slit probably used as a window. A table in the front-left corner, with my clothes folded upon it next to a wooden case. The floor around the chair was especially discolored. Soiled with all manner of bodily fluids, if my imagination allowed it.

It was all very reminiscent of a horror movie, which bordered on being too cliché to be any valid sort of threat. I smiled and tried to draw a card to cut the rope bindings. Nothing. The panic meter moved up a notch.

With the thud of footsteps close by, the door then swung open on creaking hinges. A man walked in. Stocky but strong, a dirtied leather apron covering gray linens that were grubby despite the protection. His face was obscured by a mask that was either cured leather or something made to look that way. My bare toes wiggled in amusement. He looked like a *pigman*, and I couldn't wait to kill him. So *very* eager, the other side of me salivated at the prospect.

"Ah, you're awake," he grunted, his lower mouth just about visible beneath his covered face. Wide stubbled chin and a cruel grin.

"Could have left me out for a little longer. I'm trying to sleep off a curse."

He snorted, continuing to add to the piggish similarities. "Don't have all day to wait for yer beauty sleep." His thick hands shuffled through my belongings. "Doubt anyone will buy these stupid fuckin' clothes. But the summoning item . . ." He whistled as he picked it up and waggled it.

Rage prickled through me. While I had been able to use it when it wasn't quite on my person previously, the Equipment screen confirmed that it was properly unequipped now. No cards and no summons.

"You seem too smart to sign up with the Crimson Shadow," I lied, trying to buy some time. He looked dumb as shit, and I wanted to break that hand touching my deck. Tear those fingers off. My inner monologue was on fire, the showman Max cowering away from the raging inferno building under the other, less patient one.

The man chuckled wetly. "I'm not with those stupid fucks. I *love* being here in the System, in charge of my own group. It's my playground. No authorities to come knockin'."

I winced and looked around the room, as if some less benign answer lay in a corner somewhere. "So what do you do here?"

"Black market deals. Some people pay top gold for the best items without having to farm them for themselves. Lazy, if you ask me." He shrugged and opened up the wooden case.

"Then why am I here?" Surely if robbery was their main motive, whoever had the balls to poach me in broad daylight could have just stripped me and made off with the goods.

"The gold is just the side hustle." From within the case, he withdrew a scalpel. "It's just so happens it aligns with my personal hobby." He snorted. "My *calling*."

He stepped closer, and his body odor washed over me as he blocked some of the light. An imposing figure, for certain, but I had fought worse—

The blade pressed against my bare thigh, and he moved it down toward my knee, increasing the pressure as he went until I clenched my jaw and growled.

"Good," he said, standing back up. He moved over to the case and placed the blade away.

Didn't even disinfect it first. I was horrified.

"Some people have pain resistance or regeneration Passives. The handcuff only restricts active Abilities." He tilted his head from side to side. "Yer pretty normal. Had one guy in that barely flinched even when I could see his bones. Fascinating, really."

All of that aside, I needed this handcuff when I eventually escaped. Imagine being able to restrict someone from casting Skills? Amazingly powerful. I grimaced at the trail of blood now running down my leg. *Fucking pigman.*

"You don't really know who I am, do you?" I smiled. Either the curse was working overtime on my brain, or it took a lot more than this B movie act to rustle the feathers of other Max. Shouldn't call him that, really. We were the same Max now.

"Don't care." He stooped down to pull out a little cupboard on wheels from beneath the table. "Although, soon we'll find out what you're made of."

He placed the open case atop the cupboard and wheeled it over closer to me. He wanted me to see the tools of his trade—which was unfair as he had taken mine without asking. The only *fair* thing to do would be to return the favor . . .

The inside was dirty as though it hadn't even been cleared of dried blood from the used tools previously. It had all the sorts of things you'd expected to find if a handyman and a dentist had a baby and it grew up to believe it was a surgeon but had no formal training. Or manners.

"Any you prefer I don't use?" The bottom of his wide grin was illuminated beneath his mask.

"Is that like a reverse psychology thing? I hate tricks, I hope you know." If he could see the amusement on my face, he did nothing to acknowledge it.

"Sometimes, I take the tongues first, but smart fucks *usually* change their tune. More fun to hear the pleading."

I wasn't really listening. Instead, my eyes were cycling through my Inventory. I hadn't arranged things for a while, and I might need to make space shortly. Maybe for my own severed body parts—which was an amusing thought, if not a bit macabre.

[Restrained: Cannot take Inventory items into your hands]
[Nullified: Cannot use active Abilities]

A knock at the door waylaid his hand from reaching for something from the assortment of jagged metal implements. He turned, and his wide waistline jostled the small cupboard a couple of extra inches toward me.

The window slat opened, and two beady eyes peered through.

"Sorry, boss. We've got a problem."

The piggy deflated. "What is it? I'm about to *work*."

"We were . . . We were followed?" The man's voice cracked, clearly not pleased about drawing the short straw to break the news.

"Stupid fucks." The butcher shook his head. "Go take the lads and run them down before they find this place. Don't bother with prisoners. Is it the assholes from the camp?"

"N-no, it's . . . an elf and a bear."

"I'm sure you can handle that. Fuck off already."

He turned back to me as the slat closed. "Seems your girlfriend and pet are about to . . ."

His masked face turned down toward the case, now completely empty, before looking back at me.

"I'm not too sure about *girlfriend*." I wrinkled up my face. "It's not really something so . . . *official* yet, right?"

"Give those back." His fists clenched. "You have a Passive for looting quickly. Well done. You have prolonged your suffering."

Part of me wished I had been better at escapology. I was neither a contortionist nor had the man given me an easy-to-reach knot to try to work through. Of course, at some point in my career I had given it a go, but after pulling the muscles through my back and wiggling on the floor in pain for five minutes in my flat alone . . . I had decided it wasn't for me. Didn't mean I was totally incapable, however.

"I'll trade you." I smiled.

He slowly shook his head, trying to control his anger. It probably wasn't fun for him if his emotions took over. "I'm not opposed to breaking you bone by bone with my bare hands."

If only Wolf were here, I could have made a pun. "You're out of time already. Sorry. Either you'll have to blue ball yourself by killing me right now, or your life is forfeit."

Purple electricity began arcing around my body, slightly illuminating the chamber. I could see the reflection of my bright eyes on his leather apron. Was this even a Passive? Didn't matter. The brief confusion giving him pause abated, and he drew back a fist to punch me.

A little bit of finesse was required, but his weighty fist slammed into the blunt end of the sword, the point of which was pressed against the chair between my legs. Dangerously close to my alleged magic manhood.

He was strong, although it wasn't enough to split the chair. Instead, he went to grab the weapon, but it vanished back into my Inventory. Perhaps I shouldn't play with my food. He needed to pay for touching my magic deck. *Ha.*

As he stepped back away to right himself, his foot slipped on the marbles rolling across the floor. He dropped onto his wide rear end with a growl as I stood up, the ropes dropping away like water off a duck.

"How?" He seethed.

"Short answer?" I grinned as purple energy crackled around me. "*Fucking magic.*"

Fog burst from around me, immediately filling the small room with an impenetrable dense gray. He stood, both hands bursting into red flame as he swung out for me. I wasn't there any longer, however.

"Tell me how to remove the cuff, and I won't kill you."

He swung again for my voice, but I had moved. My enraged electricity had abated so as not to give up my position, but his flaming fists left no guesswork required for where he stood.

"Fuck you! Show yourself!"

"Wrong answer," I hissed. A thunk shortly followed, with his growl of pain immediately after. And then another, and his left fist extinguished.

"*Karn!*" he yelled out.

"There's no help on the way," I whispered as the fog instantly vanished.

I pressed the triggers on both the held crossbows, splitting his mask as the bolts impaled through his face into his brain. He twitched and went to swing for me as he dropped onto the floor.

[Nullification-Cuff Key]
[Prison-Cell Keys]
[Regeneration Orb]

With a click, I slipped from the cuff and put it into my Inventory. Plenty of tricks in that magic item's future. No time to check everything else. I needed to find the rest of my Party.

Clothing looted for later and magic deck in my hand and equipped. Pact demon into my grasp and a bright grin on my face. Struck the stupid *fucking* pig-man and he rose to become Roger.

"Hey . . . Boss?" He looked around. "Fuck, what did you summon me in for this time?"

"Escaping torture," I explained. "We need to murder our way into the daylight."

The demon whistled. "Say less, boss."

From my Inventory, I withdrew Jokkar's mace. A large weapon, studded with pearl teeth. "See if you have the strength in that body."

I struggled to pass it over, but he managed to lift it with little issue. "I may cry with fuckin' happiness."

"After the violence, please." I wrenched open the door and stepped out into a cool corridor. Underground? It had that murky, damp-stone look to it. Two further cells to my right where there was a dead end, one more cell to my left, and then a further illuminated passage.

"Watch the corridor," I commanded and dropped down a Hellhound+ card to go assist him. I strode to the dead end and opened up the slat of the last cell. Empty. Then the next one. Not empty, but the mutilated figure within was long gone. I closed it and clenched my jaw. Fourth cell now, closest to my demons.

I stumbled back against the rocky wall as the hastily summoned plank of wood struck me in the face. It had saved me from getting impaled by the sword jabbed through the opened slat, so I couldn't complain, even with the blood running down from my nose.

Roger was already there, the large mace slamming into the metal door—buckling it and shattering the hinges. It struck and collapsed onto the figure beyond, knocking them to the ground. My canine pal was ready to pounce and had grabbed the struggling man by the throat before he could free himself.

The chair was occupied by a bloodied figure. Alive, but they had done some work on him already. Black mustache and goatee, shoulder-length wavy hair all matted with blood. His one remaining eye looked up at me, exhausted. Too out of it to speak.

I stepped into the room, a purple card circling around the chair to cut his binds. In my hand, a health potion. "Roger, come help this man. Protect him as you would me."

"Yes, boss."

My head hummed. Perhaps it needed covering. I went into my Inventory and shuffled my hat over into the Equipment window, and it appeared. Comforted. Back out into the hallway with Hellhound+ by my side. There were now echoes of familiar sounds, and I couldn't help but grin—oh, I was already grinning. Face muscles ached from it, in fact.

Split my cards into the air and circled them like a spinning wheel as I walked forward. Kept me on track. Follow the light, find the Party. There was shouting now, and shadows washed over the next corner in the passageway. Two panicked men stumbled backward, as if hoping to find backup from what they were running from. Out of the frying pan and into the second, more demonic frying pan.

Card through the head of the first, the second humbled by the next attack before my demon dog knocked them over. Ripping and tearing, and then something more palatable slid around the corner.

"Max!" Surprise and worry across her face. Then, confusion. "You're just in your underwear?"

"No," I slurred, shaking slightly. "I am wearing my hat."

"Dickbag." She power walked over to me and gave me a hug. "Do I need to put a leash on you?" Her grip was released so that she could burn through me with a signature glare, knowing what was going through my mind.

Mostly the curse actually. As much as I wanted to enjoy her company, I was mentally melting away. "Thanks for coming for me," I said with a straight face.

"Good thing your Party has a bear with a good sense of smell and I know a bit of tracking, otherwise you'd be . . ." She stopped and pulled a face in seeing I was out and thriving, in a manner of speaking.

"I had things under control, but I much prefer having you both around." I smiled as Roger moved up to join us, the injured man propped up under his arm.

"Fuck." Ren grimaced at my pact demon's puppet. "This was the guy who was going to . . . torture you?"

"Not even for a good reason." I yawned, the fading adrenaline taking my desire to stay awake along with it. "Just sell my items and then get off on hurting me."

"At least I let you keep your stuff, huh?" She prodded my chest and gave a slight smile. "Put your clothes on already."

Eyes unfocused, I did so—putting all my Equipment and clothing in the right slots, while she gave a heal to the rescued man.

"Wolf is stuck a little farther in, where the passageways are too narrow. But he is doing okay," she informed me. "This guy, however . . ." She crouched down to give him a look over. "Lost an eye, *maybe* use of his right arm. Trauma for sure."

I clicked my tongue. "We'll do what we can. Nobody else from the camp cared to help you?"

She shook her head, and her expression dulled before she gestured for us to move along.

"It's like they're afraid to die." I rolled my eyes. "Although, I don't think Fiona is fond of me."

"She's a hard-ass," Ren said with a shrug. "You know her opinion doesn't matter though, right?"

"Of course, I don't need to people please." I grinned, only slightly shaking as we walked down the passageway.

She raised an eyebrow at me.

"Well," I relented, "not *everyone*."

"Hey, Max!" Wolf said, his face full of apparent joy and thug gore. "Guess what I found?"

I raised my hand for him to continue, as we stepped into a wider chamber that had several mauled bodies—some of them sporting arrows.

He sat down and wiggled his head to jiggle his bowler hat for added effect.

"There's a treasure room." He pointed a paw toward a broken-down door off to the side.

I licked my lips with anticipation. *Time to loot.*

CHAPTER EIGHT

Safety in Numbers

I had skipped a few pages of the diary—left some blank as if to trick any potential reader into thinking I had died. No such peace for me yet. For most of our time spent on the island and in the first area, it had felt as though it was solely us against the world. We never got to fully appreciate the normal nature of the world around us, the sense of community that it was supposed to provide. As much time as we spent fixing things, we always had our feet in a new problem before seeing the results of our struggles behind us.

Ignoring Ren's rolled eyes at my apparent desire to actually search for items for a change, I began to claw my way through the room that Wolf had helpfully opened up for us.

"Don't have a lot of time left, boss." Roger leaned his head forward so I could see his bright-purple eyes. "Need me to stick around?"

My own eyes roved around in my skull as if he had jostled them loose from their moorings. "Uh, no, we'll be good. Thank you, Roger. Top work, as always."

"Didn't even murder anyone," I heard him murmur as he slunk away into mist, the body of my jailer dropping to the floor inertly.

"Think we could sling up our friend there, if you're okay with that, Wolf?"

"Sure."

"You alright, Max?" Ren asked from the doorway, about to help Wolf with the part that needed hands with opposable thumbs. "I mean, clearly you're *not*—but do I need to be worried?"

"No." I shook my head and then looked over at her with a smile. "You're perfect. I mean, there was nothing more that I could have asked for." My brain was not having it. The sooner I could sleep this curse off, the better. "You came here to save me is what I'm trying to say."

Her face softened. "Of course, dumbass." She went to assist Wolf, and I was left alone to sigh deeply.

Could I have murdered my way out of this den? Quite likely, once I had gotten the cuff off and retrieved my deck. Between Roger, my cards, and Hellhound+, any of these kidnappers and shady black market dealers would have been at a disadvantage in these close confines.

I thumbed through the furniture, pop-up boxes letting me know what lay inside. Mostly junk Equipment in the first three boxes. Early-level stuff that they probably couldn't sell as easily.

The fourth gave me pause, and I looted everything from it to share around at a better time. I put the gloves on right now, however, despite my brain trying to do three things at once.

[Spiked Gloves: +2 STR, +10% melee Damage]
[Gloves of the Trickster: +2 DEX, +3 INT]
[Fast Shawl: +4 AGI]
[Hardy Boots: +3 CON]
[Red Necklace: +2 AGI, +2 WIS]
[Slacks of the Wild: +2 AGI, +2 DEX]

The last chest was actually a safe. One of those where you had to turn the dial back and forth in the right combination to unlock it. I didn't know the right number sequence, and they hadn't written it handily nearby.

"Quinn is strapped up, Max." The elf reappeared at the doorway.

"Quinn?"

She nodded and stepped over to the ruined door to get closer to me. "He can barely talk. Just about said his name and then fell asleep."

"Wolf does have that effect, huh?" I smiled and returned to frowning at the safe.

"We need to get you back too." She lifted the hat from my head and placed her hand on my hair. No heal was given; she was perhaps just checking to make sure I was in one piece. "There was no combination on any of the ones we killed."

I gave the safe three taps on the top, and with the third, it vanished into my Inventory. The System would regret allowing me to do that. Even Ren's sigh was one more of apprehension than disdain. We'd crack it eventually, I was sure. She placed my hat back on my head, and I stood and turned to face her.

"I don't think you should be allowed to leave my sight," she informed me, her bright eyes narrowed.

"It's not nighttime yet." I smiled. "You're not supposed to be emotionally clingy."

As she opened her mouth to admonish me, I leaned forward and kissed her. A brief thing, but reciprocated. We parted slowly, her eyes almost immediately narrowed after. Hopefully I couldn't pass the curse on that way, although part of me considered the forward act was only due to my worn-down sensibilities.

"I'm serious, you . . . ass."

"Not keen on joining the commune then?" I tilted my head as she moved away, and we went to leave the storeroom.

"Fuck no. Fiona and Ruby are pleasant, but I can't stand the rest. Perpetual do-nothings. Especially as they can't see that they're just slowly dying by allowing themselves to be picked off."

"And what of these guys?" I extended my hand and gestured around at the corpses, picking up Jokkar's mace into my Inventory along the way. "They aren't even allied with the Lady. They're just *fuckers.*"

Ren snorted, seemingly amused enough by the rare times that I swore with such gusto. "Really? I can't believe they picked you up right outside the camp in broad daylight. Didn't even wait for night."

I nodded and rubbed at my eyes. "Normally I'm not such an easy mark, but this curse has me pretty loose. I just wanted a nap, and the trees seemed like they'd be comfortable."

"And you're okay now?"

"Bruising to my head—which is pretty standard at this point—and a cut on my leg. But he made the *mistake* of underestimating me."

She bit her tongue, clearly wanting to make some jabs but also not wanting to undermine how potentially dire this situation could have been.

I held my hand out and emptied all his horrible tools from my Inventory onto the corpse of the one who had jailed me. Even if they had a use, knowing what pain they could have caused prior to my capture . . . I didn't want them to have a career past this point.

"Nasty things," Wolf echoed my thoughts as he watched them drop to the floor.

As much as I had hated and burned to cause the death of the piglike man, there wasn't the desire to take pleasure in his suffering. We had killed plenty, often in ways that would get us locked up for life in other realities. But we didn't seek it out and revel in it. I looked around the room at the dead and wondered how much I could believe that. Better to have these thoughts when my mind was more comfortable.

Demons at least had the excuse they were born and lived through sin, beings devoted wholly to and fulfilled by evil. This man didn't have that excuse. Human, or at least adjacent to, he should have known better. *Aimed* to be better. Ren was right that the System seemed to pluck mostly assholes from their respective worlds. A reflection mirrored by the lack of assistance from the camp. No necks sticking out on my behalf just yet.

"Let's get going." I gestured for them to show me the way out. "There's nothing left for us here."

It was a simple hideout, not too dissimilar to the Thief Hideout from the first area. Built into a rocky outcropping, it seemed more likely that they had somehow taken over a System-created space than carved it themselves. Their attempts to hide it away were at least more proficient, with an uprooted tree and crushed bushes now lying where Wolf had trampled through their ruse.

Not even that far from the camp, which was a chilling thought. They may have had Abilities that made kidnapping me in the daytime a piece of cake—but if they had instead waited for the dark of night, then they may have had me for hours before someone noted my absence. Once again, our enemy's desperation and overconfidence were our blessing. Perhaps they too anticipated apathy from those around me.

"I have some Equipment for you to look at when we get back," I told Ren as we began walking back to the camp.

"Oh, *yeah*?"

We stared at each other blankly for a moment as my brain continued to hiss in the background. "Some for Wolf too," I added. My eyes turned away to focus on my System windows, as I was currently unable to accurately read social cues. The kiss had been somewhat out of character for us both, even if the sentiment of wanting to be close and safe was our unsaid normal.

[Regeneration Orb: Slowly regenerates health when out of combat]

I just needed to strap this to my head, and then I'd be invincible. Took up the Accessory slot—which currently had +5 percent spell-casting speed and +5 percent magic Damage in it—but considering it was for out of combat only, I saw no reason why I couldn't just swap them in our downtime. Even share it around. I equipped it now, shivering when I considered what it might have been used for previously.

In the den, I had counted eight opponents in total. Should things be as typical as anywhere else, that could mean there were two free agents somewhere— maybe on errand runs or looking for their next victim. The elephant poked its head out from the tree line to butt into my roving thoughts; could anyone in the camp be complicit?

"Ren?"

"Yeah, trickster?" She turned her head away from whatever she had been focused on.

"Am I being paranoid?"

Her frown narrowed, and I considered that she hadn't actually been privy to my inner monologue, no matter how loud it had to be to drown out the humming noise. If there was one thing I could rely on, it was her ability to read me like a book.

"It's hard to say." She ran her fingers through Wolf's fur. "We're used to it being us against the world. Anything that challenges that feels suspect."

It was possible that we were both paranoid then. A group of Players not allied with the Lady but seemingly not doing much to push back against the Crimson Shadow either. Some black market torture site a stone's throw away from them. Paranoia was something that kept us safe in a world that wanted us dead.

"Thoughts, Wolf?"

"I can almost taste the goat man."

I grimaced. Not exactly a sane response, but then again, I was asking a talking bear. Quinn remained in the sling, fast asleep.

Ren exhaled loudly. "I don't think Fiona is a . . . bad person."

"There's something I'm out of the loop on though, right?" I tilted my head and stumbled in that direction as my inner ear took a brief holiday.

She removed her hat to brush some of her radiant hair to the side before donning it once more. "Short version of the story," she began, as she worked her jaw. "She had a bit of a crush on me."

I nodded—another terrible action for my lack of balance. "That explains the chat she had with me then."

"When was that?" She raised an eyebrow.

"Right before I was kidnapped. Which sounds more suspicious than it probably is." Probably.

Ren sighed and shook her head, scowling out at the sparse woods surrounding us as we passed through. "She has no right. As if she has any say in what is good for me after she ran off when she couldn't accept just being friends and helping me on the island."

The fact that she was just another in the line of people who wanted to pucker lips with the elf put a wet blanket on the ire she had shown me for doubting my care for Ren. I would have rolled my eyes if it hadn't felt like I'd lose them. Not willing to help the elf with her murder spree but feeling like she had something to say about her well-being and romantic choices now seemed shortsighted, even if somewhat realistic. At least the murdering part.

"She's with the goblin now, right?" I put my hand up to my forehead. Burning up. "Ruby doesn't seem like an asshole."

"*Fiona* isn't an asshole. People just do stupid things when led by their hearts."

"Uh-huh," I said with a smile.

She scowled further. "Fuck you, Max. You . . . You *prick*."

I grinned widely and relaxed. If you ignored all the bad things, then life wasn't so bad. My feet stopped me, and I put my hand against a tree to try to prevent the world spinning out of control. They should really fix that.

The wide face of Wolf came up into my vision, his amber eyes regarding me with a tired look. "If you spent more energy on breathing instead of talking constantly, you wouldn't get so tired."

"Yerps," I slurred as sweat dripped from my head.

Ren was then beside me, shouldering my arm to make sure I didn't flop over toward the nearest rock. History did try to repeat itself. I shouldn't get in the way.

"It's not too far now. Do you have another tarp and we'll get you in a sling?"

I must look pretty bad for that to be the plan of action. In truth, I felt pretty bad—with no root to chew, the curse was slowly eroding me away into sweaty mush. How rude of the pigman to discard my medicine.

My mouth opened, but instead of words, I allowed a second tarp to fall slowly from within. A few awkward seconds passed as it unraveled into a small pile on the ground before me, the last corner of the faux vomit leaving my lips as my mouth curled to form a soft smile.

". . . I really hate you sometimes," Ren said with a sigh.

CHAPTER NINE

Happy Campers

I awoke with a bit of a start. Lying down with gray above me, my mind shouted *tent* before I could leap straight into blind panic. Soaked with sweat, and my heartbeat racing. Back in my underwear and shirt, I half expected the pig-faced kidnapper to appear over me. As if I had been drugged and the escape was all a dream.

A shadow loomed over me, and I flinched before the long hair of the elf fell over my face.

"Oops, sorry," she said softly and brushed it out of the way. "Are you okay, Max?"

"I drifted off in the sling. Fill me in." With the blanks painted over with the proper play of things, I'd be able to determine my current status.

"We arrived in camp. Ruby took Quinn, gave me something for your fever. Wolf brought you to the tent while I had some terse words with Fiona about their lack of care. Then I came back to play nurse, *again*."

No sharp edges in her expression as she told me that. Although it was more likely that she had stripped me of my suit, I found it more amusing to imagine Wolf trying to do the task without tearing me to shreds in frustration. Why that was the most important thing for my mind at present was perhaps worrying.

She could see the furrowed brow. "It's late evening now. You haven't had a full night's sleep."

"Balls," I said, deflating into the bedroll. Some manner of permanent camp, and they couldn't even get proper beds. I'd complain to the manager if it wasn't likely to end in bloodshed. What didn't though?

As if to answer my errant thoughts, Ren lay down beside me and put her arm across me, her fingers drumming gently on my chest.

"Moon is out, huh?" I asked, a smile across my face.

She sighed, her breath buffeting my bare shoulder. "*Dickbag.*"

"Go on though." Consistency was key, and I had learned to read when the darkness would bring out her softer side.

A few seconds passed before she responded, her fingers pausing their intended tune as the words found their way out. "Sometimes you scare me, Max."

"The whole purple eyes and demonic energy?" Considering the System had given her a demon-destroying Skill, that wouldn't be surprising. It made me wonder if the world had prepared us for the possibility that we'd become enemies, instead of . . . what we had now.

"No." She squirmed a little, trying to get more comfortable.

"My ability to kill without care?" It should certainly be concerning that I could put a den of people in the ground and not bat an eye.

"Not even that."

I stared up at the gray of our tent, the fading light of the day causing our interior to be dim. The large-shadowed shape of Wolf was outside the front, already sleeping. Maybe I got three guesses. I wasn't sure if she was waiting for it or if I'd never find out if I made another incorrect guess.

"It's because . . ." She eventually started to fill the silence. "You give me hope."

My brow furrowed, and I turned my head to face her. "That's a bad thing?"

"No." She moved closer and pressed the end of her nose against mine. "Just *scary*."

"I'd like to call one of those *somethings* that you owe me." I smiled widely at her.

She narrowed her eyes and moved her face slightly away to get a better picture of me.

Before she could fill in the blank with assumptions, I turned away from her onto my left to face the opposite side of the tent. "Could you put your arm around me?"

"*Asshole*," she whispered, but I could hear the smile on her face through it. She moved up close behind me and put her arm around.

Not quite as comfortable as Wolf, and I was too exhausted to ask if they could swap. If I were Ren, I'd be more worried over the fact that I was one bad day away from becoming what we sought to destroy. Even the happy campers here could see it, as if we had flashing danger signs over our heads. Kill, struggle, strengthen. The showman act allowed me to put a heavy blanket over the fact that I could be something a lot worse. I closed my eyes and hoped I wouldn't fall.

"Max?"

I opened my eyes to the bright light of day now permeating through our tent. Morning already? Sleep had hit me harder than . . . I turned over to see the elf already dressed, kneeling beside me. Her hand cupped my face, and she leaned in for a kiss.

"Survive the day and you'll get another," she said as she moved away.

Tongue-tied, I nodded and tried to put the pieces of my waking brain back into working order. Not that I wasn't planning on living through the day anyway, but that was as good a motivation as any.

"We have a guest," she continued, gesturing to my current lack of presentation. "Wolf has been hosting, but he is at his limits."

A brief amount of awkward stumbling around the surprisingly enclosed space, and I was fully dressed and ready for the first audience of the day. Why Ren had stayed to watch me rather than join the bear I wasn't sure—but it made the process of clothing myself feel more complicated than it needed to be.

But then, outside the tent I strode, dazzled by the morning light. The soft warmth was even more pleasant than the stage lights I was used to. I turned with a smile to see the rather bored-looking bear sitting beside a man with wavy black hair. An outfit of yellow and amber linens, encased with a plain leather breastplate. Black eye patch and his arm was bound with a splint and bandages.

"Max!" He smiled, his accent hitting some manner of familiarity that I couldn't place. "My humble thanks for saving my life." He stepped toward me and then knelt, bowing low to the floor. "I am forever in your debt."

"It's nothing." I waved him off with a grimace. Fans were one thing, but that was a little bit too full-on. "Luck smiled down on both of us yesterday."

Ren exited the tent to stand beside me as the man rose back to his feet. His good eye looked from her to me and then to the bear before back to me.

"Never in my time here have I seen such a beautiful Party. Truly inspirational."

I could feel Ren's disdain radiating from her even without glancing to see what expression she held. "Thank you?" I ventured.

"The great Dr. Ruby has told me I must rest until my trauma Status has gone, but if there is anything I can do to repay you, please." He gave a slight bow again. "I am at your service."

A wry grin went up the side of my face. "There is something, actually." Ren shot me a sharp glare before I leaned over and whispered my plan in her ear. She nodded her acceptance, even if her expression didn't budge.

"We are often short on receptive audiences," I began, moving to stand behind the elf. "If you could just stand and observe and give us your thoughts after, that would be a great help." I grinned widely and put my hands on Ren's shoulders.

"Sure." He shrugged, perhaps a little disappointed the task didn't involve putting himself in mortal peril to pay back the life I had apparently saved. Maybe I was reading too much into his confusion—we were *a lot*, even on the best of days.

"Perfect." I walked beside Ren and passed her over a thick gray blanket from behind me. We could really do with a silk sheet, or something velvet? Once she had it, I walked over to the pair waiting with apprehension and stood behind them. "This is our first try, so allow us some lenience," I murmured.

Ren cleared her throat and then took a deep breath. "I'm *not* doing the whole introduction thing." She grimaced. "But . . ." She extended her arms so that the blanket was beside her before it unraveled to the ground to create a curtain. "Here's . . . Max!"

She swooshed the blanket to the floor to reveal . . . me! With a flourish of my hand, I bowed.

Dazzle icons on both Quinn and Wolf, as they turned to look to where I had been—the faint mist of the unsummoned dove barely noticeable behind them. "Not bad," I murmured to the elf, as I unclipped the small perch from the back of her waistcoat, straight into my Inventory.

"Did it work?" she whispered, unable to see the icons.

"Like a charm," I said with a smile. "We'll cut the bits that make you uncomfortable though."

"Sure?" She raised an eyebrow.

"Always." I turned and walked back over to the man who was trying to get an explanation from the bear. The show worked best if you played to your strengths, the passion and drive more believable than a fake smile. Not that the latter didn't help, of course.

"Impressive magical skills, Max." Quinn turned to me. "Some manner of tele-portation, perhaps?"

"If I told you, I'd have to kill you." I grinned. "Which would make saving you pretty pointless, huh?" Although I had checked the reports and the curse had been lifted, my normal patience for people hadn't returned. The camp had me on edge, and my eyes scanned around as Quinn fumbled for a pleasant response.

"Ah—of course. I didn't mean to pry." He gave a smile and nodded to us all. "I really must be resting. I just wanted to give my thanks first."

I nodded in return. "You can repay us by being a good person."

"Meat too," Wolf added.

Silence, as I had expected Ren to add something like information or staying out of our way, but as I turned my head, it looked like she was busy in her own thoughts with something.

"Stay safe, Quinn." I turned back to him.

With another bow, he turned and went back among the groups of tents toward his own, I presumed. His eyes lingered on the distracted elf for a few seconds lon-ger than I felt comfortable with, and I watched him depart, my smile fading to an impassive glare as he disappeared from view.

"There are a lot of bad smells in this place," Wolf began as he watched the man move out of earshot. "But he is not one of them. Talks way too much though."

I gave the bear a pat on the shoulder, still unsure if that was demeaning or not. "Let's get some food in us and then find something to kill."

He looked up at me, a grin across his large mouth. "Now *those* are my kinda words."

The sound of sizzling meat hit my ears, as the elf had brought out her grill as soon as I had said the word. I turned to her, and despite the turmoil the day was sure to bring us, there was some amount of contented calm in her eyes.

"You're leaving already?" Fiona crossed her arms. Ruby stood beside her, looking a lot less put off by our intentions. In the slight background, Magnus was leaning against some crates.

"Why would we just sit around?" Ren frowned and crossed her arms in response. "Max was kidnapped from here yesterday, and you said undead attacks are regular."

I chose to sit this one out as much as I could. There was still a little part of me, hiding away in the pit of my stomach, that wanted to murder everyone in the camp. Just in case. Not exactly the most mentally stable of thoughts, so the less I could rile myself up, the better.

Ren was right to be annoyed though. Apparently Fiona hadn't exactly been as enraged and surprised to hear of the kidnappings as she should have been—according to the elf. There was a pool of apathy and passiveness that enveloped this valley, and we didn't want any part of it. Although the Equipment from the black market den was reasonable, we hadn't gotten any experience and were already underleveled for the area.

We needed to grow, not languish.

"It's dangerous." Fiona worked her jaw. "You don't know what's out there."

I could see Ren seething, and now, knowing the history between the two, it put the conversation in a much more awkward light. Whether Ruby could see the nuance or not, she didn't appear bothered. At first I had considered that two of the camp might want to join our group for leveling, but that thought soured at record speed.

"Well, we are going to find out." Ren shrugged and turned away. I followed suit, while Wolf gave Magnus a glare before following alongside us.

Fiona grumbled and complained to the goblin, quiet enough to be out of my hearing.

"Is it us or them?" Ren asked me as we walked up the hill toward the rock where the road split.

"We are removing the tumor that is draining the life from this world." I shrugged. "But we're using a ballista to do it."

Not that I wanted to start debating the morality of utilizing wholesale coldhearted murder to solve the issues plaguing the System. When the alternative was the Shadow doing the same, we were a necessary evil. Assuming the first area was now blooming with normal Players, the proof of our method's effectiveness went without question. Fiona hadn't seen what we had been through.

I shook the gloom from my head as Ren looked like she was still chewing her own thoughts.

"Let's find a repeatable Quest," I said. "I need to feel in control again."

CHAPTER TEN

Playing Catch-Up

My back clicked as I leaned side to side. "What were these again?"

"They're called Wildfolk." Ren removed her hat to rub at her forehead. Her hair caught the light in a way that drew my eyes before she covered it once more.

"Look like *meat*," Wolf added.

Not entirely inaccurate, I supposed. Although they weren't up to my culinary standards, they would make quite the meal for the bear. While their lower halves were humanoid, from their chests upward they were . . . feathered? Mostly hues of brown and the occasional white, their faces like those of owls, with small antlers from the tops of their heads.

"Are they a thing in your world?" I worked out my shoulders to limber out.

She shook her head. "No. They are strange."

Well, we'd better go kill them. I didn't say that part out loud because it sounded bad enough just echoing around in my head. The System hadn't given us much incentive as to why they needed to be culled—our adventure just taking us close enough to the area where the pop-up promised us reward for wholesale slaughter.

"We're underleveled for the area, so we should get good returns here . . . Maybe for two levels?" She removed an arrow from her quiver.

I looked around the area. Mostly unassuming. Woodlands to our left— light-brown trees with more rounded-shaped leaves. A field in front of us with the Monsters pacing around. Just to our right was a ledge that dropped down to an emptier field, with spare trees and some low houses farther away.

"Sounds good." I nodded, but my mind was elsewhere. Something wasn't right with this area, and I couldn't quite place it yet. Still, out in the relative open, we should see anyone trying to get the jump on us, and it looked otherwise quiet and pleasant—if you ignored what we were about to do.

Swapped my Accessory back to the Damage-increasing item and strapped the wand and scroll holders to the insides of my forearms underneath my suit.

"Fog wand is down to one charge. Shame it doesn't reset." Somewhat lucky of me to have stored those away during my doctor's appointment so that I could drop and activate them when I was kidnapped. Probably a waste of a use, but it was done now.

"Want to take one of mine?" She shook her own leather containers at me.

"No. Thanks though." I brought a magic card into my hand. "Let us begin the show."

Although her eyes rolled, there was less ire in them than usual. I didn't have the ego to assume I was winning her over to being just like me . . . but perhaps some acceptance was starting to paint over the gaps now that we were meeting in the middle. Sometimes to kiss.

My card wavered slightly off course as I threw it, my distracted thoughts causing it to flutter wildly at the last second to strike the first Wildfolk's feathered shoulder rather than where I supposed their neck was. They turned toward me and received an arrow directly to the forehead. They stumbled before dropping to the floor.

[Progress: 1/25 Wildfolk killed]

"Just do that twenty-four more times. Easy." I grinned at her before my eyes were drawn to two more of the Monsters, who turned toward us as the first had died.

Rather than draw weapons or charge toward us, they began to charge balls of green energy between their hands.

"You were saying?" Ren clenched her jaw and was already pulling back another arrow.

Wolf surged forward, his body glowing orange as his paws pounded across the soft grass. We had hoped to just draw the enemy into his waiting jaws, but it looked like these were all spellcasters.

My cards raced ahead of him, splitting as they passed over. One struck the Wildfolk on the right, severing some of his fingers—the second landing behind them to release a Hellhound+ from a magic circle.

Ren's arrow blazed with radiant energy as her <Smite Shot> burned through the air to strike the second Monster in the chest. Feathers soaking through with crimson, it let loose the spell before keeling over. The green orb flew from their hands and burst against the bear, singeing some fur but not doing anything too dire. He slammed into the wounded Monster and crushed them beneath his wide paws.

As Wolf bit through into his prey, the Hellhound+ came over, panting and tail wagging. He sat down in front of Ren and tilted his head with a whine.

Her face softened, and she raised an eyebrow at me. "You *sure* you don't send them to me?" She crouched down to give him pets.

"I do not, honestly." At first, I had, but after a while, they just did it of their own volition. I wondered whether they could tell how much she adored dogs or if it was part of our own bond strengthening that they saw her as an equal to me. Roger certainly had cooled on her after we had . . . Actually, I'd rather not think about the distraction, nor the implications.

Speak of the demon though. <Demonic Pact> card went out into the least mangled and chewed Monster, and it rose back to its feet. Purple ears tore the antlers from the head, and their wide eyes burst out to reveal deep pits with a small light in the middle. He held his feathered arms out and looked down at his puppet body.

"I'm a fuckin' bird!" He tried to smile with the beaked mouth, and it just looked as though he was in great pain instead.

I withdrew Jokkar's mace and handed it to my demon as he waddled over to me.

"Thanks, boss. You and . . . the elf doin' alright?" He leaned to the side to see past me.

"Still breathing, Roger. You and the family?"

He fidgeted awkwardly. "Eh . . . less said the better. What you want me to kill?"

"More of these . . . bird people. If you and Wolf split up to tag opponents, and we'll assist from range? They are magic casters, so . . . have fun?" It didn't feel necessary to warn him. I doubted it would dampen his enthusiasm to learn things the hard and bloody way.

"On it, boss." He nodded and turned to face the still-living creatures ahead, waddling off to get closer to the bear.

"We'll loot as we go, fight from the ones felled, like a chain." I tilted my head and then felt her hand on my arm. My eyebrow raised as I turned to her.

She seemed rather calm beneath that blue top hat. A slight scowl, but something more from habit than any true feeling. Whatever had darkened our souls when staying at the camp had shifted, and getting back into having a clear enemy to grind through had done wonders for both our moods.

"Fiona told me that the maximum level is twenty, and progression is tied more to Skill advancements."

It wasn't the most romantic or heartfelt thing she had said to me, but she won me over with those eyes. "Oh, so looting things for Stats will be even more important?"

She nodded. "I just wanted to make a note that you've been doing better with that."

"That's . . ." I was going to say *condescending*, but perhaps she had a point. A little bit of personal growth never killed anyone. ". . . Just one of the ways you've improved my life."

"*Ass.*" She rolled her eyes. "You've had it easy lately. Don't make me grouch on you again."

I gave her a bow just as a crunch came from downfield. Roger had broken the arm of a Wildfolk and was trying to swing his large mace around for a second strike. The blast of magic sent him stumbling back, and his attack faltered. Mine did not, as a blazing card zipped across the grass and pierced through the opponent's chest.

"You *wait* for our signal, Roger!" I exhaled through my nose as I flexed my fingers. No blood.

"*Sorry!*"

I turned back to Ren, only barely missing the slight smile fading away.

"Your eyes went purple again." She gestured for us to get back to work.

The hound ran off as I circled another card into the air. "When I threw my magic card or when I admonished Roger?"

She raised an eyebrow as she fired off an arrow. "Wouldn't you like to know?"

That was generally the point of asking questions, but I saw what she was trying to do. It had long gone unspoken that my eyes would glow and I would arc with some manner of electric power when things were most dire. When I exhausted both my mana and my emotional reserves. Whether it meant anything or not wasn't really something we had deliberated over.

None of my Passives mentioned it, so perhaps it was just an aftereffect. Something visual that didn't hint at something untoward and demonic within me. I flicked my card around the next enemy, slicing them three times before Wolf slammed into them.

[45 Gold]

[Eggs (3)]

[Chance Box]

Back to those again, huh? I'd save them until we were done fighting around here and then open them at once. The eggs felt . . . These were birdlike people . . . so I wasn't sure where my moral scale put looting their potential young. Perhaps they were unfertilized? Actually, I didn't want to know either way, so into the Inventory they went.

"Chance boxes," Ren groaned, looting through a different Wildfolk.

"Right?" I stood up and threw another card out, walking over to the next corpse. Wolf was having no issue against single spellcasters, even as more aggroed;

with the occasional heal or shield, he tore through them, taking very little damage. Roger was getting a little more beat up but changed corpses every so often to stay fresh.

I looked down at my hands. They were fine, which was a relief. No blood yet. "What do you think of Quinn?"

She withdrew an arrow, still focused on the targets ahead. "Is the context of this question you fishing to see how open I am to expanding our . . . stage show?"

"You can call it a *Party*." I wrinkled up my face. Was I asking that? Neither of us trusted new people very easily. "Not join us, no . . . but he could be useful?"

Ren grunted but didn't have any further thoughts to add.

Perhaps not a subject to tackle quite yet. I wasn't even that keen on growing a full five-person group either, truth be told. With my summons, we were practically that, without the added dynamics of inter-Party conflict. Loot shared three ways. Plus, we knew nothing about Quinn, and he might be a terrible mix anyway.

My Hellhound+ faded away, giving a short bark to us both, tail wagging, before he departed. I raised an eyebrow. "Do you think if we gave them name tags, we'd eventually see the same one?" If they even went to hell, or however it worked. I felt like they did but didn't know where that assumption came from. In fairness, I did feel all sorts of odd things on the regular.

"I think we should try." She nodded, her expression nothing but business. "Speaking of, got any tricks we can practice while we grind?"

"Sure." I grinned. "You're an accurate shot. You think you could place an arrow a foot above the next Monster?"

"Of course."

With a nod, I drew another Hellhound+ card into my hand and flung it near straight upward. Reaching high into the air, I curved it into a wide arc—way out of normal visual range of whoever was standing around. Ren drew an arrow as it started to head down toward the intended target.

Then she fired, and the arrow zipped across to strike the card exactly where we had both planned. The magic circle beamed into the air, and a fresh hound dropped down atop the Wildfolk's head.

"Summons have to land on an inanimate surface. I wondered if an arrow being an attack wouldn't work, but . . . good shot."

Ren nodded. "You can already throw them any distance you please, almost, but this way they can spawn in midair if needed."

I had done something similar before with a thrown object, which was fine for short range—but it always paid to have different options and someone else on board. With a sigh, I brought up the Map to ensure we weren't wandering near the danger zone.

The area was a rough square, with the intended progression path being to follow the main road that went diagonally from the bridge in the bottom right up to the largest town in the top left. The Crimson Shadow held most things above that line, while the resistance survived below it. I used that term loosely, seeing as the only thing they were resisting was taking action against the gang.

The necromancer and his Party were a little way to the left, away from dead center, if I excused myself the pun. We were slightly above the road but much closer to the bridge to the point we shouldn't need to worry. Chewing through the Wildfolk was taking us farther north—but we should be in the clear.

"So eager for more trouble, trickster?" She caught me glaring at the invisible screens. "You were almost tortured to death yesterday, and you're just waiting for the inevitable ambush, huh?"

"You can feel it too though?" I closed down the STAR and brought out another magic card.

"Yeah." She erased another Monster from this world.

[Progress: 18/25 Wildfolk killed]

I looked out at the woods to our left. Pretty well illuminated, with nothing hiding within other than a few of the Monsters wandering away from this field. To our right, it was clear as well. Something vibrated at the back of my mind though. An uncomfortable feeling like I was being tickled with a feather. A flare of something that reminded me of the pigman from yesterday, but different. Familiar and unwanted. My card went out, and I began to orbit us both.

Ren stopped and frowned at me.

Split them as they spun around us both, switched the direction of one, slowed the speed, lowered the height. Then I expanded the orbit away from us. Increased the speed as they got farther away. Wolf and Roger turned to see what I was doing. Blood ran down my fingers as I concentrated.

Then, there it was—a shift in the odd feeling in my head. I spun to face behind us and launched both cards to swirl around like a vortex. A dozen feet. Two dozen. To the left a little my brain nudged the cards. One stopped as it struck something as the other zoomed off into the distance.

A figure dropped out of invisibility and stumbled. Facing away from us, they scrambled to sprint away, but Ren's entangling arrow slammed through their leg, dropping them to the ground as vines curled up around them.

I stepped over, already there before I had even realized it. They turned, and underneath the shadow of their mottled-gray cloak, a singular white eye glared at me in panic.

CHAPTER ELEVEN

Demon Hunter

*C*lick.

A satisfying sound. Just as Rolo attempted to hold me away while I loomed menacingly toward him, I had snapped the nullifying cuff on the outstretched arm. The surprise in his eye was only second to our own shock, as I pulled back his hood.

Ruddy skin, two small horns, sharp teeth on an otherwise featureless face beneath the bright eye. The handprint of red was barely visible.

"You're a demon," I said. More of a statement than a question. Context clues aside, part of me knew already. A reason why I had been able to sense him despite his Abilities.

"*And* part of the Crimson Shadow," Ren added from beside me.

I suppose that part was important too. Might explain why the scout wasn't able to get a lot of useful information from the side he actually controlled. Maybe even assisted in the campground apathy by making going forward seem impossible.

"You can talk, right?" I narrowed my eyes at him.

"Fuck you, unbelievers." He hissed back, disdain starting to build behind his facial expressions.

I raised my head up to look at the elf. "It is more of a cult here, huh?"

Her brow was furrowed. "Your eyes are . . . Do you need me to take over?"

Hmm. I didn't feel particularly emotional or full of power, so it was odd that my eyes were reacting. Just looking at the demon though . . . He *needed* to die, and I was willing to do it right now. No hesitation or need for further questions. "Yeah, please do."

I stood slowly and walked backward, unable to keep my eyes off him. Warmth behind me as I bumped into Wolf, so I leaned back into his side and crossed my arms.

"Weird demon, boss." Roger was resting against the large mace as he watched proceedings. "All should obey you and follow your commands 'n' shit."

I wasn't sure why I'd get them to do that, but he had a point. This insolent demon should learn his place. A card flickered into my hand and then faded away. He needed sending back to hell, but it was Ren's turn, and I wasn't rude enough to interrupt her.

Wolf nudged me. "Focus yourself."

My eyes blinked, and I looked away from the abomination to regard the bear and his earnest amber orbs. He was right; this wasn't the normal me thinking. Or even the abnormal me. I opened up my Health Report, and it was all clear. Just an average psychotic break, perhaps.

"Thanks, bud." I gave him a pat on the side, partially to wipe some of the blood from my hands. The ploy was short-lived after I realized I was just getting Wildfolk blood on me from his fur. How the tables turned.

Ren deflated and held a knife toward the neck of the scout. The vines had slowly sunk away now, so he was only held in place by the insinuation of violence.

"I don't have much energy for this today," she began. "So play nice and I won't let Max . . ." She leaned in closer and whispered to him. His eye widened and looked over toward me.

"*Sick fuck*," he murmured.

Unsure as to what I was being signed up for, for some reason I decided grinning and licking my lips was the appropriate nail to hammer into the coffin Ren was promising. He paled and looked as though he might throw up.

Roger hopped over a little closer to me, more because of his awkwardness in moving the puppet person than because he was a rabbit analogue. "Oh shit, oh shit, boss. If you kill him, can I be him? *Be* the demon?"

I shrugged. "Sure thing . . ." I didn't get to finish my sentence as he blew away in the breeze straight after hearing the affirmative. The mace topped over to the ground, the thick handle almost landing on my toes. Maybe I wouldn't do it actually. I wasn't currently sure if I could view the demon as a friend even with Roger in there.

"So . . ." Ren continued. "We're going to do this easy way, okay? Just a couple of questions and then we won't kill you."

Not even a lie, I could tell from her voice. We'd hand him over to the camp, and he'd be their problem. If they wanted to outsource the executioner though . . . I knew someone with freshly licked lips. No, that didn't sound right. I brought up my Inventory, sorting through my items to try to keep my brain on track. Oh, maybe I could open those chance boxes—I had three of them now.

I played a drumroll in my head, ready for disappointment.

[Ring of Critical: +2% melee Crit Chance]
[Belt of the Trickster: +2 DEX, +3 INT]
[Necklace of the Quick: +2 AGI, +5% movement speed]

Not the worst haul in the world. I paused in deliberating who could use the items, equipping the belt myself, before something felt strange. My jaw clenched in anticipation.

With the flash of yellow light, a wave of warmth washed over us. My eyes adjusted to see what now lay before us. The green grass and soft dirt had been replaced by dry sand, almost endless, until it reached the horizon in all directions. The other thing to note was the large sun in the dull sky, pelting everything with continuous waves of heat.

As Ren got her bearings, briefly as confused as Wolf and I, Rolo sank down into the sand where he lay as if it were just water.

I stepped up closer to her, card in hand, as she drew an arrow.

"The fuck is this?" she said through clenched teeth, eyes darting around the empty surroundings.

"Demons of a certain power are able to cast a Domain, like a pocket dimension. Usually gives them certain powers or advantages. I would guess that this is his Class Ability, since he can't use active Skills with the cuff on."

She turned to me, confusion across her face. "How do you . . . Shit, Max? Your eyes are practically on fire."

Strange because I felt pretty calm. As to where the knowledge came from . . . It was the other Max, of course. He had dealt with other demons—killed them, in fact—as a matter of priority, usually. Drawing on the memories of that side of me. I hadn't been inside more than a couple of Domains in my time—luckily.

"I don't like sand," Wolf grumbled from behind us. "Get us out of here, Max."

"I'll . . . try."

The card in my hand empowered brighter, but in truth, I didn't know where to begin. The idea of a Domain was to give the demon a home-turf advantage. If anything, it just made me wander to other questions. Could I, or Roger, receive a Domain in time? I already knew what mine would look like, and I licked my dry lips again. Not that *I* was a demon, I was quick to remind myself.

Not in the technical sense.

"Vibrations," Wolf said, lowering his head.

"Direct me."

He sniffed at the air and then sharply turned his glare toward the left.

My card went out, twirling through the air and then carving through the sand. A trail burned through in a line before the card ran out of energy.

"He moved away, but you were close." Wolf turned slowly as he tried to track the vibrations circling behind us now.

The demon appeared to be swimming through the sand as if it were water too. A simple trick that probably worked out fine against System-created or confused Players. I knew too much though, and I was molded into the killer of demons. If anything, he was delaying the inevitable.

"Ren, apex," I commanded, throwing a card straight up above me before a second was already glowing in my hand. Her bow drew back, not needing to question my request or thought process.

Wolf began to growl at the sand as he focused. The arrow was let loose. I removed my hat into my left hand, feeling the approaching attack just as well as the bear could.

A mound appeared in the sand a few dozen feet away from us, and as we readied to attack, it zipped forward and burst out from the ground. Awash with falling sand was a giant snake, a ruddy color and with a singular white eye. The ridges of their hooded head caught the odd sunlight, illuminating the tough-looking scales that covered their body. Without hesitation, they surged forward toward the bear, large fangs dripping with venom in a wide-open maw.

Then a large fireball struck the sand it was trying to move through, the intense heat turning it to glass. My card was out and sliced straight down the middle, turning it into two sharp edges that Rolo was pushing his body between. Imp+ landed from above into my hat as I sent him away.

The sharp glass panels opened up darker crimson lines down his body as he squirmed and slowed his assault. Briefly, I wondered if my ability to push Deception also worked on physics, as that whole charade worked conveniently well. I didn't know the correct heat fire needed to be to melt sand into glass, but it seemed that neither did Rolo's Domain. The show continued despite our shared ignorance, not wanting to let a good plan go to waste.

Wolf leaped forward and clobbered the giant snake to the ground. Ren had her <Smite Shot> ready for when he gave her an opening.

I looked around. There really was nothing except heat and dried rock. Reminded me of hell, and I wasn't sure if that was some comforting nostalgia or age-old nausea rolling around inside me. Deal enough damage to the demon and the Domain would shatter away. I had no doubts Wolf was about to achieve that, even without Ren's help. It had been a last-ditch attempt to gain the upper hand, but without his Abilities still, he was far outmatched.

There was a cracking tear noise from behind me, and then everything washed away in a cool breeze, as if I had been staring at a painting that suddenly shredded before becoming ash. The bright greens made me wince as I turned to see the scout in the bear's mouth.

"Dead?" I asked.

Wolf shook his head, which just elicited sharp groans of pain from the demon.

Ren sighed and shook her head. "Never a normal day." She turned to me. "You want to try this time?"

I pulled a face. "Literally, I cannot. Won't even make it through the first question before I'll murder him in cold blood. Colder than usual."

She nodded. "Your eyes are still bright purple. How do you feel?"

"Prbbly bttrr thn hmm," Wolf said with a full mouth, to the added pain of his current captive.

"Good, actually." I frowned. Heath Report was clear. My hands were in decent shape. "It might just be a reaction to him being a demon."

"You *use* demons—friendly with them to a fault—and yet any outside your control you detest and must erase them?" She raised an eyebrow, but she already knew what the answer would be and had accepted it. As much as it needed acceptance anyway. With my shrug being the only response, she sighed. "Well, give me some pointers on what to ask him, trickster."

"Get info on the necromancer and nearby threats. See if there's anything actually untoward going on at the camp."

"Shame we can't do good cop, bad cop." Her eyes lingered on me as she walked away.

I watched her walk over, mostly unsure of how to process that. In the pragmatic sense, the pair of us could work over a mark pretty well with the carrot-and-stick approach. The continued eye contact might give rise to a secondary desire, but then again, perhaps she was just spooked by my glowing eyes. I probably would be, if I could see them. Somehow during my travels I hadn't procured a mirror.

The camp might wonder where their scout had vanished to if we played a little too rough with him. I winced as he screamed, the bear dropping him to the grass. Without proof of his betrayal, they might assume that we were out of control, and they already weren't keen on how dirtied our hands were with other Players' blood. Of course, there was also the possibility that they were in on it and admitting things would get us in deeper trouble.

There was another crunch, and Rolo yelped and started to sob. Ren was talking quietly to him, and I couldn't hear what was asked or what the replies were. Didn't really matter—despite the sounds of it, I knew she wasn't torturing him. She would assure me of such in a moment after she had got all the information she could, and then his fate was in my hands. That's just how this show was going to play out. Written in blood already long dried.

I kept my eyes on the back of us to make sure he had no way of calling backup or the Monsters didn't start respawning. The sobbing increased, and then Ren rose to walk back over to me.

"That probably sounded bad, but he did that to himself with squirming on his injuries," she began. "I wasn't torturing him. Got what information I could, so what are we going to do with him now?"

A wry smile touched the side of my mouth before I turned my face to her. "He is a Crimson Shadow, yet he was not a brainless murderer. Is he redeemable?"

"You're asking me?" She blew air from her mouth. "We're not really well equipped to be the law enforcement around here, or judge on morality."

I nodded. If the gang had a few more brain cells and less desire to murder everyone in this area, then we might have to employ a more nuanced take. What the Oathwarden said was true, however. If not killing them outright, what could we even do? Left alone, they might cause further trouble. Return to their gang. Track us down for revenge.

Before I even knew it, I had stepped around to the prone figure. Ren had followed me, and Wolf was still guarding his potential next meal. I knelt down beside the demon and grabbed him by the bloodied shirt, pulling him up to face me.

His single eye was bloodshot. While on first appearances he didn't seem to have a pupil, it was actually very light gray, and I could see it move about to regard me as I held him. Blood ran from his mouth, darker than normal humanoid blood, but very familiar to me.

"Do you know what I am? What I was?" Now that I was so close to him, I could see purple light illuminating his large orb, my own eyes full of something that he seemed to recognize.

"Hunter . . ." he gurgled.

"Yes. It is second nature for me to destroy beings like you. At least . . . in my old world. I'm willing to make a change here, but you have to meet me halfway." My jaw clenched as I struggled against the desire to kill him.

"Just . . . fuckin' kill . . . me." His breath was labored.

He wanted it. Gave me permission. I could be the killer I was trained to be and bathe in his demonic blood. Serve my purpose. Rend another life into the nether. One less demon in hell.

But that performance was rather played out. Where was the showmanship, the desire to wow and dazzle? I wavered as if my head was weighted by the conflicting thoughts.

I let go and dropped him to the floor. Stood back to my feet.

"Team meeting," I said, my eyes beginning to ache.

CHAPTER TWELVE

Pact Showing

Ren rubbed at her face before looking at the demon lying a little way off. Her eyes were tired. Perhaps already full of tribulations for the day. "I don't know, trickster. It sounds like a lot more trouble than it'll be worth."

I shrugged. It definitely would be—I couldn't deny that. "You're curious though, right?"

She rolled her eyes. "Yeah. But I'm also looking out for my own neck."

Another very fair point. "Your thoughts, Wolf?"

"I feel my morals are vastly different due to my simple nature. My heart does not care for the nuance." His eyes turned back to our injured captive. "And my stomach hungers to be filled."

I exhaled through my nose. Well, I knew it would be a hard sell. Keeping a prisoner to see what happened if they didn't get the Lady's blood, if they could be cured, was a drag both in the figurative and literal sense. Plus—the part of me that was keen to rip his head off added—they had joined up with her by choice at first anyway. It wasn't my job to fix their life choices.

Ren put her hand on my arm. "Do you think they would offer us a shred of the same leniency?"

Normally, I might argue that we should be better than them. That sort of cliché argument. But did we need to be? We'd be doing the System a favor to erase such a bad actor. Surely the Players in the first area had seemed irredeemable, and Rolo was also a demon. *A demon.*

"If you want to override our views . . ." Ren relinquished her hand. "I won't like it, but I won't argue against it. Follow your heart. I ask nothing more."

I nodded. Star of the show, I turned and walked over to the bleeding body of the scout.

From atop my head, I removed my hat and held it over him so that his face would be shaded from the sun. His white eye was half closed but still glaring at me. He was fading away and would need Ren's healing soon before his wounds took him away from us.

"Don't worry," I said softly, a smile across my face, "you're safe now."

Before he had a chance to respond, the stolen safe dropped out from the underside of my hat and crushed his skull with a dull crack. Top hat returned to my head as the large metal cube rolled off of his pulped face, and I furrowed my brow.

Ren stepped up beside me. "That was a *little* more sociopathic than I was expecting."

"Hmm?" I turned to her, slightly confused.

"Your eyes are back to normal now," she noted. "Purple eyes mean pendulum mood swings?"

I looked back down at the dead body and waved the safe away back into my Inventory. Would have been nice if that opened it, but I winced slightly at seeing the damage done. I knelt down to loot him.

"My turn after you, Max?" Wolf pushed his head alongside me to sniff at the body.

"Yeah," I replied. Leaned to the side slightly into his warm fur. Comforting. Took the magic cuff from the demon's wrist as I looked through the other items. No incriminating diary or secret letters, the usual gold and healing items.

"Some Dexterity Equipment on him," I announced out loud, intending the words to meet Ren's ears. Something inside me had . . . It felt like elastic that had been stretched too far and was having trouble resetting to the normal shape.

"I'll have a look." She came down beside me, placing her hand on my shoulder as she crouched.

My jaw clenched, and I felt like shrugging her off, although I remained steady. Her hair hurt my eyes. I *needed* to stand and move away and waited for her hand to get off my *fucking* shoulder before I . . . Oh, something was definitely not right.

"I need a minute alone." My feet were already taking me away. Not too far, just to somewhere they weren't in my peripheral. Clear fields and hills ahead of me. My eyes closed, and I enjoyed the breeze trying to calm me. *Thank you*, breeze.

To their credit, they did leave me alone. I winced as Wolf started to crunch through the body, but that meant Ren had finished looting and was probably standing and staring at me. I couldn't feel her glare melting a hole in the back of my head, which only meant that she was worried.

Was it the cold-blooded murder? Not really. It was probably the right call in the long run. We had seen what they were capable of. I couldn't take the chances of putting my companions in danger.

It was that he was a demon. I was sure of it.

Even after my souls had merged, I still felt like the normal showman Max was the one in charge for the most part. Seeing the demon drew out the deeper memories and feelings. Demon hunting was apparently a harsh and constantly stressful profession; often hunters would fall to insanity or corruption if demons didn't get to them first. I was trying to hide this from myself. Let a little mania slide through in the tricks and visceral combat, but the true horrors were locked away.

Until now, at least.

I palmed at my eyes, poor tired orbs of mine. Exhaled and turned back to the Party with a smile. The elf did have a pensive look on her face, but her arms were also crossed. I was wasting good grinding time, after all. With the mobs, to get experience, I meant.

"Anything to declare, trickster?"

"I hope to never meet another demon in this world," I said. "Now let's kill more Monsters so I can summon Roger."

I expected some rolled eyes at that, but she just tilted her head. She read me like a book, one perhaps even more miserable than the journal that I attempted to keep. Her body language was permitting me to go ahead and start killing things for the Quest, but her eyes burned for some actual answers.

My jaw clenched, but I gestured her over to me with a finger. She strode my way and stopped in front of me, arms still crossed all the way.

"The other soul really doesn't like demons, and it brought up some . . . repressed trauma, I suppose?"

She nodded. "How are you feeling now?"

"Better." I shuffled around in my suit jacket. "Fragile, still. I don't think I *meant* to kill him that way."

"It would have been more amusing in the heat of battle. We'll decompress tonight, okay?" She narrowed her eyes at me, but they were full of concern rather than annoyance. "But if you need to tap out . . ."

"I'll let you know, I promise." Although the start of our adventures had begun with me being closed off with my stability, I had learned to be more open. It made us a stronger Party to know our limits.

This time, it earned me a soft smile. A rarity and always worth the anguish of baring my issues. It faded just as quickly as she nodded toward the Wildfolk patiently awaiting their murders. "Let's go. A long day ahead of us."

Wolf passed on the demonic meal. One crunched leg and he decided it wasn't to his taste. He much preferred the comforting meal the Wildfolk could provide. I took things easier too. It gave me time to process the battle with the demon. The Domain and his transformation into a snake to try to defeat us. The way part of me wanted his death so furiously was probably part of the reason the other me swung hard the other way to try to save him. Balance, lest I fall to . . . something worse, I supposed.

For all the physical damage I had accumulated on our journeys so far, it often felt like my brain got the worst of it. The killing, bravado, mania, showmanship, anger—all bubbling around inside me as the different souls fought to become stronger. It was exhausting in a way a good sleep didn't fully satisfy. I brought Roger back out, and after a brief look of disappointment in seeing he wasn't Rolo, he got back into the violence with his usual aplomb.

Wildfolk fell to our advances. I weaved the cards around, once again a conductor moving the glowing purple objects along smooth trails. Through a head, into the eyes, hands and forearms to disarm or waylay. It warmed my hands to feel it, a soft comfort as they grew brighter. Went farther forward to start drawing in more Monsters before Wolf and Roger were ready to catch up. I hummed a tune, smiling.

The elf stepped into my view, disrupting the show. "Max?"

I dropped the cards and clenched my bleeding hands. "Yes, Ren?"

"Took you a while to hear me there. I said the Quest is ready to hand in. You're wasting kills."

My head nodded. Understood the words and what she meant. Remembered why we were doing this, but also the promise made. "I seem to be dissociating a little. Autopilot." I wondered how the System would translate that over to something she understood.

"Are you in the right mind to know when to stop or not?" She tilted her head, concern once again across her expression.

I blinked slowly and frowned. "This is going to sound strange, but could you heal me?" Although I wasn't physically wounded, there was something else knocking away inside my head.

She nodded and held her hand out, and the radiant energy flashed into me.

I winced and shirked away from it. "Ah!" My face was a grimace as I shivered from what felt like an icicle being jabbed into me. As it cooled away, whatever fever hung over my mind faded. "Thanks, much better."

"That's . . . a really unusual reaction." Her eyes narrowed at me.

"Is it? I mean, knowing where my power comes from . . ." I pulled a face. Radiant energy was the polar opposite of demonic, as far as I knew. If I was having waves of demonic influence clouding my mind, a little inoculation via the divine kept me grounded to who I really was.

Ren put her hand on my arm and sighed. "As if I didn't have enough reasons to babysit you. Just tell me when you feel you need cleansing then, okay? I'd hate to see what happens when you go off the deep end." With a pat, she moved away to go and loot the bodies.

I smiled as I watched her go, but the expression quickly sank away.

Problem was, I *wanted* to see what happened.

No doubt it wouldn't be something good for any of us, least of all me. There was this . . . pull of power drawing me in, however. Dragged through trauma and violence, I wanted to leap with both feet into the puddle and get soaked. Good way to get a cold—or my head shorn off—if I stopped miring myself in metaphor. *The show must go on.*

I shook my head off and went up to join the others, handing my Quest in along the way.

[Quest complete]
[Progress: 25/25 Wildfolk killed]
[Reward received]

[Experience gained]
[125 Gold]
[Healing Potion]
[Chance Box]

Terrible. I accepted the Quest once again and decided the chance boxes could wait until we sat down to rest. One more attempt at it and we should level up. Being slightly behind the curve seemed to make the process take less time than we'd normally be sandbagged with.

"Power token, trickster." Ren flicked it into the air toward me.

I held out my hand, and it bounced off, onto the grass. Their eyes turned to me, suspense and confusion on their faces. My brow furrowed too, and I leaned over to pick it up. As I rose back to a standing position, the long pole of the Spear of Luck came up from the ground instead of the token.

Ren's exasperated sigh was all the applause I needed. Back to normal Max. Now with the weapon fully out, I spun it with a flourish to turn it back into the token. Now the question was what to pick. It had been far too long since we had a boost in power, and I was hungry for it.

My eyes idly went from the gemstone over to my pact demon, and I raised an eyebrow.

"Hey, Roger," I called him over.

He waddled the puppet body over to me, his purple eyes glaring at me through no fault of his own. "Yeah, boss? This has been fuckin' great so far."

"You think so?" I tilted my head.

"Yeah, makes a nice change from the problems at home." He deflated slightly and propped his awkward body up on the handle of the large maul.

"I'm . . . sorry to hear that, Roger." Genuinely, I meant it. While he was an odd demon, he was part of the group, even if he was only temporary.

He shrugged. "We all got shit to improve on, right? I have a problem with alcohol."

"Oh." I furrowed my brow, trying to imagine how that worked in hell.

"Also a *tiny* cannibalism problem. But the docs say if I can stay clean, then some of the wives will let me see my kids again."

I stood for what felt like hours, trying to find the words to address any of what he had said. All the while, he just stared at me impassively. Why did he specify only *some* of the wives? Did he eat the others? Did he eat some of his children? That seemed to be what he was implying, but it seemed too rude a thing to ask for clarification on.

"What did you call me over for, boss?"

My brain clicked into some forward progress now he had jostled me out of my momentary stasis. "Oh, yeah. I was going to say that . . . you've been doing a great job . . . and perhaps it's time for . . . your promotion?"

I wasn't sure if he could read my face, as I struggled to compliment him under the revelation that his home life was perhaps just as dire as his existence here. Was this what it meant to be a demon? Perhaps I may need to reconsider my delving into this beckoning power. My eyes went over to Ren and Wolf. I didn't think I could eat them? *Would* eating an elf even be cannibalism?

"That sounds amazing, boss!" His fidgeting drew my eyes back. "No idea what that means, but it'll sure impress my probation officer."

Part of me was growing to respect the demons I could summon that didn't talk. The dogs were cute, and the birds never complained about their often-short lives. "Alright then, it's a deal." I gave him a show smile. "Best if you vanish first, I think?"

With a nod, he did so immediately, washing away in an unseen breeze to leave the corpse to topple back over.

"Upgrading Roger?" Ren asked as she came over.

"Yeah. He's been putting in work and is great for these Monster Quests. Was it even my turn for a token?" I wrinkled my nose up at her as I went through my STAR menus.

"Of course. You don't get pity tokens." She tilted her head. "You need another heal? You look pale."

"No." I gave her a smile. "Just, ah, Roger is quite the character." I wasn't quite sure how the others would take his . . . revelations, so I'd keep them as my own personal troubles for now.

**[<Demonic Pact> is now advanced: Pact demon Stats
and duration increased by 20%]**

CHAPTER THIRTEEN

Demonic Mastery

I wasn't sure what to expect, in all honesty. As I held the <Demonic Pact> card in my hand, I paused and screwed up my face.

"Feeling weird again?" Ren asked, now close enough to make out the lines of concern across the part of my forehead not covered in the gaudy top hat.

"Yes, but no." I shook my head. "Honestly, I've just had quite the twenty-four hours, and I'm not sure how ready I am for whatever the System believes an upgraded Roger should be. It can't be worse than normal Roger, right?"

She shrugged. "He isn't *that* bad."

I stared at her blankly for a few seconds before exhaling through my nose. For some reason, I didn't feel like explaining to her that my pact demon spent his free time drinking and potentially eating his own family. I'm not sure *I* truly believed it. Was the rabbit pulling one over on me?

With little excuse left, I sent out the card into the nearest dead Monster. It crackled with a familiar purple arcing electricity as it rose back up to its feet. I was expecting the usual ears-and-eyes thing, but it didn't happen. Instead, the possessed creature turned to us and walked over very competently. Their eyes were a purple hue, but not the usual pits.

"Roger?" I asked, my face already wrinkling up in apprehension.

"That's right, boss." He stopped and bowed toward me. "You have my gratitude for summoning me."

I nodded slowly. "How do you feel?" His voice was . . . calmer? Still had the edge to it but less manic.

"Fucking great, in fact. Powerful. Ready to do anything you or the mistress wills." He turned his feathered head toward Wolf. "Hello, grand one."

Ren mouthed, *"Mistress?"* at me, her furrowed brow one of confusion, to which I returned a shrug. Although he was actually remarkably polite, I had a feeling in my gut—maybe something guided by my nature—that he was just putting this on. The fact that he had more control over his puppet I could believe, but he figured he could edge his way into the show and I wouldn't notice. A sloppy performance that I wouldn't tolerate.

"Roger?" I licked my lips and stood taller.

He turned his purple gaze back to me. "Boss?"

"Kneel."

The demon paused for a second before doing so, as if he wanted to check that I wasn't running some kind of joke of my own. Down on one knee, he lowered his head in reverence.

"What is your purpose, Roger?"

"I exist to serve you, boss."

I stepped over to him slowly, my hands behind my back. "Do you expect me to have anything less than the best, Roger?"

"No, boss! I give you my all."

Beside him now, I bent over, leaning my head down to whatever kind of ears the Wildfolk had. Lowered my voice so that only he could hear. "Then you need to sort your life out. Both here and back in hell. Nod if you understand."

He squirmed and nodded.

"I won't abide any clumsy errors in my show, Roger. If you are not capable, I will find some other demon to make a pact with. *Nod if you understand.*"

Again, a silent nod.

"When I say the word, I am going to banish you. Next time I summon you, I want to hear that things are on the up. Disappoint me again and I will find a way to get to hell so I can personally tear you in half with my bare hands."

I stood up and straightened my back out. "Where are your ears?"

Without looking back up at me, the two prongs of purple energy burst out of the puppet's skull, spraying blood across the grass.

"Good, now you may stand." I watched him raise up, somehow looking sheepish with the weird beak mouth. "Do you know what you have to do?"

"Yes, boss."

With a wry smile, I nodded. "Then go." He did. The energy flowed away to leave the corpse to drop back to the ground. I watched it for a second before turning back to Ren.

She had an odd look on her face before a frown darkened whatever it had been. "Purple eyes again, trickster."

I narrowed those eyes at her. "We'll talk later."

She looked over at the dead puppet, an odd expression on her face. "Like *that*?"

As much as I would like to take a guess as to what she meant, I was currently running out of steam, partly due to my own volition this time. "Let's go back to leveling." I waved my hands to distract her from whatever her brain was daydreaming about. "You ready, Wolf?"

"Always," he said with a sigh, clearly having a much higher patience Stat than we perhaps deserved. "The feathers are tickly. Can you collect some for me?"

"Sure thing, bud." I smiled and felt about as normal as I had in the last . . . No, just thinking about it seemed to invite further madness or trauma into my life. We should just continue with the Quest and not consider what he might want with them. Other than to tickle himself.

The next card in my hand came out red and crackling—one of the rare critical ones. I flung it out and moved forward. We all watched it slice through the air before landing in the thick throat of a Wildfolk. It popped and burst a chunk of their flesh and feathers like a small explosion. The Monster gripped at the wide wound before toppling over.

"We need to get you something so that can do that more often, trickster."

Ren fired off an arrow, and Wolf thundered off. Beside us, I dropped down an Imp+ card, and the short, wiry demon gave me a nod before he started casting a fireball.

"We returning to the camp tonight?" the elf then asked, focused on her next target.

I grimaced. "Ask me again later. I'm not in the right mind. Same for Rolo's information, unless it's immediately useful." Part of me wanted to keep as far away from the camp as possible, not trusting them whatsoever. Well, a couple of them were affable enough, but still. And then the other part of me wanted to torch and burn them all down to the ground. Not in an evil way, I tried to remind myself. Just pragmatic—the fewer unknowns, the less threat we were under.

"Understood. I'm not too keen on going back myself." Her entangling arrow went out, pinning two Wildfolk that were trying to get into melee with the bear. Two seconds later, the fireball struck them, burning their feathers and scorching their exposed flesh.

"Oh?" I split my next cards as they went toward the injured Monsters. "Not eager to put on a show for our audience?"

She exhaled. "Don't be a dickbag, Max. You know why."

"Delivering the news about the scout could be bad, but then so could not showing up either." My cards hit the pair before Wolf jumped in and crushed them.

"Quite the pickle," she agreed, walking ahead to start looting.

Who knew murder could be so complicated when there were others around to hold you to account? The first area had been a neat tutorial for our macabre instincts. Crimson Shadow wanted to kill us, so we had killed them. Made the world a better place for it, clearing the path for the newer and more pleasant Players. Now that we had peers to judge us . . . it complicated how cut-and-dried we liked things.

At least, I thought that's how Ren saw it too. She had an actual connection to at least Fiona, even if not the rest. Turning up with Rolo's mashed corpse would paint us in an even dimmer light than they already saw us. We'd look unhinged.

I rubbed the back of my head as the memories of the last hours passed back through my brain.

"Got a ring here. Twelve percent Mana?" The elf was crouched by a Monster corpse.

With a shrug, I held out my hand to catch it as I went to loot the next. It was an increase, even if meager. Gold and another chance box from this body. There was a crack as Wolf tore the arm clean off the next Monster and then flung it across the ground. I had no doubt in my mind that he could solo the Quest and we could just watch and leach the progress from his efforts.

That's not how a show succeeded, however.

Stretching my back out as I stood, I brought another magic card into my hand—before the STAR on my wrist turned into a shimmering gold glow.

I turned to Ren with raised eyebrows. "Ahead of the curve?"

She held hers up to show it was a similar color. "Maybe an underdog experience bonus. We should be able to stay here comfortably to at least level ten."

Ten came with the base increase to my core Class Skill, although I didn't remember where I had learned that. Then again, at fifteen. At the max level of twenty, there was again another single Ability but something new.

We gestured for Wolf to take a break as he coughed out some loose feathers. After a quick visual check to ensure we weren't being watched or about to have the Monsters appear on us, I activated the level to see what the System thought of me now.

[Level up—<9>]
[Stats increased]
[New Ability: <Shatter>]
[New Passive: <Out of Sight>]
[New Passive: <Prepared>]

Next time that we had a chance to rest, I'd check out my Stats and see how my equipment was faring.

For a Passive Skill, <Out of Sight> actually gave a surprising amount of extra usage. I could now cast <Vanishing Act> on myself, but it only lasted three seconds. While a very short amount of time, the thoughts of potential uses bubbled up in my head.

<Prepared> gave me a +10 percent item-find bonus, which was great with how much I *loved* looting. Perhaps the System anticipated that since—as a magician—I was often finding coins behind people's ears, then that translated to me gaining more Equipment and such as a base. I wasn't about to argue with it, least of all because I knew it wouldn't listen anyway.

Active Ability for this level was <Shatter>. It was a finisher in the same vein as <Finale>, but where this one differed was that it was single target. I could remove all stacks of Dazzle from the target—shattering the illusion, essentially—at the penalty of them gaining immunity to the Status. However, for every two stacks of the Dazzle icon removed, they received a random debuff from the provided list. As much as I hated spending too much time within the screens of my STAR, I opened it up and expanded the descriptions.

[Weakened: Reduced Strength Stats]
[Lethargic: Reduced Agility Stats]
[Drained: Reduced Constitution Stats]
[Confused: Reduced Wisdom Stats]
[Astonished: Reduced Intelligence Stats]
[Fragile: Reduced defenses]
[Waylaid: Reduced movement]

That was . . . quite the list. If I didn't know any better, it seemed as though the System was keen to allow me to fool and wow people and then force conditions on them when I revealed it was all a ploy. Seemed a bit mean-spirited—I might as well just stick a card through their head and save them the humiliation. Still, against tough single targets, it could easily tip things in our favor. Against bosses, perhaps?

I caught Ren watching me think, her head tilted to the side.

"Normally, I'm apprehensive about asking what you received." She raised an eyebrow. "But now I have a professional reason to know."

My mouth turned up at the side, a wry grin at her acceptance. Nothing like more System tricks to make me feel more like myself. "Oh, some nice, simple things. A demonstration?"

"I'd accept nothing less." She folded her arms.

Tongue briefly stuck in my mouth, I withdrew an apple into my hand. "Watch this."

I threw it straight up into the air and hit <Vanishing Act> on myself. Took three big steps toward her, as I saw her eyes go up to the apple, and then down to me not being there.

After my time was up, I appeared right beside her, a flower up to her face.

"Dickbag!" She startled, her expression brief annoyance and confusion, but she gave me a quick kiss. "What is this all about?" She scowled at the red flower. No Dazzle icon, still.

Her mixture of reactions totally threw me for a loop, and my brain spun out of control. "Ah. Originally I thought a knife to your throat made the most sense, then at the last second I realized that would be even *more* inappropriate, so a flower was the quickest thing I could reach."

She rolled her eyes. "I'll repeat: *dickbag.* So you can just go invisible now?"

"For three seconds. That was just a Passive though. My new Active just turns Dazzle stacks on a single target into random debuffs." I turned my head to watch Wolf crunch up the apple. It'd be good for his digestion.

"Useful for bosses then. Or people we really dislike."

"My thoughts exactly."

Her expression relaxed, and I felt a little guilty for making her jump. She was good at sensing things, so I hadn't actually expected to catch her off guard. Not our sharpest of days, perhaps. Also felt like I had stolen that kiss through false pretenses—I had to wait till the end of the day, I had been told.

"Mine were . . ." Her eyes glazed over as she double-checked her windows. "Passives gave me a bonus to healing after killing a target, and the second one gave a bonus to damage after healing an injured target."

I tilted my head from side to side. "Overall, it increases your effectiveness, whatever you do."

She nodded. "Not very flashy—but then my Active . . ." Her eyes were now practically aglow with excitement. "<Divine Bloom>. A buff that increases friendly targets' Damage while reducing my threat."

"That's pretty good." It took a moment to click in my head what she had already envisioned the use to be. "Ah, oh . . . very good."

"You get no demonstration though." She tried to wave me away as some of the light faded from her eyes. "I'm not quite ready to act on demand yet. What about you, Wolf? Any luck?"

"Yes," he replied, staring off at the horizon with unfocused eyes. "I have . . . something to slow those around me."

"Very useful," I said. *Very powerful* is what I thought, however. The last thing anybody wanted was to be stuck in place against the bear.

My mood seemed to settle. Something about the leveling and grouping up grounded me once more. I was sure to have more states of mania soon enough. It looked like part of me was fighting against the other for control. Maybe we could do one of those weird dream things to hash it out together.

No. That was long past. We weren't separate any longer. These struggles were my own. One whole Max.

I shook the thoughts from my head and smiled at my Party. "Well, let's get back into it then. We'll level up again in no time at all."

CHAPTER FOURTEEN

When Love Dies

I had lost my diary down a ravine. My palate for starting a second one is waning . . . even as I write this sentence. Perhaps things are better lived in the present or in our fallible memories. Not everything was so dire, I am reluctant to report.

Working my jaw, I looted the fifteenth chance box from the dead Wildfolk. Putting the task of opening them up until later had just become a wall I was building, burying myself. If only there was some easy way of only seeing what was useful for me.

"Power token, trickster. This one is yours." Ren flung it through the air toward me.

I looked in its direction and looted it without moving. Already my menus were up, ready to use it without thinking about it too hard. Might start stockpiling them soon for the bigger upgrades.

[<Vanishing Act> is now advanced: You can now make two objects invisible. <Out of Sight> now lasts five seconds.]

There were a plethora of Skills and Passives I could upgrade, and truly I would never stop going over them again and again if I stopped to consider the most optimal choice. We seemed to be getting the basic tokens a lot quicker in this area, so my use was a little more flagrant.

Plus, an extra two seconds of being invisible was powerful. I used it, just to get the feel, vanishing from where I was crouched down.

"Max?" Ren asked, having me only in her peripheral. "You'd better not sneak up on me again."

"He hasn't moved," Wolf grumbled, looking over at me with a muzzle covered in gore. His form of looting looked to be filling his personal Inventory, if his glazed-over eyes were anything to go by.

I reappeared in the same position, then looked up at the bear. "You could see me?"

"Not quite." He stood up taller to stretch out. "You looked like a wiggly ghost. And you smell."

My head nodded some acknowledgment, but I wasn't too sure what to make of that revelation. Of him being able to see me anyway. I was certain that after a few hours of combat—and a slight mental break—that I could do with a wash. It's not like he smelled any better, being snout deep in the internal organs of the Monsters he had been maiming. He hadn't been able to see Rolo, so either it only worked on certain invisibilities, or was it because we were in the same Party?

"For what it's worth, trickster, I'm sure we're all pretty dire. At least the hats keep the sun out of our faces." She shrugged and looked over at the bear, whose hat was way too small to do just that.

It made me smile though. Whatever had been driving a screw into my sanity prior had sunk away and relaxed. Even as we cycled back through the Monster packs and passed the body of Rolo, it didn't chip away at anything within me. I stopped, however, and held my hand out. There was a new element to <Vanishing Act> that allowed me to see the intended targets of my Ability now that I could pick two.

My brow furrowed as the blue outline switched between the different objects around his corpse. It took a little effort, but I learned how to just use one of the charges rather than both and how to hold one target while I selected what to use the second one on.

There was something else . . . as if I could see the strings behind the performance.

"Everything okay, Max?" The elf had stopped and had been watching me glare at the body with my hand out, so the question wasn't unwarranted.

My hand shook as I concentrated. "One second." I ran my Mana down these threads, encircling and clutching at the invisible tethers highlighting my intended targets. It was a struggle, but I pulled them together, bending something intangible and beyond my understanding to my will. *I* was the one who chose how to perform *my* tricks.

The System couldn't define me.

Blood dripped from my outstretched palm as the corpse vanished.

"Balls," I said as I shook my hand. Some minor aches ran down my forearm, but I'd had worse.

"Don't tell me," the elf said as she shook her head. "You just used bullshit to invisible something you weren't supposed to?"

I pouted. "Did I ever tell you how smart you are?"

She rolled her eyes. "Save your flattery, trickster. *For later.*" She adjusted her hat. "Back to the grind."

If I didn't know any better, I may have assumed I had imagined the extra line she added in the middle. Rolo's corpse reappeared. We had one more repeat of the Quest left, maybe a second to get our level-ten and Class upgrades.

"Could we take a brief break?" Wolf requested. "I need to use the . . . woods."

My eye went out to the forest area to our side. A reasonable request, and it didn't look too dangerous. "Alright, but just roar out if there is a problem."

"A problem with my shitting?" He furrowed his brow before giving me a shrug, perhaps realizing that was a reasonable possibility.

I watched him leave. Wolf was the most hardy and capable of violence out of the three of us, but it would just take a few smart Players to catch him out.

"He eats a lot of meat," I said, turning to the elf after the bear had vanished from view. "An *absurd* amount. Are we responsible for ensuring he has a good diet?" I chose to ignore the part where most of the meat was people. Seemed rather moot when Wolf was people too, in a way.

She shrugged. "Now that you mention it, I'll feel bad if we don't." Ren removed her hat and fanned her face. "Speaking of, should we stop for some food?"

I nodded, and we walked over to the side by the ledge before the empty field. I took my boots off before I sat down and was glad for the slight calm after so much combat. Ren did the same and then sat beside me. From her Inventory she brought out a couple of pastries.

"These are pretty plain but will keep you full for a while." She passed one over, which I accepted with a nod of thanks.

We sat and ate in silence for a few minutes, just enjoying the scenery. Eventually, I couldn't hold the questions in any longer.

"When I surprised you, why was your reaction to kiss me?"

She paused her chewing but otherwise didn't move. "Is that a complaint?"

"Just curious." I grinned, clearly having caught her out.

Ren shrugged, still looking out toward the distance. "I suppose we all exit our shells in different ways."

My intention to goad her along slowly slithered away. Disarmed by her honest and plain reasoning, my next question escaped before I had a chance to think it through properly.

"Ren, are we dating?"

She snorted and finally turned her head to me. A slight scowl, but warmth behind her eyes. "Asshole. You don't really date in an apocalypse scenario." Her eyes rolled, and she sighed. "We are *together*, if that's what you want?"

I nodded. "It is. Do you want that too?"

"Of course." She gave me a pat on the leg and looked back out toward the horizon. "I know that admitting it just means tragedy will come to us, but we can at least be happy until the Lady kills us or you turn into a demon." Her head turned back to me, a wry grin at the corner of her mouth.

"Until System do us part then."

"Dickbag." She leaned against me and put her head on my shoulder. "It's too—"

"It's too early in the day for your heart to be in bloom, I know."

She sighed once more but said nothing. Too on the mark to chastise me any further. We sat and existed for almost a whole minute before the pads of Wolf's feet came from behind us. Ren pried herself from me, shooting me a soft smile before standing and brushing herself down. With a grunt, I followed suit and donned my boots, giving the bear a nod as he came to greet us.

"I feel twenty big owl people lighter," he said with a wide grin.

"There's some fruit you can have too," I offered. "It might give a bit more variety to your diet."

He stared at me blankly for a moment before nodding. "Okay."

Ren already had her bow out and an arrow drawn. "Look alive. I want to get this over with."

"Hail."

We all winced, and she lowered her shot. Turning, we saw a familiar figure moving off of the road and into the field. Quinn.

"If you murder him," Ren said in a hushed tone, "I won't hold it against you."

I tried to ignore her. As my now-confirmed elfin girlfriend, she definitely had my ear on such matters. But I also didn't need anyone else prompting me toward wanton violence. It was bad enough that half of me was fine with the prospect of coring this affable man with a card right now. We already had enough enemies. And corpses littering our wake.

"Sorry for intruding!" he continued, gradually getting close enough to talk in a normal tone. "I wasn't exactly given the all clear to leave the camp, but the good doctor was otherwise distracted." His arm was no longer in a sling, but he didn't seem to be at 100 percent yet, despite his grin.

"And you chose to come find us." A statement rather than a question, as his presence was apparent. My years of training in presenting a faux-genuine smile paying off dividends. "I was just about to go through all my chance boxes too. Shame."

"You want to open mine too, trickster?" Ren stepped up closer to me. "I have *so* many."

My whole body tensed, and my right eye twitched, as if I considered literally running from the prospect. How far could I get? That depended on how eager Ren was on sticking me with an arrow, I supposed.

"I did indeed," Quinn replied, not hearing the elf prod me with her words. "Again, my apologies for being so forward." He scratched at his eye patch, and then his view switched to just past us.

I raised an eyebrow and turned my head to see what had caught his eye. Oh. The mangled corpse of Rolo. Perhaps we should have done something with it, although hiding it sounded like it would make me feel more guilty, when currently I didn't feel guilty *at all*.

"He was working with the Crimson Shadow." I filled in the questions unspoken. "Was spying on us, which didn't work out too well for him."

Quinn whistled and stretched his back out. "Originally, I was going to ask to accompany you, but you can't help but get in trouble, can you?" He raised an eyebrow.

Did we keep falling into bad times? Or was the world steeped in them, and we were just trying to push through as nicely as possible? The truth was probably somewhere in the middle. We sought to remove the Lady, who was trying to corrupt this world, and that involved stomping through the murkiest puddles around.

"We have a job to do." Ren stepped in verbally. "And we are very efficient."

"That you are." He nodded slowly. "I will be forthright with my intentions then. Max, I seek to duel you."

"Huh, why?" I furrowed my brow.

"For the hand of the fair maiden Ren." He gave her a brief bow before leveling an earnest gaze at me.

I removed my top hat and sighed. "Really? What kind of world do you even come from? I'm not sure we have the time for . . ." I paused as Ren put her hand on my arm.

"You don't think I'm worth it, trickster?"

Her face was serious, but there was a twinkle in her eyes that said she was enjoying this way too much. My ego had been put on the line, and while I knew I had nothing to prove to the elf, I . . . had to make a good show of it? Even thinking that felt odd, despite it being something totally in my wheelhouse.

I turned back to Quinn and deflated. "Are you sure? After knowing who we are and what we've done? This isn't *to the death*, is it?"

"Just until one of us yields and is the clear winner. And I cannot deny my heart's intentions, even if you were the devil himself."

My eyes found themselves rolling. How close to the truth he might be. Well, not that close—I shouldn't prop myself up so high. I looked him over. In *reasonable* shape considering he was still recovering from his ordeal. Probably a few levels higher than me. A drive in his eyes that was foolish and misguided. Even if he won, Ren would sooner put an arrow through him than be won over.

But then, he *wouldn't* win.

Even as I nodded my acceptance, I felt the warmth inside me drain away. My face sank, the chill of what must be done ready to take the reins.

"Ten paces. The beautiful elf may count us down."

He turned around, awaiting me to join him. Dagger to the back of his neck right now would be the easy answer. Our world was figuratively cutthroat when it wasn't literal, and these sorts of games just made me feel ill. Like it was a mockery of what we had suffered through and overcome.

But I could only win by playing by the rules. Stepped up and put my back against his. Some of the humor had left Ren's eyes after she had clocked my expression. A day with enough mania and turmoil, I should perhaps be eager for a little slice-of-life action. But part of me couldn't accept it. Wolf looked vaguely interested in the strange ritual, perhaps a little disappointed the loser wouldn't be filling his stomach.

"On three then." She stepped farther away to avoid our potential bullshit.

Quinn had a rapier now drawn and an oddly shaped leather pouch on his hip, which screamed flintlock pistol to me—but I could just be buying into clichés.

"One, two, three."

We moved, taking ten steps away from each other. My hat was still in my hands. All I needed, really.

Ten steps and I turned, throwing the hat as he raised his sword to deflect it— or what it might be harboring.

Confusion struck his face in seeing I was no longer there, right before my forehead then also struck his face. The invisibility canceled as I made the attack, hands in my pockets. He dropped back to the ground like a sack of bricks, his weapon falling to the grass as he grasped at himself.

"Fucking *ass*." I removed a pocketed hand to clutch at my head. "Why is your nose so fucking hard?"

Ren stepped up to me and gave me a heal, the throbbing pain soothing away with warm comfort. "As much as I am pleased with the outcome," she began, her eyes narrowing. "That was a little underwhelming."

I shrugged and looked down at the sobbing Quinn as he clutched his bloodied and broken nose. Didn't really feel like smiling at what I had accomplished. Perhaps she was right. "I've got the rest of the day off. No autographs."

The elf crossed her arms. "*That's* your one-liner? You need to stop hitting your head on things."

As much as I would have liked to disagree, I couldn't. The grip of cold within me faded away, and I sighed. Now I had to deal with the injured man. It was much easier when we only had to kill people. In saying that, however, it wasn't like Ren had healed him either.

She moved away, as if she could read my thoughts, and crouched down beside Quinn. "Hey, dipshit. I'm not a trophy or possession to be won. Be thankful Max didn't kill you because I'm sure he will have no such reservation if you piss him off again." She shook her head and then stood up. "And I'm not healing you. I hope your pain is fertile enough ground for the roots of humility to take hold."

See, now *that* made the brief effort worth it. While she had become soft to me over time, I had almost forgotten the rose still had thorns for others.

"Come on, Max," she said as she passed me, a slight smile at the corner of her mouth. "Let's finish leveling up."

Wolf nudged up beside me, my top hat held gently in his mouth. I gave him a brief bow as I retrieved it, noticing his forlorn look toward the injured man before he went to join Ren.

With a shake of my head, I withdrew a healing potion from my Inventory and threw it down on the grass beside him.

Better a humbled fan than a vengeful critic, after all.

CHAPTER FIFTEEN

Tentative Expression

After taking my potion, Quinn healed up relatively well. His ego might need a little more time, but after getting back to his feet, he had decided to sit on a withdrawn chair and give us space to work our magic. Or at least kill a few handfuls of Monsters.

A process we performed with little flair, just doing the bare and most efficient things necessary to drop the Wildfolk to the ground. I would feel slightly amused at us being less dramatic now that we had an audience, but the voice in the back of my mind held a grudge with the overtly annoying man.

Couldn't kill him though.

Eventually, we mopped up the last required System-created for the System to labor us with experience and chance boxes. I rolled my shoulders out, already aching from the prospect of having to open them all. Didn't even want to look at how many I had accumulated.

The STAR on my wrist began to glow a radiant gold. We had reached level ten, only a couple of days behind where we should be. While the pragmatic part of me considered that killing these Monsters again and again could be a safe way to get another level or two over the next day, it was actually exhausting just to think about. I needed some variety just as much as Wolf's diet did.

[Level up—<10>]
[Stats increased]
[Class Keystone upgrade: <Demonic Magician>]

I ran my eyes over the words, about to bring up the details, right before I was interrupted by Ren. Stepping up to me, she put her hand on my chest where my heart would be.

"Is this part of your Oathwarden upgrade, or . . . ?" I raised an eyebrow, trying to determine whether the warmth I felt was natural or not.

Her expression didn't change, but she tilted her head to the side. "You'll never know." Without allowing me even a glimpse of a smirk, she then removed her hand and stepped away.

All things going well, I probably *would* know in due course. Her Oathwarden Ability had kept me alive at least twice . . . maybe more . . . in the past. No doubt if she had added functionality to it, I'd find out exactly what in the most painful way. Ah, now I'd put it out into the world.

Back to my own screens, I brought up the detailed information.

[<Demonic Magician>: Damage bonus per Dazzle icon increased. Defenses also increased per icon.]

The exact numbers weren't really groundbreaking, but an overall Damage increase was certainly nice. Now I would also receive a minor boost to my defenses, which would be nice for not getting my skull caved in mid-combat as often.

"What's up next?" Ren asked, lowering her hat to obscure her eyes.

While the weather had been rather pleasant, hours of combat had us overheating—especially in the clothing we chose to wear. We had earned ourselves a proper rest even though there was so much to do.

I rubbed my chin. "I'm not eager to go fight the Shadow right after meeting the bare minimum of this area. If we could find some Quests . . . Get to twelve at least?" See what other kind of bullshit the System could give us, maybe work on a few more tricks together.

"Alright." She brought up her STAR menus to look at the Map. "I think we've earned a rest, but I'm not too sure how I feel about going back to the camp."

That was the elephant in the field. In the end, and much to my amusement, I decided that we shouldn't live in the shadows. Like the bad guys. Much unlike the showman's stage.

"Let's bring them the body. Tell them what happened." I looked over at Quinn, who still hadn't gotten the courage to come back up to talk with us. "Better to have tentative allies than ill-informed enemies."

She nodded. "And if they don't take our side?"

I smirked. "You know the answer to that."

Another nod, this one briefer.

Wolf was stretched out on his back, almost like he was sunbathing. A wide grin spread across his face as his tongue hung out. "I can eat goat man then."

"You content enough with your upgrades, Wolf?" I changed the subject while we were certainly close enough for Quinn to overhear the bear's overzealous desire to consume the campers we were about to go meet.

"I am now a bear *plus*." He rolled over back to his paws and shook himself out.

He was mostly clean of gore now, and I realized that there was probably no issue for him to clean his clothing using the System button. Although that usually did Cosmetic outfits. Maybe it saw his fur as his worn clothing? I wondered, if I were naked, would I be able to use that option to clean myself rather than bathe?

"A lot on your mind, trickster?" Ren was a few feet away but had clearly seen my mind was running away from our current focus.

"Just thinking of myself naked. Shall we go talk to Quinn?" I turned away from the bear and gestured toward the seated annoyance.

She didn't reply and took a second before she joined me in walking over. Perhaps busy with something in her System menus.

Idly, I brought out a coin into my hand. Flicked it up into the air and held my hand out to catch it, but it went straight through my palm to fall among the grass. Just a matter of looting it as it struck me while dropping a new one located on the underside of my hand at the same time. Through practice, the positioning and timing of my Inventory swapping had become almost flawless.

Something I took pride in, even as much as it would be handy to kill things from great range like Ren. Or heal injury like Ren. A broken mix of Abilities in her own regard, she helped us function as a trio—with the unopposed strength and hardiness of Wolf. Sometimes I felt like the third wheel, even knowing how effective I was at dealing Damage from near or far.

Quinn held his head low as we approached. If he had truly feared us, he would have run away like a rat. The fact that he had stayed put either meant he had a lick of honesty in him, or he thought he still had a chance with Ren. *Just kill him now*, the other me—who was just me now—said. One day, I'd take responsibility for my own thoughts. Right after the *other* me did.

"Sorry about your nose. I don't really know how duels are supposed to work." I shrugged and avoided the rolling eyes of the elf at me for starting with an apology.

"It is not often I am humbled in such short order." He spoke toward his lap still. "To be struck down in a single blow brings me great shame."

I exhaled through my nose. "I wouldn't worry about it. A tree almost killed me."

"And a horse," Wolf added from behind.

Ren perhaps wanted to add to that list, but with the two obvious accidents pointed out, she had to scrape through her memories to find something else to dredge up. My heart had stopped the first time she gave me a full smile, but that was neither here nor there. Definitely not here.

"The point is," I continued, before she grabbed hold of something, "life here is fleeting, and you drew up against someone who has killed dozens of people. You didn't know what you were getting into, and knowledge is strength in this world."

He nodded slowly and then looked up at me. His single eye filled with a sadness that I didn't think was possible. Or appropriate. "For you to be so wise, and also show me leniency over my transgressions . . ."

"There's no need to oversell it." Ren crossed her arms. "I assume you are waiting for something other than a round two?"

Unable to meet her gaze, he shook his head. "I am still in your debt. My intention was to offer my services as a guide for your leveling process."

I raised my eyebrow. "After you had won over Ren by besting me? That seems shortsighted." How he could expect anything but animosity from me should he have won was beyond me. In fact, if he had won, he would probably be dead by one of our hands shortly after.

"I am a fool." He returned to groveling. "A simple man unable to learn from his mistakes."

We waited in silence. There was clearly some backstory he was about to labor us with, and as little patience as I had, I felt bad for him. Able to resist the call of the Crimson Shadow, yet still flawed and willing to court death. For what? To try to woo a beautiful woman in a way that was antiquated by . . . Well, it seemed more like fiction, from where I stood.

"The portal . . . I found it when trying to escape from the local baron and his men." Quinn looked off to the side. "They sought to kill me, or worse."

"For womanizing the wrong woman?" Ren's expression was rather dim.

"Something like that." He nodded and lowered his gaze. "Alas, my heart seems to take me to dangerous places."

"Not sure that's your heart making decisions," the elf murmured under her breath.

I turned to see Wolf looking bored out of his mind. Perhaps trying to decide whether he had the time to nap or if we were going to give up and allow him to eat the sorry sap. The problem with Quinn was that he was too easy to read—it made me want to trust him. He'd had the chance to do something more dire than challenge me to a fair duel but hadn't. Then apologized profusely.

Ultimately, the decision was Ren's. It was her safety and comfort I cared about, more than having to fight off any potential betrayal.

My eyes narrowed toward him. "What manner of skills do you possess? Class and level?"

"I am an Arcane Fencer, level fourteen. Most of my combat Skills are around quick sword strikes and evasive magic."

For all the good that specialization did him. "We're not going to make a decision right away. Allow us to talk in private back at the camp, and we will let you know then." I raised an eyebrow at Ren, and she nodded her agreement.

Someone who could point us in the direction of useful Quests to complete or knew of an efficient route to travel to level quicker would be worth their weight in gold. Not that we had much use of that as of late. If his plans took us too far north of the main road, then we could assume something was up and not take him up on that danger.

The fact that I had humbled a man five levels higher than me using solely the front of my head didn't really surprise me. We were a few steps higher up the ladder than most, for a variety of reasons. Neither did it work for my ego much. A protracted battle where I emerged the victor would have tasted sweeter, but I didn't want it to turn into anything palatable. There was an ugliness to our adventure that I had accepted.

We had seen it in the eyes of the first group of normal Players. Reviled almost as much as the Crimson Shadow, I didn't expect thanks. The first area was now working as expected, and the warmth that gave my heart kept the furnace burning. Kept us striving forward.

I turned to the elf and gestured for us to start moving. The pair of us went over to Rolo's corpse and somehow shuffled most of it into one of the sheets. There was quite a mess I had made, but you could make out the handprint on what was left of his head, kind of. Wolf didn't seem too pleased with being a wagon for the dead body, perhaps because he had no interest in eating the demon.

"I'm still surprised about Rolo," Quinn said from a good fifteen feet away, clearly not too keen on being any closer to the corpse. "He had a lot of sway with Fiona and the others."

My brow furrowed. "How do you know?"

"Just the . . . impression that I had. When recovering." He idly played with the grip of his sheathed sword.

I wasn't sure how much I liked that. There was a timeline I had to get straight in my head to avoid slitting his throat right now. My right eye twitched as my internal warmth cooled and sank away. The gears in my head clicked around slowly so that I could start building the questions that might save his life.

Level fourteen, so he would have been in the area at least a week, by approximation. Longer if he was solo . . . Was he solo? And if so, why? Nobody at the camp seemed to recognize him or knew he had been taken by the underground marketeers. In the . . . handful of days the Lady had ruined this area, what had he been doing?

"You usually adventure solo, Quinn?" The first chamber had been loaded. A game of roulette was a terrible decision for a man that didn't gamble. Except when it came to my own life.

"I hardly adventure at all lately, if I'm honest." He shrugged and looked sheepishly off out toward the horizon. "I had a Party. Two of us died trying to do a Quest we weren't prepared for. We kind of . . . split up after that. Haven't seen the other two since before all this Crimson Shadow business. Then I was kidnapped, of course."

All reasonably believable.

"What have you been doing instead of adventuring?" Ren asked, securing the last knot of the sling.

"Hiding, mostly." He didn't meet our eyes. "A great shame for one so filled with bravado and passion for the open world. But I was a little lost after everything that happened. Found a System-created house with an attic, barricaded it, and kept to myself." His hand went up to rub at his eye patch. "They grabbed me when I was out looking for food."

I exchanged a glance with Ren, and she shrugged. As much as I was in no hurry to have what little trust I had to give out broken, the story seemed to make enough sense for my hand to stop tensing around the hidden card by my side. Ren and Wolf could see that I had been holding it, and their poker faces were commendable. Considering my questionable grasp of sanity on occasion, it was surprising how easily they were complicit with my decision-making.

"Let's get going then." I smiled as I dusted off my empty hands. "Time to test how critical our reception truly is."

CHAPTER SIXTEEN

Unwelcome Gift

We were mostly quiet on the walk back, which was a small blessing . . . though I could tell that Quinn wanted to fill the silence. Perhaps a little unfair of me to allow him to be miserable. Well, not *unfair*. Something usually unlike me, however.

My need to impress and woo everyone had been tempered by the need to keep the three of us safe. Humbling him was a mercy compared to what the bad side of me wanted to do. There I went again, trying to separate myself into a good and bad. A normal and an *other*. I wasn't even truly sure what a soul was, let alone understood how they could be merged or what that meant long term.

I had settled into being a necessary evil with an unnecessary amount of flair.

Tiring of feeling like I was dragging around a sad puppy, I turned a scowl over toward the failed duelist.

"So Quinn. How do you propose to assist us in leveling that we couldn't do ourselves?"

Ren glared between the man and me, either annoyed that I was engaging him, or perhaps she just didn't like him enough to even entertain the fact that he could be useful. I didn't blame her and shared the same views. The silence had kept me bouncing around thoughts I didn't want to have though.

I had pictured a future where Ren was kidnapped and Wolf wounded by the Crimson. In anger, I would become untenable. Closer to a demon than ever and driven to murder everything solo in an attempt to rescue her. It soured my already dim mood, but I at least hoped that thinking it out so clearly would prevent the world from putting it into action. Wouldn't be narratively interesting to hit the replay button.

"There's a Dungeon. I know of all the traps and secrets in it." He kept his eyes on the ground, not willing to do more than grovel with his potential knowledge.

"How far?" I wasn't about to be dragged toward a Crimson Shadow trap.

"Southwest of the campground. Near the coast."

My right eye twitched. Well into the supposed safe area yet the entire prospect of a Dungeon had images flickering through my mind. The ambush. The risk. The bloodshed.

Still, lightning wasn't supposed to strike twice in the same place. I think that was the idiom anyway. We'd need to have a proper Party chat about the prospect before any concrete decision was made.

"Is that it?" Ren asked.

"No." He shook his head but still didn't meet either of our eyes. "There's a Quest chain that can also get you a whole level in a short amount of time. I know where it starts and the steps required."

I sighed and looked up at the rock we were coming up to. Where we had first seen Rolo sitting. Shame we couldn't get some answers out of him before I pulped his head in. It was dangerous to make assumptions, but if he wasn't part of a group from the camp, then he was probably part of a Shadow group. They would know he was now deceased.

Whether that could be a problem or not didn't seem to matter to me right now. He had been spying on us, so our presence was probably known. If the Lady had told this second area about us, then we should expect more sloppy assassination attempts coming our way. Then again, she might have hoped the countless thugs she had around her little finger back on the other side of the bridge would have killed us off by now.

Little did she know I was developing an immunity to death by constantly smashing my own skull in. What didn't kill you made you traumatized.

We circled the rock and took the switch in the pathway. The campground ahead of us, there was already a handful of people out front by the barricades. A small amount of tension filled me. Ready and willing for the worst, but too emotionally spent to wish it to be anything but acceptance and accolades.

"Let me talk, if you want?" Ren offered. Her eyes looked exhausted at the prospect of the looming conversation.

I nodded. "They might be more receptive to you." While I had happily fit into the slot of being the Party face, the elf had a bit of rapport with Fiona and might take the news easier than if I strode in and waved around my accusations. Plus, I didn't feel much like talking for a change.

It came as no surprise that the fighter was one of the figures waiting at the gates. Magnus and Ruby were there too, plus two others I hadn't seen before. A lithe woman with deep-red skin in an amber robe and a muscled man in thick black leathers. He looked tense, and the pair of knuckle-dusters in his hands made him look ready to tussle, despite the relatively relaxed stances of everyone else.

Naturally, as the group of us were in clear view, we became the focal point of all their attentions. How could we not be? While most of them were between bemused and indifferent, Fiona and the goblin didn't look too pleased at our arrival. How I hated to disappoint them further.

"I see you hired another clown for your group," the fighter said, rolling her eyes.

Ruby had her arms crossed. "Quinn, I told you to stay put, and now you've gone and gotten roughed up. Too soon to adventure while you still had mild trauma."

I felt a little twinge of sympathy for the man. Not so long ago, I was in those boots. Not those specific ones. I was being more figurative. They didn't look my size and would clash with my suit. Hmm. A nap sounded good after the current performance was complete.

"Thinly veiled insults aside," Ren began, choosing her words carefully. "We have something to show you."

"If it's some trick, then I don't care for it."

I noted how Fiona had not looked toward Ren at all during this interaction. Always a scowl solely leveled at me, as if the conversation was only between us. Maybe she was asking me to kill her with her eyes. Is that what they were saying? Begging for it? I shook off a chill as I saw Ren looking at me. Although she was gesturing toward the sling, I knew what else she was saying behind those pools of bright blue.

Terrible time for me to start losing it.

Exhaling, I crouched down and untied some of the sling. Tried to do the reveal with the least amount of clown flair possible. I barely survived the process.

As the corpse dropped to the ground, tensions hit the ceiling. Which was currently the sky, so that was quite high up.

"You killed Rolo?" Fiona seethed, her hand gripping the handle of her sword tightly but not drawing it. Still glaring at me, as if I was the only one here. Magnus had moved up, anger on his face as well. Ruby just looked confused.

"I suggest you approach this with a calmer head." The words came out without too much thinking, but I was able to cut myself off before I added, "While you still have it."

Her right eye twitched. "Then I suggest you start explaining, clown."

The pair that had been part of their prior conversation had stuck around, unsure as to whether a fight was about to break out or not. Slightly put off by the mangled corpse I had brought to display. I knew we got our hands a little dirtier than most, but I found it odd anyone could have gotten this far while still being a little squeamish.

I gestured for the goblin to come have a look, which she did after a brief glance at the fighter. Trusted us enough to be close, at least. Wolf had been statuesque since we got here, his eyes focused on the lion man and zero interest in taking part in the little chat we had in full flow. Likewise, since Quinn had been admonished, he had looked like he wanted the earth to swallow him up. The ground *was* often hungry, but its maw was only six feet deep.

"We caught him spying on us," Ren offered as Ruby stepped over beside where I was crouching.

Fiona bared her teeth at me, as if it had come from my lips. "That's his job!"

She hadn't taken my advice on being calm about this, and I didn't feel like engaging and escalating to anything more than getting called a clown. The goblin was apprehensive but had a cooler temperament, possibly a more clinical view of things. I adjusted the body to show more of his pulped face. Cards on the table.

"Mark of the Red," she said, pulling a face. "Fucker!"

I nodded. "Right?"

Fiona was practically grinding her teeth down. "This doesn't mean that . . . Ah, fuck's sake." With a growl, she turned away from us and put her hand over her eyes. She sighed deeply. "No wonder we haven't been able to gain any ground."

Ruby then turned and put her hand on my forehead, pushing back my hat. "You've had quite the day, huh?"

"It's been . . . an effort." I grimaced as she looked down at me. It would be nice to stand back up, as my legs were cramping, but it felt too rude if she was diagnosing me or something.

"You have a bruised head, and sunflower over here has a swollen nose, bruising around his eyes." She removed her hand and put them both on her hips. "I don't have any special power to see the past, but looks like you won a duel."

I raised an eyebrow up at the man before I finally stood. Wasn't much to imagine he had either done something similar in his short time here or perhaps was just loud about his intention to try to court Ren. Something that would earn the ire of Fiona, for sure.

Ren gave Wolf a pat on the side as she finished untying the rest of the sheet from him. "We thought bringing him here to explain would be better than just running off."

Now the fighter turned to regard the elf. "You're right. If we had found him and you'd gone, we'd have hunted you down."

I yawned louder and longer than necessary and stretched my arms out. The temptation was to vocalize what needn't be said. *They couldn't even dig themselves out from the Crimson Shadow. How were they going to hunt us down?*

Fiona could read between the lines, and despite the renewed scowl in my direction, she seemed to calm. Or at least it didn't anger her further. "I am unsure about how much I can tolerate your presence." She exhaled slowly as she looked between the four of us. Somehow Quinn had been lumped in as our plus-one. "Allow us to discuss it, alright?"

With a glance at Ren, she gave me a nod. Wolf was still mentally absent, hoping he could eat the probably very pleasant Magnus. "We have our own things to discuss. We'll head out just around the corner to give us all air to breathe?"

"Acceptable. We will send someone over when matters are decided. Hopefully, you won't murder them too." She turned, avoiding Ren's heavily rolled eyes and started off back into the camp with the rest of the onlookers following.

"I'll heal you both up once you're allowed in." Ruby gave us a smile and a nod before following along.

I sighed and leaned against the bear, who snapped out of his focus.

"Well, that was underwhelming," he grumbled.

Quinn shrugged. "I'm at least glad it didn't resort to violence."

With a slight smile, I looked down at the destroyed corpse we now had to go bury. "Why's that?" I asked, turning my grin toward him. "You don't know which side you would have been on."

CHAPTER SEVENTEEN

Freshly Unearthed

I stood over the hole dug by large paws. The earth upturned and grass roots torn from where they had grown. With a grunt, I slid the body of Rolo across the ground and into the shallow pit. The cracked face and split eyeball slowly turned toward me as I stared down at what we had done.

"Don't you want to know my secrets?"

My head slowly shook at the whispered words his broken mouth somehow spoke. I did not want to know.

"Don't you feel like a demon too?"

I wanted to say no, but my tongue caught in my mouth. My vision was dimming, and I couldn't look away. Perhaps he was right. If he moved over, then there would be room for both of us. Safety and peace.

"Safety and peace."

"Max?"

Light bloomed in my eyes as I blinked, the soft breeze and glow of midafternoon washing away the focused gloom that had been clouding my vision. I turned my head away from the corpse to look at the elf. "Yeah?"

"I'm honestly worried about you. You need a rest." Concern painted over her usual scowl. "You were just ignoring us and staring at the body in silence."

"Just paying my respects," I murmured, wondering what secrets the talking dead body could have wanted me to know. "But"—I held my hands up—"I admit you are right."

She rolled her eyes. "Obviously. Quinn, help Wolf with the body. I'm going to discuss things with Max." The fencer looked as though he might argue why he had to get involved with a corpse he didn't help create, but one glare from the elf and he was straight into it.

I stood, and we walked a little farther across the field that flanked the campsite. After removing my hat and rubbing my eyes, we found a fallen log to sit on under the shade of a couple of trees. The other two were still in view, but I tried not to stare and see how well they were getting along.

"What a fucking day." Ren sighed and kicked her boots off. "We'll die of stress at this rate."

"You're telling me." I closed my eyes and deflated. Wrinkled my face up when she pressed a hand on my forehead. "People seem to like doing this to me."

She grunted and swiveled around closer so that she could get a better grip on me. I wondered if she was about to crush my head in or twist it around on my neck. Either way, I wasn't going to resist it. Her hand moved away after a few more seconds, and she instead pressed her own forehead against my shoulder.

"I thought I'd be able to tell if something was up," she said and sighed. "But there's no evil energy or anything. You don't feel like you're in trouble."

"Maybe that's because you're here," I said, opening my eyes back up.

Ren sat back up straight, removing her head from me. She looked tired now, some amount of exhausted calm on her face for a change. "You still have a good handful of hours before I'll be swayed by that." She prodded my arm with a finger. "Back to business, if you have the sanity for it."

"Camp drama and Quinn's proposal?"

She nodded.

"I'm . . . willing to stay at the camp tonight if you're fine with it." I tilted my head from side to side. "It's a place of relative safety, and as much as Fiona would like to snap me in half, I don't feel like the majority of people are hostile toward us."

"She holds a lot of sway though." Ren moved back around to be sitting beside me. "I think what you didn't say *was* true: If they can't fight back against the real threat of the Shadow, they'd stand no chance against us."

I smiled and relaxed. Not that it would be that easy, of course. But I admired the confidence she had in our group—me especially. She had no reservations about me dueling Quinn, not knowing anything he was capable of. "I really like how you can read me so well."

Her head tilted as she looked at me, her expression impassive but soft around the edges. "Something about you just clicks, Max. It wasn't easy at first, but things just feel . . . natural now." She placed her hand atop mine and held it.

"We met halfway, right?" She still had some way to go to being a natural magician, just as I needed to work on my leadership skills, but the efforts so far pushed us together to be stronger.

"Yeah."

Although her answer was simple, she gave away a lot more with her face. Both of us books that the other could read where others would struggle. She was fighting the urge to be soft, despite the time of day. It seemed like she was losing that battle, as her other hand came up to cup along my jaw and run through the hair at the side of my head.

I leaned forward, ready to kiss her—when she moved away.

"What's this?" Her frown couldn't hide the amusement in her eyes as she withdrew her hand from behind my ear, now holding a gold coin.

"Very good." I grinned. It was a shame we didn't have more downtime to practice things, but that was just the nature of our current adventure. Maybe one day, once things were normal, we could become quite the duo. Magically.

She flicked it into the air, and my eyes followed it. I stole it from the air without moving just before it landed back in her hand, which she still closed as if she had caught it. With an eyebrow raised, she opened up her hand to reveal a sweet cake.

"Extremely good," I said and also considered giving her some applause.

"You ass," she began, putting the treasure straight into her mouth. "Isn't it a rule that you're not meant to mess with another magician's trick?"

I feigned a shocked face. "Mess with? That was merely a collaboration. If we had an audience, it would have looked as though it had been all you."

Her eyes rolled, but I saw the glimmer of excitement in them. With the cake already eaten, her face wrinkled up. "Do we *want* an audience?" She was looking over to Quinn, who had been complaining to the bear about getting mud on his sleeves. Wolf had not eaten him, so perhaps our large companion was meeting us halfway too.

I mean, we didn't *eat* people.

"That's a tough call." I rubbed at my eyes. "The downsides being that he is annoying and might constantly try to flirt with you."

"He wouldn't dare." Ren kicked the side of my boot gently. "You'd fuckin' tear him in half, trickster."

Something about the light in her eyes and choice language used told me that she quite liked it when I used my overwhelming power to show off how strongly I felt about her. A potentially deadly hobby, yet . . . I did like to see her happy.

"Well . . ." I tilted my head from side to side. "If he doesn't make you uncomfortable, then having the knowledge to level us quicker would be nice. Can kill the Shadow quicker."

She nodded. "I'm willing to give him a chance, with the threat of violence if he misbehaves."

I looked back over to the man as he seemed to now be regaling Wolf with a tale that the bear could not care less for. "He's not the sort of person I'd usually associate with, but he seems to wear his heart on his sleeve. He's perhaps the most trustworthy Player we've met."

"You get that impression as you broke your skull on his face?" She raised an eyebrow. "That said . . . I do agree with you. It could be an act to appear harmless, but I've been trying to read him, and he mostly comes off as lost and misguided."

I'd certainly say that. He came at me while still suffering from the trauma Status, something that hit close to home. "Maybe when he is fully recovered, we could have another duel."

Ren didn't respond. She knew I didn't mean I was putting her hand on the line again. Quinn seemed to take things to heart easily, and my humbling of him could turn him toward something destructive in the future. Having my demons be subservient was one thing, but if we were to trust him as an equal, then he deserved to squirm out from beneath my boot. He'd have to earn it, of course.

"Hey, Wolf," I called out to the bear and waved him over. Quinn looked our way and deflated. Now he stood, awkwardly shuffling some last remnants of dirt over the grave.

"Thank you," Wolf said as he reached us. "I felt like my brain was becoming some kind of mashed food that I would need to eat."

"Not a fan, then?" I tilted my head.

"I feel like eating Quinn would give me a stomachache." He lazily looked back toward the man. "But other than being a bore, he isn't like the bad people."

Ren nodded. "Any disagreements to letting him guide our next couple of levels?"

Wolf shook his head. "On the condition that I don't have to engage him in conversation."

"I'll probably hold the short straw in that regard." I sighed but then smiled to them both. "Trust doesn't come easily to us all, I know, and we still have an ache over what happened to Hannah. Having some normal connections would be nice for when this is all over though. We don't want to be friendless mass murderers."

The bear grunted and lay down. "I forgot how much you talk as well."

Ren patted me on the arm. "Go give the good news then, Mr. Speech-Giving Leader."

I rolled my eyes but stood. "Equal partnership," I reminded them, pointing my index finger between them both.

Although I had accepted being the face of the group and using what charisma—real or imagined—I possessed to talk to the many oddballs on our path, I didn't want to be seen as the leader. It was not a personal vendetta that drove us but a shared agreement that our quest to stop Lady in Red from making a mess of the System was the most important thing we could do here.

Whether that was true or not was something else entirely. Had we really achieved much? So far, we had tidied up the mess on the starter island and in the first area, but our true aim was to nip her progress in the bud. How she had gotten so far ahead was something I wondered if we'd ever find out, but the assumption was one of her Skills gave her power or experience beyond her level.

"Quinn," I said, finally reaching him after my mental dialogue ran out of physical space that my legs could buy me time for. "Great shallow grave. I'm sure Rolo appreciates it."

"I'm . . ." His face contorted. "Are you mocking me, Max?"

My right eye twitched, and I exhaled. "I've had a difficult day, and my sensibilities are rough around the edges. I do hope you can forgive me."

"Of course." He gave me a low bow. "Think nothing of it."

It was partially true, but I also wanted to gauge his reaction. He was taking what I said to heart, either keeping his issues with my attitude to himself or earnestly allowing it to slide after my reasonable apology.

"We have agreed you can be our guide for a short time," I managed to say without walking it back. "With three conditions."

"Of course, please tell me them." His eye was practically glowing with excitement.

"You are to guide us to the most efficient way to leveling, nothing more—no side agenda. Do not engage with Wolf with anything not mission critical unless he initiates conversation with you. And last, absolutely no flirting with Ren."

He opened his mouth to speak, and I held up a finger to silence him.

"Breaking any of our rules gives us discretion in either firing you from your position . . . or *killing* you." I tilted my head to the side, not clocking how loose and fatal the terms of service sounded. "I also have one question for you, should you accept."

He knelt down on the muddied grass and held his head low. "I promise to uphold those three rules, on pain of death or humiliation. What is your question, Max?"

I met his eye as he raised his gaze back up at me. A smooth smile crept across my face as I felt nice and cool inside. Calm spread through all the muscles whose aches I had been ignoring. Exhaustion took a brief respite as a bulb of intrigue lit up inside my chest.

"Tell me, Quinn. What weapon do you possess in that side holster?"

CHAPTER EIGHTEEN

Open Sesame

I could see the apprehension on his face, clear as day. He didn't want to let me in on what he had holstered to his side, yet knew that he had to if he wanted to accompany us. He'd rather make friends than enemies at this stage, knowing what we were capable of.

On the other hand, I was rather cool on the idea. Starter-island Max would have been bending over backward to accommodate the man, and I'd have tried my best to make him a fan of my work. Nowadays my work involved a lot more loss of life, which anyone with a healthy mind shouldn't be a fan of. I glanced back at the other two members of my party, both of them in quiet conversation.

"This is my Class Keystone," he informed me, popping a clasp on the leather holster. "I have told few of its capability, and even fewer have seen it in action." He paused, about to lift the flap up. "Possibly the other way around."

I narrowed my eyes, ready to see a flintlock pistol or something similar. That would be a step up over the more medieval weaponry we had come across so far. If you discounted the guy with twin chainswords. What I hadn't been prepared for was it to actually be something so visually basic.

From within, he took out what appeared to be a small boomerang. Polished light wood, lacquered and smooth.

"Oh," I said politely. "I wasn't expecting that." It didn't seem exactly what a fencer or musketeer-looking fellow would have been carrying around in his old world.

"When I throw it at something," he continued, "at my command, it will explode."

"Oh," I said, some confusion now on my face. Something else I did not expect, and even less likely for a duelist to wield. Perhaps this was the arcane part of his Class and he was essentially showing me a magical grenade.

"It only works once per day." He shrugged and placed it back away. "The kidnappers took my good sword but thought my Class weapon to be something more banal. A shame I couldn't show them its true purpose firsthand." With a glum smile, he gave me a brief bow to signal his duty to fulfill my request was complete.

I held out my hand to shake. "Glad to have you on board, Quinn." Although I smiled, I mostly wanted to see the weapon in action and possibly involve it in my act somehow. Our pyrotechnics were few and far between—a once-a-day big bang could be just what we really needed to . . . blow up the Crimson Shadow?

He took my hand with both of his, and we shook, a warm smile across his face.

"One last thing," I added. "No adventuring if you have the trauma Status."

"It is mild at present, Max. The doctor assured me rest would cure it in no time at all."

"That was before you came to fight me, yeah?" I raised an eyebrow.

His one eye took a glance over at Ren before he nodded sheepishly. "I tend to act brashly and follow every spark of passion that erupts within me. Part of the reason I decided to hide myself away was to limit how much danger I would get myself into."

Otherwise, he'd be with the Shadow or broken underneath their boots, no doubt. A stroke of bad luck to have been picked up by the marketeers. Traveling solo seemed like a large risk—another thing I couldn't help but feel bad about. My brow furrowed as thoughts and questions started to bubble within my mind.

I took a glance in the direction of the camp before gesturing to the fencer. "Come sit with us while we await our fate. Knowledge is power, and perhaps we can drag you up to our level."

Although the pair didn't look too pleased as I brought him over, it was wise to be wary of a new face. We had agreed to travel with him, so some amount of acceptance was required—and as we sat in a loose circle, the tension slowly melted away as I began to speak.

I told him our history, what Ren and I had accomplished back on the island. The Lady and her effect on the first area. Meeting Wolf and fighting off the various ambushes. Despite it being in my nature, I didn't embellish the facts. Told him all, everything up to the small village here and meeting Fiona and her group.

He sat in patient silence, an enraptured audience if ever I saw one. His eye widened at certain parts, and his expression changed slightly between disbelief and awe, but by the end he seemed rather mellow compared to his usual self.

"Incredible," he said, deflating in his chair. "It is . . . almost beyond belief, yet I do believe you—wholeheartedly."

I nodded, glad that he was now caught up to speed. "If you want to back out now, that is an option."

"No judgments," Ren added.

He shook his head. "No. I . . . I thank the stars to have crossed paths with such a fated couple." His eye went down to the bored bear. "*Trio.* It surely cannot be chance we have met. I feel invigorated and honored to be part of your journey against the dark forces that plague this world."

"Great," Ren murmured, "now there's two of you."

An unfair jab, I felt. While I certainly had my moments of drab introspection or labored them with a weighty phrase about our situation—I wasn't unnecessarily poetic about it. I hoped anyway. Was his showmanship clashing with my own?

I narrowed my eyes as he smiled warmly at us. No. The difference was he didn't need to impress or draw acceptance from people. He was just outwardly this insufferable because he was already so sure about himself. Nauseating.

"The plan is," I began, "to rest for the remainder of today and head out tomorrow. While there are plenty of hours left in the day, I am one bad incident away from having a mental break."

"That makes a change," Wolf added. The elf shuffled slightly, probably to hide the amusement in her expression.

"Instead," I continued, ignoring the pair, "I have some questions to open up to the group." Dramatic pause to ensure I had their attention. "First up, whom were the marketeers selling stuff to? It can't be the groups at the camp, right?"

"Unless they are part of it," Wolf grumbled. "A honeypot to draw wayward Players in." He licked his lips.

His fixation on food aside, it was a reasonable point to bring up. I deferred to Ren for her views on the idea.

"It's . . ." She wrinkled her face up. "You need to remember I didn't know Fiona for that long. It doesn't seem like something she'd do . . . But then, look at us."

A stage magician with more blood on my hands than tricks as I slowly lost sight of myself to what? A demon? There was something I was keen to avoid addressing at this stage. Perhaps I would take a leaf out of Ren's book and allow my internal thoughts out once we had some privacy under the night's sky.

"Could be any of them in there," Quinn added. "Not to cast any aspersions on the fine folk who nursed me to health, but there are a lot of unknowns."

I nodded. "We'll put a big question mark over the camp for now until we know how they feel about us. If not them, then who? My kidnapper didn't seem keen on the Crimson Shadow, but coin is coin, right?"

"What do they even need gold for?" Ren scowled at the grass. "It's not like the System requires us to spend it on much."

"Shame the adventuring taxes are so high," Quinn said before sighing.

"Taxes?" I grimaced. The uncomfortable word had me wanting to call for Reggie.

"Yeah . . . What, you *haven't* been paying them?" He leveled a blank expression at us both before his poker face cracked away and a wide grin emerged—before we even had a chance to buy it. "Sorry! Just a little joke, ha! The fair Ren is correct, however. There isn't much opportunity to spend gold unless you head to one of the main towns."

I brought up the map. "There's what . . . Four towns?"

"Three smaller and then the main hub," he said with a nod. "Although I have not made it all that way myself."

The closest was down on the southern coast, back to the east a little. If only we had gone that route rather than be distracted by the village taken over by the gang. In fact, the towns were almost placed in each corner of the area. Assuming north of the road was controlled by the Crimson Shadow, then that left the southwest one our safest bet—with the central hub just before the third area up in contention.

"Why are the Players camping here instead of staying in the town?" I raised an eyebrow, the question more just my out-loud thoughts than a shovel digging for answers.

Quinn shrugged, his time with them just as short—if not more so—than our own. Perhaps a question I could jab them with should they decide not to turn us away. Looking over, I could see that Wolf had fallen into a nap. Under this pleasant shade, I couldn't blame him. We'd had an active day and definitely deserved some downtime.

Even thinking and knowing this, I craved to continue. At my personal detriment, I felt the need to level more. Gather Skills and tokens, and . . . My brow furrowed.

"How powerful is your Class Keystone, Quinn?" My head tilted to arrange my thoughts into one useful pile rather than be spread out.

He screwed his mouth up, and his eye went between each of us. "If I set it off where we currently sit . . . all would die. Except maybe the venerable Wolf."

My eyebrows raised. I had tried not to consider myself becoming more of an assassin with my teleportation, invisibility, and penchant to survive any odds . . . but he had a throwable satchel of C-4. The things I could do with that. The damage. *The death.*

Licking my lips, I gave him a wry grin. "I have a job for you then, should you have no current use of your Ability today?"

We stood back out in the field, a little farther from the camp so as not to worry them. Ren didn't seem too enamored with my explanation that Quinn had a magical grenade, even if the System translated that into something she could understand. Wolf had been grumpy at being awoken but had soon fallen back asleep on arrival at our destination. Shame it wouldn't last.

I walked a good fifty feet away from the elf and bear with the fencer by my side.

"What Stats does your Class require, Quinn?"

"Agility and Intelligence main, Strength minor."

Shame, but that made sense. We'd be competing on Intelligence gear, perhaps—but it was interesting he didn't have Dexterity as a main Stat considering his fencing background. Then again, we hadn't seen him fight properly yet.

I stopped and withdrew the safe from my Inventory to place on the grass. Tilted it on its back so the locked face looked up at the sky. Up at its reckoning.

"What do you think?" I asked him.

He rubbed at his goatee. "Ah . . . It is not impossible. You have piqued my curiosity, Max."

"Twenty-five percent of the contents." I shot him a smile. "We are all equal here." Although I hadn't run this past Ren yet, I was sure she wouldn't disagree. If he was going to risk life and limb to assist us, it seemed fair to treat him as we did one another.

Plus, I wasn't going to waste any more brain cells on trying to open the thing. It could be useless junk.

From his pouch, he withdrew the small wooden boomerang and placed it gently atop the face of the safe. We both turned and walked back toward the pair who were uninterested in whatever we were getting up to. I had to admit that Quinn was growing on me. Where Ren was too closed off and trying to crawl out of her shell, the man was too overt with his feelings and needed to dial it in.

Wolf was quiet and considerate but very plain and forthright when asked. And me . . . Well, I was pretty sure I was slowly going insane—but I put a good show on, at the least. I was entertaining, for those not being crushed beneath my heel.

I shook those thoughts away as I caught Ren's blue eyes. Quinn and I stopped, his face a slight grimace as we looked back toward the otherwise inconspicuous item atop the metal cube.

With his hand extended, he whispered out a word that the System did not translate.

CHAPTER NINETEEN

Pop!

The resulting explosion was something both impressive and underwhelming at the same time. Perhaps too many movies and living a life full of theatrics had given me a disjointed vision of what a blast really did. However, the power and damage it wreaked was awe-inspiring, even if the loud bang did earn us both glares from the elf and bear.

We walked back over to the safe, now sitting in a small ditch of brown mud. Grass smoldered on the edges of the circular pit that was easily a dozen feet wide.

"It's been a while since I've used it last." He grinned, clearly as enamored with the destruction as I was.

"I can imagine. It's not exactly subtle." I licked my lips, trying not to think about what I could do with that kind of power. Explode people, probably. Once per day.

Any worry that even that was not enough washed away quicker than the smell of charred metal and burned dirt hit our noses. The poor safe lay facing the sky still, the door now buckled and smoking. Warm to the touch, but the locking mechanism had given up the ghost, and the contents were ours—assuming we hadn't ruined them either.

It popped open in my grasp, and I was vaguely disappointed to be presented with a looting window rather than have anything tangible on the inside. System liked to ruin my mood.

[8,345 Gold]
[Socket Setters (2)]
[DEX Gemstones (3)]
[AGI Gemstones (2)]
[Skill Book (1)]
[Power Tokens (12)]

I whistled. Partly because I wanted to build anticipation, and I was amused to see the other two members of the Party moving toward us.

"Worth alerting the rest of the area to our location?" Ren asked, her arms crossed.

She couldn't hide her desire to know what was inside though. I could read her like a book. Nevertheless, I didn't want to drag the suspense out longer than necessary just in case she set Wolf on me. He seemed even less impressed with the loud noise that had woken him up.

"First off," I said with a wide grin. "There was a bunch of nice meat." I caught the elf's look. "And fruit."

From within my Inventory I withdrew some pork chops, a pair of apples, and some carrots in quick succession. Carrots weren't a fruit, but hopefully it was enough to persuade the bear.

As he crunched through, my eyes quickly went over the newer items to see what they did before I did the big reveal.

Socket setter added a socket to a piece of gear—which enabled a gemstone to be affixed. Another way for gear to boost Stats. *Two* wasn't exactly an easy number to share around. These gemstones gave a +2 to their respective Stats, and I was sure I'd found a Mana one at some point.

"Three power tokens and two thousand gold each," I said, mostly to give them a figurative bite to eat while I finished off reading things. There was a little rounding of those figures, which I'd work out eventually, I was sure.

A Skill book gave you the option of three random skills to choose from. Random meaning outside of your normal Class choice. Limited to a certain list, and mostly utility skills. I pouted, trying to imagine how we would divide certain things up fairly.

"I can see that look on your face, friend." Quinn gave me a soft smile. "If there is anything rare or important you cannot share, I understand—I am new to the group and the tokens and gold are more than worth the cost of being part of this."

I raised an eyebrow at Ren, and she shrugged.

[Quinn has joined the Party]

"I was hoping for more Equipment." I stood from the spent metal container and stretched out. "But there's some Dexterity things for you, Ren. Also this."

She tilted her head as I held out the book, as if I was about to do something strange with it as part of some trick. With a suspicious glare toward me, she took it and brought up the description.

"Hmm. Pass." She handed it back.

I raised an eyebrow but nodded. I understood her reasoning. Max, the man of many tricks, could probably do better with something extra—even if it was something mundane. Instead, I traded over her tokens, gold, and socket items.

"Now this is better, thank you." She gave me a glare that lingered before I was able to tear myself away and distribute the rest of the plunder to the others.

"Someone approaches," Wolf mentioned, turning his head as he licked his chops—his meal finished, including the fruit and veg.

We turned to see that he was correct. From the direction of the campground, a male figure dressed in plain brown leathers. He was alone, which meant he came to deliver a message rather than run us away.

"Clive, right?" I grimaced and raised an eyebrow at the elf.

"Yeah. I get the impression you're not a fan." She shrugged. "Seems pretty normal to me."

"That's the point." I tried to scour the approaching man for a sign of . . . anything that was remarkable about him. "It's like his Class is just *generic human*."

Ren nudged me to get me to hush, but I could see a wry grin at the side of her mouth. Quinn looked apprehensive but didn't seem to have any preconceptions about the man.

"Hello," he greeted us, now close enough to speak at medium volume. "You may remember me. I'm Clive."

I nodded. "Yes." For the day that I'd had up until this point, I prided myself on not adding anything sarcastic to that acknowledgment. I was just about to dig through my tokens and the Skill book.

"The meeting has concluded. You are free to stay." He stopped and held his hands behind his back.

Ren narrowed her eyes. "There's no addendum or conditions on that?"

"No." He remained impassive.

I considered the ramifications of killing him outright. Probably a bad example to set for our new temporary Party member. Ren and Wolf might play along, but making enemies of every Player in the area would be pretty shortsighted.

"Okay," I relented. "Thank you, Clive. We'll finish up here and circle back when ready."

"As you wish. Best regards." He turned and started walking calmly away, unaware that I was staring the worst daggers imaginable at the back of his perfectly normal head.

"I can see why he'd be your mortal enemy," Ren said, turning to me. "Given that you're opposites."

I rolled my eyes. "Like any of you are any less of a spectacle." From my Inventory, a chair appeared as I sat.

Quinn furrowed his brow, looking down at his garish yellow outfit, before then glancing at the chair that had appeared a lot easier than he was used to.

"Team meeting . . . again, I suppose?" As much as the morning had been spent between grinding Monsters and avoiding a mental break, the late afternoon seemed to be sinking into conversations about . . . Hmm, my brain had started to slow down.

I looked up at the three as we sat in a loose circle once more. Adding a new voice and complication to the dynamic was an issue we had been avoiding for a while. Quinn seemed trustworthy, almost up to a level only Wolf could reach. The extra power for our group would help us against the unknown. Being a party of three had made us easy to ambush.

"Say, Quinn," I began, "you haven't really seen what I can do, right?"

He shook his head politely. "From watching you fight the Wildfolk, you are a ranged spellcaster, with a gambler or jester theme."

I caught Ren squirming slightly. Even though her face hadn't budged, I knew that was a tell that she was holding in a laugh. "*Magician*, but close enough. The card attacks are one part of it . . . but maybe I can give a demonstration?"

Wolf perked up, perhaps assuming the trick would end up with him getting some meat. Well, I couldn't disappoint him. Quinn seemed apprehensive but was attentive. Ren was glaring at me but was eager to see what I was about to come up with. What a crowd.

"Do you have an orange, Ren?" I smiled at my protégé.

She nodded, withdrawing it into her hand before lobbing it over to me to catch.

Only I didn't. With my eyes narrowed, the orange stopped in midair over my lap. It hovered there, bobbing up and down for five seconds. I then clapped my hands together over it—nothing there—but when I drew them apart, I now had an orange in each hand.

Wolf and Quinn both had a few Dazzle icons, but unsurprisingly, Ren did not. She gave me a brief nod, but I knew she was more impressed by tricks that didn't involve me moving things in and out of my Inventory. This one was a little different, in that I focused on quickly dropping the same thing in and out as quickly as possible in the same place to give the illusion of floating. It was hell on my eyes, however.

"Some manner of conjuration." The fencer looked half ready to give me some applause. "I am impressed."

I spun an orange in my hand, and it turned into a roasted chicken. Off to Wolf it went, with the other orange.

"You should see him do that in the middle of combat." Ren raised an eyebrow. "He kills people with that kind of bullshit."

Amusing to note that Quinn winced as the elf swore. I'd have to clue her in on that. No doubt he saw her as many did—a beautiful elfin princess. And she was, in a way, but so much more of a person outside of that. She caught me smiling at her, and I slowly turned my gaze back to the present, my train of thought trying to find the right rails.

"Ah, so we're allowed back to the pleasant camp." There it was, got it in one.

Ren deflated in her chair. "No doubt Fiona said a lot more than it was just okay."

"I for one am glad to have a safe space to sleep tonight." Quinn scratched at his eye patch. "I'd prefer some solid walls, but it's better than a dank chamber where they remove eyeballs."

I grimaced. Not far from that fate myself, depending on how quickly Ren and Wolf had arrived. Although I had made it out mostly unharmed, Quinn wasn't so lucky. "How are you other than the trauma?"

"One eye fewer is a detriment to my fighting ability." He looked down and shuffled in his chair. "Another reason why I was keen to find a place in your Party."

Ren and I exchanged a look. We had hardened ourselves to do the worst things necessary to fix this System and find some closure to what the Lady had done. Quinn was the breath of fresh air to remind us of our humanity. Or whatever elves had. Elfmanity. Not built like us to rise above the struggle but strong enough not to have fallen. He was the sort of person we were doing this all for.

"You know . . ." Ren began. "Not that I'm pushing you away, but you could always go back to the first area."

I nodded along. "There's new Players coming in that could use guidance, and we're pretty sure we got rid of most of the rot there."

He looked between us and furrowed his brow. "I feel like I have a lot of growth to do as a person before I could act as a mentor. But perhaps that is a noble goal for me, once I am ready."

Quinn may have his flaws, but he didn't seem dreadful on the inside. The Crimson Shadow were terrible and violent, and the campers were apathetic and lax. From the few newer Players we had met, he seemed a lot more well-adjusted. I wondered if we had managed to appear during a period of people with terrible attitudes being brought into the System. Would be bigheaded, but part of me was willing to believe I was here to fulfill a purpose.

To kill the infection that the Lady was soaking through the land.

We settled into a silence as we each went through to use our tokens, although Wolf was perhaps just going back to sleep. Three was a decent number, and I was tempted to save them up to get the next upgrade on my main attacks—or perhaps one of my summons. Still, waiting around for seven more when we could die the next day seemed foolish. Better to have power today than be a corpse with unrealized potential.

My eyes rolled over all my Abilities and Passives. A tough problem to chew on, but I dove in face-first.

[<Demonic Transposition> is now advanced: Mana cost is reduced by 30%. The switch can be reversed within two seconds of using the Ability.]

Although it sounded like a one-way ticket to getting dizzy, the reversal seemed way more important than the Mana usage of the Skill. The first example that came into my head was putting a dove up by a chimney, switching so that I could drop something down into the house, and then reversing back to wherever I was safe. Also, a novel way to Dazzle or confuse an enemy while in combat.

[<Master Summoner> is now advanced: Summons have an additional 15% Health and Damage]

This brought them up to 25 percent bonus to both. Shame it gave no further effects—but the locked expert stage of the Skill seemed to hint that it was more than just a Stat boost. Even with Quinn on our side, we'd get good use out of my demons, and they'd earned a little boost of their own.

Trying not to glance at Ren out of guilt, I upgraded the next Skill.

[<Bloodletting> is now advanced: Maximum Health drained converted to Damage increased by 15%. Spell Crit Chance increased by 5% when bloodletting.]

The extra 5 percent Damage wasn't really worth it. It was hard to imagine this being a good pick if I didn't have the Headband of Woe, which increased Damage with Mana used. However, Crit Chance was very nice—and 5 percent was much higher than my current bonus. Sure, it meant pushing my Health and Ability to the limit, but when I could possibly get more of those critical cards in clutch moments without wasting Mana on normal cards . . .

It seemed like a something pretty useful. <Shatter> was now my only active Ability not upgraded, and I was pretty neutral on it until I saw it in action.

"Do you have any expert skills, Quinn?" I raised an eyebrow as I brought out the Skill book.

"Ah, just the one." His eye was still on his menus. "Something that helps me avoid projectiles."

I nodded. "Shame I didn't just attack you with cards then. Things may have gone differently."

His eye moved away from whatever he was looking at to seek me out, a warm smile crossing his face. "Perhaps. I expect you are a lot more than meets the eye, knowing what I do now."

If Ren hadn't also been in her Ability menus, she probably would have rolled her eyes. It was a reasonable response. Quinn was still malleable. Once we saw how he fared in the fires of the forge, we'd see if he could be tempered to play the role we were destined for.

I activated the Skill book, unsurprised all that opening it did was bring up menus to select options.

[Pick one:]
[<Analyze>: You can see the level and basic Class of a target]
[<Terrain Expert>: You can determine the nature of the surrounding terrain]
[<Battle Observer>: You can see Status-effect icons on nearby targets]

Clucking my tongue, I gestured to my selection with nothing but a thought.

CHAPTER TWENTY

Healthy Skepticism

While all three Skills had some use or another, I didn't need the System to talk to me about mud and trees. Likewise, basic Class was just a rough approximation of what someone's actual Class was. For me it would be Wizard. Most opponents dressed in a way that made it clear what sort of role they functioned in on the battlefield.

There had already been a few times where I hadn't been able to see other debuff icons that would have been helpful. Like, knowing Jokkar had stunned the other two and not killed them would have been less stressful. I raised my eyebrows at my Party now and accepted <Battle Observer>.

Quinn had an icon. A red *T* on a gray background with a small number one in the bottom-right corner. The first level of trauma, I assumed. At least he had been forward about it, and now I felt like a bit of a creep for being able to see this about people. Maybe it suited the magician part of me, to help Dazzle or win over people if I knew what ailed them. Time would tell.

Ren had nothing over her. I was partly ready to guess that she had something that made her immune to being dazzled or something that perhaps hid her Status effects—but then again, that wouldn't necessarily be something I could see with this Ability anyway. She tilted her head in seeing me narrowing my eyes at her.

I switched to Wolf, who had two icons over him. The first was a red square with the outline of a stomach in black upon it. Second was a light-blue color with an upward arrow in black. With an eyebrow raised, I found I could bring out the descriptions of these, since I was apparently close enough.

[**Hungry: You require food**]
[**<Energetic Boost>: STR and CON increased at the cost
of increased hunger (On)**]

Well, now that made a lot of sense. I wasn't sure whether or not I should tell him, however. Depending on how good the boost was, I'd be happy to continue filling the bear with food if it increased his efficiency. Still, if he was doing it out of ignorance, it wouldn't be fair of me to keep a secret for myself.

"Wolf, are you aware you have a buff Skill toggled on all the time?" I tilted my head but clocked Ren's raised eyebrow at my question.

"I know some of those words," he grumbled, his eyes currently closed and chin resting on his paws.

"You have something that makes you more powerful but requires you to eat a lot more. You could turn it off when not in combat to remain satiated for longer." He probably knew *all* those words if the System was doing its job of translating everything for us properly.

"I like eating."

Ren rolled her eyes and came at me with a question of her own. "What did you get from the book then, trickster? You can see all icons now?"

"I'm not sure about *all* . . ." I leveled a blank stare at her to see if I could read anything from her expression. "But generally, yes. I can see Quinn's trauma Status."

"Anything on me?" she asked.

"*Should* there be?" We both remained impassive, perhaps the two best poker faces in the System.

Quinn cleared his throat. "Ah, speaking of my Status—if we have the grace of Fiona et al., it would be nice to get some rest."

I slowly broke eye contact with the elf before addressing the man. It was getting close to dusk, and if we were going to have a busy day of traveling and leveling tomorrow, then getting some good rest sounded like a solid plan. Plus, I had survived the day and had a kiss coming my way if I played my cards right. Which I *always* did.

"Good idea, Quinn." Other than having to deal with the other Players. "Any objections to heading to the camp for the day?"

Ren didn't seem too enthusiastic but shook her head. Wolf grunted and murmured something about hoping they had some food. It was all as expected, really. I stood from my chair, giving it a glance so I could put it away. The other two did the same but much slower. For a moment, I just turned and took in our surroundings. Amber light from the waning sun had started painting the landscape a different hue.

Beautiful in a way. Again, I found myself in awe of the System to some degree, coming from a world that was often just the glow of the stage or the drab gray brickwork of civilization in twilight. It was enough to remind me of what we were fighting for. All who found themselves here with enough earnestness in their hearts deserved a pleasant world to grow and thrive in.

Ren put her hand on my arm, jostling me from my thoughts. "Everything alright, Max?"

I smiled and put my arm around her, surprised briefly that she allowed it. "It will be, Ren."

She followed my gaze out to the fields, now almost golden with the sunset approaching. "Wasn't angling for a romantic moment, but I'll accept it. My worry was . . . I just had a *feeling*. Like back at the Dungeon."

My hand slid away from her back, and I turned to face her. "One of your Skills gives you some kind of premonition powers?"

She shook her head. "Not as such. I didn't know you were going to be kidnapped, so it's not something related to my Oath." Her face wrinkled up. "Maybe it's just been a long day."

I nodded, and we turned to join the other two. She was trying to downplay it, but I trusted her instinct entirely. Probably a good idea to tell her. "I trust your instinct entirely."

She rolled her eyes. "Really trying hard for that kiss later, huh? But thank you. We'll need to be on alert then."

"We will be." I smiled and ignored her playful jab. As much as it might be true, the prospect that something bad might be around the corner had thrown a wet blanket over the possible flames of our blooming romance. It felt awkward to call it that, but she had officiated it, so she only had herself to blame.

Wolf chuckled loudly. A rumbling thing from ahead of us. He and Quinn had apparently found some common ground to talk about. The snippets I caught seemed to be about food, but I was way beyond being surprised.

"You made a good call with Quinn."

I raised my eyebrows at her. "Oh?"

"We've been through a lot." She exhaled and looked out to the trees as we rejoined the main road. "Your choice shows that you're not . . . You won't become a monster. Cold and indifferent."

"Hmm." How correct was she on this? My actions with Rolo sparked a truth of what I was capable of. We had already slain our way through enough people for it to be hard to believe I had a clean and good soul. In the fort, she had told me to not lose sight of myself, and this was what she'd meant.

I had no doubt she would follow me, even if I had killed Quinn. Even if I had killed through the camp. There was a limit, I was sure, where she would put the demon-killing arrow through the back of my neck. I was in no hurry to get close to that line. In fact, the farther away from the line I could be, the better.

"I'm fallible," I admitted to her. "But glad I have you to keep me pointed in the right direction. If I was alone in this, I'd . . ."

"You'd be like I was on the starter island." She hooked her arm around mine as we walked. "Dissociated, bitter, and angry. Fiona drew me out of it a little, but then it compounded when she left. I . . . was not in a healthy place."

"What changed when you met me?" I relaxed as we fell into step. "Other than being swayed by my charisma and good looks, naturally."

"Honestly? It helped that you weren't *entirely* an asshole. You seemed earnest about wanting to help me, and I was desperate for a conclusion. Something to put an end to the constant torment." She sighed.

"And I was desperate for someone to show me the ropes in this world and find some safety." I smiled as she shot me a scowl.

"You're competent enough, trickster. I treated you like shit, and I'm glad that didn't push you away."

"We are both good at reading people. I could see your intent behind the scowls and disdain for how I beat out the odds with childish flair." I grinned to myself as we were almost at the large rock before camp.

She let go of my arm and straightened out her waistcoat. "*Now* look at me." She tilted her head and gave me a soft smile. "Seeing me beneath the layer of grump was an easy way into my heart. Hadrian, Fiona, other nameless jerkoffs—they just thought I was pissed at them all the time."

"They were all assholes," I said diplomatically.

Her eyes rolled, but her expression was content enough. "*You're* an asshole sometimes. So am I. I'd be more worried about you if you weren't a dickbag."

Our conversation petered out as we rejoined the two ahead of us as they stopped on the path leading into the camp. No surprises that Fiona was awaiting our arrival, but interestingly enough, it was only her there.

She looked as though she was chewing on some manner of insult or gibe to throw our way, but it melted away. "Group decided to trust you. I'm not going to welcome you with open arms, but you're free to stay as long as you need." She raised an eyebrow at Quinn. "Some of you may need healing. All we ask in return is you help take watch. There's a gap tomorrow night."

"Smaller camp tonight?" I asked.

She nodded curtly. "The pair you saw earlier, their group is going out to the west. Against my advice, but adventures do what adventurers do."

I gave her a low bow. "I appreciate your discretion."

"Whatever." She sighed deeply. "Thank Ruby, mostly. The world is too full of shit for us few to be so up in arms." She held out a hand toward me.

I took it and shook. "Tensions are naturally high. What matters now is the way forward."

She narrowed her eyes at me but didn't want to address the comments. "Same tent is available to you both, and we have one for Quinn nearby."

He gave her a low bow too, a mirror of the one I had performed. I saw her jaw work, but she gestured for us to follow on in.

Ren stepped ahead of me. "Do you have some way to bathe here, Fiona?"

"We do, back left. There should be some water left in the shower." With one last put-on smile, she waved us away. "I'm on front-gate duty for a while longer unless Clive comes to relieve me, but perhaps we can speak further in the morning?"

The elf put her hand on my shoulder and leaned into my ear to whisper. "As much as I'd like you to keep an eye on me, I'd prefer you kept an eye on Quinn."

I nodded as she moved away, totally unflustered by the mental images now fighting for brain space. "Wolf, go and protect Ren with your life. Extra rations for you." He seemed happy with this.

As I watched her walk off, I could have sworn there was a coy smile at the side of her mouth. I exhaled and turned to Quinn. "Come on, let's go and see the doctor."

He hadn't been gazing after the elf when she left with the bear, which was a good sign. Party dynamics would get messy if he still held a candle for her. Liable to get burned. It seemed the luster was just on the surface layer, and the run-in with me had set him off on a more realistic path. Still, she wasn't about to take the risk of having a Peeping Tom while she showered, and Wolf would definitely keep her safe from that.

The pair of us went to the side of the camp where the medical tent was. A lantern illuminated the inside, but the opening was down. I screwed up my face in being unsure of the procedure here.

"Knock, knock?" I said with all the confidence I could muster while still having it come out as a question.

There was movement, and then the flap was moved to the side to reveal the face of the goblin. "Oh! If it isn't my favorite pair of patients. Come on in."

I shrugged at Quinn's raised eyebrow. We hadn't been here long enough to be a favorite, and it didn't sound sarcastic enough given how often I was prone to getting myself in trouble. I allowed him in first before I followed into the tent.

"Take a seat, both of ya." She tutted and crossed her arms. "What's wrong with you now, Max?"

I sat on the edge of the bed and raised an eyebrow. "Nothing, I think? For a change." Rather sane and undamaged, for the present moment. Just tired.

"Perfect. Then I can give you this." She withdrew a potion bottle from a wooden case on the side table and handed it over. Dark green in color with slow swirls of purple when I moved it.

"Oh, thank you. I thought you mostly dealt in goop?"

She grinned before giving a brief curtsey. "Oh, it's *totally* goop. Barely a potion at all, given how viscous it is. System should give you a heads-up though."

[Grand Arcane Potion: +100% Mana regeneration, +20% magic Damage, +5% magical Crit Chance. 20-second duration. Inflicts Mana exhaustion.]

I whistled. "I'd hate to be in a situation where I'd need this." It was bound to be soon, I was sure. Mana exhaustion meant my power recovery would be all but nothing for an hour after the potion wore off. "I am to understand that we have you to thank for allowing us to stay?"

"Eh." She shrugged and went to the cabinet for something. "Fiona gets stuck doubting her own decisions. She is smart but not really a leader. She just does it because . . . someone had to, you know?" Ruby turned back to us and drew a box over toward Quinn.

It was understandable. She was trying to create a space where people could be safe. One of the towns seemed like a better place, however . . . Perhaps a question for the morning.

The goblin spread some dark goop across Quinn's forehead. "Told you to stay put. Now look at you."

"My humblest apologies," he murmured, looking down at the floor.

"Broken nose too? Trauma Status is like a force multiplier for bad times, you know?" She tutted and moved his head around to observe the damage I had caused.

"That was my own hubris." He winced as she prodded the sore-looking area.

She shook her head and hopped down to dig around for another medicine. "*Always* hubris. Gotta be careful out there."

We looked at each other and gave small shrugs, smiles across our faces. Through all the turmoil, I may have just made another friend.

The tent flap flung open, and the armored figure of Fiona stomped in. She turned to me, her eyes narrowed and burning with some emotion.

"I want to know how you did it."

CHAPTER TWENTY-ONE

Night Showing

I paused and looked at the fighter. Quinn and Ruby had also turned to observe her entrance and pointed question. Wasn't too sure *what* she had actually asked. Surely she didn't mean Ren again? Not with the goblin present?

My mouth opened and closed, but all I could manage was a look of confusion.

Her expression dulled. "You said you killed Velkos? Guy with the chainswords?"

"*Oh*, yes." Relief and understanding flooded through me. She just wanted to discuss the man I had murdered, rather than explain the nuance of how I'd won over Ren. It wasn't troubling at all that I found that the easier option to talk about.

Fiona crossed her arms and waited for me to drip out the details. He'd obviously left his mark on her in more ways than one. I took a deep breath.

"He was in the fort. Dueled him for a bit and poisoned his arm with some witch's potion."

Ruby tilted her head, looking like she had some questions there but didn't want to interrupt.

"The poison caused his arm to be inert, so he had to cut it off. While he was distracted, I put an attack through his back and heart." I left out the part about taking his weapon to bisect one of the other combatants. It sounded a lot worse the further from the act I had grown.

The fighter grunted. "Would have liked him to suffer more, but I believe the story. Although, you dueled him without taking Damage?"

"Ah." I grimaced. "I am rather evasive if given the chance. But . . . could I ask what happened to make him . . ." I gestured to her scars in the politest manner I could muster—which was not at all.

Her eyes narrowed before she softened and seemed tired. "Something stupid, believe me. We Partied briefly but had an argument. Somehow, we agreed that a duel would settle matters." Fiona shuffled uncomfortably. "He took it a lot more seriously than intended."

"Duels are a great way to be humbled," Quinn agreed before turning his head away from her glare.

I took down my top hat to place it beside me. "It's no wonder he joined the Lady. Sounds like he was an asshole."

Fiona looked as though she was going to give a sarcastic response, but instead she sighed and let her arms relax. "Yeah. System is full of them, myself included." She held a hand out to be shaken. "I'm not sure I trust you fully still, but you have my thanks for killing that fuck."

I extended my own, and we shook once more. "I understand your trepidation and will do my best to be an asset to the camp."

"Eh, just don't be a weird ass." She shook her head. "We'll talk more in the morning with everyone present, but I just wanted to give you a heads-up. We've had a message back from Candlekeep up in the northwest."

That was the town Hadrian had said the Lady intended on getting to next.

"It sounds like they've rebuffed the Lady's attempt at a take over there. They said . . ." She screwed her face up. "She had been growing in strength up until the last couple of days, and she's been weaker?" Fiona shrugged. "As accurate as that is."

I nodded slowly. That gave me something to think about.

"Well, I'll be off. Rest well. I'm sure tomorrow will be a long day." She gave Quinn and me a nod before shooting the goblin a brief soft smile, and then she left.

My brow furrowed as we fell into silence. Why would the Lady have gotten weaker? The answer was right in front of me; I was sure of it. Her impossibly quick ascension through the areas and then . . . running out of steam. I raised an eyebrow at Ruby, who had been patiently waiting for me to pay attention so that she could ask me a question.

"You fought the witches?" Her eyes twinkled with interest.

"We did, yes. Did you?"

She shook her head. "Looked fun but dangerous. We heard some other group lost a couple of members in there."

I raised an eyebrow. It would be unfair to say we had found it . . . easy. But it *had* been. Just how far ahead of the curve were we? "It was a coven of three, some decent loot."

"I'm envious. We played things pretty safe." She idly tapped a finger on a glass container. "Not that I'm complaining about being alive, ya know?"

It made me wonder—if Lady in Red had come through when they were leveling in the first area . . . would their group be dead or converted? I shuddered to think that they could have fallen—but then again, they hadn't now, so perhaps they were fine.

I watched as the goblin wiped a different color goop on the fencer's face. "Are you happy here, Ruby?"

She raised an eyebrow, pausing the application of whatever medicine Quinn had earned. "Happy? Hmm. With Fiona? Yeah. With the camp? Eh. With the System? We make do the best we can, ya know?"

"Yeah, I know." I nodded along. Replace Fiona with Ren and that was mostly my thoughts too. "System isn't great, but we're trying to keep it stable."

She grunted and continued to slather the foul-smelling mixture over Quinn's nose and around his bruised eyes. "I had an okay life in the old world. Some that come here are trying to escape from bad situations. S'pose I just . . . help people wherever I go."

It cooled my mood that people were rather nuanced once you spent five minutes not considering killing them. At this rate, I'd find out that Clive was a reasonable chap, and we'd become fast friends. I grimaced at the thought. *Over his dead body*, the normal bastard.

"No head goop for you, Max. The bruising isn't too bad. Just avoid hitting your head on things for a couple of days." She gave me a grin as she cleaned her hands off.

"Ah." I gave her a short bow. "You don't know what impossibilities you ask of me."

"Well, just don't die." She gave Quinn a pat on the leg. "Ain't no goop that can bring you back from the dead. I think. Fuck knows, really." Ruby shrugged. "You're both free to go. Hopefully, a brighter day tomorrow, aye?"

"Hope screams eternal." I smiled and picked up my hat, leading the quiet fencer into the gloom of early evening.

"It's been quite the day, Max," he turned to me and said without hint of anything but earnest exhaustion.

I stepped a little farther away because the goop wasn't pleasant. "I'll say. Lots to do tomorrow as well."

"Then good night to you. I hope the others rest well." He gave me a bow and walked off toward his tent.

I stepped through the darkened maze of other tents to find that Wolf was outside our designated one. Ren must have finished already. The bear gave me a grunt and shuffled to the side to allow me entrance but seemed more interested in getting some sleep than giving me a verbal update.

Lantern was on low as I entered to find the elf already under the covers. We had managed to make the approximation of a double bed with our bedrolls and blankets, which was a nice sight to come home to. "How was it?" I asked quietly.

"Cold as fuck." She pulled a face.

I put my hat down and lay beside her. She did look cold but at least reasonably clean. Her hand came out and pulled my face forward, and I received the kiss earned for surviving the day. It was a long thing, a soft conversation gone unsaid, before she eventually pulled away.

"That's all you get. I'm not sold on the privacy we have here." She pressed a finger against my nose to move me farther back. "Plus, *you* stink. I left enough in the shower for you."

"My savior," I said with a grin. "Oh! That reminds me."

I stood, stooped slightly at the low apex of the tent, and began to disrobe. Ren glared at me with a furrowed brow, which only increased as I got completely bare.

"I'm all for a performance," she said in a loud whisper, "but *what* are you doing?"

"Hmm?" My eyes went around my menus and Equipment screens, trying to find the option. No, it seemed as though it didn't work for me as it did with Wolf. I turned to her and put my hands on my hips. "Well, Ren Moonflower. I'm trying to break the System, as usual."

"*Moonflower.*" Her face screwed up before her expression relaxed. "Well, I don't *hate* that, as far as pet names go, but . . . how about you act normal for once, *Max Dickbag*?"

I snorted and shook my head before grabbing up my clothes. "Maybe the best compliment I've ever had."

She groaned, not intending it the way I had taken it. "Just . . . hurry back, okay? There's only so much night before I will fall asleep."

With that on my mind, it was perhaps the briefest and worst shower I had ever had in my life. With the promise of some heart-to-heart time with Ren, I wanted to rush the process. The fact that the night air had a brisk chill to it and the small amount of shower water was practically ice cold did little to bring me comfort. Certainly woke me up, but the wrong time of day to be alert. My suit kept me warm enough for my return trip through the dozens of tents.

A few were lit by low lanterns. The occasional murmur of conversation coming from a couple. Near the back was a small campfire with two figures sitting, although I couldn't see from here who they were exactly. Back to the tent, I nudged the bear aside to squeeze back in.

Thankfully, she was still awake.

Into my sleepwear and I got under the blankets beside her. "You were right," I said, "the temperature of that water was criminal."

"Right?" She turned over to face away from me and then shuffled back against me to spoon. "Better share body heat so we don't die."

I put my arm around her, receiving a healthy amount of hair in my face. "What does your heart say tonight, moonflower?"

She put her hand on mine and squeezed it. "I'm still on edge, knowing that danger is coming."

"We'll get through it. Fiona mentioned that the Lady might be weakening."

"Really?" Her fingers tapped on mine. "You know why?"

"I have an idea." I moved my mouth up to her pointed ear and whispered. "She gets more power the more followers she has."

Ren was silent for a moment as she considered it. "And we've been killing a lot of them, right?"

I nodded. "Mm-hmm." It was one of the few explanations that made this all make sense. There wasn't any way we could know for certain, but if she was destined to be some kind of cult leader—then believers making her stronger would tie together her speedy ascension through the areas. She had lucked out in having soft minds to convert in the first area, but after we had taken down the fort and started gnawing on the second-area baddies, we had set her back.

"I'd like that to be the case," the elf eventually said. "It makes everything we've done even more worth the pain."

"One day there won't be so much struggle." I leaned in and kissed the back of her head. "Just you and me, Ren, and anyone else that we can drag along for the ride."

Her hand squeezed mine. "Call me moonflower again."

I smiled. "*Moonflower.*"

She sighed and pulled my arm in close against her. I waited for any further conversation, but none came. She had fallen asleep, and I didn't blame her after the day we had endured. While my own eyes were getting ready to drift off, I made the effort to check over my Stats quickly—and regretfully put off the chance boxes until the morning. Such a shame.

[Stats]

[Strength—8]

[Constitution—9]

[Agility—8 (7 + 1)]

[Dexterity—25 (19 + 6)]

[Intelligence—40 (19 + 21)]

[Wisdom—10 (8 + 2)]

[Luck—14]

Given that my <Pick a Card> Damage was reliant on my Intelligence Stat, it seemed to be a good idea to stack my gear toward that. Dexterity had fallen behind a little, but other than my crossbow usage, it shouldn't affect too much. <Sleight of Hand> already pulled enough weight when it came to manipulating my System Inventory and items.

I yawned and partially considered going through the boxes to see if I could replace some of the remaining area-one gear I still wore. Going through my

Inventory, it seemed as though I had accumulated twenty-two of the blasted things. Eighty-three feathers as well, which I'd have to remember to give to Wolf tomorrow.

So, I could lay here and put myself to sleep as information box after information box filtered through my vision . . . or I could just enjoy being here with Ren and fall asleep in her warmth. I went with my heart in the end, making the most of how close we had grown.

In fact, those thoughts punctuated my dreams. Or at least, I thought they did.

I awoke in darkness. The vision of Ren and me out on a date on a pier near the beautiful ocean sinking away from my brain just as soon as the sounds of shouting struck my senses.

Yells and flashing lights in the darkness. Ren awoke in a confused state beside me as we tried to gain our composure and prepare ourselves for whatever was going on. As if on cue, the deep voice of the bear silhouetted against our tent entrance rose over all else.

"We're being attacked," Wolf growled from just outside.

CHAPTER TWENTY-TWO

Darkness Against Us

The confusion had briefly allowed me to panic, right before the colder side of me closed the hatches and nailed them shut. Questions still remained, but I calmed. Was this a ruse by the camp, and they were planning on finishing us off in the night? Had the remnants of the marketeers come back for vengeance? Somehow it felt more likely that the answer was the simplest one.

Crimson Shadow.

We had both burst from the covers and switched to our Equipment, weapons drawn. I took the lead and pushed out of the tent first, emerging beside the growling bear. It was dark out still, aside from the blooming lights of Skills and roving lanterns that had been turned up.

My eyes struggled to adjust, and I pressed a hand against the bear as Ren came out beside me. "Report."

"Smells like death," he growled. "Rotten death."

I turned a glance toward the elf. "Zombies."

There was fighting and yelling coming from the entrance to the camp. One of the voices was definitely Fiona. From our right, a figure stumbled toward us— the bright yellow giving away that it was Quinn and not a walking corpse.

"From one nightmare to another," he said with a grimace. He looked pale and rather panicked. His trauma icon was gone now, which meant it was early morning and he had recovered. "There's fighting at the gates. Shall we assist?"

My brow furrowed. The question was him deferring to my leadership rather than supposing that the alternative was that we didn't help. I turned to Ren, as she seemed hesitant.

There was a brief glow around her head, a faint radiant gold we could only pick up due to being in near darkness. She looked up at me and shook her head. "There's more . . . I can sense them. Through the woods to the west."

I had no reason not to believe her entirely. Part of her Class was holy adjacent, and while she hadn't mentioned anti-undead Abilities, it made sense if something was making the connection. They intended to flank the camp after everyone had been drawn to the entrance. Surround us.

"We'll hold this west side. There's a small clearing before the trees." We were already reasonably close to that part of the camp, which made me wonder if the attack was intending to catch us. Despite the looming trouble and unknowns out in the darkness, I still felt remarkably calm.

We demolished a couple of empty tents to give us more room. Ren to my left, Quinn to my right, with Wolf just in front of us.

Our attacks ready, we stood tense, eyes trying to adjust to the darkened woods. And then—movement.

"I can see them. Zombies, at least a dozen," Ren said as she calmed her breathing.

Small orbs of dim yellow started to appear among the shadowed shapes. Their glowing eyes were now visible as they drew closer. I put my hand on the back of Wolf.

"Stay with us, friend. They might want to try to draw you into the woods. Here, together, we have safety." His response was nothing but a grunt.

The elf turned her glance to me briefly. "You ready for the show, Max?"

I licked my lips and gave her a quick nod. But despite being prepared as best as I could be, the next part of the act was beyond anything I could have imagined.

"Only fools hide in darkness," Quinn murmured. "Let us see the strength of their convictions." He held out his hand, and a spark of amber shot forth. As soon as it reached the tree line, it bloomed into a bright light, persisting over the area and illuminating the woods.

For a brief moment, it felt like show lights, giving me false warmth. Our stage was bright and unavoidable. The crowd was a little more lifeless than usual and unlikely to be dazzled, but we worked with what we had.

Quinn gave me a pat on the shoulder. "We're right behind you." I could feel the glow of energy as he buffed me. An increase in Mana capacity and regeneration. Elation filled me.

Wolf took a deep breath in and then roared. Louder than I'd ever heard him vocalize, I was surprised that I didn't receive any negative effect from the volume. I saw icons pop up over the approaching zombies as they stood and wavered. Dazed, it said.

Beside me, Ren cleared her throat. "Corpses and cadavers! Introducing, in a special late-night showing, the one and only Max the Great!" She flourished her hand toward me, her recently acquired Damage buff flooding through me. As her eyes met mine, I could see that her face was flush.

It was almost too much for me. I raised my hands up as a purple card split, so it appeared as though I held one in each hand. Shame to waste such an introduction on mindless undead, but any crowd was worth the practice. No tricks tonight, only survival.

I flung both cards out and zipped them through the trees. On my attack, Ren pegged one with an entangling arrow, holding them all in place. Quinn had drawn a crossbow, which he fired before winding a crank to reload it. I kept my cards powered and danced them like a conductor, weaving throughout the walking corpses.

"Keep an eye on backstage," I instructed Quinn. Although his manner of flair was different from mine, he had settled into a role rather easily.

An Imp+ would be a poor choice, as we didn't want to set fire to the forest. Hellhound+ might be okay, but without knowing how zombies functioned in this world, I didn't want to risk one. Roger wouldn't work in a reanimated corpse, even if it died again. The System was keen to tell me this even as I continued my assault.

No matter. Most things died from enough brain injury whether the trope was true here or not. My cards spun in figures of eight, slashing through necks and into temples. Occasionally I'd only hit a shoulder or chest, but with Ren getting head shots, we made quick work of the attempted flank.

"Ten down, six to eight remain," she confirmed.

Quinn went up on tiptoes to try to see farther. "Front gate looks managed. There may have been more that way."

"Any sign of a ringleader?" I asked, smashing through the skulls of two more of the undead.

Wolf wasn't too anxious to get into the fray now that he had seen them. The rotten flesh and loosely put-together bodies didn't seem quite up to his standard— not that I'd allow it either. The last thing we needed was the bear becoming infected with something or turning into a zombie himself. A softer expectation that he might just throw up the undead parts was equally appalling.

"Nothing I can see," he replied. He turned to face the east side of the camp. "Forgive my eye. Perhaps Ren can see better . . . but eastward."

The elf planted another arrow into the skull of a zombie before turning to allow me to conclude this section of the performance. I could see her glaring that way out of the corner of my eye. "Fuck, I think there's more."

Into my hand, a large glass bottle of water. "Radiant." I handed it to her, and she whispered a word in Elfin, causing a golden glow to filter over it. We were bending the rules a little here, but the System was sloppy about such things. Back in my hand, I turned to her, my purple card cutting down the last zombie on our side. "Call it."

Her blue eyes narrowed up into the air. ". . . Now."

Then I was gone, switched places with the hell bird Ren had been watching. Away from the light and into the darkness. Away from the soft ground and into the cold air that whipped through my suit. Away from my stage and over the fresh audience. I threw the bottle down as a group of yellow eyes looked back up at me. Then, just as I had left, I returned to the safety of my Party.

Quinn whistled as he observed my act. Dazzle icons, which seemed more of a pleasant formality than anything useful at present.

"Can you move the light?" I asked, fingers flexing and ready to bring out more cards.

With a quick nod, he gestured to the orb of amber illumination and moved it down as if it was on a string to follow over us. We then stalked across the campground, among the tents toward the other side where they had tried to pin us in. A large amount of zombies. I wondered if the attacks were usually this aggressive.

"We should warn the others," Ren mentioned, her eyes going up to where figures were fighting more undead.

"Allow me. I can cast my voice." Quinn cupped at his mouth. *"More undead, east of camp, Max and Co. engaging."*

Even from here, I could see the slightly confused looks on a couple of the figures as they tried to seek the source of the voice. It looked like Ruby was at the back, and she waved an acknowledgment at us.

Our orb of light illuminated a group of melted zombies that our loose approximation of holy water had hit. There were still a handful or two, but between us we made short work of the shambling corpses. The last one dropped in no time at all, and an odd silence then fell over the camp. The crackle of a fire near the north entrance, and the wail of someone in pain. We watched the south of camp . . . but nothing came.

Quietly confident that the attack was over, we took a deep breath and relented to going up to the gate to check on the rest.

"Very impressive," I noted to Ren.

"Hmm? Oh." She pulled a face and looked away. "Not sure where that came from, really. But you thought it was okay?"

"How do you feel about constructive criticism?" I smiled.

She turned back to me with a slight scowl. "How do you feel about a knife between your ribs in your sleep?" Her expression softened. "Go on then."

"I did like Max the Great, but alliteration can work wonders. But that is to say—I'm not tied to any stage name at present."

"So like . . . Max the Misguided, or Mild Max?"

"Point taken."

Any barbs we were playfully clashing soon melted away at the sight of the northern gate.

In one chair, Clive sat, head lolled to the side. Three arrows with purple-feathered ends protruded from his chest. Likewise, on the ground, the elfin man lay, blood pooled from his head.

Fiona was sweaty and stressed, her weapon caked with gore. Magnus was the same way, resting up against some of the crates, while Ruby rubbed healing goop on his wounds.

"I'm too . . . I can't even be angry," the fighter said, still out of breath. "As much as it is like me to lash out, I know that without you here, we would have been overrun. You fought groups in the east *and* west?"

I nodded.

"It's usually just a medium group at the front." She closed her eyes and sighed. "No Rangers to pick off the watch. No flanking tactics. This was meant to wipe us out."

I crouched down by the elfin man. "Arrow too?"

Ruby stepped in. "No, some kind of magic. He wasn't . . . dead when we got here. But there was nothing I could do." For the first time since meeting her, the goblin looked sad and withdrawn.

Not entirely knowing why, I placed my hand on the back of the body's head. Something . . . Something felt odd. A chill ran through me, and my brow furrowed. "Did you know Rolo was a demon?"

Fiona shook her head. "He kept covered up. We knew he was different, but not . . . a demon."

"Do you know of any other demons?" My hand was shaking. The magic used had a familiarity to it. I should know, of all people. It had left a residue around the impact site that I could almost feel tangibly, and I hated it. *So much.* "Ren, come here." The words came out more of an abrupt command than I was intending.

She knelt down beside me and looked me in the eyes. Hers were concerned, and I could see the glimmer of purple reflected at the back of her blues. Not much needed to be said after that, but she turned to the corpse and put her hand on his head. Brow furrowed. She nodded her head slowly as she looked back at me.

"You want to tell me what the fuck you're doing?" Fiona grunted. "Getting doe-eyed over the corpse of my friend is not a good look."

I stood and lent a hand to help Ren up. The cold sank away as I moved farther from the body. "He was killed by demonic magic."

The fighter's eye twitched, and it looked as though she might have a sarcastic comeback for that, but instead, she just nodded.

"Any of you injured?" Ruby asked, a bottle in her hand already.

We gave her the negative. Wolf huffed. "Didn't even get to do anything." His eyes were affixed to the lion man once more, and strangely enough, so was Quinn's.

"It was probably the best introduction I've ever had." I placed my hand on his back. "All of you did well."

"It was a pleasure to serve." Quinn turned and gave me a brief bow.

Either it was my tired mind trying to catch up to reality, or it was rather suspicious that Quinn's Abilities seemed to fit into the group. At least, his utility Skills were very useful. Then again, without seeing him in actual combat, we couldn't truly know how he'd jell with us. He might even be more of a support Class than his title alluded to.

I furrowed my brow, taking a break from stroking our own egos, realizing there was an elephant in the room. "Where's the other group?"

Fiona shook her head. "Fuck if I know. We saw them head down for the night. We'll check tents before we . . . I don't know. *Fuck's sake.*"

With a scowl, I looked out to the campground. I had seen people sitting at the back after my shower. Where did they go? And why?

It made me irrationally angry, something unlike me. We had found a small enclave of relatively normal Players who had avoided the corruption of the Crimson Shadow. Sure, they were ineffective, but they were troubled individuals with faults. Now they had been attacked, with one group leaving earlier in the day and the second after nightfall. It didn't add up, and it made me sick to try to work my head around.

I turned back around to see everyone had been looking at me. For what? Had I sprouted horns or been laughing maniacally?

No.

Magnus was wounded, and Ruby was melancholy. Fiona was exhausted and overwhelmed. Her eyes still held some ire for me, but now there was something else even stronger I could read in between the lines.

She was desperate for my help.

CHAPTER TWENTY-THREE

Headliner

I sat and stared out into the darkness, unsure as to why people seemed to turn to me for guidance. Especially after calling me a clown or jester. Running a show wasn't really leadership experience—I was but a spectacle propped up by those around me. The part of me that killed demons on the regular was just as solitary, so my position now was just . . . bizarre. Confusing.

In seeing the look in Fiona's eyes, I had offered to take watch. Partly for that reason, at least. She was exhausted and grieving. Rest could help with some of that. The other part of my offer was just in case the demon showed their face again and I could ram my fist down their throat and pull their organs up like many handkerchiefs tied together. See how long that trick worked for.

Wolf and Ren were nearby. They hadn't left my line of sight, which was comforting. The bear had curled up just below the camp entrance, and the elf was sleeping against him, a blanket covering her. Out of sight of any potential arrows, or worse. Quinn was taking watch with me, sitting on a chair opposite, across the opening to the camp proper. The remaining other group had moved their sleeping arrangements closer. No point being spread out when we could be assailed from any side.

"I see that look, Max." Quinn turned his eye to me, speaking quietly. "You feel undeserving."

"Am I that easy to read?"

He gave me a brief smile and nodded, gesturing toward the sleeping pair not so far from us. "I see now the bond you all have. It's humbling. They would not trust you if you were not deserving."

I nodded, but I wasn't sure I believed it entirely. Ren and Wolf, sure. Love and companionship formed over struggles and conflict. Quinn and Fiona? Earlier today, I was a murderous weirdo that could be challenged to fruitless duels. Now I was worthy to lead?

The colder part of me had an inkling. It wasn't about my decision-making or the way I held myself. I had strength. I did what needed to be done. I survived it. Faced with dozens of walking corpses, we had made it a show—probably something beyond the pale to the group ambushed and just trying to survive the night. My Abilities had taken me flying through the air and back. We weren't just struggling to survive the System; we were making it our own.

"What do you think of this . . . situation?" I asked him, more to keep myself awake than anything.

"Can't see the camp being tenable any longer." He rubbed at his eye patch. "As for the absent groups, I do not have any good words for them."

I had tried not to think too hard about it. The most generous reasoning I could come up with was that they had a forewarning about what was about to happen and left to save their own skins. But then, why not warn Fiona's group? *No.* I felt the anger rising up again. I'd save my seething for tomorrow.

"In my old world," Quinn said softly as he looked out into the darkness, "there's a saying. Faux bravado may be an empty box, but enough can build a sturdy wall over time."

"I have something similar." I smiled despite the circumstances. "Most of my adult life is built on empty boxes."

He shook his head. "Yet you do not see that you have filled them. With competence. With love. With power."

It was nice talking to Quinn. As much as he seemed like something from a more antiquated world than my own—and has his own share of overt bravado— there was a soft sadness to him. His simple machismo hid something more poetic and emotionally intelligent, which I respected. It was still a distance before he was trusted on the same level as the other two, but I didn't consider him a threat.

"Max?" He shuffled awkwardly. "Do you think that Magnus likes men?"

My brow furrowed. "What, to eat?"

A wide grin crossed his face, and he relaxed in his chair. With a deep sigh, he looked up at the stars overhead. "One day, I hope to find happiness in this world. Peace and happiness."

I turned my tired eyes out to the darkness. The slight hue of brown promised a potential sunrise over on the horizon. What would it take for me to be able to get to that point? Remove Lady in Red? What if there was worse than her in this world? If there was no escape, what would I have to do to make this System habitable?

These thoughts ticked away in my head, counting up my exhaustion until the darkness took me.

"Max?"

My eyes shot open, the light of day far too harsh.

"You're okay. Quinn woke me and Wolf, and I have been on watch." Ren's hand came over to cover my eyes as her radiant hair drooped across my face. "Calm your eyes, trickster. But there's something you need to see."

I considered that she wasn't offering anything pleasant, but I nodded, and she released her grasp. Somehow the act helped with the tiredness that the sunlight threatened to burn into my skull. I looked up at her, and she gestured out of the camp.

With aching legs, I stood as Wolf grunted his good mornings. Up the road, away from the camp, the large stone had been toppled to block the road. Burned into the stone was a word or . . . no, a phrase.

"Can you read it?" Ren asked.

I nodded slowly. It was in Demonic. Could I always read Demonic? Probably. My brain felt like wet compost. "Loosely it means "brother killer," but more . . . There's a stronger bond there."

"A twin?" Wolf asked, looking up at me.

"That would fit." I pulled a face. "Rolo's twin then?"

Ren crossed her arms. "It's not a threat or proper message then, just giving us a label?"

"It means they weren't happy their deceit was found out." I shrugged. "Until we know why the other groups left, I'm not certain how much I want to commit to saying or believing."

She gave my shoulder a squeeze. "I'll go get some coffee on."

I turned my gaze to watch her move back into the camp slightly and set up her grill. Still constantly scowling at nothing in particular. If it wasn't for the aches in my muscles, I'd easily believe the fight during the night was a dream, and she hadn't actually given me a big introduction to the walking dead.

My eyes closed again so that I could try reliving it. Any other circumstance and I would perhaps be enamored beyond belief. I still was, I had to remind myself, as I stole a gaze at the grumpy elf. Quinn's utility really set the stage, and I would have to pick her brains on what she thought about that. Right after the looming meeting.

I turned back to the message inscribed on the rock. There was a demon out there, allied with the Shadow. I'd need to put them in the dirt so they could be closer to their twin. Even now, part of me wanted to ride into the jaws of death. Seek out the demon and necromancer and erase them both as a matter of urgency. The part of me now pretending to be a leader put a wet blanket over that idea. As powerful as we were, we still had to play by *some* of the System's rules.

Quinn had filled me in on a few details that we were too busy being drenched in conflict to soak in. This area was for Players to get up to level fifteen, then the next was to eighteen, fourth to twenty, and then the last area was solely for max-level

Players. We had been ahead of the curve in terms of power but low when it came to the numbers required of us. There was an element to it that felt . . . arbitrary.

At least, until I was humbled by a higher-level Player, I'd think that way. Then again, I'd probably be *dead*—which was the reason why we'd go leveling instead of straight for the Crimson Shadow. A nice circular thought I tied up, good as done. Now it would be time to address something not so easily sealed away.

I turned back to Ren as she brought a mug of coffee over but looked past her as the trio of the other Party had emerged and were working their way to us. Quinn was still asleep, and I didn't blame him considering he was sleeping off the trauma, even if the Status icon had gone.

The elf turned to the others after passing me the warm cup. "You three want coffee too?"

Fiona and Magnus nodded, but Ruby shook her head. "Makes me a little too wild," she said but looked sad to be left out.

"How'd you sleep?" I asked them as they joined us up near the camp entrance.

"Like shit." Fiona shrugged. Her eyes definitely told the same story. "But thank you for taking watch so we could get some, at least."

I nodded. "I wish I could have done more."

The fighter paused for a moment before bringing out a chair from her Inventory to sit with us. Ruby followed suit, while Magnus leaned against the nearby crates and scowled out up the road.

"What's done is done," she eventually said, the energy having sunk from her usual fiery attitude. "This changes things, but I think it's time enough for that meeting."

I withdrew an apple into my hand and threw it over at Quinn. His hand grabbed it from the air before his eye opened, surprised and bleary, confused to be meeting the bright light of the morning. My eyebrow raised at this act, but nobody else seemed to be paying attention. Curious.

Ren finished up the coffee making, passing one to Quinn as he stretched out and nodded his greetings to those gathered, his eye lingering on the lion man a little longer than the rest. With the formality of sharing the life-giving yet scalding liquid out of the way, we all settled into a loose circle and awaited Fiona to begin. Wolf continued to look out onto the road, either not excited at the prospect of a long conversation or not keen to tire his eyes out by staring at Magnus.

"First off . . ." Fiona sighed, deflating in her chair. "An earnest apology to all of you. I realize that I have been a huge asshole."

I nodded slowly but waited for her to continue.

"My time here has been . . . I came to this world avoiding conflict." Her tired eyes dropped to the floor. "I was a soldier. My unit was overrun, and I was trying to escape pursuit when I found the portal. There was . . . I was never built to be a *leader*." Fiona looked up at Ruby before looking past the goblin to the arranged tents.

With another sigh, she turned back to us. "I tried to build a place of safety and do what I thought was best. But I kind of fucked it and, if anything, just made things worse. You three looked like a threat to our status quo, so I tried to push you away. Maybe if I had been more accepting . . . things would be different."

I exchanged a look with Ren, and I could tell her thoughts mirrored my own. With a glum smile, I nodded again to the fighter. "We understand. This world is not easy, and you did what you thought was best for those you cared about. We hold no ill will against you for that."

Fiona looked again at the goblin, then back to me. "You're pretty reasonable for murderous oddballs."

"It's kill or be killed," Ren said. "I'm surprised the Crimson Shadow haven't tried harder to get rid of you."

"They either recruited or killed every other Player in the first area," I explained. "And . . . really fast."

Fiona nodded. "Other than the group pressuring us here, there might be more farther north . . . Honestly, knowing that Rolo was betraying us, it puts a lot of our information into question."

We'd have to play it by ear. The assumption would be most remaining Shadow would be en route to Candlekeep where the Lady was heading, but we couldn't be lax with our defenses. "The two groups who are usually here . . . might be a problem."

Ruby screwed up her face. "They can't have turned against us, surely? We had no bad blood, even if we did get on one another's nerves sometimes."

Fiona shrugged. "I am beyond assuming their intent. If it was betrayal . . . then they're as good as dead, right?" There was no threatening tone to her question as her eyes went between Ren and me.

We nodded, and the elf answered. "Yeah."

"Rest assured," I added, "we will avenge your fallen, whether it was the act of the ones under your care or the Crimson Shadow."

"Wish it could be by my own hands." She gave me a wry smile, but the exhaustion still hung heavy in her eyes. "Instead, we've decided to . . . yield."

I raised an eyebrow. "How so?"

"We're going back to the first area," Ruby explained. "Just to breathe easy for a change, get our bearings before we return."

Fiona nodded. "Would be nice to see what supposed good you have done over that way too. If it's really as you say, then I'll owe you an even deeper apology."

"Water under the bridge." I held my hand up. "All that I want is for you all to be safe." Rather diplomatic of me for a change, but as much as the fighter hadn't been a fan of me up until now, there was no point holding grudges over potential allies for the future.

Other than being grouches, they hadn't done anything *terrible* toward us.

She just sighed in response. "I had hoped people would be more trustworthy. When it turns out the ones I most expected to be dangerous were the only ones we could depend on. Without you here, we'd probably be dead."

Ren shuffled in her chair. "Are the attacks usually that dire?"

"No. The attacks have been increasing in severity since the Crimson Shadow rolled through."

I tilted my head. "The necromancer has been a problem since before?"

"A nuisance at first," Ruby said with a nod. "Like he was just toying with us. Either the Shadow have made him give more of a shit or have given him a big-ass power boost."

Zombies weren't a great threat unless you were distracted or they had support. If they hadn't assassinated the two on watch, then it would have been easy enough, even with the other campers abandoning the place.

My eyes went over to where I had seen a pair of figures by the fire the night before. I was no detective, but it would be an idea to give it a once-over before we moved on. No doubt we would come across at least one of the two groups in our travels, and some manner of conflict would need to be resolved.

Almost exhausting to think about. I raised the hot coffee up and took a sip. Slightly burning my lips, but I needed to feel the pain to sharpen me. Ren might have the ability to perceive the occasional ambush, but I had been growing a lump in my stomach for this second area since arriving.

And I knew the worst was yet to come.

CHAPTER TWENTY-FOUR

Bowing Out

Fiona planned to abandon the camp after scouring it for anything of use. The group that had gone west during the day had taken everything with them— not entirely odd given we had an intangible Inventory to hold everything in anyway. The ones who had left in the night . . . had left remnants of their existence.

Which *was* odd.

Ren stood nearby, her hands on her hips as she scowled at the spent campfire. "They were here, sitting on these two chairs?"

I nodded and looked back in the direction of the sectioned-off area where the shower was. Even in the darkness, they would have been able to see me come and go. They waited until I was back in the tent perhaps, but there still would have been someone at the front entrance on watch. Why Fiona expected most assaults to come straight down the road rather than flank through the woods as the zombies had done was neither here nor there. No point beating up someone already broken.

"Anything you can track, Wolf?" I looked back at the bear, and he started to sniff around the chairs.

"There *are* some tracks." Ren blinked at the ground where grass had been scoured away. "West. At least . . . to start with."

"That's where we're headed too?" I raised an eyebrow at Quinn, and he just nodded in response. If they had joined the Crimson Shadow, then I would have expected them to have gone north to join the others or head toward Candlekeep to assist the weakened Lady.

I grunted and withdrew some paper and a pencil from my Inventory. "Quinn, could you go prod Fiona or Magnus about any details on the two groups? Classes or Abilities. We'll head out soon. I just want to gather what information we can."

"Of course, Max." He gave a brief bow and took the things before walking away.

"Can never have one normal day, can we, trickster?"

I gave the elf a slight smile. "It's hard to imagine there is such a thing, given the company we keep."

In an odd display of something other than disdain for the waking day, she instead just pouted, still with hands on hips. No quip or further thought was offered.

With a sniff of his large nose, Wolf shook himself out and looked up at us. "Two stronger scents, male. There are a handful of other weaker smells that I cannot place."

"Handful," I repeated. It was possible that, other than the group of five, people could have walked this way just as we had. "And they head west, like Ren says?"

He returned his snout to the ground and started to move, trying to draw out any scent over what I imagined was a campground full of undeath and desperation. He wasn't wearing his hat or waistcoat today, and I'd prod him on why once business was over. Or perhaps I'd just accept his choice—like a good leader.

"I feel bad for Fiona," Ren eventually said, relaxing her arms. "I considered asking them to travel with us. System might limit parties to five, but we can move about as more than that, right?"

I nodded. We may still be reeling from the inclusion of Quinn to our stage show, but it seemed coldhearted to leave others to the wolves just because we had a theme we had attached our mental safety to.

"But . . ." she continued. "You could see it in their eyes too, I bet."

The wind hadn't just been knocked from their sails; the whole mast had been torn off and thrown into the endless sea. "They don't have the heart to fight."

She nodded, and anything else didn't need to be said. Better they be safe and have time to grieve than to be dragged along in our wake. Being drawn to conflict was one thing, but we were steeped in it. Taking on all odds because we believed we were better than them. That we could survive them because of Wolf's indomitable constitution, Ren's unerring aim, and my complete inability to let the System tell me what was possible.

Oh, and Quinn could blow things up.

"You want to see them off to the bridge though?" She looked back at me, and there was some amount of sadness in her eyes. Not something I'd seen often, and even if my initial answer would have been no, I melted under that gaze.

"I'd feel a lot better if we did." I smiled. The first area would do well to have a few higher-level Players about in case something untoward was going on.

She smiled, if only briefly. "We're becoming soft, trickster."

The way my stomach did a small flip at being referred to as a we signaled there may be some truth to the statement, yet I did not want to admit it. "Your perception of time may be awry, Ren." I gestured for us to walk after the bear. "Was it not yesterday we killed hundreds of Monsters and I murdered a demon?"

"That's barely anything, in the grand scheme of things." She shrugged and followed along. "If you're not killing whole Parties and swearing violently while your eyes blaze purple, then it's all rather . . . pedestrian."

The glint in her bright-blue eyes told me she rather liked the dangerous side of me. I did too, I supposed. Ordinary magician Max wouldn't have made it this far, of that I was certain. Demon-hunter Max had the skills to keep us afloat, despite his rough edges. I just had to temper the two sides of me so that I remained affable and intact.

"Pedestrian is nice sometimes," I eventually said as we reached the bear. "Gives us time to work on our . . . entrance."

She avoided my look, so I turned to Wolf instead. "Thoughts?"

"I feel like shouting at the enemy isn't the best way to reveal ourselves." He looked up at me with his amber eyes. "Plus, for that one, I have to be stationary. Which is boring."

I nodded slowly. "And the tracks?"

"They head into the woods and then are harder to track. Either because of the zombies or they used something to hide better." He shrugged his large shoulders and then sat down on the dirt.

The rejuvenating energy the coffee had provided was starting to wane already. While I rubbed at my temples, I freed my mind to wander. The undead were most likely System-created that could be summoned and controlled. Although I had glossed over their details during the attack due to the tired surprise of their arrival, they had all looked rather generic.

As if they were all made from the same three to four Villager presets from one of the towns. All human, plain clothing, and no remarkably outstanding visuals that would give away that they had been Players. Something of a relief. The world was terrible enough without worrying about the corpses of those fallen coming back for a second time to try to bury me.

"No sense chasing ghosts," I said eventually, giving them a shrug.

"Pretty sure they were zombies, trickster." Ren turned away from me, perhaps to hide an expression of amusement, but I followed her gaze to see Quinn approaching us.

"Got the list for you, Max." He smiled and handed it over. "Magnus was very helpful."

"Fantastic. We found that the second group left this way last night, but the trail goes cold." I took the list from him and had a cursory glance before placing it in my Inventory. Enough to recognize the groups if we saw them, but I'd study their known Abilities later.

"We're actually going to go back and escort them to the bridge," Ren added. "Make sure they get there safely."

He nodded. "Very kind of you both. I believe they are about ready. They wanted to speak with us anyway before we parted."

We left the edge of the campground and followed him without much to say. Plenty was going on within our heads. I gave Wolf a pat on the side as we went through the tents. He was a little grumpy about not being able to chew through the enemies last night, I could tell. There would be plenty of enemies ahead, even if we took a step back and focused on leveling on Monsters.

As we circled around the last of the tents, we came across the trio of survivors. They still looked weary, with exhaustion and guilt on their faces.

"Anything?" Fiona asked.

I shook my head. "They left toward the west, but there's no solid trail outside of the camp."

She nodded slowly. "Was hoping for . . . I don't know, honestly." With a sigh, she put a hand on the goblin's shoulder. "We'd like to stay in contact, if that's okay? We're no good to you at present, but the future might be brighter, even if bloody."

"Of course." I smiled.

Her brow furrowed as her eyes unfocused, looking at her STAR menus. "It's not letting me add either of you as a contact?"

I exchanged a glance with the elf. For once, she seemed just as confused as I was. "There are contacts . . . and a way to message in the System?"

Fiona looked away from her screens and narrowed her eyes at me. "Yeah . . . Pretty early on there's a questline that . . . You didn't really do Quests, did you?"

Ren tilted her hat down slightly. "Guilty."

Ah. So there *was* a way for us to stay in contact. We had just blazed past it in trying to level and address the Crimson Shadow problems. Somewhat awkward, and it made me wonder if there was anything else important we might have avoided in our ascension.

Quinn cleared his throat. "There might be a way I can help you there. If you give me your details, I can then pass them on when the others have it unlocked?"

The fighter shrugged. "Reasonable. I hadn't assumed you to be the responsible one of the group, but perhaps you can steer them straight."

He didn't appear to want to bear that burden but gave us a sheepish grin as he exchanged details with her.

"We're going to escort you to the bridge," Ren said to change the subject away from our incompetencies. "If that's okay?"

Ruby nodded while Fiona was busy in menus. "Of course. That would be nice actually. Ah . . . We haven't buried the other two yet." Her face contorted into a grimace, something unlike her.

"Quinn and I are journeyman grave keepers. We'll help you there." I winced, not intending for that to sound so casual and humorous.

Wolf grunted. "I will assist."

I noted he wasn't currently staring at Magnus for a change, although Quinn had taken up that mantle. Despite it still being so early in the day, I felt spent already. A new morning and more enemies and hardship. Still, places we could improve and a clear plan for us to go ahead.

Part of me was itchy to get into combat again. Sometimes that made things easier—you often knew where you stood in a fight and didn't have the time to be morose over the fallen and state of the world. Or how we'd missed out on a key point of the System. We'd have to pull Quinn aside and see if there was anything else we had avoided along the way.

Fiona nodded. "We'll do it together. They were our Party and friends, but I will not turn away any assistance in putting them to rest."

I wanted to believe that death took us somewhere nice after. Back to our own worlds, maybe. That opened up questions on what the System was, some things that I had been putting away in the back of my mind so that I didn't go mad thinking over it. My own suspension of belief was often hard at work to allow me to function here.

"We're leaving the camp as it is," Fiona continued. "Take anything left that you want, but I doubt there's much useful."

"I have a few potions you can have," Ruby offered.

I held up my hand. Letting me loose around the camp to loot all the oddities I could use in my tricks was prize enough. "I don't want to deny you anything you may need. We'll be fine."

"It's okay, Max." The goblin withdrew a pouch stuffed with six glass vials. "I can replace this stuff no problem once we're settled back in the town."

I smiled and took them, giving the small goblin a low bow. "I thank you then." As I rose, a sheepish grin took my face. "Which makes me feel terrible, as all I had to offer you three was a request."

"Oh?" Fiona raised an eyebrow. "What would you ask of us?"

"Once you're all settled, if you could make sure the area is going well for new Players? Get the bridge cleared properly. There's an outpost that needs rebuilding if the System hasn't done it . . . I know it's a lot to ask."

Her expression relaxed. "We'll do what we can and keep you updated. You've got a good soul under all that gaudy asshole stuff, huh?" Her eyes briefly went over to Ren before returning to me. "Some things make more sense now."

"I'd prefer that violence wasn't the answer," I lied, "but the Shadow keep asking the wrong questions where I have no choice." Well, not a total lie. A life without hardship would be preferable, but until that was possible, I'd do what it took to survive.

Ruby rubbed her pointed chin. "If you could get in contact with someone from the third area, they might be able to come help you with the Lady? We don't know of anyone, unfortunately."

I nodded. That would be preferable—there must be a decent number of max-level Players in the world. Having them roll through and crush the Lady's uprising would be a lot less stressful for our little group. Although . . . something about that had a weird taste to it. Not that we wouldn't get the glory, but the third area was an unknown. How populated was the System? I felt whatever answers I'd eventually get would be uncomfortable and dire.

Perhaps I shouldn't let the mood control the unknowns.

With little else to share, we agreed to go off and do the needful to put their fallen to rest. Having shuffled them around the outside of the camp toward the place Rolo was buried wasn't the most secure given we were dealing with a necromancer, but in the stress and grief of the aftermath, it was all they could manage.

I turned back to look at the camp as we reached the gates. Seemed odd with it being so empty now. A place abandoned under the constant pressure of those ruined by the System.

Quinn put his hand on my shoulder as the others passed ahead. "In time, new life will bloom here. I believe it."

I wasn't so sure, but I gave him a brief nod, and we caught the others up.

Ren had turned, giving me a scowl. Something wasn't right.

I approached to see the trio tense. Confused. On the ground, the corpse of the elfin man they had left. But he was the only one.

Clive's body was missing.

CHAPTER TWENTY-FIVE

So Soon?

Between us, we put the present body to rest. Thankfully, this one did not try to talk to me or lull me into sharing the shallow grave with it. What was meant to be a solemn moment for their group had been tainted by the unknown. Where and how had Clive's corpse gone from where it was left?

We hadn't seen anything during our watch. The bodies were out of our line of sight anyway, but we had decent visuals on part of the road. I just didn't see the reasoning *why*. Stolen for the necromancer? Maybe he had a skill that worked after death. There were parts of our fights in the first area that painted it to be something grim in my mind.

While the trio paid their respects, I brought up the list that Quinn had gotten and read it from the System.

[Party One—went west in the daytime]
[Dwarf male, gray hair, beard]
[Male, black leathers, twin blades]
[Female, red skin, magic user—fire??]
[Ranger, black hair]
[Healer, plant based]

[Party Two—vanished in the night]
[Female Paladin, silver armor]
[Male spellcaster, red hair, robes, defensive magic]
[Male Thief, ranged weapons?]
[Female spellcaster, purple skin, black hair]
[??? not sure, maybe another caster]

I worked my jaw, briefly intrigued at how the System also translated our written words, not just spoken. A soft jab from Ren took me from my musings.

"Any thoughts?"

As much as I would have liked to have a concise point to share, I shook my head. "We'll get them to the bridge and then have a meeting." A small pang of panic rose up through me before I realized she was holding my hand. Nothing as intimate as our fingers intertwining, but she was clasped on like a radiant anchor.

We had seen enough death—and caused plenty ourselves—but burying those we were allied with always brought back the . . . humanity in us, for lack of a better word.

With one last sigh, Fiona turned to us. "Let's head out. The day is long, but we shouldn't stagnate."

I nodded, and as one, we started to make our way to the road. Ren relinquished her grip on my hand but gave me a neutral glance before moving up to walk beside the fighter. A soft enough expression compared to the default. It settled some of my thoughts. Time to focus.

Time to *open those boxes.*

By now, I had become somewhat proficient at seeing what would be useful for me based on the suffix or prefix the System gave items. As such, it was easy to knock away the notifications for things I didn't care for and focus only on the things I would use.

[Arcane Necklace: +3 INT, +5% magic Damage]
[Leggings of the Trickster: +2 DEX, +3 INT]
[Spear of Greater Luck: +3 Luck]
[Crossbow+: +2 DEX, empty socket]
[Plain Ring+: empty socket]

It seemed the upgraded Equipment meant that the item had sockets. The spear was a straight-up upgrade to my previous one, and the crossbow would be handy for when a shot really counted. If I could get a gemstone to put in there that had Luck or Dexterity, then that'd be really nice. I didn't equip the plain ring+, but in seeing it was inlaid with a bright-blue spiral of something, I had to keep it aside for . . . reasons.

The rest of the items weren't useful for me—some I would put toward the rest of the Party at some point when it would be less rude to talk shop. I caught Quinn looking at me as I closed down my Inventory.

"There is something more to your skill set, isn't there?" His eyebrow was raised, but there was no judgment on his expression.

I nodded. Perhaps he had seen the purple eyes or clocked our demon talk when we had found the dead watch. "I can summon demons. You would have seen the bird last night."

"Demons?" He tilted his head and looked up ahead at the rest along the road. "That is certainly an odd . . . theme."

"It's a long story." Well, not that long. "There was a second Max that came through the portal at the same time. We are the merged result."

"Ah." He didn't seem convinced.

"The other me was a demon hunter with a demonic patron who fought demons in hell."

He grimaced. Maybe it was the fact I had said demon too many times in the same sentence. "I'm not a superstitious man, Max, but perhaps that is a reason why you have so much trouble avoiding conflict."

It was hardly *my* fault the Crimson Shadow was here. If you excluded the point where Ren and I had pushed the Lady off of the starter island and allowed her to gain whatever Class Ability had boosted her through the land corrupting people. Aside from that, I welcomed peace.

"Perhaps," I said diplomatically. "Just a heads-up though for when we get into an actual fight."

"You don't consider the zombies to have been an actual fight?"

Wolf nudged himself in between us. "Max means against Players. That is where he excels."

I was briefly speechless at the random compliment from the bear but also had to pause my train of thought to consider what that implied. Truthfully, I got the most use out of my Inventory manipulation when faced against other Players. They were just more of a challenge than System-created Monsters were. I needed to be on my best form.

"It's not pleasant," I concluded, if only so I didn't sound insane. "But it feels like I am geared to deal with problem Players."

Quinn grunted. "There's a story I heard that gets passed around here. A Player with a Skill that increased their damage by a certain amount until they made their next attack—if they lost a duel." He raised up a finger. "You may assume he would just appreciate a good bounce-back Ability, and duels don't really come up as often as the System would think, right?"

I nodded along.

"But no. No hubris too great. He had a better plan. He would lose as many duels as possible. Hundreds, if not thousands—if he could find the chance. Stacking the bonus way beyond the intended limit." He rubbed at his eye patch. "The fool intended to punch the ground and destroy the System once he got powerful enough."

My brow furrowed. "Is this person you?"

"Heaven's no." He smiled. "The Player died when his opponent went a little too far with the duel."

Wolf looked up at him. "So he spent his whole time here getting beaten up and then died?"

Quinn shrugged. "If the tale is even true. My point was one of caution. Do not bite the hands that feed."

I was willing to concede that he might have something of a point. Whether that would stop me on my path was . . . Well, no. I wasn't about to stop pushing my Inventory and magic bullshit to the limits, System be damned. Perhaps that would come around and make me regret the choice in the future.

"My question is," I began, changing the subject. "How did you catch the apple while still asleep?"

He turned his good eye to me, a twinkle within it. "You are not the only favored child of the System."

"Can you catch *arrows*?" My eyes narrowed.

Quinn grinned but didn't answer. *I bet he could.* That seemed unfair, for reasons I couldn't think of right now. We'd have to do some practice when we had more downtime—although, attacking him with arrows might not be the best look if it wasn't a guaranteed science.

We fell into a silence as we continued on, past the fields where the Wildfolk were and getting closer to that first small village we had cleared. Ren was in low conversation with Fiona, and it was nice to see them getting along again. Magnus was leading at the front. He had been near silent since the attack last night but seemed keen to act as guardian for the rest of us. Ruby was beside the fighter, and Wolf continued to stick between us at the back.

It *did* feel like we had a long day ahead of us. Having to head back west after this toward the Quests and Dungeon Quinn intended on helping us through. A couple of easier levels wouldn't go amiss though. The more power we could grab onto the better.

To our left, the village we had freed. Now the System-created Villagers moved around, doing their set daily tasks, making it look lively and . . . normal. It comforted me that we had achieved something with that bloodshed, although I wondered what Fiona and her Party had intended to do if they came upon our corpses with the Crimson Shadow the victors. An odd thought, but the simple answer would be they'd turn tail.

Now we just had to pass over the crest of the hill, the horizon already glimmering sea and the edges of the forest surrounding the first town. The group ahead of us paused at the pinnacle before the path weaved downward toward the bridge and us three at the back caught up.

Immediately, my stomach sank as quickly as my body temperature dropped. We had found Clive, at least.

His body was propped up like a flag at the top of a wooden pole, planted in front of the bridge. He was facing away from us, however. Toward anyone intending on making the journey across from the first area.

Five figures stood around him, now noticing us with some surprise in their eyes. Red handprints on their heads aside, they were clearly the group who had left in the night. Group two on my list. Betrayers.

They didn't know they were already dead.

"Motherfuckers!" Fiona seethed, stepping forward.

I held a hand out to stop her, earning the ire of both her and Magnus.

"Why stop me?" Her jaw was clenched, but she now trusted me enough not to ignore my order to hold. "There's only five of them."

"Believe me," I said calmly. "We will kill them, but we have the advantage here."

"The road is trapped," Ren added.

The fighter and lion man settled, trying to scour the pathway for what the elf may have seen. I had felt there was something off but didn't know for sure. Now that we had been spotted, one of them had cast a barrier spell. A manner of thick wall made of magical energy. We had the high ground, so that was probably a good bet if they didn't want to get picked off by my ranged attacks.

"What's your plan, Max?" Ruby asked. She looked even more tired now and not too keen to get involved in the potential fight. They weren't much for Player-on-Player violence.

I rubbed at my forehead, trying to keep the cold side of me from taking over. "The area is too open. They'd see my dove going in. Quinn?" His boomerang could be an option.

"Might damage the bridge." He had drawn a crossbow and was staring down at the group with intense focus.

We couldn't have that. Dropping myself behind them would be a good plan if they didn't expect it, but seeing me coming would be a short trip to getting stabbed in the face. One of my least favorite places to receive stabbings.

"Looks like two of them are holding the barrier up," Ren said, an arrow already up to her bow. "Might not be able to wait it out."

"Another meal too far away," Wolf grumbled.

I considered our options. This was taking up valuable leveling time and had annoyed me that we bumped into the traitors so soon. How short-lived their self-serving interests were. Why the first port of call of the Shadow seemed to be to hang corpses around in hopes of scaring people away, I did not know. Perhaps those with fear in their hearts were easier to turn.

Quinn put his hand on my arm, and I realized I had been wavering. My eyes felt warm, and I figured I was learning the tells for when they were glowing. After a brief nod of thanks to the fencer, I turned to the angry fighter and her group.

"There is something I can do . . . but you will not like it."

Fiona scowled. "Do anything you need. As long as they die."

I ran my tongue across my lips as I withdrew a card into my hand. "I'll hold you to that." With a nod to Ren, she readied an arrow.

Hopefully Clive would forgive me too.

CHAPTER TWENTY-SIX

Double-Booked

I hummed a tune without melody. Ren had asked if I wanted an introduction, but I had declined. Unlike me, certainly, but I didn't want to be the main focus. Sometimes in an act, getting the skeptics unsettled first made the ground fertile for what was to come. Right now we had to erase five Players who had betrayed the trust given to them and had desecrated the corpse of one of our allies.

Still, it wasn't much better than what I was about to do.

"Magnus, throw this." My new spear dropped to the side of me and slowly tilted toward the lion man. "Aim for just beyond the pole."

He grunted and took it from me.

"Everyone else, ready what ranged attacks you have for the shield. We want them hunkered down at first."

Acknowledgments filtered into my ears, letting me know the stage was ready and raring to go. I split the cards in my hand. A tough task for them both to complete . . . But by this stage, we were natural. As one.

My Mana reserves hit empty, and I started drawing into my Health with <Bloodletting>. I couldn't help but grin as I felt cool and calm inside. A placid lake before the tidal wave of dopamine washed over me. Could have gone on forever in this state, just edging the elation soon to arrive. No.

"Now."

Ren fired an arrow, a second drawn even before the first reached the glowing energy of their tall shield. Quinn fired a crossbow. Fiona leveled an arrow with a shortbow. Ruby sent out a small bolt from her magic staff, accompanied by a tinkle of the bell. Wolf had made it over to the steep rocky side next to the downward path, and his feet glowed a bright green.

Magnus threw the spear—and he threw it well.

As the flares of light from the shield illuminated the pathway just before the bridge and distracted them, my cards were out. Through the air as fast as I was able. One relatively straight to the intended target. The other had a more complicated path to take, but it had a job, perhaps even more important.

The fingers on both my hands clenched as I tried to maintain control of the empowered card. Blood ran down my hands and soaked into the arms of my shirt. I needed the power for the speed. I needed the speed despite the control. I needed the control to *fucking* succeed.

A second volley went out, slightly staggered to keep their attention.

"Quinn," Wolf growled. "Hop on."

If a wide grin wasn't already painting my face, I would have smiled wider.

The spear struck the trunk-like pole holding up the body and clattered to the cobblestone road behind the group of Players. Shortly followed by the dead body of Clive that I had cut loose.

I could hear the gasps and confusion of our allies as their former companion stood up to his feet awkwardly. Bright eyes of purple flowing from his impassive face as two long ears burst from the top of his skull.

Wolf growled and thundered down the rough terrain beside the path, avoiding the traps set. While normally a dangerous route, his Skills seemed to make the decline of rough stone and shrubbery nothing but a smooth passage. With the fencer on top, they hurtled down toward the melee about to begin.

"What the fuck . . ." Fiona whispered, lowering her arrow.

I had already apologized in advance and didn't have the faculties to do so again mid-performance. My eyes were burning bright, I could tell. They could hate me or abandon our pleasantries once more after the fact. All I had now was an audience in need of . . . having the shit murdered out of them.

Roger picked up the spear, just as one of their group noticed his presence. The female Paladin turned away from scowling at us to bring her shield up to face the sudden appearance of an enemy behind them. She called out to the Thief, who held a crossbow of their own.

My pact demon had no intention of fighting the armored foe in melee, however. At my command, he instead lobbed the spear past her, her reactions too slow to stop it.

"As soon as the wall is down, I'm in there," I said, a card already out.

"I can get the traps, man," Magnus offered, his jaw clenched.

"You can," I replied softly. "It might be over by the time you catch up. I'm sorry for hogging the limelight."

The wall went down. One spellcaster with a spear in their back. My demonic dove interrupting the other. I switched places before anyone could respond to me.

I arrived in a flash of vertigo beside the wounded caster. They were trying to give themselves a quick heal, confused at the presence of my demon—and now me. I grabbed the back of their brown hair and pulled their head back. Made my dagger vanish within his neck. *Ta-da!*

Then Wolf arrived. Quinn leaped from his back and caught the crossbow bolt shot by the Thief from out of the air in a flash of red. The bear swiped the attacker to the side before turning and charging in a burst of amber into the second spellcaster, knocking them to the ground.

Now up close, I could see the fifth member that we had little information on was a . . . bugbear? I wasn't sure how I had that knowledge. They were a head taller than me, hairy, and with excessively long arms. A sword of flaming green in one hand and some kind of spellcasting focus in the other. Maybe a Battlemage?

They strode toward me, sword pointed forward as if to cast a spell.

I went invisible.

Confusion went across their thick brow right before an arrow struck them in the chest. Entangling vines grew up from the ground, pinning them in place. A quick glance to the right showed that the Paladin had been stuck only briefly before casting a Skill to escape. It had given the wounded Roger some time to back away now. He needed a weapon. No, he needed to assist me now.

The bugbear turned their eyes up toward the Oathwarden at the top of the hill. Their final mistake. Invisibility dropped as my split cards went out, cutting at their face. Blinded them, if only briefly. From my side, the stabbed spellcaster came in with Jokkar's mace, cracking the skull of my opponent with a heavy downswing.

I turned my burning eyes to survey the battlefield.

"Keep her alive," I told the bear.

Quinn had killed the almost-disemboweled Thief. The bleeding remains of what was the second spellcaster's pulped skull was Wolf's doing as well. Now the Paladin was lying prone, a heavy paw threatening to buckle her plate armor and crush her chest.

"Boss." Roger knelt and bowed his head low.

"You may rise." I ran my tongue across my teeth. "Tell me, Roger. Did you take my commands to heart?"

He stood up but kept his gaze on the ground. "Yes, boss. I can confirm I am working on my substance abuse issues and no longer desire to eat my own kind."

I wavered in place, some heat of energy dissipating as the show finally wound up. "And your family?"

"Still early days, but things are improving."

"See to it you maintain that direction." My tired eyes went to the path, where the rest were carefully making their way down. "You may go now. Thank you for your service."

"At your command, boss." He gave me a bow and vanished, leaving the spent corpse to flop to the bloodied road.

A little cold toward him, perhaps. I was all for a little levity, but I needed to keep a firm hand on the rudder. Especially in current company. Once he was more normalized, then we could be a bit more casual. I sighed deeply.

Quinn came up to me. "That was . . . shorter and more visceral than I had anticipated."

"Yeah." I frowned and then snapped back to my normal self. "Players aren't usually prepared for fighting against other Players. We're not balanced that way."

"Your efficiency is—"

"Well practiced due to necessity." I gave him a glum smile and then turned to greet the others.

Fiona's expression was nothing but a thunderstorm, and she came directly up to me, even ahead of all the others who were still making sure there was no last trap. She didn't even yell or speak until she was standing two feet away from me.

"You're a fucking monster," she said in a hushed tone, so only the three of us heard. "And I'm thankful as fuck that you're on our side."

"I'm still sorry," I offered. Too exhausted to be intimidated.

She looked past me to see the pained Paladin and the spent corpse of her fallen friend. "You found his body and got us someone who can talk. We'll leave the rest in the past, okay?" Her hand extended, and I shook it.

My eyes blinked away a slight haze. "How do you want to do the questioning? We usually avoid torture."

Quinn raised an eyebrow. "Usually?"

Fiona worked her shoulders before looking back at the approaching three. "Not sure I trust my temper to do anything other than beat her to death. Can I defer to your experience?"

I smiled. "Let me confer with my protégé."

The fencer shuffled before whispering, "Is that me?"

Ren approached with the other two, my hell bird sitting atop her head. I let it go with a thought to return to mist. The elf's eyes were . . . bright and glad to see me in one piece, perhaps. Hmm. My lack of injury was odd. Something felt off here.

"Ren," I began, "dibs on bad cop."

"Asshole," she said and deflated. "*Fine.*"

Magnus and Ruby still seemed either annoyed or unsure of me but were either too emotionally exhausted to engage or were following Fiona's lead in this.

With Ren beside me, we stepped over to Wolf. "Thanks, bud, you alright to take down this terrible pole and clear the road?"

He growled at the woman beneath his paws, putting his nose up to her face. "Certainly. This one isn't quite cooked enough."

I wasn't sure if he was alluding to the fact that we were about to grill her, but it amused me nonetheless. As he backed away, I summoned a Hellhound+ beside her, who immediately snarled and looked ready to tear her face off.

"Sometimes I wonder if the System gave me <Speak with Dead>," I began, grinning as I stood over the Paladin. "Due to how often I get to chat with walking corpses."

She glared up at me, but no response.

Ren crouched down beside the woman, her brow furrowed. "The least we could do is sit her up and make her a little more comfortable?" Blue eyes came up to me, an earnest desire in them that I almost believed.

"Why?" I pulled a face. "She isn't even going to talk. I owe her no leniency."

"Please, Max? *If* she agrees to talk?" Her worried expression turned to the prone Paladin.

The woman's eyes went between Ren and me. They were an interesting amber color and not entirely trusting of either of us. "Let me heal myself and sit on a chair."

I raised an eyebrow and gestured Quinn over. "Can I borrow your Class item for a second?"

He hesitated at first but stepped over and withdrew the boomerang. Gently, into my hand it went. I then knelt down and pulled on the Paladin's armor, lifting her from the floor slightly, so that I could jam the item down the back behind her neck. I let her drop to the ground and stood up straight.

"You may do so." I placed out a chair. "The item I have put behind you is an explosive that will destroy you if you do anything we do not like. Do you understand?"

She grunted and nodded briefly. Slowly, she moved herself up to her feet, grimacing and groaning from the pain she was in. Gradually, she made it to the chair and sank into it with a deep sigh. Raising a single hand, letting us see what she was doing, a radiant light pooled down her plated fingers and sunk into her torso. An icon temporarily appeared above her to show that it was a gradual heal over time. No other icons were present.

It would be a shame for Quinn to waste his Ability this soon in the day, against a lone foe, with Ren and me possible collateral. That was a risk I would take, however. The *baddest* cop.

"See," the elf gestured. "That wasn't so bad."

I clicked my tongue and crossed my arms. "Waste of my time."

"What did you want to know before you kill me?" The woman lowered her hand onto her lap. Some resignation in her face. Acceptance for picking the wrong side, perhaps.

"I think the branding on your forehead is answer enough as to why you left the camp last night." I tilted my head. "Was the betrayal worth it?"

She looked past us to her dead Party. "Currently, no." Her face started to redden as her eyes filled with tears. "They told us we'd be safe. They'd spare us if we left and didn't tell anyone."

"The necromancer?" Ren crouched down beside her, sadness in her own expression.

I was more tense with her being that close to an unknown agent, but I trusted her judgment. Crimson Shadow didn't usually exhibit this amount of remorse or regret for their choices.

"Yeah." The Paladin sniffed as quiet tears rolled down her cheeks. "We were meant to leave earlier, but we . . . We struggled to do it."

"Bullshit." I shook my head, the outburst surprising them both. "You could have said something at any time. You knew we were at the camp too."

She looked at the ground. "Fair. We were told the camp would be overrun, and our silence was the only way for us to live. We had grown so tired of just . . . barely getting by in this world."

"You wanted to be part of the winning team?" Ren asked softly.

The Paladin nodded, her mouth turned down in barely contained misery. "They said . . . They said if we strung up the corpses after, we could join them . . ."

"You're not actual members?" I asked, dropping the act for a moment. "Haven't drunk her blood?"

Her head shook, and Ren and I exchanged a glance.

The woman was just a normal misguided asshole.

CHAPTER TWENTY-SEVEN

Nuance

Most of the Crimson Shadow had been easy to erase from this world. Even when faced with what they had done, or stood for, they continued to be unrepentant. Would squirm and claw their way from under your thumb to gnash and bite at you. Rabid animals.

Now that we had met someone only one foot in the pool of blood, it made our usual binary approach a lot more difficult.

I looked back at the corpses we had created. A harsh punishment for those whose only crime was . . . Oh, no—they had abandoned us to die in the camp. Trying to keep themselves safe was one thing, but knowingly putting us in danger was nearly unforgivable.

Ren was waiting for me to proceed, to see if I changed tact with this new information. In all honesty, I wished I could make the decision to just kill the Paladin and move on. It was only by virtue of how the fight shook out that she was even alive—the plan *was* to kill them all.

Then what were my choices? Give her up to Fiona to decide her fate? Let her go atone for her terrible choices? Start a prison and judicial system to put these sorts away for their crimes? None of those really ticked a box that made me comfortable. Neither did killing her in cold blood.

With a sigh, I clicked my fingers, and my hound went to sit in front of her. I turned and gestured Ren and Fiona off to the side.

"What's the matter? Cold feet?" The fighter raised an eyebrow once we were partly out of earshot of the Paladin.

"Eh." I pulled a face. "I kill the Crimson Shadow and demons. She is neither."

Ren had a scowl upon her face, but she gave me a nod. "The nuance is important."

Fiona sighed and rubbed at her short hair. "So you're trying to think of a humane option that doesn't leave us with a potential enemy? She can't be trusted though."

I looked back at our captive. She looked miserable and withdrawn, her face lowered and gloomy. Resigned to joining her companions across the ground in short order.

"Take her into your Party," I said.

"Fuck you." Fiona shook her head. "Take her in *your* Party."

"I can't. The Paladin seeks safety. We aren't about that." I looked toward Ren to see her reaction to my proposition. Not overly eager, but she understood my angle.

"She *betrayed* us," the fighter seethed. "Strung Clive's corpse up."

I leaned forward, closer to her. "And how many lives did you doom with your inaction? What of your own sins in trying to do your best?"

Anger flared up in her eyes, and she bared her teeth. "You fucking *dare*?"

"Yeah, I do." A wave of cold passed through me. "What you have now is a chance to prove you can lead, can do better than the Shadow. Or are you a monster like them? Like me?"

I could see her tense up, trying to decide if hitting me was a good idea. Her incensed eyes went between me, the elf, and the Paladin.

"You don't have to bend over backward for her," Ren said. "Allow her the safety of the first area and time to grieve. She will repent, in time."

"And if she betrays us again?" Some anger had died down in Fiona's expression.

I stood back up, away from her. "Kill her and mail me her head. Or don't actually; that would be weird." I shivered as my body temperature returned to normal. "Feel free to exact your revenge on me personally."

Her eyes rolled. "We both know how unsuccessful that would be. Let me talk to the others . . . But this is fucking stupid." She left to go meet with Magnus and Ruby.

"I think it's the right call, trickster." She watched the woman leave before turning to me. "Also, threatening her was amazing. I was almost giddy."

I raised an eyebrow and smiled at her. Her expression hadn't really changed throughout the whole exchange, but I believed every word of it. "I'm starting to think you like that side of me."

"*Every* side of you." She pursed her lips. "Now go sort this mess out."

With a brief bow, I turned and walked over to the Paladin. How funny that the parts of us that changed for us to be a better Party and companions were also the things that we loved about each other. Oh, the *L* word. Better keep my head in the show.

I crouched down in front of the seated woman and gave my dog a pet. Lower than her to be less threatening. I looked up into her dissociating eyes. Although I hadn't gotten the go-ahead from the other team, I had a feeling they were following my stage directions. It was the only way things could work.

"Do you know how many Crimson Shadow my group has killed?"

She didn't meet my gaze but shook her head.

"Me neither. Three or four dozen by now. Cleared the first area of them, as far as I know." Crouching this way was actually slightly uncomfortable. "I have a proposition that you might not like."

Her amber eyes rose to meet my own. "My life is already forfeit."

"No. You have one last chance at penance. At safety." I sent the Hellhound+ to get pets from the elf before he vanished.

The Paladin just looked confused.

Footsteps came up beside me. Metal boots. A gloved hand rested on my shoulder and gave it a brief squeeze. Fiona had accepted my proposition. Either that or she was about to lop my head off, which would be rather amusing in retrospect.

"Fiona here is willing to accept you into her Party. They are heading into the first area to rest and recover. Taking time away from the conflict."

She looked up at the fighter, even more confusion and sadness in eyes that didn't understand, her lips unable to get out any words.

Fiona shifted from behind me and crossed her arms. "Strength is repairing those broken around you, not discarding them. You will have to earn your place, and our trust . . . But if you truly seek it, we can offer you a second chance."

The Paladin burst out into tears and held her hands up, practically praying for the opportunity.

I stood and walked around her to retrieve Quinn's boomerang. The man had been leaning against Wolf, the bear close to napping and seemingly unbothered by the fencer's casual closeness now.

Stepping back over to Fiona, I gave her a brief nod. "This is where we part ways then."

She grunted, and tiredness filled her face. "I still hate your fucking guts, Max. But I respect you."

I grinned. "I won't ask for a hug then."

"No, fuck off already." She smiled and shook her head before turning to the Paladin.

My feet took me away from the situation. I shook the large hand of Magnus and got an awkward hug out of the goblin. We waved the group of four off as they started to cross the bridge.

"Thoughts Ren?" I asked.

"Things sure were easier when it was us against the world. I almost feel guilty for the four we killed."

Almost.

Under different circumstances, they may have all lived and followed a path like the Paladin. This was the crux of it though. Much like Fiona could become a good leader if she wasn't so afraid to make mistakes, the would-be Crimson

Shadow group had reaped the consequences of their actions. Not an easy lesson to swallow, but the stakes were high.

"They had opposed us," I said flatly. "Perhaps soon the world will run out of fools."

"If only," she replied, undressing me with her eyes.

I *really* needed to keep up this false-bravado stuff. Instead of buttering up the elf more, I turned to the other two in our group. "Pole and bodies into the river. Best not to leave such a mess."

"Don't forget to loot." Ren jabbed me forward with her finger.

Relenting to peer pressure, I joined the others in clearing the stage. Not usually one for the dirty work, I at least gave it my all when roped into lending a hand. The blood would hopefully wash away with rain or scour away under the glare of the sun. With their pockets thoroughly shaken out, we dropped the bodies and pole over the edge of the bridge and into the fast-flowing river.

"Anything good, trickster?"

[6,343 Gold]
[Brilliant Robes: +3 INT, +3 WIS, +5% magic Damage]
[Cloak of the Caster+: +5 INT, +5% magic Damage]
[Warrior Ring: +2 STR, +2 CON, +5% Health]
[Health Potions (8)]
[Antidotes (4)]
[Note]

How sad it was that breaking open Players like piñatas was the surest way of getting good loot compared to doing Quests or Dungeons. No wonder the System was in such disarray. I moved my current cape to my Cosmetic slot—the ability to hide the movements of my left hand was worth more than any Stat in the same slot.

"This," I said, withdrawing a piece of paper to hand to her.

Her brow furrowed further as she read it. "Where they planned to meet someone from the Shadow to get their blood and proper introduction?"

As much as she was good at reading between the lines, those were the actual lines of the letter, so she was equally as good at reading those as well. Hmm, something had come loose in my brain, perhaps.

Quinn stepped over and stretched out his back. "What's the location? Far from here?"

She handed it over to him, and his eye ran through the text.

"Tomorrow."

I nodded. As much as I liked it when the bad guys put their intentions down with ink and paper, this didn't add up quite nicely. The thought swirled around in my head, but I couldn't put a finger on it to keep it in place.

"You know," I said, instead of letting the thought fester. "You could have joined them. Fiona's group, I mean."

He cast his eye back down the bridge, the wooded first area visible just past the heap of broken fort parts. He turned back to me and passed the note over with a smile.

"No. I feel my destiny lies with the three of you. Hopefully to die saving your life, Max, and fully repay my debt."

I groaned. "You know, saying things makes them more likely to come true, right?"

"Superstitious, trickster? Or overly pessimistic?" Ren stood with her arms crossed.

"Neither." I shrugged them off and gestured for us to get moving. "It's a subconscious thing. Makes you head toward paths that your mind has already cleared."

"Like how you can force a card pick?" Her eyebrow raised.

"Yeah." I smiled.

Wolf grunted. "That's why I always talk about food."

As if he didn't get enough already—even with his debuff causing him to require sustenance more often. Still, it had been a tiring morning so far, and we hadn't gotten stuck into our original plan for the day yet.

"Let's get somewhere less painted with death and take five for elevenses, then?"

They agreed, and Quinn pointed out a location closer to the coast that had a Quest that might help unlock the Chat function. Plenty of tired disdain in his eye that we had managed to skip that on our way here.

Still, power had been more helpful, and Ren and Wolf were never too far from me if I wasn't getting kidnapped. Now that we had cautious allies, some way of telling them our last will and testament before we dashed ourselves on the rocks of our hubris could be helpful. Quinn especially seemed happy to have the details of Magnus, compared to Wolf, who was indifferent to the notion.

"Going to be a long day," Ren said to me as we walked side by side. The other pair were slightly ahead, Quinn again delivering an animated tale loosely food related to capture the bear's attention.

"They all seem to be lately." I smiled at her, another pang of brief panic as her hand held on to mine again.

"We're growing though. Maybe not in power, but in strength." She had a calm to her expression as she looked at the pair ahead.

Quinn had been an unexpected addition. That much was true. Our morality had been tested, and I'd like to think we made the best choices for a pair of killers. Although penned in by the framework of the System, our camaraderie and personal character growth had clearly found a good place to farm experience . . . as we were thriving in that respect.

I felt more confident in taking the role of a decision-maker. Ren had swallowed her pride to put on an act or two to support me. Wolf was the glue that kept us stable. Quinn had his flaws, but he was open with his feelings in a way that was admirable, when not annoying.

It wouldn't last, I was sure of it. Even as the breeze brought across a smell that signaled we were near the shore. The daylight was soft and comforting, and the scenery seemed calm and lush. This was just another quiet stage before the bubble popped.

Conflict rose from the meager shadows to follow us wherever we went. Sure, today might just be a day of beating up System-created . . . but tomorrow we knew where Crimson Shadow would be meeting the Party we had just ruined. The necromancer, Tyler, and his ilk might make a move south of the road knowing that the camp was all but overrun. There were probably more enemies just waiting in the wings for us to make a misstep that we hadn't even heard of.

But looking into those bright-blue eyes, and holding Ren's hand . . . I—

"Hey, Max!" Quinn called from ahead, the clouds of rosy pink surrounding me dissipating. "You should come see this."

CHAPTER TWENTY-EIGHT

Playing for Keeps

Despite my gut instinct telling me otherwise, part of me was flattered by it. Somebody had created an effigy of me. Well, the assumption was that it was *me*, however the culprits had a difficult time finding any sort of fabric that matched my gaudy outfit. Instead, dark-purple linens wrapped around what looked like a scarecrow. Just off a beaten path rather than in a field.

"I have trouble telling you apart," Ren admitted.

"They made him far too handsome," I said, narrowing my eyes at the loose ball of dried straw.

Quinn was pulling a face, not too enamored by our casual response to someone making a dummy out of me. Someone other than me, for a change.

Wolf went up to it and sniffed. "Not a scent that I recall. Nothing fresh."

"Interesting," I said, although my thoughts were a little further from that statement. That meant that it was put up during the time we were in the first area, most likely. "Anything else in the area you can note?"

He huffed and made the show of circling around the area. "Some . . . Monster tracks, I think. Something odd, but also very faint."

Nothing I was currently worried about. It reminded me of the drawing one of the Crimson Shadow had of me for tracking purposes. This was just a poorly designed statue in the middle of relative nowhere, however.

"You must have really made an impression on Lady in Red," Ren eventually surmised, giving me a glare as if that could have been through my own fault. We hadn't even seen each other face-to-face.

Quinn unfocused as he looked at his Map. "There is no spell attached to it. The only other thing I can think it might be used for is . . . target training."

I raised an eyebrow and turned to the area behind us. If the Lady wanted me dead, then whatever lay down this south side of the area might have been told a man like this—but more handsome and awe-inspiring—was to be killed on sight.

In fairness, I expected that reaction from most people we met, so other than being slightly more alert, I wasn't worried.

"Top prize goes to whoever kills my would-be assassin." I grinned.

"What is the prize?" Ren and Wolf both asked in unison, while Quinn looked as though he was getting there a second too late.

"Prize will have to be tailored to the recipient." I shrugged as I continued. "Although . . . if I kill them, then you'll all owe me a favor."

After a couple of grumbles, they eventually accepted my proposition. Now I had three others looking out for my safety even more than before. Not really a trick or the intention of my proposal . . . but things worked in my favor, as I designed it that way.

"I see right through you," Ren said, her eyes narrowed as we started back down the path.

"Of course," I replied impassively. "That's why you're my most trusted ally."

Her eyes rolled, and I noted her hands were busy holding her bow and an arrow. She must clearly want that prize more than she was letting on. The question then was . . . what was she hoping to get from me?

I smiled and looked out at the scenery. More trees, but they were starting to become sparse as we headed down toward the coast. I could see the ocean out on the horizon over the short hill on our left. The sunlight reflected across the soft waves, totally paling in comparison to how enrapturing the blue of Ren's eyes was. I made a note to say that sometime.

"Say, Quinn," I began, if only to distract myself from the radiant elf beside me. "Before all this hardship came upon the land, were there a lot of Players?"

"Compared to now? Yes." He rubbed at his eye patch as his eye searched the terrain for anything untoward after me. "It had always been relatively quiet though. Depending on what your Party was doing, you might see one or two other groups during the day."

"First area was like a ghost town." I pulled a face. "No friendly groups at all."

"Much must have happened during the time I was shamefully hiding away," he said, accompanying the statement with a shrug. "Quest is just to the left here."

Ren seemed keen to protect our rear, which made it awkward to exchange glances with her. Given that was 60 percent of our interactions, I felt a little put out.

"Roger behaving better now, trickster?" she asked, just outside of my peripheral.

I nodded and looked out to the horizon, as Quinn took us down a stepped path. "Seems my stern voice works on most people, huh?" As much as I would have liked to see her expression, sometimes it was more fun to try to pick up on any changes in body language.

A slight change in pace as a brief hesitation waylaid a single footstep. The longer exhale as her mind wandered to a replay of the time I gave my pact demon a dressing down. Perhaps it was unfair to try to break down our interactions like I would a trick. These things always had more nuance, and I was enough of an unreliable narrator without reading into things in Ren's normal movements that weren't there.

Her hand touched my shoulder, and she leaned in close to my ear. "I can't wait until we have some more private accommodation."

As soon as the words finished exiting her mouth, she was away from me. I turned with a raised eyebrow to see her with a neutral scowl out at the surroundings.

"Eyes on the steps, trickster," she said, narrowing her eyes. "Don't want you tripping and opening up that delicate skull again."

I did as she said and tried to discern if I had imagined some of that or not. She *was* good. My churning internal organs aside, we would actually need to decide on a plan for the evening. Camping near the coast sounded about as safe as we were able to get . . . or perhaps *in* the Dungeon? I couldn't remember if there was something that would prevent that or not.

Before my brain could even process the thought of more private and structural lodgings, the edge of my boot clipped the corner of a step that was slick with something vegetative. Not even Ren's quick reflexes could save me.

This was my end.

Pain went up my left ankle as I hopped down the next couple of wide steps, almost barging into Quinn. I had beaten the odds and avoided dashing my brains out on the rocky decline. I would have been even more elated if I could put weight on my foot.

"Fucking asshole, Max!" Ren stomped up beside me and held me steady. As much as she was glaring at me, there was no anger on her face. Maybe just sad acceptance over the amount of bullshit constantly present in my existence.

"In fairness," I began. ". . . Ah . . ." I frowned back at the step, hoping to find it was a trap laid for me and it wasn't just idle clumsiness that brought me to this malady. No, I bore the blame alone. I just shrugged instead of finishing the sentence.

"Just a sprain, right?" She frowned down at my boots as if that would give away the diagnosis. "I don't think my heals would do much for that."

"I'm sure I can walk it off." With a sheepish grin at the fencer, I shrugged. "I have a habit of getting myself into near-fatal and totally avoidable accidents."

Wolf grunted. "That's unfair. If you hadn't fallen out of the tree, then we'd never have met."

Very true. How different our lives may have been without Wolf at our side. We'd probably be dead, no doubt. I took a step and stumbled as my foot gave way, almost sending me off into the bushes. "How inconvenient," I murmured as everyone watched me with a mixture of exhaustion and worry.

"It's not much longer, Max." Quinn pointed down the trail. "Look, you can see the bottom, and there's even a bench there."

"There is?" I raised an eyebrow and smiled. "Last one there owes me a sweet cake."

Before they could interject, I was gone. I sat down on the bench as my demonic dove fluttered around them where I had been standing. Now that I was out of the tree line, I could see a few houses nearby. Open skies and the sound of waves in the distance. An immense feeling of calm.

I withdrew the potion pack that Ruby had given me and looked through at the contents.

[Potions of Gradual Healing (2)]
[Greater Antidotes (2)]
[Action-Speed Potion]
[Nature's Defense Potion]

Nothing in there to cure me of being an accident-prone show-off. I put it back away and turned my head to see Ren slide across the stone paving to a stop. Wolf wasn't too far behind, whereas Quinn was red-faced and disappointed. It amused me that they took things that seriously. We needed the levity.

"Should have known you'd win, Ren." I gave her a warm smile. "You never let me down."

"Stuff it, trickster." She rolled her eyes and came to sit beside me. "Where's my sweet cake?"

I raised an eyebrow. "Perhaps you misheard. The loser owed *me* one."

Her bright-blue eyes bore into me as she checked her memory for the truth. Eventually, she turned to the fencer with a narrowed glare. "Where's Max's two sweet cakes, Quinn?"

The man deflated and walked over, shooting a side-eye at the bear. "While I do not believe that was a fair challenge, due to the unscrupulous actions of those I will not name . . ." He looked over at Wolf again. "I am a gracious loser, and thus . . . here is your prize. *One* sweet cake."

Into his hand, the promised goods. Further scowls from the elf in being denied part of the prize. Wolf had an amused look on his face. He must have pushed the man out of the way and then used his bulk to prevent him from over-taking. Ren, being sprier, had avoided the clog before it could happen and made quick her escape. Wolf might have even assisted her in winning, which tickled me, even if it wasn't true.

I put the sweet cake into my Inventory. "Not hungry right this minute, but thank you, Quinn. I always appreciate a good sport."

Ren was pouting, but her ire had diminished now with the hope that I had put the cake away so that I could share it with her later. I *would*, and that was indeed the reason. How we had run out of them already, I wasn't so sure, but hopefully once we got to an actual town we could stock back up with all this otherwise useless gold.

"The town is to the east again now, right?" I brought up my Map to see that we had gone west away from it, toward where the fencer had promised us places to level.

"Correct." He stretched out and tried to cool himself off. While our outfits weren't great to fight in—even with the adjustments made—his almost equally flamboyant padded long-sleeve shirt looked like it would hold in heat more so than our shirts and suits.

I wiggled my foot around. Better to a degree. The rest had certainly helped deal with the initial . . . inflammation? I wasn't actually sure how it worked. Only that I preferred it when my foot was more functional and allowed me easier access to getting where I wanted to be.

Ren put her hand on my leg and pulsed radiant healing through me. I noted that she could cast the spell from range, so the contact wasn't a necessity. "That's better." I nodded slowly, even if it didn't do much. "Still aches, but I could probably move now."

As a demonstration, I stood up. Could keep weight on it now, at least. I took a few steps, only some brief pain radiating around the joint. "Not . . . perfect. How far is the Quest, Quinn?"

He narrowed his eye and raised a finger to point at one of the houses about a hundred feet away.

Ren stood up beside me, a wry grin forming on her lips as we looked at our destination.

"Double or nothing?" she asked.

CHAPTER TWENTY-NINE

Always Ahead

I slammed through the door of the house, stumbled, and clattered onto the floor like a mangled pile of limbs. Groaned as I turned, just in time for Ren to repeat the action, tripping over the step just before the door and landing right on top of me.

Would have been rather romantic in a cliché way if her elbows didn't knock the air out of me and her head hadn't collided with mine. Before I had a chance to react, she stole a quick kiss and then rolled off of me.

A large shadow cut off the sunlight coming in through the open doorway. The whole building vibrated and creaked in pain as the enormous form of Wolf slid sideways into the wall.

I groaned again and put a hand up to my sore head. My aching foot could not stop me from being the headliner, as much as my body was regretting the need to win.

"Should have known you'd get ahead using bullshit," Ren murmured, sitting up and rubbing her own head.

Pretty much par for the course at this stage of my life, and her own fault for challenging me despite knowing my capabilities. If anything, I was surprised she was able to keep up and stay ahead of the bear, who had some Skills geared toward charging forth. Quinn got the short straw once more, and I'd perhaps feel bad if he hadn't tried to trip me near the start. We did what we could to survive.

Up to my feet and I stretched my back out. Getting too old for these kinds of games. My eyes went to the back of the room, where two figures stood watching us, as my hand went down to help the elf up.

Wolf moved away from the building, allowing light to pool back in, illuminating our observers.

A man and a woman, looking around middle-aged and surprisingly weather-worn, considering they probably spent most of their time in this building. Our interactions with the System-created people of the first area were mostly limited, as the uncanny-valley aspect made me uncomfortable.

I dusted myself down to at least look presentable and waited for Quinn to join us before I went and messed things up.

The fencer stepped into the room, redder in the face than before and potentially second-guessing his decision to join us. It was curious that he didn't have any speed-boosting Skills, but perhaps that was an unfair judgment to make.

"Ah, seems I owe you a second cake, Max." He gave me a low bow. "Your abilities stand unequaled. However, I do not have a second on my person at present."

"That's no problem." I smiled and held out my hand for him to shake. Needless, but he seemed to like the more antiquated formalities—the only person bowing more than me in this world.

Returning the shake seemed to settle his thoughts and bring him some comfort, as if any annoyance was washed away by the action. He truly was rather flitting with his emotions. "I had not imagined we would be having such fun and games. Certainly not after the other . . . activities of the morning."

"We don't usually." Ren tilted her head. "But given how much trauma we go through, it's a good way to not be miserable constantly."

I nodded. Ren had always been my spark of sunshine during the darkest days, and now that we had another in our Party, we had to play a little harder, to work a little harder. Wolf seemed ambivalent about whatever we got up to, but I'd pencil in some time to check on him soon enough. Right now, it seemed the exertion had brought his next nap up on his schedule, and he was guarding the building with his snoozing form.

"Well, I hope to partake in further levity, although maybe things that don't involve Max beating us in rigged games." His smile put to rest any inclination that he might be sour about it.

"I do need humbling every so often." Before I could receive a response, I gestured toward the patient Quest givers, mostly to avoid being reminded about the times I broke my skull or apparently had trouble walking in a straight line without injury. I put a pin in thinking of more games I could rig in my favor.

"This one is nice and simple. You just need to talk to the kind madam there." He gestured toward the woman. "The Quest requires you receive a message through the Chat, so it might force the unlock?"

Even if it didn't work, I at least got two sweet cakes out of the venture. And no permanent injuries. Maybe I shouldn't count my chickens.

"Hello, adventurer," the woman began. "I'm expecting my great-aunt to visit today, however I have not heard from her recently. If I give you her details, could you try to contact her and make sure she is safe?"

My brow furrowed. "Why can't you do it yourself?"

"Only adventurers have the ability to send magical messages." Her expression didn't change as she gave me the obvious exposition.

"So . . ." I removed my hat to rub at my head where I had collided with the elf. "Is your great-aunt an adventurer?"

"*Max*," Ren interjected, "quit engaging the Quest givers and get this done with."

I rolled my eyes. Forgive a man for wanting to learn more about the world he lived in. "Sure, Miss . . . Quest Giver. I will contact your great-aunt, and we'll see just how *great* she really is."

[Chat function now unlocked]
[Contact: Great-Aunt Ulla added]

"It worked." I snapped my fingers and bowed away so that Ren could repeat the process.

Quinn nodded, and with his eye unfocused, he sent me over the contact information for the three from the other group, along with his own.

Not wanting to get further behind the curve, I decided it was time enough to give it a go and let the fighter know we were contactable. No doubt so that she could scream murder at us once the Paladin did something bad . . . assuming she lived through it. An intangible keyboard appeared under an empty text box. My <Sleight of Hand> made it child's play to tap out my intended message—more of a stenographer than I kept telling myself, it seemed.

[Max: Here's my contact. How's the first area?]

I waited a few moments as the elf and woman spoke in the background, slightly worried I wouldn't get a response—before a gentle ping only I could hear signified a message had been delivered. Something else to get used to.

[Fiona: Peaceful and . . . thriving.]
[Fiona: You really unfucked it, it seems.]
[Fiona: Take care and stay alive, clown.]

The slight jab at the end seemed unnecessary, but I was mostly sure that it was a little amount of banter. However . . . I was relieved to hear the first area was doing fine. Our time spent there among the bloodshed was worth it, after all.

Quinn then sent the same details over to the elf, and I smiled at her. "Just spoke to Fiona, and she says the first area is looking good. She used the word *thriving*."

"Really?" She seemed genuinely pleased, although some confusion passed over her face when trying to unfocus and look at her own Chat windows.

It was easy to forget that she came from a world that didn't have instant messaging or emails. Our current existence put us somewhere in between my modern world and her fantasy one. Although, I was again using my own definition of *fantasy*. To her, it was just normal. My mind idly waltzed over to thoughts of taking her back to Earth and having to teach her about . . . cars and coffee machines. Cliché rom-com stuff.

"Not a fan." She grimaced at the windows. "Of the whole Chat thing. It's useful though. Wolf, get your ass in here and get the Quest."

A loud grumble came from outside as the bear shifted to his feet and stuck his head in the doorway. "Why? I will not use it."

"Are you declining a potential trick avenue?" I asked, faux surprise on my face.

He paused, unsure as to how paired to the magician life he truly was. Eventually, under the five eyes leveled his way, he gave in and tried to squeeze through the doorway. A tough ask, and I wondered if I would eventually get something that could manipulate my allies. Ah, maybe with better phrasing than that.

Only slightly buckling the doorframe, he entered, muttered through the dialogue options, and then begrudgingly worked through getting the contact details from Quinn as we left. It seemed more pragmatic to keep walking rather than stand around and do it. It meant the pair were otherwise distracted, but I didn't feel we were in any present danger.

I walked alongside Ren, something we seemed to fall into naturally now that there were four of us in the group. Not that I was complaining, of course. It made it easier to ignore the ache and occasional twinge of pain in my ankle, at the least. Racing our way to the building was rather shortsighted with my injury, but I could perform under pressure.

"Apologies if I've now shared my head-injury curse." I smiled at her.

"We're doomed if that's the case." She wrinkled up her face. "Didn't bruise, did I?"

I lifted her hat, watching as the sunlight illuminated her hair. "Nope, perfect as always." She smiled as I returned the blue top hat atop her.

"Always with the charm." She shook her head. "And with only a brief cold shower after all the exertion over the past few days, I feel like garbage."

"A little more struggle and then I'll personally find you a house with a working bath."

"My hero," she said, her eyes going back out to our surroundings rather than digging into me further.

I found myself living for the juxtapositions. The murder and threat on our lives flashing against an odd romance that I now found myself wanting more of. As much as I yearned to save the world for moral reasons, as the days went by, it was becoming more likely I was aiming for something a little more selfish. A chance to really be with Ren and see if we were anything more than trauma bound.

The small gathering of houses gave way to a built-up area. An odd seawall of gray stone that blocked out the view of the beach and rolling tide. Didn't do much to prevent the smells of sea air and warm sand from reaching us, but the apparent promenade made the next leg of our journey a lot easier.

"We'll move away from the coast again shortly," Quinn said, tilting his gaze back to us. "Up a hill on the right in about ten minutes. I just thought the fresh air made a nice change."

"It certainly does," I said as I tipped my hat toward him. The sounds of the waves lapping at the shore were comforting, even though I hadn't spent much time near the coast in my old life. Between soft sunlight and pleasant scenery, I felt lost . . . but in a good way. Tired but at peace.

If the System had been perfect, then this would be like a slice of paradise.

"Something to fight for, isn't it, trickster?" Ren caught my relaxed gaze, probably having similar thoughts on our situation.

"I already have enough of that, right here." I raised an eyebrow, unsure as to why I had said that.

She tutted. "So early in the day too. You invite malady on me, dickbag."

I turned away with a sheepish grin on my face. She was right, of course. Openly gushing about my feelings would soon have destiny frowning at our happiness and prompted into action to put an end to that. We had managed to skirt any potential tragedy by having me take the brunt of fate's punishment. Survived only mostly through bullshit.

But then, it *was* what the System allowed.

It was a shame to leave the coast and head back up into an area more wooded. The higher vantage point gave us a good view of the golden sands and blue ocean that went on until the horizon, and I made the mental note to return here once we lived in better times. My ankle had all but recovered, the scenic route giving it something to reflect on and remind it of its purpose.

To take me forward into more trouble.

As if by narrative fiat, Wolf and Quinn stopped just ahead of us. The fencer's hand went to his sword pommel, and I could tell by the bear's body language that something was up. Steeling myself, I stepped up to them to see what they had caught eye of.

An open field . . . filled with Max scarecrows. Perhaps a dozen of them, all dressed in different shades of purple.

More interesting, however—albeit less flattering—was the creature standing in the middle of the field.

As we stood taking in the interesting scene, the large Monster turned and looked at us.

Well, mostly at me, naturally.

CHAPTER THIRTY

Having a Blast

There was an odd anger in the eyes of the Monster that now stood before me. A *Troll*, the System was keen to tell me.

His rough clothing and the surrounding ground were already stained with blood. Tears throughout the muddied brown sack he used as a waistcoat exposed scarred flesh. He seemed tired and irritated.

The reason was rather clear. Each of the odd Max scarecrows had metal spikes wedged into the area around them. I could imagine the System-created trying to attack the approximations of a bedazzling magician and just cutting himself up in the process. He was System-created, so I wasn't sure he'd even remember or understand why. Just more needless cruelty.

And for what? They thought they could foster a Monster truly angered at me? That he could hold a grudge and track me down, kill me without hesitation for what the Man in Purple had done? It sickened me that they were so . . . thoughtless.

The troll dropped to the ground as drops of blood from my hand did the same. I let the fully powered card vanish away, hardly even registering that I had made the attack.

"You must have quite the fan club, Max," Quinn said quietly.

"Be a lot cooler if I did," my murmured response came as I stepped out into the flattened field. I took some of the purple fabric from the nearest scarecrows. The others kept a wary eye around the area, expecting there to be someone watching . . . or perhaps just an actual threat to whatever this constructed area was meant to be.

Quinn ran his hand through his goatee as he slowly turned. "Perhaps this was meant to be something more, but the perpetrators have left?"

Made sense. If the Lady was making a push for Candlekeep and needed extra hands, any petty grudge held against me would fall to the wayside.

"I think she must be scared of us," Ren said with a shrug. "To keep telling her underlings to look out for us."

Another fair take. We hadn't seen the woman since she escaped us on the island, yet she had given fair warning to plenty that I was a danger to their plot. It just made me wonder if she had tabs on us . . . knew if we were ruining her parade back here still. Then again, if her power was based on how many followers she had, then she'd know something was up.

I turned to the bear to see what his take was on this.

"They don't even look like Max. He is more than just a gaudy attention seeker."

With a nod, I decided not to engage that any further. He wasn't wrong, on all accounts, but there was enough bouncing around inside my brain without putting my sense of self into doubt.

Instead, I stepped over to loot the Troll. Part of me expected it to raise from the dead—a trick set up by the necromancer. They weren't that smart, however, and even if they were, I doubted that we would have much issue. I paused briefly in thinking of what evils I could get up to if I was on the wrong side. I'd best not put that out into the world lest it was something that came into being.

I was only the wrong kind of murder away from being as bad as the Shadow.

[342 Gold]
[Bandages (4)]
[Unlucky Maul]
[Note]

"Hmm." I stood and unfurled the page. "They left me a note."

"Some baseless threats that will go nowhere?" Ren rolled her eyes.

I shook my head. "Well, threats are a given. I'm not sure how they anticipated me coming this way. Seems like wasted effort, if you ask me." I caught their glares in wanting me to get to the point. "It's actually a notice to offer me help, should I remove the necromancer's group."

Ren and Quinn exchanged a glance. "Does it say who from?" the elf asked.

"It's signed by . . . the Eternal Wardens."

The fencer grunted. "Such a false name if they require our action to do anything."

I found myself agreeing with him. While more proactive allies sounded good on the surface, the requirement that we got our hands dirty before they'd lend aid soured any anticipation I had held. They could be apathetic like the camp-ground groups. Or something worse.

However, it seemed as though it was neither a trap nor an attempt to scare me away. It was, in fact, a beacon. A way for me to get information without the newfangled Chat system. That could only mean my exploits had been found out by others . . .

That meant I had some manner of *fame* brewing.

I grinned as Quinn led us away from the field and to the small village beside it. The murdering side of me had been getting too much attention lately, but the showman part was starving for something greater. The only thing better than a wanted poster drawn by your enemies was a wanted poster drawn by your allies.

In fact, other than Ren prodding me to make sure I was fine every so often, I survived on these fumes of elation throughout the whole process of the Quest that Quinn dragged us through. It was perhaps one of the most boring things I had suffered through in my entire life.

Talk to this person. Move objects between other people. More talking.

Zero combat, and I gave up trying to impress the Villagers before even arriving. I tried to speed through any dialogue options, only to be chastised by Quinn for missing out on some exposition that was important for answering a question further down the chain.

Ren made mention that killing Wildfolk all day might have been just as useful, given that we'd also get power tokens. I agreed, but I didn't want to linger around the same area for too long. We could be found, and the experience would start to be a poor use of our time. The Dungeon after this Quest would also give us a level, and then we could think about power again.

Of course, I was more eager to put the necromancer in a grave. Killing Players didn't seem too difficult, whatever level they were, as long as you struck first and in an important part of their physical body. In saying that, it wouldn't hurt to have a couple of extra tools in our arsenal before going in on the offensive. Options gave us lifelines.

Just two more parts of the Quest—Quinn was eager to encourage me—as I held out a screwdriver as if it was a fouled diaper. Didn't want to accidentally steal one of the important Quest items. A little danger-free leveling wasn't the worst thing, on reflection. Sure, my ankle pain flared up a little from all the walking, and Ren looked sour about the whole experience . . . and Wolf grumbled throughout, but we did it without any harm.

In fact, a wave of relief passed over me as the final turn-in was done, and a beautiful golden glow illuminated my STAR.

[**Level up—<11>**]
[**Stats increased**]
[**New Ability: <Demon Cannon>**]
[**New Passive: <Stage Help>**]
[**New Passive: <Quick Dealer>**]

Ren was just behind me on the last part of the Quest, while Wolf was a few back. Plenty of time for me to go over the Abilities the System had granted me, unless I had to step in to stop him from eating an NPC again.

<Stage Help> was thematically amusing. For every 5 percent Health I was missing, my Party would gain a 2 percent Damage buff. I assumed the intention was that if I were floundering up on stage, those waiting in the wings could prop me up with some enthusiasm. Or violence. I could already force myself to drop 15 percent Health using <Bloodletting>, assuming I didn't let Ren know. That would be a good way to get a small Damage boost.

Not content enough with just empowering my cards past the limit that was usually possible, <Quick Dealer> increased the maximum velocity of them by 10 percent. Not a huge amount, but most Passives seemed to sit contently in the neat-bonus range. Very few were game-changing, but they all added up to increase my capabilities.

I left the active Ability until last. Partly because it was becoming tradition, and partly because that's the order the System delivered them to me. The third reason was that the name gave me the chills. I almost wanted to check around to make sure nobody was watching my screens—even though they couldn't.

The System had granted me a new summon. A literal cannon that was somehow demonic. Without trying it out, I imagined it had little horns on it . . . either near the front or the back—I couldn't decide. Once summoned, I could use it to either fire something from my Inventory if I was nearby or just a blank confetti shot at any range. The confetti shot would Dazzle enemies, but either way, I could only fire three times and after the three shots, the cannon would return to . . . cannon hell.

Perhaps the longest description box yet, it notified me that it was stationary but could be rotated in a full circle. Having this for the fort would have been useful . . . I only had to be within line of sight to fire it but beside it to load it with something from my Inventory. Of course, with <Demonic Transposition> I could have the bird sit on it and—

"You okay there, Max?" Ren disrupted my thoughts. "You're staring off at the horizon and smiling."

"That's because our distant future has great things in it." I grinned wider as I waited for her inevitable disdain.

"Our future *together*?" she asked with a poker face that could win awards.

I held her gaze for a couple of seconds, suddenly feeling like I needed to wait for nightfall to say what was on my mind. "If you play your cards right," I eventually managed to eke out.

There was a slight twitch in one eye, but she maintained composure, only giving a brief nod in response to end that part of the conversation. "System give you any bullshit?"

"Yeah." I clicked my fingers as if I was about to show it off, but I didn't want to just yet. "Some ranged support and minor Passives. How about you?"

"A healing ward, increases to my shield's defense, and armor piercing of my arrows." She shrugged and turned to watch Quinn try to convince Wolf to hurry up for the last part of the Quest.

There were no decent rewards from the chain, aside from the experience. I had grabbed plenty of random things going around the village, which the occupants didn't seem to mind. More tools at my disposal were always better than some loose change and chance boxes.

Still, I was getting itchy. Not just because of the lack of action in the last few hours . . . there was something bigger afoot. Like static in the air, I could feel it tingle the small hairs at the back of my neck. I often had the egotistical notion that I had a purpose in this world. That I was curated to deal with something. To solve a problem. Now it felt closer, but I was still unsure of if it was real or just my fractured mind trying to cope or find solace somewhere here.

"Now you're staring at the horizon, but you look . . . constipated?"

I turned to the elf and deflated. Her neutral expression had the cracks of a smile at the corners of her eyes. "This *Wolf diet* is really no good," I complained.

"What's that about eating me?" The bear himself stepped up beside us, a tired scowl across his face. "I will literally raze this village to the ground if I have to maintain another droll conversation."

We both looked over to Quinn, who appeared to have had much worse threats leveled at him during the waning stages of the bear completing the Quest.

"Alright to take a break for food, Quinn?" As much as I wanted to keep pushing forward, it wouldn't do to go without sustenance. The village seemed like as safe a place as any.

"Certainly, Max." He gave me a nod and regained his composure. "I have a Skill that can put down a campfire?"

I nodded eagerly. While the day was still too young to enjoy the warmth of it, there was something naturally comforting about sitting around the fire. I had far too many chairs in my Inventory; it took me a second to find my favorite, while Quinn picked a clear area to set it down without inadvertently damaging anything.

"You have a lot of utility Skills, Quinn," Ren noted.

"Ah, yes." He looked up from her from where he was knelt down. "Much like how Max has different demons he can summon from the same Skill, part of my Class has useful survival skills."

That seemed reasonable. Although <Summon Demon> was an active Ability, the System had given me the demonic bird as a Passive. I assumed that was how the Classes that had crafting Skills worked. A mix of combat ability and functional utility. Quinn had told us he was an Arcane Fencer, but perhaps that was a fib and he was something more mundane.

I narrowed my eyes as my brain tried to slide parts of the jigsaw puzzle together. The Abilities and the accent, there was a familiarity there that I—

"Hey, Max." Ren moved her chair next to mine rather than arrange so we'd be equally around the fire. "Want to run through a few introduction tricks with me?"

She turned in her seat to face me, and I furrowed my brow. Hand out, I removed her hat to inspect for damage. "Perhaps your head is even more fragile than mine."

"Ass. I'm being serious." Her hand went up, and she pushed her hat back on. "Against the zombies, it was fine because they were slow and unresponsive. Against a real audience, we need to be snappier."

I agreed. "Trouble is introductions are generally long-winded to build up to the reveal of what a star I am. I've always been a fan of 'now perish,' however."

"Oh, like a one-liner? Hmm." Her head tilted in thought.

No greater bravado than a good one-liner before thrashing someone. I'd even used a couple in my time in this world—although I couldn't remember a single one of them. Perhaps it was better that way, rather than to force a catchphrase.

Just as I was about to float some ideas, Wolf shuffled up from where he was lying, his snout sniffing at the air.

"Footsteps approaching," he growled. "From the north."

CHAPTER THIRTY-ONE

A Good Deed

Nothing soured a mood quite like uninvited guests.

As soon as Wolf had made mention of impending visitors, we were all to our feet with weapons drawn. I maxed out the card I was holding and found it interesting that I could see the icons above the rest of the Party to signify that they had the new Damage buff from my drained Health.

A few moments later, and even I could hear the movements and low voices of those approaching. It would have been a good idea for us to get into some manner of cover or defensive position rather than standing like statues around the small campfire, but we had not. There was something about the voices that was off . . . Nothing bad—but yes, that was it. *Nothing bad.*

Ren's arrow now fully primed and ready. My hand relaxed a little. Not enough to dispel my card that still itched to be released.

Around the corner of a house stepped three figures.

Immediately, I recognized them—the other Party who had left the campground the day before. But not all five of them. No crimson handprints on their foreheads.

"Halt lest you perish where you stand," I said, wanting to get ahead of proceedings.

To their credit, they paused, surprise on their faces. The emotion pushing away what looked like stress and grief. It was the woman with red skin and amber robes, the burly man in black-leather armor, and the dwarf with a comically large white beard.

"We're friendly." The woman spoke first, raising her empty hands into the air. "You're not with the Crimson Shadow, are you?"

Ren shot a glance toward me, her bowstring relaxing slightly but waiting for me to take the lead.

"No, we are not. You left the campground yesterday—why?"

They were on edge. Something had been weighing on them, and they seemed uncomfortable being put under duress. Eventually the woman spoke again.

"We wanted to level up. Fiona kept telling us it would be too dangerous but . . . Well, maybe we should have listened." Her eyes went to the floor, emotion filling her up.

"You don't know what happened at the camp last night then?" Ren asked.

They turned to her, confusion on their faces. Too good to be putting on an act—and I should know about that sort of thing.

I sighed and dispelled my card. "Come, take a seat and we'll get you up to date. Just be warned . . . Any funny business and you're dead."

Despite not looking like they appreciated threats, they did as I asked. Slowly getting out their own chairs, they sat down as a trio on the other side of the fire from the rest of us. Naturally, they looked pensive, but I couldn't exactly blame them. I wouldn't take so easily to threats on my life. We told them about the zombie attack, the fallen party, and Fiona going back to the first area. They reacted with shock and sadness, and at the end, they were genuinely crestfallen.

The woman introduced herself as Leyla. "It seems nothing but turmoil drenches this land. We are just returning from . . . Two of our Party have been captured."

"Captured," I asked, "not killed?"

She shook her head and looked at the other two. "We can still send them Chat messages, which means they are alive. But they don't respond."

I opened up my Map as she spoke. We weren't near where the necromancer's group was meant to be.

Quinn crossed his arms. "And you couldn't get them back, even at the cost of your own lives?"

"They're being held in a fort," the dwarf, named Urist, said. "It was supposed to be a System-created place, but Crimson assholes have done something to it."

"Corrupted the guards there, made it their own," the man said, a wide-eyed stare not really focused on anything. His name was Yuri, and he seemed to have taken the whole event harder than the other two.

If anything, it caused a thrumming in my head. I was too far gone to play hero . . . but erasing the gang was my calling. Farther from the Dungeon and supposed easy level up. Yet, the System had just given me a *cannon*. How fortuitous that a fortress needed assailing now. Too convenient.

"What was your plan now then?" I asked the question to slightly delay the inevitable—that I'd have to ask my troupe what they wanted to do.

Leyla exhaled. "We hoped to go the easier route near the coast back to town and rouse up some help from the camp."

I managed to stop myself from laughing. "Really? Perhaps you fell into luck by running into us instead." My jaw worked as I raised an eyebrow in question to my fellow Party members.

Wolf shrugged, content enough to get to fight and chew through things. Quinn gave me a nod, a valiant quest if ever there was one, something up his street. Ren was apprehensive and took a moment to consider it before giving me the nod too.

I turned to the gathered three and gave a soft smile. "We will help you reclaim your friends. Send me the location, but we need to eat before we go." Wasn't about to die on an empty stomach, and Wolf might actually eat *me* if we didn't start shoveling food into him. He'd been very patient.

Although the gathered three didn't seem supercomfortable sitting idle while we ate, when their alternative was going to be being turned away by Fiona, a handful of minutes wasn't the end of the world. Might be the end of their friends' lives, but if it was at that stage, then we couldn't really be blamed.

"You want coffee, Max?" Ren withdrew the kettle into her hand, not even needing to wait for my response.

"Please," I replied as she was already hanging it over the campfire.

"Quinn?"

He shook his head. "My thanks, but I will have to decline."

I narrowed my eyes slightly at him. Not that avoiding caffeine was a particularly heinous crime—not until I became king—but he seemed cagey around our new associates. Whether that was just pragmatic caution or he sensed something untoward, I didn't know. In fact . . . I wanted to find out.

[Max: Getting a bad feeling?]

I watched as his eye went to his intangible screen, then to me, before back to the screen. Although they couldn't hear the notification, if they had their wits about them, he probably made it obvious what we were doing.

[Quinn: just caution^]
[Quinn: we've had a lot of . . . eventful meetings lately^]
[Max: Agreed.]

As much as I wanted to ask him why he ended his sentences with an up arrow, I decided it was more fun not knowing. Wasn't even going to make a guess at it—and it was just the two lines, so might not even be a trend.

He was also right, comparatively. He had spent some time hiding away before being kidnapped, and then it was all downhill from there. Fighting against zombies and Players alike, and now the prospect of taking down a fortress just for some people we barely had a passing acquaintance with.

Almost talked myself out of it there.

Certainly, with the campground group now in shambles, things looked pretty dry here. If not us, then who else? There must be plenty of other Parties that hadn't been corrupted, but we just hadn't met them yet. Would they be useful to our cause? I sure hoped so.

I turned in my seat to face the patient trio. "Roughly what kind of Classes are you three?"

"Ice Wizard," the woman said, despite being red and orange all over.

The man was a type of Thief, and the dwarf was a Cleric. Their Class composition gave me some things to think over once we got moving, but all of that was drowned out by a question I just couldn't shake from my brain.

What could I fire out of my cannon?

Ren stood before me and handed over the steaming mug. "Everything okay, trickster? You look . . . antsy?"

"Yeah." I nodded. "I just have this big cannon, and I don't want to get it out in front of anyone just yet."

She paused to stare blankly at me for a couple of seconds before sitting down on her own chair. It wasn't that I was shy, of course, but it would take some luster out of the surprise if everyone got to see it in action before I was ready to use it. I furrowed my brow at my coffee while my mind clicked around.

Atmosphere around the camp was tense and quiet. We ate, which was nice. I felt reinvigorated after such an odd morning and fueled for what was probably going to be an even odder afternoon. Everything was packed away in short order, and we gathered to set off.

"So what can you tell us about the fort, Leyla?" I asked.

"It's a reasonably tall stone outpost, probably used during a time the Crown was at war?" She pulled a face. "Or designed to look that way."

"Three floors? Square shape?"

"Square, sure. Raised with a short staircase up to the entrance door. Four floors, if you include the top battlements. And there's a ten-or-so-foot wall that goes around the area—squarish as well."

I nodded. "And all the System-created there are now hostile to any non-Shadow?"

"Yeah."

Ren beside me, we exchanged a glance. The ramshackle building defending the bridge was easy enough to assail due to it being flammable. I could drop myself atop the battlements of the stone fortress, but it probably wouldn't give me much advantage—unless the Player controlling it happened to be standing at the apex unguarded.

Given how brainless many of them seemed to be, that was likely.

I had nothing in my Inventory with the right shape or density to be a cannonball stand-in. The question would be how the cannon decided to engage with real-world physics and if I could fire smaller objects without losing most of the force from the . . . demonic gunpowder? I supposed that if it worked in *demon* ways, then it should let me.

So eager I was to try.

"Can't break through stone walls," Wolf grumbled from ahead of us.

"They have a gate?" I asked.

"No, just an opening in the walls near the front. It's guarded by plenty of System-created, however." Leyla sighed.

Ren rubbed at her forehead. "Enough to be a problem?"

"Not on their own," she replied. "A good team could slowly work through them. It's the addition of the Players that makes it impossible."

It wouldn't be fair to say that the System-created were two-dimensional . . . although fairness didn't really come into it given what they were. But they *were* basic. You'd could almost guarantee what path they'd choose or how they'd react to you. Being smart and patient could get you through any such problem. Players were not only a lot more powerful but had the advantage of fully functional minds—even if they didn't use them.

"We were fighting through, thinking it was just a normal Quest, up until we got inside the main fort building." The dwarf spoke up. "Some manner of blast sent us back out the door as the other two were caught up by a trap."

"Then a barrier went over the door, and we couldn't get back through," Leyla added.

The Crimson hadn't killed the pair; they were sure of it. So what purpose did they have for keeping them alive? At first, converting them forcibly sounded like the most obvious answer—but so far we were pretty sure that everyone had willingly joined up at first. If not that, then what? Ransom? Something much fouler?

Either way, it soured my mood. Pleasant weather and pleasanter company excluded. I felt worn thin. While having the good times made up for the bad, moving back and forth had me tired of the process.

The truth was I wanted to wage a war.

Pick the land clean of the Lady's influence without rest or remorse. Just keep at it until it was done. Then whatever ruins remained could be paradise for all of us. Especially Ren and me.

Trouble was I had learned from past mistakes. The magician burned out on his day job but unable to quit had been buried long ago. Perhaps one of the head injuries had helped things move along, right next to the corrective glares of the elf. Burning out on wanton destruction would be swinging the dial in the opposite direction.

The show must go on, but that just meant abiding by the rules. We needed the downtime between sets and a break from the limelight to work on ourselves. It's what made it survivable in the long term.

Now look at the troupe I had gathered. Oh. *There* was the energy coming back . . . We were about to put on a great show—I could feel it humming through my bones. The four of us, plus some extras, could put everything we'd learned lately into practice.

In no time at all, we'd be *killing* it.

CHAPTER THIRTY-TWO

Blast Radius

I stood, arms folded as I glared forward, and sighed.

Our travels had taken us to the intended destination in no time at all. I didn't care to check the Map to see if it really was a short distance or if my roving thoughts had made it seem as such.

I was mostly just annoyed.

The outpost was just as they'd described. A pathway led from the main road up to it—an opening in the wall guarded by four System-created. Behind them, the courtyard that seemed busy, although I couldn't see most of it. The fort itself rose up, a tower of gray stone blocks and small slit windows.

But the thing that was grinding on my very soul was the *decor*. The Crimson Shadow had made no attempt to daub it with blood or furnish their own banners to replace the pale-blue-and-silver ones that were currently present. Even the guards showed no sign of being corrupted or controlled. Glowing-red eyes would have been nice. Or just a scowl or two.

For all intents and purposes, it looked like a nice, friendly place.

"I can see your apprehension," Leyla said, tilting her head toward me. "That's what caught us off guard too."

"They *are* Crown guard," Ren noted, clearly having read a little more world lore than I had, "but they'll attack first if we get closer, I take it?"

The woman nodded.

Ren grunted and turned her eyes my way. "Plan of action, trickster?"

I smiled. All the possibilities had been blooming around inside my mind like fireworks. Once the brief annoyance of the stage being subpar had abated, an almost giddy excitement had started to bubble deep within. Even the worst stage and props could be fashioned into a dazzling show with enough pizzazz. And I was chock-full. Bursting.

"Yeah," I eventually confirmed. "I have one."

I stopped in the tree cover and removed my hat to fan some of the heat off of my face. Just a little preshow nerves. Placing it back upon my head, I turned my eyes to the elf. While I was clearly tense about the looming performance, she had sharpened. A piercing glare from her bright-blue eyes skewered straight through my chest. Well, slightly to the left.

Her eyebrow raised. "I assume you brought us back here alone for more than just fooling around together?"

My mouth opened and closed, the prospect not even touching my soft brain during the planning phase. The front door just seemed too obvious—we needed to make more of a surprise entrance. So I had dragged her along with me to the back of the fort where—

She pulled on my suit collar and brought me in for a deep kiss.

It might not have been part of my plan, but it seemed to be a workable addition. Ren moved away and smiled, briefly blinding me to anything but her.

"Let's go blow their fucking minds, Max."

Well, I'd have to now, wouldn't I? Wolf would be waiting for our signal. While the road in was too obvious, sometimes you needed to play to the expectations so that when you came along to subvert them, it was more effective. While eyes focused on the group of five, the real tricks were being done out of sight.

We made it to the back wall, the shadow of the fort obscuring our movements. My back against it, I placed down a chair in front of me and then held a plank across my arms. Ren hopped up both to peek over the wall. Face full of her knees, I was surprised at how easily I held her in place. Either I had more strength than the System Stats pretended I had, or maybe elves had hollow bones or something. She stepped back down, knocking my hat forward slightly.

"There's about two dozen guards that I could see, maybe a handful more blocked by the building itself." She tilted her own hat back and blew at her hair.

Chair and plank back into my Inventory for now, I adjusted my hat and pulled a face. "Not too bad. Players must all be inside then."

"Seems that way."

Most likely they would be notified as soon as the guards got into combat—if the sound of fighting alone didn't alert them. I rolled my head back and forth. "No back entrances on the fort?"

She shook her head. "I can already tell you want to drop in on the roof and do some bullshit, but that's too risky here."

Correct on both accounts, but I just nodded in response. Things had worked out in the bridge fort due to most of it being destroyable . . . and a little overconfidence on our part. A solid building with five to seven Players—if they'd converted the captives—sounded like a good way to get trapped and not have the help of the Party.

My eyes cycled through my Inventory, arranging things to the first page of grid boxes for easy access. Never knew what could be used in a show, but I had a good amount of confidence in what was likely. Mostly multipurpose things that were reliable, with a handful of wild cards.

"Alright." I took a deep breath. "Are you ready for the show?"

Ren gave me a bow. "Born ready, trickster."

Everything in order. The crowd quietened down as the lights dimmed. Cool energy flowed through me, mixing in with the explosive adrenaline waiting to escape. Suspense weighed down on me, and I couldn't leave it any longer.

We landed on the inside of the wall together, back-to-back. A bright card of white-hot power left my hand just as an entangling arrow went out in the opposite direction. Before we drew the ire of the whole area, Wolf howled out and burst into the opening from the road, shortly followed by Quinn and the three tagalongs.

My card was out; the full power mixed with the new speed increase was difficult to control at first, but I quickly got used to it. Through three throats before it dissipated. Hellhound+ went out next, an arcane circle appearing on the wall beside a startled guard as the canine leaped out atop him. Next was Roger, emerging from within one of the fallen.

Ren had killed another two behind me and was drawing for a third.

"Roger, Ren, with me," I commanded, striding my way to the main building. Wolf was too big for the door, and I wanted Quinn to pair with him—there weren't many places safer than beside the bear. There was a chance our quarry would try to escape or the fight would spill out of the structure—so having them right there was a win condition.

Sneaking was never a true option, even though I was practically an assassin that could go invisible and teleport. They held too many cards, and we weren't even aware what game we were playing. The only option was to flip the table over.

Up against the main fort on a slightly raised stone walkway, the three of us stepped around to see Wolf mauling through a handful of guards. Quinn darted in toward the wounded, skewering them with his sword before stepping back into the cover of the bear. I could see a pairing building there—a bond to efficiently chew through enemies.

I sent the Hellhound+ away as we rounded the corner to the closed and barred wooden door. It looked thick and designed to be able to take a battering without relenting. The others might be able to be spotted from the windows on the next floor up, but we would be unexpected . . . unless they had some magical form of detection anyway.

From my Inventory, I withdrew Jokkar's mace and handed it over to Roger. He nodded his thanks but knew well enough to keep his mouth shut. Leyla had said that, when they had escaped, a Player had stood up at the top and was using a crossbow to fire down upon them. These sorts of things had a way of repeating themselves.

Into my hands the tin of yellow paint.

An empowered bolt of energy shot down from above, Ren's shield absorbing it as it struck Wolf. That was my cue—time to do some magic.

I switched places with my dove almost directly above me. The breeze jostled my footing as I stood atop the battlements. Possibly the record for the highest peak of my career. It would have been nice to observe my surroundings—see the beauty of the forest and look out to the ocean . . . but other than trying not to fall from this precipice, I had little time to work with the surprised individual.

A man with rusty hair and pale skin, the signature handprint on his forehead. He looked up at me in shock, suddenly seeing this purple-clad magician holding a metal tin in his hands. The tin vanished, and then so did I—to be replaced by my dove once more.

Ren raised her eyebrow as if to question my success.

I winked at her and then clicked my fingers. An unnecessary flourish, but it painted the scene, much like the—

From atop the battlements, my cannon rang out. Summoned just behind the man and loaded with the tin, as I had been near enough to facilitate the process. I had only a brief glance at my new weapon, but it didn't appear to have horns. Only a slight purple sheen to the dark-metal body. All eyes turned upward at the noise as the shadowed figure of the man was flung over the lower wall of the upper floor and tumbled down onto the solid ground with a hard splat.

Yellow paint pattered around him as the remnants of the can bounced across the stone. Sure, it didn't get us into the door, but . . .

I stepped in front of it, my brow furrowed. Bird and cannon unsummoned. Wolf might be able to break in, but they would be expecting that. Roger could maybe do the same with the large mace, but that would be a slower process that they'd for sure take advantage of.

Something blipped inside my head, and I brought up the Chat message.

[Quinn: I can use my skill to open up a new entrance?^]
[Max: Please.]

If his boomerang could open up the safe, it should be able to make a hole in the fort. The trouble I had with the plan was not knowing where the captives were being held. More fool us for not considering the possibility that the Crimson Shadow might have them tied up against the wall we intended to blast through or would even use them as human shields if knowing our plan.

It was designed to resist being breached, of course. Leyla's Party even said there was a barrier that was summoned to keep them out. What this meant was . . .

even blowing through the door—the ones inside were likely still able to keep us from getting in. We'd have to take the risk with Quinn. My initial acceptance was correct.

[Max: At the back if you can.]

From near the entrance still, he gave me a nod, and his hand went to his side pouch. I prodded Roger and gestured for him to go inspect the dead body, hopefully to draw any eyes his way so Quinn's Skill wasn't intercepted. Although, I wasn't sure the demon could loot, so his acceptance of whatever he thought I may have meant was concerning—but a problem we'd cross when we got to it.

Ren was tense, and so was I. Standing outside the front just waiting and trying to not get caught . . . It wasn't how we usually did things. Where was the pizzazz?

From one of the windows above us, a jolt of lightning shot out and struck Roger. He convulsed, the skin across the puppet's neck and face now charred and split to expose redness within. With a scowl up to where his assailant had attacked from, he flipped them the middle finger and growled.

"The fuck is that?" The voice came muffled.

An explosive blast rocked the back of the building, and with a quick nod, Ren and I skirted back in that direction. Looping past the corner, we could see a billowing cloud of powdered rock blowing away from the impact site. Hopefully it made it all the way through and wasn't just superficial damage.

I got to the impact site first and turned to see that there was indeed a hole—not especially large but good enough for us to head into if we ducked. Card out into my hand, I dropped it as <Card Fan> went up to protect me. The blast knocked me back across the debris-strewn path and onto the dirt ground.

Ren was there and fired an arrow off, but it just ricocheted off of a glowing-amber barrier that went up across the wall.

"Trying to sneak up on us, huh?" the voice cackled from inside. "I'd like to see you blast through *this* wall, asshole."

I righted myself back to my feet and brushed the dust from my purple slacks. Would need to clean up shortly. A smile crossed my face. They thought themselves impenetrable and safe—but hunkering down in one place just meant it was easier to surround them. Corner the beast and starve it out.

"The fuck is that?" a second voice from inside yelled out right before the growls of my Hellhound+ vibrated through the space.

"Looks like there's no door between the first and second floor," I noted to the elf. A little practiced precision had my card circling to the side of the building through the slit windows, placing my canine friend on the floor above the two with foul mouths.

From the other side of the courtyard, Wolf roared and thundered toward the barred door. No escape for the Crimson now. We only had to hope that we'd get in there in time before they did something to those being held.

Ren could see that was my line of thought. "Go back to the roof, trickster. We can take the ground floor."

I nodded. She didn't need to say any more than that.

With one last brief bow, I ascended to be the star of the show once more.

CHAPTER THIRTY-THREE

Sandwich

With a rush of air I was once again at the roof of the fort. A spray of yellow paint decorated part of the battlements where the man had been standing previously. To my right, a staircase that led downward.

Using the dove meant that I had to drop my Hellhound+ that had been harassing the occupants of the ground floor. Hopefully he bought enough time for the others to gain some advantage. Away from the light breeze, I walked down the stone steps. A wooden door, slightly ajar, in my way.

I stepped through it after activating <Vanishing Act> on myself. It looked like some manner of sleeping quarters for the System-created. Bunk beds with plain green linens covering them, beige pillows at the end of each. There were also six guards in this room. Swords already drawn but inactive, and an exit door was across from me to lead to the next floor below.

Just before my invisibility faded away, I split two cards out. Eyes turned to me as I strode toward the exit, arterial spray ejecting as my cards darted round their necks, my fanfare. The *magician* had arrived. As their bodies slunk to the floor in near unison, I swiped things from the room on my path to the door.

Two pillows, a small chest, three sheets, a metal helmet, and an empty metal cup.

Not exactly a lion's bounty, but we made do with any prop that came up. Couldn't exactly be picky in a world where—

As my hand went for the door handle, it instead flung open, narrowly avoiding hitting me as it revealed the perpetrator.

A wiry man by all accounts, with a full beard of black. Pale, sickly complexion in contrast to the red handprint that sat over his pale-blue eyes. There was a tiredness to him, alongside an unhealthy amount of potential anger. The two blades he held assisted in painting that picture. This close, I could clearly see the debuff icon over his head. A red square with black handprint within—Unfaltering Faith it was called.

Confusion illuminated him briefly. "You're not Gharra?"

"No." I drew a card and flicked it toward him. That must have been the man on the roof. Odd that they hadn't clocked the body that Roger had been standing by was their friend.

He dodged the card and leaped at me, <Card Fan> coming up to block his attack as I took a few steps backward.

I smiled as I flourished my hands. "You're not the first group of insects hiding away in a nest that I've then burned to the ground." Into my right hand, my newer Spear of Greater Luck.

"Quit talking and die," he growled, a crackling blue energy now covering his blades.

It had been a while since I had fought a good one-on-one battle—it was easy to forget that people were full of Abilities and differing Skills when you could cut their throats from fifty paces. I felt calmer in this situation than I had against the rat with the dark sword or in the fort against the chainsword guy.

This man was much quicker though. Higher level and more experienced. But then again, I wasn't such a slouch myself. Despite putting some of my better tricks on cooldown already, I felt I had enough in me to win out. The others would be relying on me after all, and I couldn't allow any disappointment to mire my performance.

He burst forward, another Skill powering his movement. I threw the spear, although it turned into a pillow as it left my orbit, the weapon returning to my clutches straight after. He batted the object away with one hand, the electricity on that blade fading out. As his other hand came in, my left rose up with the helmet on it. A dull sensation went down my arm as I barely blocked the attack, but now we were face-to-face.

That just meant there was so much of the room he couldn't see.

I was knocked back again, nearing the staircase back to the roof. The warmth of freshly bleeding cuts soaking through my shirt. I didn't appreciate it when my suit got ruined, despite it being a natural part of the day at this point.

My right hand rose up to point at him, a purple card leveled in his direction. Mana and then Health pooled into it, causing it to glow brighter before turning white. He had made the decision to wait with his guard up, sure of himself that he had a Skill that could dodge whatever I was about to throw at him.

"The trouble with the stage," I said softly, "is that it is always so damn hot."

His eyes narrowed right before he was engulfed in flame. My Imp+ back behind the door at the other end gave me a devilish grin and started to charge up another fireball. Shadow flinched, and my card went out.

Waves of energy went over him as he prepared some of his most important defensive Skills—I assumed anyway. But my card did not strike him. Instead, I curved it through the bed frame beside him, causing the top bunk to tilt and eject a dead guard out on top of my opponent.

His defensive auras flickered as he stumbled across the room, pushing the corpse to the floor. A second fireball was almost ready—he found himself in a terrible place between two attackers. Still, he wasn't totally powerless. Two swords of blue electricity appeared above him, and he entered a martial stance with his own two blades up.

"I've never fought someone with four swords before," I cooed. "There's just one problem though . . ." I flourished the spear around, tuning it into the Blade of Shadow before again into my Knife of the Trickster. "You had no chance from the beginning."

With a wink, I used <Shatter>. The Dazzle icons faded away to be replaced by others. Slower movement speed and lower Constitution and Agility.

He could no longer be fooled by my tricks, but they were no longer required. I blazed with purple energy as I darted toward him, drawing his focus just before the second fireball struck him. The smells of charred leather and singed fabric hung heavy in the room as I lunged out with my knife.

I found purchase in a forearm raised to protect himself. His other blade came forward, but I already had a trusty plank of wood in the way to block it. Instead, my left hand jolted out and grabbed him by the throat. <Card Fan> came up as the two ethereal blades jabbed down at my face. We let go of our weapons and wrestled for a bit. It felt as though it went longer than it probably did—mere seconds of trying to overpower each other in the brutal old-fashioned way.

Pain wracked his reddened face as he collided with something metal around waist height. We weren't near the beds though, and he was rightfully uncertain about current proceedings.

Fog suddenly filled the room, obscuring our vision, and I managed to push myself away from his grasp in the brief confusion.

A blast rang out through the room, dulling my hearing as I was sprayed with warm liquid. There was a wet slump as something dropped to the floor, and then comparative silence. Sent the Imp+ away. Sent the cannon away. Stood in the dense gray for a few moments to regain my composure.

Chat dinged me a message.

[Quinn: We are on ground floor^]
[Quinn: Two dead^]
[Quinn: Barrier prevents ascension^]
[Max: Another dead up here, will work my way down.]
[Max: No eyes on hostages.]

I hummed to myself as the fog vanished, and I dropped the spent wand to the floor. It did not clatter, however, which was greatly disappointing, and I was tempted to pick it up for a do-over. It had landed on the top half of the man bisected by the demonic cannon. System really didn't know what it was doing, giving me something that powerful.

From one of the dead guards, I pulled up Roger, drawing him from wherever he was below. Purple eyes rejected the prior occupant's as the skull split, pushing the helmet off of the puppet's head to reveal long ears of glowing energy.

"Boss." He peered around at the carnage. "Looks like you've been doing well."

"Any injuries downstairs?"

Roger shook his head. "The big dog got some bone splinters in his gums, and the new guy looked like he had bitten off more than he could chew too. Is he, like . . ."

"Like what?" I asked, gesturing toward the door and passing him my spear. His mace would have been left downstairs. I dropped a Hellhound+ card behind us.

"Like . . . Is this, like, a harem thing you have going on?"

I paused at the threshold of the doorway and gave him a tired look. I *was* tired. Not built for melee combat, despite ending up in it regularly. Perhaps I could get some training off Quinn when we had some easier days. "*No*, Roger," I said.

He just shrugged in response.

As I didn't really want to encourage him any further, we continued down the stairs as I rolled a bandage around in my left hand. My first use of <Shatter> was reasonable. Not exactly the same flare as <Finale>, but then again, how could you beat the pinnacle of a show? It had slowed him down enough to where I could avoid being stabbed and position him in front of a hastily summoned cannon loaded with a plank of wood. At least I knew now the force wasn't dissipated when used to fire something unusual.

He had left the door open here too, and we stepped through into a room with two figures sitting against the left wall. Bound with hessian sacks over their heads. There were also four guards, which turned toward us, anger in their eyes.

I stepped over to the bound pair while my demons dealt with the filth. A card out, I cut through the ropes restraining their hands and feet. Pulled the hoods off to reveal the faces of the two that matched the descriptions we knew of them. They seemed out of it . . . Drugged, maybe? No handprint debuff, but nothing else to give me a clue either.

[Max: Hostages located. Will clear remaining Crimson.]

No use waiting for the reply. As I stood, I watched my demons finish off the last of the guards. Told the hound to guard the prisoners and Roger to lead to the next floor.

They were trapped now. Desperate, most likely. Holding off the rest of the Party below, they were probably waiting for theirs to come back down the stairs at any moment. Now on the stone steps illuminated by torchlight, I slowed and let Roger get farther ahead. We reached the closed door, and he turned to give me a brief nod before opening. I nodded in return, our final act coming up.

He swung it open before taking a step, immediately becoming impaled by shafts of glowing white light. His puppet body twitched before he slumped over, dead. That was a shame.

I stepped over his spent body with my hands in my pockets. Invisible.

The man at the other side of the room was almost a caricature of an evil wizard. Long graying beard that hung from a peaked hood, robes a dark black with red skulls emblazoned up the sides. A wild mania in his eyes, panic mixed with fury. Signature handprint. One hand held up the barrier over the door beside him, the other outstretched toward me, anticipating me following in Roger's footsteps.

He seemed almost eager for me to do the inevitable, and my strides took me across the room in a couple of seconds.

Click, on the outstretched wrist. The barrier immediately dropped. My invisibility dropped. Nullifying cuff prevented his active Skills from working.

Confusion twisted at his face as the hand turned to me, attempting to cast a spell.

"Show's over, sir," I said softly. "It's time to go home now."

Against better judgment, I gave him a swift headbutt, knocking him both to the floor and unconscious.

The held door swung open, Quinn and Ren there with weapons readied, before seeing it was just yours truly standing alone. They filtered in to allow Leyla's group to follow suit.

"Next floor up," I said, and they rushed past with little word.

Part of me had expected worse. To find the bodies dissected or used in some weird ritual. Something ten times as macabre as this. Perhaps I shouldn't wish ill or assume the worst. Not everything had to be dark and miserable.

As if hearing my thoughts, Ren came up and cupped the side of my face with her hand. "Report, trickster."

"Some minor injury. Mentally I am fine. This one here is still alive." I shuffled my boot to gently kick the prone wizard.

"Your eyes seem normal." She removed her hand and gave me a pat on the chest before her warm heal sank through me. No real discomfort, which was nice.

"I will keep Wolf company, if things are safe here," Quinn suggested, not needing to say that the large bear had issue with coming up the stairs.

I sighed as he departed and removed my hat. "Not bad for a rescue mission."

"You almost sound disappointed, Max."

With a smile, I affixed my hat and stood tall. "Far from it, Ren. Sometimes you need an easy crowd to get some practice in."

She rolled her eyes and gestured to our captive. "I don't know why you want us to struggle, but let's get this one out front ready for questioning."

"Dibs on bad cop."

"Fuck you, Max. *Fine.*"

My eyes searched around the room as we knelt to grab onto the figure. Not for valuable loot. Not even for clues. Not even for the extra props I could use.

I searched for a way to end this all. For us to stop repeating the same death and destruction wherever we went. As we hoisted the wizard up, the answer seemed the same as it had always been.

Find and kill the Lady.

CHAPTER THIRTY-FOUR

Best Cop

I crouched down near the wizard where he had been propped up against the stone wall. The courtyard had been completely cleared of any roving guards, and the other Party were currently trying to help their rescued others down the stairs.

A shadow crossed me, and I looked up to see the elf standing with her arms crossed. "It's not good for the brain to be knocked out for this long, is it?"

She shrugged. "Not sure he was using it anyway."

A fair point, but even so, I wouldn't want to be on the receiving end of such trauma. "Perhaps I should stop hitting people with my head."

"It is rather unbecoming," Quinn added from the side, a neutral expression on his face.

Part of me wanted to apologize to him for that, again. He had earned it and gotten what he deserved, however. Would ruin the lesson to make amends more than we already had. He was right about it being unbecoming. I was a *magician*, not a tavern brawler.

We turned as Leyla and the others came down and out of the fort, into the light. They all looked tired and relieved. She stepped over to us while the others jostled their dizzied friends toward the road out of here.

"I honestly can't thank you all enough . . . If we hadn't been able to rescue them today . . ." She looked back at them. "Well, this was probably our only chance."

I smiled and stood up to talk to her more politely. "It was a pleasure. We can always be counted on to fight against the Crimson Shadow."

"Even so, I'm not sure how we can repay you." Her brow furrowed.

"Contact details would be a start." I gestured my head toward the fort. "One day we might call on your aid in return."

"That is acceptable." Leyla smiled and sent her contact information over. "We will be staying south of here, probably go to the town until we're recovered before leveling again."

I was glad they weren't turning tail and running back to the first area. While it was unfair of me to look down on Fiona and her group after all they'd been through, I still did. Leyla and her Party might be a few rungs lower than us, no matter their level, but if things started to become more than a five-person job, it would be handy to have others to call on for assistance. A little army.

Not that we were even five people, of course.

We shook hands, and she gave regards to the rest of the troupe. Smiles and nods until they were out of sight, back onto the road.

"That wasn't so bad," Ren said before deflating. "Killed a few people, made some tentative allies. Have a captive for questioning."

"We ought to search the fort for information," I said, mimicking her expression. "They adore writing things down. Plus, looting the bad guys."

"Thought you almost forgot." She looked down at the Wizard before back at the stone structure. "Let's get this one sorted out first, then we'll do things as quickly as we can. Getting to the Dungeon today would be nice."

Quinn squinted his eye up to the sky. "Assuming there are no other distractions, it should not be an issue."

"Perfect." I cycled through my Inventory until I found a bottle of water. Popping off the cork, I emptied it onto the Wizard. It just made him wet and soaked into his robes. "Huh, I was led to believe that sort of thing worked."

"Maybe if I start chewing on him?" Wolf offered, only one of his eyes open lazily, as a nap threatened to take him out of the investigation.

I shook my head. As much as that would be an easier option, these had been some of the least effective of the gang that we had come up against so far. Seemed unfair to punish them further. Well, they were mostly dead now, so perhaps that thought should have come a lot sooner.

Ren shifted beside me and kicked the man in the shin.

He stirred, his brow furrowed as he tried to get a hold of his senses.

"Didn't actually think that would work," she murmured before getting ready to put on the good-cop act.

I was already in the mindset, and I crouched down in front of the Wizard, grabbing him by the collar of his damp robes and pulling his face closer to mine. "Wakey, wakey, fucker. Time for us to have a talk."

"*Max!*" the elf complained. "Give him a chance first. He might cooperate."

"The only thing he needs to do is stay alive while I get the information out of him." My body temperature dropped, and I felt my eyes begin to glow. "You can do that, right? You prefer fingers or toes?"

"Fingers," Wolf said with his eyes closed.

"Wha—?" The wizard looked confused, still trying to put the puzzle pieces together.

"Here, let me try first." Ren gently pushed me away, so I'd let go of our captive. "We just want to know what you were up to here."

"H-holding strategic locations," he murmured, unable to make eye contact with the elf.

"Oh, that's good!" Her bright eyes tried to search for his avoidant gaze, seeing where his weakness was. "The Lady having you guard her progress as she marches on Candlekeep?"

He nodded but tried to lean away from her, as if her eager stare was melting him. It was amusing to watch—as the good-cop routine was seemingly uncomfortable enough for him to open up about the details yet dislike the process.

Ren leaned in closer to him as he near flattened himself sidewards on the floor.

"Anything more you can tell me?" she purred. "What were you going to do with your captives?"

"C-convert them forcibly," he murmured, his own eyes closed now.

"By making them drink her blood?" I asked.

No response.

"I bet you were waiting on the extra supplies, huh?" Ren pouted, despite him no longer looking at her.

He nodded and grunted.

We could really do with finding out how she managed to transport so much blood, never mind how she came up with the stuff. It seemed unlikely it was literally from her body given the amount she would have to lose for everyone to get a regular sip. If we could disrupt the supply chain, then we'd potentially starve out the rest of the corrupted groups here. I quickly sent that message over to Ren and watched as her eyes unfocused to read it before she again looked at the Wizard.

"Just one more question—you've done so well!" She almost smiled. "Whom or where do you get your deliveries from?"

He was silent for a moment, squirming as if he wanted to work his way away from her and the pointed question. "Can't say."

I held my tongue. While I did enjoy being bad cop and leveling threats, Ren pretty much had this in the bag, and any attempt I made at stealing the limelight would just dampen what she was achieving. The greater show was better than my own accolades. *How I'd grown.* The rest of us might as well be invisible with how much presence the elf held over our prisoner.

"Can't or won't?"

A little more squirming, and he sighed deeply. "Won't. They'll kill me."

Ren rolled her eyes before returning to the act. "We could keep you safe. We're much more powerful than any of her Parties."

The Wizard sucked at his teeth. It was undeniable that we were strong, having taken over their fort with little damage of our own aside from a dead Roger and the few cuts I had amassed. It was clearly a sticking point that he wanted safety. Perhaps with us, he could have it.

"We have space in the Party," Ren continued. "We were all enemies or disliked one another at the start but have grown to be a strong team. You could be just what we need."

I pulled a face. We were all fast friends immediately, as far as my brain could remember. Sure, Wolf wanted to eat us, and Quinn was potentially something greater than an annoyance . . . Ren had even been a little harsh on me at the start . . . I forgot where I was going with this. Plus, she was putting on an *act*—I shouldn't forget that.

His eyes opened, but he was still unable to look at her. Not her face anyway. I narrowed my own eyes at him.

"R-really?"

"You have to give up that information first." She held a finger up and wagged it. "We need to trust you, right? I *want* to trust you."

The Wizard licked his dry lips. Panic still in his eyes, but some exhaustion weighing in there from stress. He looked between me and the elf a few times. I remained neutral, not wanting to push him back into his shell.

"There's a group of three. They're fast. I'll . . . I can send you over their route information?"

"You could? Wow!" Ren's eyebrows went up, clearly impressed with how far he was willing to go. Her eyes unfocused as she looked at her Map. "That's . . . amazing—oh, we didn't get your name? Mine's Ren."

"Thallen," he said, nodding energetically at the deal almost being completed.

"Well then." She smiled, illuminating the area . . . or perhaps that was just my heart. "Welcome aboard, Thallen."

She extended her hand out to lift him to his feet. He accepted, still some awkwardness in making physical contact with the elf. Ren stood and helped him up with her left hand. Her right hand came up quicker, burying a dagger in his neck.

Pain and confusion went over his face before he dropped to the ground, a river of red darkening through his robes as they soaked up his blood.

"Ugh," she said, stowing the knife away. "Next time, you're the good cop."

"Sure," I replied, a smile on my face as I looted his body. Mostly because I was recalling her smile, but deep down, I respected the violence. Probably an unhealthy thought to have, actually.

Quinn shuffled awkwardly. "Every hour that passes, I thank your graces that I only walked away from my folly with a broken nose."

Ren shrugged. "You're not evil, Quinn. Just a dumbass. You'll note the only people we kill are the Crimson Shadow."

I nodded as I brought up the Wizard's loot.

[605 Gold]
[Intellect Mittens: +4 INT]
[Mana-Expert Ring: +15% Mana, +15% Mana regeneration]
[Clasp of Regret: +10% magic Damage, –10% physical Damage]

The rest was surprisingly worse than what I had—or at least the Stat distribution wasn't optimal for my build. Ah, who had I become? With a sigh, I stood and dusted myself off. Would need to repair my suit when I had fewer eyes on me.

"Let's get this fort searched through then." Ren gave me a prod. "Wolf and Quinn take the bottom floor and keep watch. Trickster, you're with me."

I gave her a bow in response, and the other two grunted their acknowledgments. It wasn't our fault that Wolf couldn't make it up the stairs, so as far as making this go as quickly as possible, the split made sense.

It was actually nice to step into the shaded area of the bottom floor, out of the light of the day. Something about being constantly in and out of combat made even a middling day seem humid. Plus, wearing a suit all the while didn't help.

"Start from the top and work our way down," Ren instructed me, to which I nodded. Pragmatic.

I led the way up the steps, past the dead bodies and furniture strewn about, our eyes glancing around for any obvious things to make a second pass over on our return. Eventually, for my thankful legs, we made it to the top, where the bunk beds were in the guard barracks.

"You really made a mess up here, huh?" Ren tilted her head at the group of corpses, blood painting half the room, and the Crimson I had split in half with the cannon.

"I guess I do what needs to be done." I gave her a sheepish smile but then was caught off guard by the intense glare she was giving me.

She took hold of my shirt in her grip and pulled me over to one of the beds.

"Yeah you do," she said.

CHAPTER THIRTY-FIVE

Grand Display

One might assume that being surrounded by bloody corpses wouldn't set the right atmosphere for acts of passion. However, it turned out that everything became background noise under the right circumstance, and whatever feral mood had overtaken us both seemed to be just that. A surprise, especially during the daytime, but clearly something we both needed.

I crouched down beside the dead bodies to loot them, in my underwear, while the System repaired my suit. *Convenient.* In my peripheral, I caught the bemused look of the elf, watching me in my state of undress as she tied her hair back up.

"Even though it's becoming easy to see past the scars and grime, I would *literally* kill for a hot bath."

I nodded. It was a wonder I wasn't dehydrated with all the sweating I'd been doing today. It must be near lunchtime now—we'd certainly earned it. I was sure we could press Quinn into having a detour to somewhere with a bath or shower.

My suit completed and popped back into existence. Comforting even if a little stifling this time of the day. I stood and turned around as Ren had moved over to me.

A tight embrace. She pressed the side of her head against my shoulder as my arms also wrapped around her.

"You do weird things to me, Max."

I rested my head against hers and caught her falling hat as I jostled it away. "Ah, I don't know. That was pretty vanilla."

"Asshole." She sighed and gave me a squeeze. "You know I meant emotionally."

Of course I did, but some levity gave her an out in case this was heavier than she wanted. There was no need to clarify. We just held each other for a moment or two in silence. A brief respite from the hardships of the world, and a place of safety for our hearts.

"Let's get back to it, moonflower." I moved back away and gave her forehead a peck before replacing her hat. "They'll start suspecting something, if they don't already."

She gave me a coy smile as she turned to go loot the rest of the bodies.

Strange how life seemed to be taking me on a downward spiral, yet I felt far above it. On cloud nine. I stole a glance at her while pretending to look through the top half of the man I had bisected. There was no denying I was besotted with her. The pointy ears were cute, but I hardly registered that she was an *elf*. She was just Ren, unlike anyone I had ever met before. And we were changing into ever-better versions of ourselves that I couldn't help but love.

Those words found purchase on my tongue as I watched her, apprehensive and ready to burst forth.

Before I willed up the strength to, a beep signaled a Chat message had just come through.

[Quinn: All okay up there?^]
[Quinn: Nothing much down here. Wolf just sleeping^]
[Max: Working our way, ASAP.]
[Max: Set a destination for somewhere we can eat and refresh?]
[Quinn: As you command^]

It wasn't really a command, so now I started to wonder if I was too controlling over the Party.

"Am I too bossy with everyone, Ren?"

She looked over and shook her head. "If anything, you need to ramp up that assertiveness. Maybe tussle with Wolf and put him in his place."

I stared at her blankly for a few moments, trying to see how much of that was just her egging me on. I knew she had a spark for Max the Leader, but she didn't really want me to wrestle the bear for dominance. Well, in saying that . . .

She sighed. "No, trickster, you're fine. You're our headliner and dictate the show—it's good to have one clear idea rather than everyone pulling in different directions."

I pouted, mostly because it was sweet when she used show terms with me. Unnecessary, but appreciated—she truly had been putting more effort into the performance side of things.

We finished up the looting with little fanfare. A couple of things for Wolf potentially, but not much else. Down the stairs and we sifted through things double time so as not to keep the fencer waiting. Again, very few things useful to us other than some potential props for my ever-growing collection. There was, however, a diary. Or at least a collection of notes wedged together.

I read through them as we stepped out back down to the ground floor. Wolf was blocking the doorway, sleeping, while Quinn had his feet up on a crate while he leaned back in a chair.

"Anything good?" he asked, eyebrow raised at what I was reading.

"Potentially," I murmured. "Let's walk while I finish reading. I'd rather not have the guards respawn on us."

He nodded and stood up from his seated position. "There's a place that might accommodate us about twenty minutes southwest."

"Perfect, I appreciate it." I gave him a warm smile. Possibly odd after killing so many in cold blood.

At the doorway, he nudged the bear. "Move it, furball."

Wolf grunted and shifted himself out of the way, having a big stretch as soon as enough space had been made for us to filter out.

Ren rubbed at her eyes as the daylight scoured us once more. "So we know the location of the necromancer group, a group intending on meeting the Paladin's Party tomorrow, and the route the blood deliverers take."

"My brother was in the military," Quinn began, "and he would often say going after supply lines was the way to win a protracted conflict."

That sounded reasonable to me. As little experience as I had on the matter, I could see the benefit of delaying all blood to any Shadow in this area. Even more so than outright killing one of the other two groups, although the necromancer owed me his head for disrupting my sleep the other day.

"Disrupting their blood deliveries would weaken the whole lot of them," I eventually agreed. "Might make fighting the groups easier on us. Send me the route, Ren."

She nodded and did so, and I lowered the pages held so that I could bring up my Map. No surprise they were avoiding the main road. Even as overconfident and foolhardy as they seemed to be, getting caught out on the singular wide road that bisected the area diagonally would be on a different level of nearsightedness.

It weaved back and forth, almost parallel to the road, and mostly on the northern side of it, aside from a couple of places.

"What do you think, Max?" Ren asked.

I could tell she was prompting me to lead again. At this stage, I was happy to play the role she wanted me to fit in—in fact, I was growing to enjoy it. As much as we were a team, I was the sparkling idiot that was pulling them forward to eventually get at the Lady. In saying that, however . . .

"We'll rest up. Get some lunch and, hopefully, a bath. Maybe some downtime? Hit the Dungeon in the evening and then make plans for intercepting the courier in the morning." I tilted my head toward the fencer. "Quinn wanted to show us through the Quests today and the Dungeon—we can avail him of his duties tomorrow."

He pulled a face, unsure how to react to that. Sure, he had lent his help in bringing down the fort to rescue those other Players, but I wanted him to know he still had an out before things got dire again. I wouldn't even hold it against him.

There was an amount of . . . killing that the Party had grown into. Just straight-up murder that made me realize we weren't exactly the *good* guys. Quinn was just an asshole, like everyone else. A fool who acted on his heart's whim. The rest of us were . . . just like the Crimson Shadow, but opposite.

I hadn't even made note of how easily and without care Ren had killed the Wizard, partly because I would have done the exact same thing. We were the enemy of the enemy, but it didn't mean we were palatable for those on the side-lines. Leyla's group hadn't minded because we'd saved their lives. Fiona hadn't trusted us, even after we'd proved dependable. We were just good at one thing . . . Well—I glanced over at the elf—*two things*.

"Not going to finish your reading, trickster?" she asked, her face a scowl, but only put on for appearances. We didn't want to become insufferable to the others as our mush gradually seeped out into the daylight.

"Just giving my eyes a rest," I lied. "It's been a long day, and I've seen a lot of things that need processing."

She rolled her eyes in response and looked ahead, walking a little faster to sidle alongside the bear.

Quinn fell into step beside me, some amount of anxiety or troubles written clearly on his face. With a hand up to stroke his beard, he turned his eye toward me.

"I have not yet decided when we will part ways, Max."

With a smile, I nodded. "There's no hurry. As long as it's not mid-battle, you are free to choose when to leave."

He grunted and looked back out to the greenery now illuminated by the midday sunshine. "What would I even do? Ever since I was a boy, I had dreamed about exploring the wider world. When I first found myself here, I was elated."

"You were?" My arrival was mostly confusion and head injury, shortly before being attacked by the Lady's gang members.

"It was akin to arriving on unsullied shores. A brand-new world unlike any-thing I'd known. My passion was overflowing."

I tilted my head as we walked down the stone path. "But?"

Quinn smiled. "Always a *but*, isn't there? I'm not a fan of numbers and of feel-ing gated away by the leveling process. I prefer things to be free and open, like my relationships." He chuckled to himself before sighing deeply, returning a tired look toward me. "I feel as though if the Crimson found their way to me before you did, I would have easily fallen under their sway."

With a nod of my head, I gave him a pat on the back. "I'm glad we found you when we did, Quinn. The Lady is promising false hope to those desperate for some closure and asking for so much in return."

"Burning the forest down to stay warm is no way to live," he agreed.

He was definitely in my top three people that we had met, excluding the Party. Depending on how the Dungeon went, he might even hit the top spot. Dependable or accepting allies were few and far between, so I had to let a little water under the bridge to stay afloat. Attacking me in the duel was a dick move after I had saved his life, but a little conflict had drawn us together, and he had found a place in our group.

Still didn't trust him completely, and his admission that he would have fallen to the Lady was cause for concern even with how understandable it was. I was no fool, and my guard would remain up around him. Then again . . . perhaps a fool would trust Ren as well. I narrowed my eyes at the back of her as she talked quietly with Wolf. Just because we locked lips on occasion didn't mean that . . .

I stopped myself and shook away those thoughts. It was too easy to fall into the dark pit when we skirted the rim so closely. No point stressing about the near improbable when we had plenty of actual problems to deal with.

It didn't take long before we could see the small group of houses ahead of us. The possibility of a bit of rest washed away any foul feelings that had been stinking up the corners of my mind. The only hope was that there was a place to scrub my physical form.

With the sun clearly overhead now, I removed my jacket and placed it in my Inventory before rolling my shirtsleeves up. A little bit more of a casual appearance, but the top hat still did the heavy lifting for the theme.

"Dibs on the bath," Ren said, turning her head back to us.

I smiled and shrugged toward Quinn.

"Ladies first, naturally," he said.

I opened up my Chat.

[Max: Found the other group. Not corrupted.]
[Fiona: Thank fuck.]
[Fiona: How are things there?]
[Max: Five more CS dead. Have some good leads.]
[Max: There?]
[Fiona: It's been a couple of hours, shit all has happened.]

With a smile, I closed it down. That's what we wanted to hear—no news was good news. We had a slightly warped sense of time, given that our waking hours were stocked full of activities. Usually violence.

"Something doesn't feel right," Ren said from the front, her bow drawn into her hand.

I sighed, my tired eyes roving over the nearby houses. Nothing immediately obvious. No dead bodies or living ones aligned with the Crimson Shadow. The elf wasn't wrong, however; as much as the small clump of houses seemed pleasant . . . there was almost an odd texture to reality in this area.

Into my hand, a card at the ready . . . just in case.

Despite the good weather, it seemed that when it rained, it poured.

CHAPTER THIRTY-SIX

Worlds Apart

An unease had settled among us, despite there being no obvious problems with the houses. No System-created, but no signs of any struggle or violence. Eventually, any caution took back seat to our exhaustion.

While Wolf sniffed at the air, we slowly pushed our way into the nearest residential building. I stepped in first, card at the ready. Empty, aside from the expected furniture. The others filtered in behind me, their weapons lowering at seeing how mundane things were. The bear struggled but eventually squeezed in through the door without bringing the wall down with it.

"Quinn, check the upstairs with me." I gestured with my head. Normally I'd take Ren, but I didn't want it to become a thing where the Party would keep splitting along the obvious line. Plus, I didn't think I had the fortitude for anything more than a cordial handshake. Even then . . .

He fell into step behind me, sword in one hand and the other up, ready to cast a spell. I'd need to pry open his mind to see what he was actually capable of at some point. Although, with a less-violent-sounding metaphor.

Wooden staircase led us up from the open downstairs area and onto the upper floor. Open doorways, only two rooms. A cold breeze that only I could feel steeled any nerves I had, and the slow and steady pace was only for the slight chance of getting the jump on anything that may be lurking in the shadows. Or to avoid traps, I supposed.

The first was a large bedroom, which looked like a small slice of heaven. A door on the right side gave promise of an en suite, and fully expecting the jump scare to arrive at this juncture—I pushed it open to see. Small tub alongside the usual restroom facilities. Nothing untoward, but the relief that washed through me made me shudder. I couldn't wait for my turn.

"All clear," Quinn reported from the doorway of the second room.

It didn't help shift the awkward feeling this place gave me, but I relaxed somewhat in knowing we had a brief reprieve from the wider world.

We returned downstairs to the pensive elf, and I let her know the good news about the bath. She was gone before I had even finished the sentence, doors closing behind her.

I sighed but smiled. "Let's cook up a feast. You any good with food, Quinn?"

"I'm great at eating it," Wolf murmured to himself, curled up beside the closed front door like a guard dog.

"Not exactly," the fencer scratched at his bearded chin. "I have an Ability that can turn less desirable things into a reasonable meal but have no real hard skills from my previous life." He shrugged and gave me a sheepish grin. "Servants, you see. I was born into some wealth."

I nodded. That sounded like it made sense and explained some of his foppish attitude and immaturity when it came to matters of the heart. Not that I could be a judge of such things, having been a loner until very recently. The dangerous love I had with Ren still hadn't settled in. It would be good for me to keep my head on properly and not let my emotion start driving the narrative. Oh, there was that *L* word again.

"Can't say I'm much better," I admitted, "but let's get this stove fired up and see if two heads are better than one."

He gave me a brief bow and gestured toward the back of the downstairs area where the open-plan kitchen was set up. Even from down here, I could hear the water flowing through into the bath, and I was slightly envious. I bet the elf looked contented and relaxed.

I blinked away the mental images as Quinn lit the wood. "You have a *lot* of survival or utility Skills," I noted.

"That's what I get for being an Arcane Fixer, I suppose." He smiled before his eye unfocused to search his Inventory for some food to cook.

"*Fixer*," I repeated. "Not . . . Fencer?"

"Hmm? No, Arcane Fixer."

Oh. Perhaps one of my head injuries had knocked something loose in my hearing. It should come as no surprise that I was an unreliable narrator in my own life—even ignoring my rather drab journal entries—but mishearing an important detail like Quinn's Class was rather embarrassing.

Then again, that made perfect sense. I wondered if the System was smoothing something over there, as Fixer was a rather odd name for a Class—yet a *very* fitting title for someone with as much utility as he brought to the show. Things were a little too convenient sometimes.

Using a rapier had added to the deception—not that I could rightfully call it that. A Dazzle icon probably earned, as I had tricked myself into believing something not quite based in reality. I ruminated over my folly as we threw some meat into a pan and cut up some vegetables. From behind us, I could practically hear Wolf salivating.

Right on time, just as the food finished cooking, Ren returned to the ground floor. Radiant as ever, with her outfit fully repaired. Not quite a smile on her face, but with the cloud of the day's activities now washed away, she seemed much better for it.

"Would have lived in there forever, but the food smelled too good." She narrowed her eyes, as if we had done her a disservice by cooking too well.

"Feels like forever since we had a proper cooked meal," I said before smiling. Now I didn't know whether I wanted to bathe first and look as sparkling and fresh as the elf or sit and gorge myself on the food while it was still hot.

My stomach won out in the end, and in short order we were then sitting around in the living room area digging into our meal. Any trepidation about the group of houses sank away as I became more relaxed than I had felt in days. I finished eating first so got the pleasure of bathing next.

It went by in a blur, as if the steam clouded away my memories of the minutes that passed. Gave myself a thorough scrub down while my suit repaired once more. Although I didn't have the cooked meal to draw me away from the warm tub, I was keener to not be alone for too long. Not out of nerves, but . . . I was used to having people around at all times now. Such a change from my previous life.

I stepped back down the stairs and grinned at them all. They had been in conversation about something but stuck a pin in it on my arrival. Quinn grunted and stood, not so eager to get himself in the bath next but resigned all the same. As he worked his way upstairs, I went and sank down onto the couch opposite to where Ren was sitting.

She seemed calm, which was as good a look as any considering the life we led.

"Coffee?" she asked, already on her way to the stove before I had the chance to nod.

Wolf yawned and stretched out. "Wake me up when there is killing or eating to be done."

I tipped my hat to him as he settled down for a nap. A weird dog analog while my faux wife was in the kitchen. Domestic life seemed like something . . . unattainable with how the System wanted us to live. But in this brief moment, I felt accomplished. The showman act had always been seeking a greater audience, more accolades and acceptance . . . but it couldn't have a good ending. Self-destructive in my desire to burn the candle from every end.

A life where I settled down and could be content was as alien to that Max as this world was. The demon hunter was no different—it wasn't a career where you kept friends or were able to hold down relationships. How amusing that the two souls weren't so different, despite being worlds apart. I wondered how many other Max souls there were out there . . . but felt uncomfortable in knowing the answer already somehow.

"Here you go, Max." The elf snapped those thoughts from my mind as she passed me a mug.

I hadn't even heard the kettle whistle. "You are an angel, as always."

She gave me a soft smile and sat beside me instead of returning opposite. With a sigh, she sank into the couch while cradling a mug of her own. "Quinn is growing on me."

"Yeah? Out of all the assholes we've met, he's probably the most reasonable."

Ren nodded and blew the steam from her coffee to cool it. "He's a jerk, sure, but he is pretty up-front about it. He was just telling me that Magnus rejected him."

I tilted my head and raised an eyebrow at her. "How'd he take it?"

"Much the same as with us. Sulked for a few minutes, and then it was like his passion for life came back and he was looking forward to finding love elsewhere." She pulled a face, clearly unimpressed that he could be such an extrovert with his feelings.

Perhaps we were just lucky to have found each other. Certainly, if I ever did imagine whom I'd end up with, it wouldn't have been with a grumpy elfin princess from another world. I had my delusions—but *that* had never been one. Still, my brow furrowed.

I opened up the Map and zoomed out. The small world of Othea was displayed before me . . . or at least this singular continent we were currently on, the starter island just off to the right-hand side.

"Ren, what was your old world called?"

"Hmm? Oh, Othea."

That sounded . . . Maybe there was a translation thing that the System was doing. Othea could just be the word for *world* or *earth* in the shared language.

She seemed interested in this change in conversation. "Why? What was yours called?"

"Earth," I said, trying to zoom around to find anything else lurking in the large ocean surrounding us.

"Oh." Ren looked up at the ceiling. "I wonder why the System has the same name as mine then but not yours."

"It's *not* translated then." My thought came out verbally. A statement that might not make a lot of sense without context, but the elf caught hold of it with a firm grip.

In less time than anticipated, Quinn was already done with his bath. The door closed upstairs before he started down toward us, a sheepish grin on his face. "Something about a hot bath always rubs me the wrong way, but at least I no longer carry the sweat and stress of the day."

"What was your home world called, Quinn?" Ren immediately went in for the question, skirting past his statement.

"Othea," he replied, moving over toward the chair opposite us.

She hummed and glanced toward me.

"Don't forget," I added, "both of me came from different worlds. So there's probably more than one Othea. Aside from these with Systems anyway."

The fixer looked very confused as to what the conversation might be about but didn't seem keen to ask us to get him up to speed. In truth, I wasn't sure what it all meant either at this stage. Not that a clear answer would affect our current lives in this System, but the whole portal thing was something I had put out of my mind early on and then tried not to think too hard on. Not like I could leave, and at this point . . . my eyes wandered back to the elf . . . I didn't think that I wanted to either.

"True," Ren replied. "Some of my memory is fuzzy still, like I can't remember names of places I used to know."

I tilted my head and found that I had a similar issue. All these tours to so many cities . . . but I couldn't remember the names. Anything with more granularity than just Earth drew up a blank—although I also knew hell, for as helpful as that was.

"Same here." Quinn rubbed at his goatee and furrowed his brow.

Ren held out her hand. "Paper and pencil, trickster."

Although I wasn't a supply closet—Ah, who was I kidding? With less flare than usual, I withdrew the requested items and handed them over. She gave me her mug to hold, and she set about finding a blank page and began drawing shapes.

Quinn raised an eyebrow, but I just gave him a shrug.

After a few focused minutes, she was done. Turning it around, she showed the fixer a page full of shaped blobs. "This look like Othea to you?"

Confusion across his face as he nodded. A finger extended, he leaned forward to point to one of the blobs. "Apart from this bit here, it's one big landmass instead of the smaller islands you've drawn. But I come from . . ." His finger went to the lower-right corner. "Whatever this one was called."

Ren leaned the page back to look at where he was pointing. "Oh. I'm from up here." She tapped the blob on the top left. "Worlds apart, even if our worlds *weren't* different."

I glanced over at the sleeping bear. Even if he wasn't still napping, I doubted that he knew what Earth or Othea were or understood the concept of continents or world maps. For some reason, I felt confident in guessing that he would be from one or the other.

My narrowed eyes brought up my Chat.

[Max: You're from Othea, right?]
[Fiona: . . .]
[Fiona: Yes, how the fuck did you know?]

[Max: How many of your group are from Othea?]
[Leyla: Three. One from Earth and one doesn't remember.]
[Max: Who was from Earth?]
[Leyla: Yuri.]
[Max: Thanks. Send me his contact details sometime, please?]

I closed the windows down, leaving Fiona on read. The replies had taken a few minutes to go back and forth, and Ren and Quinn had been trying to describe landmarks or vague historical events to see if any information could be gleaned. It appeared not, if their expressions were anything to go by.

"Alright, focus, gang." I clapped my hands together, disturbing the bear enough that his ears opened, even if his eyes resented me for the interruption. "Other-world problems for another time. Let's talk business. Leveling and getting ahead of the Shadow. Quinn?"

"Dungeon is about an hour away," he replied. "It can take a couple of hours to complete if we are careful, so my advice is to head there soon rather than leave it too late."

"Don't want to get caught out in the dark on our victorious return," I said with a nod, which he acknowledged.

I stood, about to rally the troops to make ready our intention to travel right away . . . before stopping.

From outside the front door came an odd sound, as if the ground itself was splitting and tearing like dry vegetation. Getting closer. Louder.

Right outside.

CHAPTER THIRTY-SEVEN

Lock Removal

The building groaned, not even giving us enough time to move. Wood splintered and burst as the front of the house and any structural points were pulled away as if sucked down into a hole. Of course, I had little time to react or see the perpetrator due to the upper floor collapsing down upon us.

Pain and darkness washed over my body. Warmth from something bleeding, but otherwise I felt cold. Near freezing, despite the body of Ren lying beneath me. Perhaps I could have done something more useful than throw myself on top of her—for all the good that it did. A wooden beam had skirted my body and struck her. I could see an icon above her head in the darkness. Unconscious.

With my elbow, I broke the healing charm I always kept in my belt. Warm radiance flooded through me, and I felt slightly less dead. Couldn't move the weight of the wooden beams covering me. Chat came up. Avoiding my technophobia for a moment, I drew up a Group Chat with all the Party.

[Max: Report in?]

Nothing but silence and the continued clatter of remaining house parts settling into a neat pile around us.

[Quinn: Leg fucked, one arm trapped^]
[Wolf: o]
[Max: I'm pinned, Ren is unconscious.]

None of us dead, at the least. I imagined that Wolf either couldn't work the Chat or didn't care to. That he hadn't burst from his position in angered rage meant he was probably trapped or injured as well.

I had always wanted to bring the house down, but this was . . . Well, perhaps neither the time nor place for such a joke.

"Think that killed them?"

"Doubt it. Lady wants the two of them alive, yeah? Can leave the other two."

"Fuck no. After they killed Rolo, I want to have some fun."

If I hadn't felt cold previously, I was practically frozen now. Two male voices, but I anticipated a group of four. No doubt my companions could also hear the discussion but kept quiet. A good performance was tight and controlled.

"Think I saw purple over there. Let's dig the asshole out." Third voice, this one was female and oddly soft considering the context.

Ren began to stir, the icon fading away as her tired eyes opened slowly. Confusion over her face as I put my finger against her lips. She unfocused as she went through the chat messages.

[Ren: What are we dealing with?]
[Max: Rolo's group. Intending to capture us.]
[Quinn: You two anyway . . . ^]
[Wolf: O ooo o]

Footsteps crunching against the debris as figures approached us. Purple light illuminated the dark space where Ren and I were trapped, as my eyes were incensed at the approaching evil. Her bloodied hand rose up in the pocket of space that the couch had allowed to run along the side of my face.

No words spoken, but I could tell by the look on her face. It was time for another show—a little improv required, but we'd recovered from worse. Determination. She seemed to visually cool off when it came to looming violence, just as I did. It's what made her the perfect protégé.

"If they're lucid, just zap them with your stun, and I'll net them." First male voice—gruff but intelligent.

"Uh. If they struggle and we accidentally kill them . . ." Second male voice—older sounding but with an odd inflection to it.

The woman sighed. "Perhaps stop verbalizing your plans . . . They may be listening in."

With a grumble, the gruffer voice spoke in a murmured tone as he started to shift the wood away from where we were trapped. "Think you're so smart because you didn't have to take the red."

A follower of the Lady that didn't need to take her blood? Perhaps I wouldn't kill them all as quickly as possible. I still fully believed there was a fourth figure standing there, being quiet. One that didn't need to talk—or didn't like to unless necessary. This was quite the pickle we found ourselves in . . . and they were all waiting for me to make the first move.

As planks, ruined furniture, and whatever tiling was previously on the roof was noisily removed from where we were entombed, there was currently only one thing I wanted to do.

Fighting against the weight and pressure of the wood on my back, I shifted slightly, so that I was more face-to-face with the elf. She looked rather miserable. Not even sad or pained, really. Just fed up—perhaps annoyed that we were already bloodied after just having a bath. System just couldn't allow us anything nice.

"Your head is bleeding," she whispered, barely audible over the grunts and moving debris.

"Ren." I took a deep breath, which hurt in a way the adrenaline and nerves didn't seem to dull.

"Max?" she responded, her scowl softening. It was dark in this small pocket of relative safety, after all.

"I . . . love you."

For all intents and purposes, this could have been the end of me, and I would be rather content. Crushed under the shifting house, blasted away by the Skills of our enemies, heartbroken from—

"I love you too, trickster." Her hand came back up to cradle my face.

Just the first two options remaining then. I leaned down to kiss her, agony twitching through my torso. Pretty sure that I was tearing muscles as I fought against whatever had me pinned. But I sealed the deal, at any cost. The show wouldn't have it any other way.

We parted in the gloom, and she delivered a heal to me, fixing the damage I had done to myself and bringing me to near full. Her hand went down to pop her own charm, and I could see the relief on her face as some of her wounds cleared up. I felt for the other two, but Wolf was hardy, and Quinn was resourceful.

I was just slowly angering. Every inch closer the Crimson Shadow got to us, my fury rose up a couple of notches. It wasn't as though I could burst out from the ruins with my untenable rage, but if they thought I would be easily caught, then they were about to receive a short lesson in why you don't *fuck* with Max.

Ren's brow furrowed as she continued to watch me. She could sense it too—it wasn't just the glowing eyes . . . Mentally, I had grabbed the crowbar and had started popping open the other-Max boxes that we tried to keep nailed shut. Even in the worst times, I tried to keep a tight grip on it.

But no longer. I had something greater to protect now.

I allowed it to consume me, flood me with the memories and experience that I had gained in killing demons in hell. Practically humming with energy, I felt the true shape of things. Knowledge of truths that I'd kept hidden even when they had been so *fucking* obvious. I could almost laugh out loud, if it wouldn't tip off the soon-to-be-murdered dipshits.

Demon-hunter Max had used a last-ditch ability to get out of a bad situation in hell. A portal to anywhere conjured up by my pact demon. It saved my life and brought me here just at the same time as the magician Max came through.

But the System had put two and two together and gotten five.

For my demon was bound to me and came through too, in a way. Not a real person or humanoid capable of becoming a Player, the System had melted them down and swirled them around inside my joined souls.

I wasn't a demon, but something within me could be.

Right now, I planned to test that theory.

"Just set fire to the other two. Leave it too long and they'll get out. The bear is going to be tough as fuck if he gets free."

"Get the others out first," the woman replied. "I'll not have accidental collateral."

Not taking the blood had left her with some common sense. Shame I was going to split her head open and mash whatever misery lay within all over the dirt. I ached and fidgeted. Wanted out. This was maddening—a sour feeling when I had already let whatever sanity that remained sift through my fingers.

They were getting closer now. Some of the daylight started to make through the smallest of gaps. My heartbeat pounded in my chest. Eyes darted up through my Inventory, cycling things even faster than usual. Both souls were aflame and passionate to put on a display—something they'd never forget. Or remember.

A cold sensation ran up my neck, and I realized Ren had put her hand upon me there. It felt oddly uncomfortable, yet I didn't shirk it away. There was an energy in her eyes. She had seen the tide vanish and knew there was a tsunami coming. Excited her half as much as it scared her.

"Kill them all. Kill them *for me*," she whispered.

I said nothing but smiled. Such a dangerous request, yet so alluring. Who was I to deny such a simple request from the one who loved me? Ren loved me, and I loved Ren. Such a juvenile thing to amuse my overheated brain with right before the stage lights came on . . . but it was as good a motivation as any.

"Getting close now. Careful," the gruff man warned. "The magician is supposed to be tricky."

"One jab with my spear and he won't be a problem," the other man responded.

[Quinn: I'm afraid I cannot offer assistance^]
[Wolf: oooopooiio]
[Max: Be ready.]

And there it was. The heat of my rage hit a limit and was released as steam, cooling me. I felt the glow leave my eyes, our space returning to dim shadow, yet I still felt different. More . . . complete.

Ah, I had truly accepted that I was one Max. Not just pandering to the worse half of me; now that the cat was out of the bag, there was no getting it back inside. This was who I was now. How fortuitous that it happened at the same time that I was able to be honest with Ren about my feelings. Coincidental, I was sure.

More sunlight streamed through as bigger chunks were removed.

I played dead for now, just waiting for the right moment. Ren was tense, ready to assist me however she could. While they were all pinned, I would mostly be on my own. Four Players . . . with unknown levels or Skills. Almost too easy.

From my Inventory, I withdrew a blue flower to drop into her hand. A sweet gesture, which she appreciated—I could tell—but there was a secondary purpose to the action. She also understood this—and I wished I could gush to someone about how amazing this elfin woman was who could read me as though we shared thoughts.

[Max: Ren is *really* amazing.]
[Fiona: What? What does that have to do with Othea?]
[Fiona: Answer me, asshole.]

I closed the Chat.

All in all, I didn't feel too bad about the whole collapsing-house thing. It had forced my emotions out with Ren. Gotten me to truly accept being a Demonic Magician. Given us someone with more than two brain cells who we could . . .

"If I don't kill one, I'll need to be bad cop . . ."

Ren scowled at me and pouted. "*Fine.* Dickbag."

Clarity breezed through me just as a beam of sunlight came through and struck her hair. The radiance was usually uncomfortable when I was being like this, but now it was . . . stunning. Even more than usual, it was like a beacon—a rallying flag for me to go above and beyond.

"I see purple . . ." the gruff man announced and paused. "Unmoving, possibly trapped or injured."

I closed my eyes and smiled. All those things were true. I was humbled by simple wood and an ambush, injured and unable to move more than a little without breaking myself.

My eyes opened as two cards bloomed into my hands.

Still, the show must go on.

CHAPTER THIRTY-EIGHT

To the Max

Music was something I had an odd relationship with. It wasn't that I didn't enjoy it—I was human, after all. So much of my adult life had been hearing the simple fanfare tunes that brought me out onto the stage or sent me off. They permeated my brain, eager to push forward into my active mind when I tried to recollect any kind of song.

As such, the humming in my head was one of these pleasant intros, getting me ready to arrive on stage. As the cold glass of the grand arcane potion touched my lips, I resigned myself to getting the deed done in twenty seconds. A little deadline pressure just made things all the more interesting.

It also *was* goop, albeit not unpleasant to the taste buds. Like bread or sweet dough, perhaps. Energy flooded my System, Mana illuminating through my core as if it was a stage light itself. The tune hit the peak, the crowd holding their breath at my impending reveal.

And thus, it began.

As one of my audience pulled another beam off of me, the wooden debris covering my body burst outward. The small pocket of space expanding violently as something rose to fill it.

"The fuck is—"

My demonic cannon cut off his sentence with a loud blast of confetti—filling the nearby area with small squares of colored paper. Dazzle icons popped up around them all.

"Stab him!"

The spear of the slim man darted past the cannon, finding purchase and breaking bone and flesh. He withdrew it to find the hell bird impaled on the end of his weapon. Confusion painted his sweaty face. Slim mustache and short dirty-blond hair. His armor was cloth and leathers.

Beside him, the gruffer man in chain mail looked no happier. His round face starting to panic, deep-brown eyes trying to search the shadowed space for where I was hiding.

On cue, Ren threw the flower against the cannon, using her entangling shot with the gift as an intended projectile.

Invisibly, I stepped past the two men as roots came up from the messy floor, pinning their legs in place. The woman was wearing half plate, a cape of red hanging behind her. The silvers were muted and matched the black dress she wore beneath her armor. Her brow was furrowed, eyes ablaze as she went to cast something.

Second blast of confetti, pasting the two men with more fanfare, icons nearing the double digits already.

Click.

Nullifying cuff on the woman. I was correct—there was a fourth character in the audience. Tall and masculine, they looked like some manner of lizard man, but they weren't scaled . . . More of a hammerhead shark look. Dim-gray skin, dark and uncaring eyes. Two barbed blades in their large webbed hands.

Applying the cuff seemed to count as an attack, which was unfair but beside the point. I had planned the performance with that in mind already. The supposed attack dropped my invisibility a second early, so I used my momentum to headbutt the woman. I really needed to stop doing that, but it had worked out well enough, and she fell to the ground.

A third blast of confetti signaled the approach of the shark man, blades bursting into blue fire as a Skill launched him toward me.

"He's behind, fuck!" The gruff man twisted and tried to turn toward me right before my Hellhound+ leaped out and grabbed onto his arm.

With a click of my fingers, <Finale> washed through the area. Colored spotlights swirled around before focusing on me. Rapturous applause filled my ears as everything faded away. A crescendo building up to a high point in the performance.

The shark man stood stunned, aware he was now an important part of what was going to happen. Audience participation could go either way, but he seemed pretty receptive to what I had intended for him. Didn't really have a choice, actually.

My hand rose up to show the crackling red critical card, and with the potion flooding my body with power, I sank everything I had into it. It vibrated and shook in my grip as blood ran and dripped to the dust-laden floorboards. Eager to escape and fulfill its purpose.

Now it was time.

As my cannon faded away, I released the card toward the stunned Player. It moved like a flash, akin to the one back at the first-area Dungeon. But this was critical. It did not just cut the odd humanoid. It burst halfway inside his chest, cratering most of his insides to fall out in a chunky spray to my feet. An odd bouquet. The applause grew louder, and I smiled.

His inert body dropped to the floor, and the effect faded away. The stun wore off, and I had to earn back those Dazzle icons on the remaining few. Gruff had been broken out of the stun early by my overeager hound—but that was acceptable. I admired the gusto.

Time was running short. I was on a schedule here. Two cards in my hand and out toward the man assailed by my demon. He managed to block one, but the second cut across his face, blinding him.

Thinner man sent out a magic projectile toward me, which <Card Fan> blocked. Movement behind me as the woman had risen and drawn a melee weapon to strike me from behind.

Keep the woman alive.

She yelped out in shock as the maimed body of the shark man grabbed her, purple ears flopping down over her face.

I felt myself nearing the edge. Not of switching to the dark side or growing horns and becoming a demon . . . Those days were long past. The edge was just the stage; it bordered what I encompassed, what I drew my power from. I knew my limits . . . and finally, I knew what I truly was and could accept it. That level of comfort just meant the show was smoother. There were no doubts left.

I loved Ren. I cared for my Party. I would erase the Lady and any of her ilk without a thought.

My feet took me closer to the thin man as the vines faded away, freeing both the captives. Spear in one hand and a knife of magical energy in the other, he darted forward to meet me. Crackling white light, his longer weapon surged toward me before striking a thick piece of wood that emerged in front of my torso.

If anything, this just infuriated him further, and he grew more desperate.

In total opposition, my face was calm apathy. I had danced like this before, and he was off-key to how the tune was playing in my head. Cards split and circled behind him, taking the gruff man in the arm and neck. Panic across my opponent's face as he heard his accomplice fall to the growls and gnashing of my demon.

I stepped backward, further planks going up and blocking each of his leveled attacks. And he was fast. I could not deny that. Energy from his Skills blurred his movements as he lashed out, turning with the blade before jabbing with his spear.

All rather droll, in honesty. I placed my hands behind my back as I felt the potion wear off. Mana exhaustion hit me, and I felt empty. Devoid of anything but desire for rest, for the show to be done already. My head tilted as I continually brought up and put away planks to block each of the continuous attacks leveled at me. You'd think that he would change tactic, but no.

It was too late now anyway.

The pile of debris beside me—now a lot smaller than when I'd first stepped beside it—burst apart as the bloodied and angered bear leaped out. Empowered by his own Abilities, his large paw came down and smashed the surprised man into the floor.

Show was over, as far as I was concerned, and I turned away. Foregone conclusion once you had Wolf atop you. Instead, I strode over to where Ren was still pinned and started to vacuum up all the debris that I could, ejecting it out of my Inventory off to the side every time it got too full.

Couldn't have done this from underneath without risking having more collapse on us, at least unless it was a last resort. It didn't take much for her radiant hair to bloom out from the darkness, and she sat up on the clearing couch to rub at her head.

"You did it, trickster." She gave me a pained smile, looking back out at the carnage.

A heal came my way, and I realized I had actually taken some damage during the fight—although I couldn't pinpoint exactly where. Maybe the wood hadn't blocked all those strikes. I went over and began excavating Quinn. The hound jumped up on the couch beside Ren for cuddles, while Wolf started to eat some of the man he had pulped.

Roger dragged the captive woman closer to us. Panic and anger in her eyes, but without the blood, she at least had the sense to not try anything stupid.

"These fuckers come out of the woodwork like hell roaches," the demon growled, not used to the weird body he was inhabiting.

"Yes," I replied, turning a cold glare toward her. I dropped a chair from my Inventory and kicked it their way. "She can sit. If she tries to run, break her legs."

"Yes, boss."

I uncovered Quinn, and he was looking worse for wear. Bloody and pale. He wasn't overselling it when he said his leg was fucked. With his arm now free, he withdrew a healing potion, shaking as he brought it up to his lips.

"Ren, help Quinn out." More of an order than I intended, but she gave me a firm nod and stepped up out of the loose pile of wood to move closer and assist him.

I took a few steps over to the seated woman. Maintaining eye contact, I made a show of taking Jokkar's mace out of my Inventory and handed it over to Roger.

"Normally we do a little good-cop, bad-cop thing," I explained, my tone low and flat. "However, we're all rather injured and tired . . ."

"There are worse things than a bad cop," she said, able to see where I was heading with this.

"Clever. It's refreshing, albeit disappointing, to meet one of her minions that still has half a brain. You have a name?"

"Tanya." Her eyes looked to the floor as the reality of her situation sank in. "She certainly undersold your abilities."

I stretched out my shoulders. Plenty of ache in them after the brief combat and residual pain from being buried beneath the house. "Rolo let her know we were here, however?"

She nodded. "He was hoping to stoke the bad blood between you and Fiona."

Would have been a shame for me to have had to kill the fighter, eventually. Wouldn't have taken much to stoke those flames, I was sure.

I turned my head to watch the groaning fixer exit his tomb, aided by the elf and her heavy scowl. Still had use of his leg, but it looked tender. Both of them were bruised, with various bloodied cuts across their bodies, alongside an unhealthy amount of dust and wood fragments.

"You didn't have to take her blood to join?"

Tanya shook her head. "My Class Keystone makes me immune to it. It was join or die, either way."

"Lots of death in this world, isn't there?" I sat down on my own withdrawn chair, the exhaustion catching up to me in waves.

She glanced up at my pact demon as he stood with the large mace ready to pulp her if I gave the word. "If only you had been here sooner, you might have been able to save my life."

I'd have to give this to her—she had a way with words. Perhaps it was because most of the Crimson Shadow had been unrepentant bastards, but her self-awareness was a novelty, if not conflicting.

Behind me, Ren stepped up and gripped at my shoulders to work in a slow massage. Part of me died right there, completely at her mercy. Divine.

"Why'd she keep you around if she couldn't control you?" Ren asked, still turning me into demonic putty.

"Somebody needs to boss around those on the lower rungs." She shrugged, maintaining eye contact with the elf. "Perhaps death would be a mercy to me after I've had to shepherd around these imbeciles."

"Your flock looks fucked," Roger added. "Shitty shepherd."

Tanya didn't respond to my demon, but some of the light left her face. She had a strong will. I could see that. A character of gray where we tried to keep things black-and-white. The Paladin on the bridge had been an easier answer, as she was barely ankle-deep in the Crimson . . .

This Shadow had dirtied hands. It was perhaps a mercy that I couldn't currently summon cards.

"You have us at a disadvantage," I admitted. "It is a rarity we get to have a reasonable conversation with someone who wants us dead."

She nodded slowly. "I accept I am on borrowed time. Please allow me one thing before you decide to kill me."

I raised an eyebrow. "What is it?"

"Let me tell you everything I know about the Lady so you can stop her."

CHAPTER THIRTY-NINE

In Control

rust was a word with a lot of weight to it—far too much for only five letters. Tanya was offering us up information, knowing that we would probably kill her right after. Of course, some of it might be a trick or an attempt to guide us down the wrong path. Was there any true point to that? I prided myself on being able to read people, and she seemed to be on the level.

Ren and Quinn pulled up chairs beside mine, and Wolf replaced Roger as my demon sank away back to hell.

"Your eyes," the elf said, her brow furrowed slightly more than usual. "They are different."

"Purple?" I asked. They couldn't be glowing, as I felt calm now. My energy—demonic or not—was spent.

"Yeah, but . . . the irises are purple. Like they've changed color. No glow."

Hopefully she didn't mind, as I think that was just me now. A complete person accepting of all past, present, and demonic parts. Didn't even need to hit my head for the realization to sink through my thick skull. In saying that, I might have taken a plank or two to my brainbox while protecting the elf.

I looked between my worn and dirtied companions before giving Tanya a wry smile. "You know, we had only *just* had baths after going without a good wash for a few days."

"That almost seems like a worse crime than trying to kill or capture you." She exhaled. "Such a fanciful world, yet I miss the creature comforts of where I came from."

"Earth or Othea?" I asked.

Her brow furrowed, and she looked at me, tilting her head. She looked pretty human, but that could mean either, as far as I knew. Cogs were whirring in her head, a pregnant pause in the air for what should be a simple answer.

"*No!*" She opened her mouth in surprise. "I've seen you before, on the television."

My eyebrow raised, and an odd shiver ran through me. Not just because I had a potential fan that recognized me, but that she could have come from the same Earth as I had. Or at least a different one where I was still a prominent magician. "You . . . know of me?"

"Barely." She shrugged apologetically. "Magic isn't my sort of thing, but I've caught you in passing. The purple suit more than anything."

Okay, so maybe not a fan. That put her imminent death back up to a possibility again. I caught the glare of Ren from my side—but it wasn't my fault I was famous. Ah, perhaps it was because I was losing the thread of the conversation.

"As far as I can tell," I continued, reeling things back together. "People either came from Earth or Othea, but there appears to be different versions of each world. Well, I know there's at least two Earths as . . . I had different professions in each." Didn't need to give her the full picture.

She nodded. "I did some time in the military and now work as a virologist."

That explained the Class Keystone to be resistant to curses or afflictions, I supposed. Based on her outfit, I would assume she was a Battle Cleric or something similar. "Is that why you joined up with the Lady? You wanted to go back?"

Tanya rubbed at her forehead. "I mean . . . *sure*, I want to go back. She seemed pretty convinced she knew how to reverse the portals or whatever."

Ren crossed her arms. "And that is worth ensuring others can't return, so that only those loyal could?"

A shrug was the only given response at first before she sighed and looked up to the open sky. "At first, it didn't seem like I'd get into too much trouble. I'd only recently joined the Party and wasn't privy to what they'd been up to prior. I was happy enough being an individual and just forwarding on her orders. The full-Party rule was then mandatory recently, and I was lumped in with these half-wits."

I nodded and steepled my fingers together. "But then she got word we were here, and she sent you after us?"

"Yeah." She gave me a humorless smile. "She seemed to have a lot of apprehension and ire for you, and I guess it's not unwarranted, given that you practically wiped my whole Party on your own."

My fingers flexed against each other. I saw her reasoning for wanting to talk and bare all to us now—it humanized her. Made her appear as more of a flawed but relatable person and not just a murder-hungry monster. I'd been scouring every expression and sentence uttered for a hint of betrayal or lie—and I knew Ren would be doing the same.

Quinn would . . . I turned my gaze toward the man. Just as expected, he looked rather smitten with the woman already—his eye alight with interest for every spoken word. Back on the other side and Wolf looked bored and annoyed. Either hoping he could eat the woman or he could get a clean and nap instead.

"Despite our proficiency, the Lady always stays several steps ahead," I eventually said, not wanting to eat up the compliment leveled toward me.

"For now. But you know how it works, right? She is literally a cult leader that grows more powerful the more believers she has."

I nodded—we had guessed something like that. It had been how she catapulted into the second area while we were barely getting the sand out of our boots.

"But now, we've been killing enough to slow her down?" Ren asked, her arms still crossed.

"She didn't say that exactly, but that was my impression." Tanya snapped her fingers. "In a way, I did you a favor by feeding you these imbeciles to kill."

I couldn't help but roll my eyes. She was smart enough to know we wouldn't be swayed by her trying to make it sound like she was working to our benefit. There was something about the fact that she was maintaining her composure and humor in the current situation that . . . I liked? Or respected, at least. I imagined that she would have seen some things in the military and at least learned something about life and death even if her System life hadn't been too drenched in conflict.

With a deep sigh, I sank into my chair. I was unprepared for a sympathetic villain. Or at least an affable one. If only there was a prison . . . But then we'd need a court and justice system too. Neither were things I cared to take responsibility for. I couldn't save the world and fix society at the same time.

I gestured with my hand. "Time to sing then, canary."

She shuffled in her chair before returning a nod. The inevitable was accepted, but the human desire to not perish still remained. It was only natural.

"The Lady believes that in order to fix the System, it needs to be united. Preferably under her rule. That's why she is working her way to the Crown." Tanya rolled her eyes. "One of her group is able to do something to convert System-created, but they're finding resistance at Candlekeep."

Quinn grunted before remembering his manners. "Like at the fortress."

"Oh?" She tilted her head. "You've been past there? No wait, let me guess. You killed them all already?"

The fixer grinned and nodded eagerly.

"They had captured a pair from one of the campground groups," I said. "We took them back."

"By killing them all," Ren clarified.

Tanya nodded slowly, a wry smile at the edges of her mouth. "Impressive. I clearly hitched my horse to the wrong wagon. She told us you were important to capture, but I don't think even she knows what you're currently capable of."

Ren narrowed her eyes. "Why does she want us alive?"

A shrug was given in response. "Maybe to torture you or make you suffer. Force you to convert or fight one another—who knows? That was plan A anyway."

Seemed to me that such a plan was doomed to fail, which meant that . . . "Plan B was just to kill us?"

Tanya gave a half nod. "Naturally. Once she eventually gets wind of my group being wiped out, she'll send one of her more competent Parties your way."

I smiled. "That doesn't mean much, knowing how quickly they fall."

"Eh. She has two main groups with her. Actually competent and high level, with useful Skills. The rest of us are spread out, doing her bidding. Those with more competent Classes are assisting at the city, but there's a few characters bumping around you wouldn't want to stumble across unaware."

The elf still didn't seem too content to be sitting here talking. "And you haven't tipped anyone off so far?"

Tanya shook her head. "You're both rather astute, correct? You'd be able to tell if I went to my Chat windows. I know when I have been bested, and I'm glad that you're standing in opposition to the Lady. As . . . difficult as that may be to believe."

It *was* difficult to believe. I hated that the longer we talked, the less I felt like putting a card through her neck. If anything, I was trying to find the line between distrust and paranoia. Sitting among the wreckage of the collapsed building while trying to make these moral decisions wasn't helping my mood.

I rubbed at my temples and brought up my Chat to see that I had a missed message.

[Fiona: I hope you know you're a dick.]

Seemed pretty obvious at this point. A magical one—if the rumors were to be believed.

[Max: Did I make the right call with the Paladin?]
[Fiona: . . .]
[Fiona: Is there really nobody else you could bother?]
[Fiona: *Yes*. Unless she slits my throat in the night, you did.]
[Max: You hold an important position now, and my respect. But I will no longer send you messages, as per your request.]
[Fiona: Asshole, that's not what I meant!]
[Fiona: Firstly:]

I closed the Chat down and wrinkled up my face. That didn't really help me decide on what the right call here was.

"Calling for backup now?" Tanya asked, her eyebrow raised.

"Hmm? No. Just liaising with the one I put in charge of the first area." I rolled out my shoulders, wishing Ren was giving them a rub again. I'd have to ask her nicely later.

"A resistance force, like a militia?" She cocked her head to the side. "You sure are full of surprises. I bet the Crimson there are having a tough time if it's someone you trust."

Ren shook her head. "There are no Crimson Shadow there. We killed them all before coming across the bridge."

"And new Players have been coming across from the starter island," I added.

"Huh." She looked taken aback by this, some genuine surprise in her expression. "You're . . . actually doing it. Fixing the System, I mean."

I turned my head to the elf. "How many have we killed in this area so far?"

"Fourteen Crimson, four potential recruits, eight marketeers."

Tanya blinked, her confusion now washed away to leave something completely blank. "I'm honestly at a loss for words."

More than anything, I just wanted to have another bath. Just redo the whole nice-house part without the ambush that destroyed it. The sun had dried out all the blood and dust on me, and I just felt crusty. With Mana exhaustion, it was like I had a large caffeine crash and my body was going to be just a husk for the next hour or so.

But I was the leader. I got to *decide* things. I stood from my chair and vanished it away.

"Take Tanya to the next house." I leveled my finger toward the next intact building. "We may have to delay the Dungeon while I think on some things."

"Like how much information is enough before you kill me?" the woman asked, maintaining eye contact.

I shrugged and gestured for Wolf and Quinn to escort her. The bear had been quiet, but he looked twice as exhausted as I felt. We needed time to heal up and mentally recover. Maybe food and a hot drink?

We walked over the warm flagstones of the small village, Ren sticking by my side more than she usually would, her glare constantly on the woman. Door open, we entered the soft shade of the interior. It was mostly the exact same as the destroyed house, albeit the furniture was arranged slightly differently.

"Alright," I turned and placed the chair back down in the middle of the room. "You may sit and exist for a little while longer. Anything weird and Wolf has permission to eat you."

"The bear is called Wolf?" she asked as she sat down gently.

"A story as long as my digestive tract, if you care to hear it that way," he grumbled before lying on the floor and staring at her.

"Ren, upstairs with me," I ordered. "Quinn, if you could get any important Map locations from Tanya, that would be appreciated."

"Of course," he nodded.

With little fanfare, I turned to the staircase and led the elf up. We'd need some privacy to discuss these important matters—I couldn't make the decision alone and carry the weight inside my head any longer.

Straight in through the bedroom and then into the en suite. Over to the bath and hit the taps. I turned back to her with arms folded as she closed the door.

"Get in," I told her. "I'm going to scrub all that filth off of you."

She said nothing as her face flushed, blue eyes aglow as she started to unbutton her blouse.

It felt good to be in control.

CHAPTER FORTY

Mind Made Up

The warmth of the bath was almost as comforting as the body of the elf resting up against me. Although we had started the event with impassioned undressing, as soon as we hit the water, any carnal desire washed away. Thankfully, so too did all the stress and tension the house collapse had labored us with.

So instead, we had washed our healing wounds and removed the dust clouding our hair and skin and just soaked together. Selfish when we had the others downstairs with our captive . . . but I *wanted* to be selfish and take what *I* wanted. Life was too short.

"I've fully accepted the other side of me," I said softly. "There are trace amounts of a demon that has become part of me."

"Explains the eyes then. How do you feel?"

I was currently in the most relaxing bath I think I'd ever had. A naked elf who loved me was currently cuddled up beside me. I had recently bested a group of people intending to kill me, hardly breaking a sweat.

"Pretty okay," I undersold it.

"You've come a long way since the awkward showman from the first island." Her fingertips ran across my chest.

Awkward wasn't exactly a fair take on things, but I thought back to when we had first met. She had undoubtedly saved my life—or at least prevented a lot of personal injury—by interrupting my fight with the two thugs. I had latched on to her as a point of safety in a world that was strange and wanted me dead. Even agreed to murder people to grease the wheels of our partnership.

I had never imagined it would have amounted to this.

"Couldn't have done it without you by my side," I said.

She exhaled through her nose. "I know." Her fingers gripped against me softly, and she pushed away to look me in the eyes. "Think the others will be pissed we ditched them for this?"

"Maybe." I shrugged. "Let them be. Quinn can have his turn after, and I'll overfeed Wolf." With my hand, I pushed the wet hair from her face.

"And Tanya?"

I sighed and pulled a face. "Caught me. The real reason I came up here was to avoid making a decision."

Her bright-blue eyes rolled. "Your constantly wandering hands tell a different tale, trickster."

With a smile, I ran my fingers behind her head and pulled her toward me. "Shh," I hissed before we shared a soft kiss.

A signature scowl returned to her face as she moved back away. "Did you just shush me, asshole?"

"Yes, I did."

Her eyes narrowed. "You and I will have words later tonight."

Three little words, I was pretty sure. We had settled into a new stage of comfort, our feelings out in the open. Other than the playful jab at me quietening her, she hadn't had so much as a frown since we'd stepped into the bathroom.

"What are your thoughts on her?" I returned the subject back to what was more important to the brain, even if less to the heart.

Ren groaned and moved away to sit against the opposite side of the oval tub. She pouted and crossed her arms. "Pass. I was hoping you'd do all the heavy lifting."

"In exchange for the heavy petting?" I winced as she flicked water at me. "Your opinion is important, Ren. You have the ear of the king."

She rolled her eyes again. "Honestly? Killing her in cold blood would be pragmatic but doesn't sit quite well with me. We're trying to erase the Lady and her negative influence on this world, but that means cultivating good Players too, right?"

"You're saying that Tanya hasn't taken the blood, so she could change and do right for the world?"

Ren pulled a face. "I'm saying I'll stand by whatever decision you make, even if you regret it or it brings us ruin in the future."

Sounded more like she was still delegating the hard part to me but was self-aware enough to accept the consequences for her just being the greater woman standing behind the great man. She knew I could read that from her, so there wasn't much need to extrapolate.

"Alright." I sighed. "Let's leave this slice of heaven and see what mistakes we can make for future us."

Other than tripping out of the bath and almost cracking my head open on the floor, getting dried and dressed was an uneventful part of this process—where I only stole a dozen glances at the elf repeating the same motions. With a bright smile, she gave me a nod, and we both sighed before we opened the door.

As we headed down the stairs, five eyes narrowed our way.

I leveled a scowl back at them. "What? I just had a house dropped on me and had to kill our aggressors. I'll take a bath if I *want* to."

Quinn immediately dropped any ire he might have felt toward the pair of us, some surprise in his eye at my curt response. Wolf relaxed but still seemed put out at having to babysit our captive. Curiosity had filled Tanya's expression, but other than that, she didn't speak up.

I felt Ren's hand on my lower back, either gesturing me forward or supporting my tact.

"Update me, Quinn, then you can go bathe or take a break however you see fit. Wolf, find something to fill with food and I will overburden it."

That won them over. Had to lead them with the stick and show them an easy route to the carrot once they did something for you. The bear was almost immediately searching around for the largest container the house could offer. Quinn licked his lips, his eye going into his STAR menus to send me something.

My Map opened up, and several coordinates were highlighted. I furrowed my brow as I shared it across to Ren.

"Quinn here has already told me about the groups you have dealt with," Tanya began. "These are the rest, as per my update yesterday."

There were a few more than I had been expecting. Not that it seemed realistic that the necromancer's group would be our only obstacle before reaching Candlekeep, but I had underestimated how many people were in this area. "Is everyone now Crimson or dead?"

She shook her head. "No. There are two Guilds offering resistance and the occasional unaffiliated few who have not taken the blood."

We knew of one of the groups who wanted us to meet them at some point— the Eternal Wardens.

Ren crossed her arms. "You couldn't have joined one of them?"

Tanya shrugged. "Hard to be indecisive with a blade to your neck, and they have a dim view of desertion. Not that I had any opportunity—the guy your demon inhabited was essentially my handler."

I grunted. Would have to go through the Map properly when I had the patience for it. With the bath long past me, my mood cooled.

"Alright, everyone at ease. Tanya, with me to the side room." I gestured to the door just before the kitchen.

Although I received some cautious glances from my team, Ren gave my arm a brief squeeze before I followed our captive into the other room.

Some manner of study, or something. Bookshelves on one side, desks on the other. Small table with a pair of chairs in the center as if it had been prepared for this purpose. A soft low couch was beside the bay window at the far end. I shut the door behind us, turning the convenient key in the lock.

"Sit," I requested, and as she did, I sat opposite her at the table.

She shuffled uncomfortably and sighed. "Could you at least make it painless? I'm sure you know a few good places to cut to end me quickly."

I said nothing, but from my Inventory I brought out my Knife of the Trickster and placed it in the center of the table. Point end facing me. Her jaw worked, and she looked between it and me.

"Hands," I requested.

Tanya's expression remained stoic as she placed both hands with palms down on the table.

I rolled my head around on my neck. Forgot to ask Ren for that massage— the bath had all but melted away any such thought, but now I felt tense again. Oh well, I had already made my decision.

With the wave of my hand, the nullifying cuff was unlocked and then looted, as if it had just vanished from her. It reappeared on my own wrist. Dazzle icon.

She furrowed her brow and rubbed at her left wrist where it had been. "Why? I don't understand."

"Words mean little to me," I said, relaxing into my chair. "You've said a lot in the short time we've had you captive. About wishing you hadn't signed up with the Lady."

Her head nodded slowly as she tried to put the pieces of the puzzle together. Trying not to look at the knife that lay between us.

"Thus, I give you this gift." I smiled and tilted my head. "I have Mana exhaustion, so I cannot cast anything for a good twenty or so minutes still, even without the cuff. The door is locked. I have provided you a knife, and you could probably escape through the window."

Tanya looked over toward the thin glass where the quiet daylight sat in pensive expectation.

"You could kill me," I continued. "The Lady would be happy, wouldn't she? You'd not be a failure. One of her favored, I'd assume. One of the first to go home . . . if she could even be successful."

Her right eye twitched. "Why are you doing this? You're going to give me the alternative option now, right?"

I shook my head. Usually that would be how this cliché would play out, but I didn't want to force her between two choices. Perhaps she knew that I still had a chance to defend myself even without my magic, but I wasn't about to prostrate myself any further.

"This is all about your legacy, Tanya. What you want for your life and this world."

Internal conflict had her frozen with a wrinkled face. I could see now that she was a little older than I had first thought. No grays in her black hair, but the tired experience now weighing on her eyes told me a lot more. Late thirties, early forties perhaps. Her fingers were tensing at the edge of the table, either trying to get a grip on her emotions or perhaps mimicking the motions for grabbing the knife.

"There's someone you want to go back for, isn't there?"

Her eyes came up to meet mine, and any stoicism had now washed away. The sadness of the truth too much to bear. "Husband and daughter," she replied.

The simple three words painted enough of a picture. Motivation for the necessary evil even beyond saving her own skin. If it wasn't for her Class Keystone, no doubt she would have taken the blood and just been another raving cult member, too deluded and full of hate to reach what they desired. It made my hatred for the Lady double.

"I'll not lecture or make any promises," I said quietly. "Your burdens are your own, and I am in no place to change the course of your destiny."

If the Lady really did have knowledge and capability to get us back, then I would accept taking a knife to the neck so this mother could be reunited with her family.

Her hand went slowly across the table and gently took up the handle of my blade.

CHAPTER FORTY-ONE

Full House

Tanya turned the blade around and held the sharp end, pointing the handle toward me.

"I'm not going to kill you, Max. Not sure I even could if I wanted to."

I nodded and took the blade. Rested it horizontally in front of me instead of putting it away. Part of me was anticipating some trick or reversal, even if she didn't go for the immediately obvious play of putting the sharp end of the weapon in the soft parts of my neck.

"What *do* you want to do then?"

She tilted her head but maintained eye contact. Her eyes were a warm brown, but there was a sharpness to them. As much as her family was a weak point in her heart, she seemed like someone who would act logically if given the chance. There was some intrigue in there too. Like she knew I wasn't so softhearted to just let her go free because we had a nice conversation, so she was trying to see my angle.

"Living would be nice, actually." Tanya raised an eyebrow. "Is that an option?"

I shrugged. "It could be. Want to know how Quinn became part of our group?"

She gestured for me to continue.

"Came out and challenged me to a duel for Ren's hand."

Tanya chuckled and shook her head. "You let him tag along after that?"

"Trust is a difficult thing to hold on to in this world. It was either see everyone as an enemy or take some chances to hopefully achieve our goal." I looked out at the sunlight streaming through the window. Oh, to go back to the times when my next trick was the most concerning thing on my mind.

"Am I not your enemy?"

I smiled. "Depends what you do when I unlock that door. Unless you intend to escape through the window."

She rolled her tongue around in her mouth. Already made some kind of decision, I was sure. Not entirely convinced that she wanted to speak it out into the world yet, it seemed. Tanya exhaled deeply, and the words eventually worked their way from her mouth as I allowed the silence to settle.

"Allow me to help you."

"You've done quite a lot already." I continued to smile. The locations of the Crimson Shadow groups were a huge boon—allowing us to go on the offensive rather than wait for the inevitable ambushes. Who needed to level more when we could pop into their camps at night and kill them with a fucking demonic cannon?

She pursed her lips together. "You are right, Max. It would be too much to ask for your group to trust me after today. It probably seems shallow for me to say I believe you four would be able to take down the Lady and her Guild."

"It *does* seem shallow." I nodded. "We don't need our asses kissed. Can you do taxes?"

Tanya pulled a face. "My husband is an accountant. I picked up some basic things over the years."

"We are planning on killing off the blood couriers. We have their route. Would you know when they'll be at certain points?"

"I would."

Part of me hated what the other part of me knew. It almost seemed to be something fated for our group. The final puzzle piece that we were missing. Against every fiber of my being, I didn't want it to be true, but it was almost as if the route was well lit by the bright lights, taking me to center stage.

"Death and hardship follow us, every day." I grit my teeth together. "Are you willing to kill and risk it all for the rest of us so that we can eventually succeed? It's all or nothing, Tanya. Either you are with us or you stay *far* out of our way. Preferably not six feet underground, but we've buried better than you."

Her mouth opened and closed, taken aback.

I took the dagger up in my hand. Purple electricity started to arc around my body, flickering as my mood cooled. "Even on our darkest days . . . this is who we are . . ."

With a quick action, I stabbed the blade down through my left hand, pinning it to the table. As she shuffled back in shock, I drew out my blood into the air to form a magic card. With no Mana, I was purely using my own life to create it. I couldn't be curtailed by the System.

The door burst open, splinters of wood scattering to the floor as the weak lock shattered from the setting. Ren appeared with her bow up and her <Smite Shot> glowing radiant light.

"Hold," I commanded, and she relaxed the held tension ever so slightly. "Tanya wants in on the show, Ren. Thinks she can help manage us, make us more efficient."

The semicaptive woman winced and pulled a face. It wasn't really what she had offered—and certainly not in those words—but destiny knew different. Either that or my mind was partly spinning out of control.

"Is she also able to stop you from breaking your skull on things? Because my attempts have been for naught." She glared at me, and my heart did a little flip.

Oh, it might also be because I still had a knife impaling my hand to the table. I threw the card to the floor, having it appear as a Hellhound+, who immediately began wagging their tail at the sight of the elf. A wave of my free hand and the knife and cuff went into my Inventory. I took out a bandage to top me off, not wanting to bother Ren for a heal right this moment.

"I can . . . try?" Tanya replied, looking remarkably unsure as to what was actually being asked, her eyes darting toward the aggressive elf and my partially insane self.

"Good enough for me." Ren sighed and put down her bow so she could pet the summoned canine.

"You'll have the same terms as the rest of us," I agreed. "Equal effort, equal risk, equally shared loot. Don't give us any reason to terminate our partnership."

"I'm . . . Are you really . . . ?" Her brow was furrowed. The last couple of minutes a bit too much of a fever dream for her mind to process.

Perhaps I shouldn't have maimed myself to make the point—but it was pretty clear. Hadn't even signaled anything to Ren, but she knew when I was in pain and was ready and willing to erase the woman with no questions asked. Not only that, but if she had tried to kill me, I still would have the ability to summon cards, even if it detrimental to myself. In truth, the cuff wasn't even on properly, but a little illusion never hurt anybody.

[Tanya has joined the Party]

"Don't overthink it," I said as I waved her away. "I'm *fucking* ravenous though." Up and away from the table, I stepped past the elf coddling my hell pup. "I hope Wolf found two containers."

Quinn stood up from the chair he had been occupying, not quite as energetic as Ren at coming to my defense, but he didn't have the same sixth sense. "Ah, I saw that the good lady Tanya has j—"

"She's married," I said as I waved him away as well. "Where's Wolf?"

As if on cue, the bear shuffled in through the back door—struggling somewhat as his round rump hardly fit through the small frame. Walking backward, he dragged a shallow wooden trough in behind him—bringing plenty of dirt and foliage in at the same time.

"That's a planter, Wolf." I sighed and shook my head. "Not exactly the best thing to eat out of."

"*But you promised*," he murmured through teeth clenched on the end of the frame.

Well, I couldn't let him down now, could I? As he tried to maneuver the long object into the kitchen, I gestured for Quinn to help him out as I went through my Inventory. Ren stepped in through from the side room, somehow carrying the Hellhound+ in her arms like it was still a puppy. Tanya came in after, still uncomfortable and trying to process her acceptance.

"Any good at cooking, Tanya?" I asked as I sorted through the loose stacks of uncooked meat.

"I know a thing or two," she said with a shrug.

"Perfect, we need a little feast for all the talking we have done and are about to do."

Ren scowled at me from behind the panting held canine. "Something wrong with my cooking, trickster?"

"No." I smiled. "I need you for something else."

She raised an eyebrow expectantly.

"My shoulders are killing me, if you could give them a rub?"

"*Asshole.*" She sighed and put the dog down, giving him a last pat on the head before I sent him away.

I grinned and turned back to the bear, who was now sitting on his backside and looking at me—awaiting his just rewards in the long planter he had arranged in the kitchen.

We had a full house now, and I was apprehensive despite the gusto I had been putting on. My natural confidence was at an all-time high—that *wasn't* an act. It had been a long day of hard-fought wins and easily expended emotions . . . but I felt good about it all. Whether I could trust the newer pair was something else but not exactly why I felt a little on edge.

Ren and Wolf had been the perfect matches for what our Party needed to be a near-invincible trio. Well, if you didn't count all the times we nearly died. Becoming a five had been a shadow looming in the back of my mind ever since I knew Parties were a thing. Did the other two fit in?

A little too well.

The System had smoothed some of the lines between our Skills, but Ren's acceptance to be my protégé was something she had come to naturally. Wolf was far from a performing animal, but he hit some of the same markers. Quinn being full of rugged utility . . . a *fixer*, according to the System, was odd enough. Now that I had shuffled Tanya into the same box Reggie had once held, I wondered how much of this was fate and how much was my mind rounding off the edges to fit reality into something that I could accept and understand.

Either way, I was mentally burned out from the day we had endured.

Hand extended, I expelled a healthy selection of meat, fruit, and vegetables to spray down and fill the trough Wolf had brought. I'd need to stock up again soon.

"Still have those feathers when you want them," I murmured as I turned to go sit at a chair. No sooner had I, Ren's hands gripped at my shoulders and plied my muscles into less-tense shapes.

Tanya sat opposite, unclasping the side of her breastplate so she could sit more comfortably. She gave a tired glance between each of us, then sighed. "I feel like I may have gotten myself into something I am woefully unprepared for."

"We're each a little weird," I said, totally at the mercy of the elf breaking the stress from my body. "Perhaps a better introduction is in order? My name is Max. I was a magician and demon hunter in my previous lives. Now in the System, I have demon-summoning Abilities and am a dab hand at Inventory manipulation."

"Demon hunter?" she repeated. "Thought we were from the same world?"

"I'm actually two different versions of me stuck together." I shrugged, as that didn't seem to budge her confused look.

Ren gave one last squeeze before moving from me. "Give her an example of your Inventory stuff, trickster."

I clicked my fingers, bringing forth a card into my hands. A plain, normal one, from the many part decks I had collected. Ace of hearts, purely by chance. After letting them both see which it was, I flicked it straight into the air. Only it turned into a dagger as it ascended. Hat down from my head to catch it. My spear then slowly rose up out of the hat, the ace of hearts impaled at the tip.

"Impressive." Tanya tilted her head. "At first, when they said you were a magician, I assumed it was just a different name for Wizard."

With a shrug, both objects vanished, and I put my hat back on. Could have done something a lot more spectacular, but I'd had enough for today. Having found the ability to give myself limits, I *would* make use of it on occasion.

"Ren," the elf said, sitting down near me. "Ranger with healing and defensive Skills."

"I'm a bear," Wolf said, his voice rising from the kitchen where his mouth was still half full. "And I do bear things."

"Called Wolf," Ren added. "Which I believe is partially my fault."

"Quinn," the man said from my peripheral, giving her a low bow. "Utility specialist and jack-of-all-trades. I owe my life to Max and have sworn to assist in any manner asked until I can repay him."

A little more exposition than required, but it fit his personality well enough. I gave Tanya a brief smile. "I have a pact demon who makes a regular appearance. He was the one who restrained you—Roger."

She nodded slowly, taking this all in. "Tanya, as I'm sure you've worked out. My Class is focused toward buffs and debuffs. I told Max this, but in my normal world, I am a virologist with a military background."

I made note that she was still using the present tense throughout our conversations. As if her reasons for joining the Lady weren't clear enough, she was obviously still holding on to something we had long let go. For us, it was always *old* or *previous* world.

Tanya was like a ghost who hadn't moved on and accepted that she had died.

Not that I was here to show her the way to heaven, of course. For as long as she proved her loyalty, then we'd be here to support her coming to terms with those things being behind us. Focus on the Lady now; we'd worry about the *after* when we got to it.

Her eyes unfocused as she glanced over to her STAR menus, before her eyes dimmed and expression hardened.

"They know my group is dead," she said. "But that I live."

CHAPTER FORTY-TWO

Start to Manage

The air in the quaint wooden house grew a little chillier. Although, that could be because Wolf had left the back door open. All eyes were on our newest recruit, waiting for her to do something. Maybe explode. At this stage, I wouldn't discount anything.

"What do you want me to reply?" she asked. Her eyes had left their unfocused state and were looking at me, so I knew she wasn't secretly typing.

I drummed my fingertips on my leg as I exhaled. "Who are they?"

"Handoff group for once we captured you. Drent was going to update them. That's the shark person who has a lot more holes in his head than usual." Tanya raised an eyebrow.

Even though I had just put my hat back on, I removed it to place on my lap while my fingers ran through my hair. Still a little long—I'd have to ask one of my troupe for a cut eventually . . . But which one?

"Our sleep was interrupted by a zombie attack, and we have fought against three other Parties, and a troll." I added that last one for effect, even if it wasn't that much effort. "What do you suggest we do about this?"

A bit of an ask to put her on the spot this early, but it served a dual purpose. Well, a trifecta of purposes if I took my exhaustion as truth—which it was. Another opportunity for her to prove her switched allegiance wasn't weightless but also a test to see how she thought. If I was putting her in the manager box, she'd need to show me she was able to function in that role and guide our efforts when we were rough around the edges.

She clicked her tongue and made the point of removing her breastplate fully now. Although her black dress wasn't particularly combat worthy, it was rather plain and—surprising to me—padded underneath. Catching my intrigue, she grimaced.

"Lady thought I'd fit the theme better in a dress. Can finally switch to something more practical . . ." Her eyes went between us all again. "Unless there's a different uniform requirement here?"

I shook my head. "Wear whatever makes you most comfortable." My hand went out to gesture for her to get back to the matter at hand.

"Best thing to do is kill them," she said. Her stoic and calm expression was refreshing. With that attitude, she'd fit right in with us. "I'll give them a half-truth. Tell them you captured me and are trying to get information out of me."

My head nodded slowly. "Bring them to this location and ambush them?"

"At night would be best," she agreed. "If they think you're asleep, they'll be less apprehensive about attacking."

I gave Ren a glance, and she gave a brief nod in return.

We liked that plan. Killing off another Party of Crimson Shadow where we weren't on the back foot for a change was worth losing a bit of our sleeping time.

Tanya cupped her chin and looked down at the floor. "I know their levels and rough Classes too. This area has decent terrain for an ambush, but we'd want to move on after, just in case they let any other groups know they were coming here."

"Sleeping in the Dungeon is still a possibility," Quinn said, leaning against the wall as he rubbed at his eye patch. "It means traveling in the dark, but it will be safe once we arrive."

Wolf lifted his face from his meal in progress, tongue lapping around his mouth. "I could eat," he said.

"Sounds good to me, then." I clapped my hands together. "Time to take the fight back to them. Oh, what level were you, Tanya?"

"Fifteen," she replied. "You all are too?"

"Eleven, but Quinn is fourteen."

Tanya looked a little surprised to hear that answer. "Only eleven? How long have you been here?"

"Couple of weeks for us." I gestured to Ren, ignoring the fact that she had spent three months in misery on the starter island. "We sped through things and came to the second area at eight."

"That's . . . actually quite efficient." The woman shrugged. "Shouldn't take you long to get to the fifteen cap then. We can plan tomorrow?"

Ren furrowed her brow. "Level cap was twenty, I thought?"

"In the wider world, sure, but . . ." Tanya trailed off as she looked between us. "Of course, you haven't been here long enough, so you might not know. There's been a barrier preventing access to the third area, and you need to do some Quest that way to get higher than fifteen."

That opened up a whole casket of questions, wriggling around like dirtied worms. Where to even begin? We had avoided what little lore the world had tried to push our way and filled our brains with our own heroic quest to rid the System of the Lady. For certain definitions of heroic anyway.

"Why is there a barrier?" Ren asked, her normal scowl comfortably back on her face.

"And who put it there?" Quinn added, saving me the hardship of doing the deed myself.

"To answer . . . who . . ." She flexed her fingers as she thought. "The King and Queen, I believe."

I raised my eyebrows. "They are Players with actual control or part of the System?"

Tanya pulled a face. "As far as I know, it could be either—but it's something like that. I was here after the barrier went up. The reason for it . . . Well, I've been told it's because of Lady in Red."

My brain was two steps behind still. That information made sense for why no higher-level Players had come through and gotten rid of her. It didn't make total sense, however. "She's only been causing trouble for a couple of weeks though?"

A shrug was the response. "I don't have the full picture, I'm afraid. Someone told me that PvP wasn't enabled at some point—but something changed. As luck would have it . . . one of the chaps paying us a visit later might know some more on it."

I nodded slowly. More of the full picture had been revealed, even if it wasn't quite perfect. "Alright . . ." I glanced again at Ren to make sure she was on board. Seemed that way. "Make arrangements, Tanya. I'll need a report on what we're going to be up against."

"Of course." Her eyes unfocused as she went to put the plan into action.

Or at least, I hoped so. There was still the chance she could be double-crossing us. Set us up for something even worse than a single-Party ambush. It wasn't very likely though. Not being under their corrupting influence put her a few intellect points over the others, and she was probably exhausted dealing with the violent half-wits.

I mean, we were a little better than that. Maybe.

Ren stood up and placed her hand on my shoulder briefly as she passed. "Anyone else for coffee?"

Tanya almost leaped from her chair with how she shuffled to focus on the elf. "You have coffee? Should have said from the start. That's reason enough to join you lot." Without a chance for anyone else to reply, a mug was already in her hand at the ready.

I smiled and settled into some form of comfort. We'd need to keep an eye on her still, but the woman seemed almost happy to be among us. Appearances could

be deceiving—I of all people should know this . . . but it was nice to meet someone who didn't want to run away, call me an asshole, or split my head open.

The piercing whistle of the kettle drew my attention to the kitchen, where I
could see Ren leaning against one of the counters with her arms crossed. Despite
her scowl at the group of mugs now ready to receive the magical liquid, she seemed
relatively relaxed. It put my mind at ease, as the times where we were both wrong
about something were few and far between.

Wolf had somehow managed to finish off his bounty of food and immediately decided to have a nap right in the middle of the open-plan kitchen. Quinn
appeared to be focused on something in his STAR menus, and I wondered if having one eye made the process more awkward. Probably.

"It is done," Tanya said, drawing my attention back to her. "Group of five coming at one in the morning."

I heard Ren groan as she poured the hot water. Another night of terrible sleep.

"They're not suspicious that you can reply to them?"

"Not particularly." She shrugged. "I'm not sure there's much that can stop
Chat messages unless I was unconscious. Plus, they're the *Crimson*."

They were. I nodded. The sun was starting to set now, so we still had a few
hours to make our plans. Although I had kept a poker face, I felt the same way
about the lack of sleep as Ren did. Still, I turned and smiled as she came to pass
me a mug of coffee.

"It's a struggle to get this stuff," Tanya said, nodding her head in thanks at
the elf as she received her own. "Especially as an outlaw."

I sat and enjoyed the warmth of the cup for a moment. It probably wouldn't
keep me as awake as I would like, and resting in the Dungeon didn't seem that
comfortable either. In a time of relative safety, the groups of us could split off into
different houses. Live like normal people, if even for one night. Part of me just
wanted to focus on the relationship with Ren and not have to deal with all this
violent bullshit, but . . . I needed them both, in some way.

Tanya blew the steam from her drink and then tilted her head. "I told them
you were holding me in this house, so perhaps we should make arrangements to
not be here."

"Alright." A grin slowly rose up on my face as I raised my voice. "Everyone
gather round. We have a show to put on."

"*Trickster*," Ren whined, an uncharacteristic sound coming from her. The end of
her bow jabbed into my side as she tried to get my focus.

It was nighttime now, and we lay on the grass under the dark sky. After going
through our plan a couple of times and spending more time with Tanya and
Quinn, things seemed more . . . normal. While the fixer had emotions clear on
display, our new Party member just seemed to be very . . . pragmatic and

straightforward. Her singular focus was getting back home, and some time spent chatting about things from our past world had tied her to our cause greater than any threat could.

Not that we could promise to send her back, but she had come to the agreement that the Lady had no clue either. Certainly this mysterious King and Queen might have answers if anyone did. Not that I expect there to be a way to return to Earth, given that—

My right eye twitched as I was jabbed again. "Yes, moonflower?"

"I love you," she whispered, her bright-blue eyes picking up the moonlight.

Any tension washed away in seeing her expression. "I love you too. You grow more ridiculous by the day." I thought we had reached the ceiling of her emotional expression, but it seemed the nighttime had to be a step above at all times.

"It's not ridiculous to state the truth," she said with a huff before turning her gaze back to the center of the small village. While she didn't scowl, I saw the businesslike seriousness return to her. Her feelings aside, she was still the same Ren underneath.

We had made the pact that our relations wouldn't hinder our goal. Something she had agreed to with a pout, but she was fully on board. Already accepted that love was an invitation for tragedy, we still needed to be cautious that we didn't stumble into worse through our distracted sensibilities.

But then, that's why we were laying in thick grass under the cover of darkness instead of in a soft bed under the cover of . . . well, just a blanket, I supposed.

That our plan had involved us being paired together was just coincidence.

Slightly out of the village on a small mound that could barely be considered a hill, we had a slight height advantage while still being able to see the front area of four of the houses. The ruined one we'd almost died in. The nicer one we had rested in. The two others who were now part of our plan.

"I'm sorry," she said, even as my mind had moved on. "Been a very straining day. I'm rather eager to live a life of those good times, and I've started putting the cart before the horse."

"If only we could be so gluttonous and satiated with what we desire as Wolf often is," I replied.

She looked back at me and smiled. "One day, trickster."

A beep of my Chat brought me away from saying anything further to the elf, and after shuffling whatever Fiona had said out of the way, I brought up the message from Tanya.

[Tanya: They have updated me. ETA 10m]
[Max: Understood.]

I switched to the Party Chat we had now included her in.

[Max: Ten minutes. Prepare.]
[Quinn: Ok^]
[Wolf: o]
[Tanya: In position, at your command.]
[Ren: Ready.]

Closed everything down and looked back at the elf. Her eyes were trained back on the dark village, only illuminated by the lanterns we had left as decoys in the house. The shadow of the corpse Wolf hadn't chewed up sitting in a chair near the window across the dirt and dull grass. I'd save my own prodding for postbattle.

It was a simple reverse ambush. Assuming Tanya wasn't screwing us over—a prospect that seemed less likely by the hour—we'd wait for them to assail the house before springing our own traps on the group hoping to catch us sleeping.

She had advised to try to keep the more knowledgeable Shadow alive if we wanted to ask questions about the third area. A frogman who was a type of Arcane Knight. Heavy armor and some spells. More trouble than it sounded worth—to try to incapacitate rather than just outright kill—but I said we'd see what we could do.

Quinn and Tanya were in the closest building to our right, on the top floor to send out supporting Skills through the windows. Wolf was in the house farther away but still on the right. Ready to repeat his entrance that we used in the first village in the second area. Our trap was in the closest left, while the ruined building was farther left. With Ren beside me, we could quickly rain down powerful ranged attacks, and having a good view of the stage would allow me to dip in and out where I was most needed.

Any looming excitement was jostled from my overworking brain by the jab of the bow end again. In raising an eyebrow, expecting more soft words, I caught the sharp glare in Ren's eyes as she gestured out to the darkened road.

Two small orbs of light bobbed closer before being snuffed out.

Curtain was about to rise.

CHAPTER FORTY-THREE

Just a Taste

We had invited unknowns into our little group of safety. Yet, in lying here in the darkness awaiting the looming conflict in the small village, I didn't feel as on edge as I should. If anything, it gave me hope. While such a thing had scared Ren when she saw it in me, I was comforted. A Party of five had seemed untenable at first—we were too closed off. But now . . . our capabilities had grown, and I had even more of a strong feeling that we'd be able to take the Lady down.

Time would tell if that would bear fruit or if things wouldn't work out as expected. Even so . . . as I watched the darkened figures approach the house . . . I expected *everything*. Slowly planned for every eventuality. No longer repressing half of myself, I now found that everything felt clearer and more concise. Ready to be erased.

The group of five split. Two crept toward the front door. Avoiding the light of the lantern, I could still pick out a larger figure with an odd gait. Probably the frogman. The other three circled around to the back of the house, two out of sight while the last came past this side of the building.

It felt nice to have my Mana back and usable—how odd that it was something I had an attachment to. I didn't feel bad for using the special potion Ruby had given me already. No doubt otherwise it would have sat and collected dust in an Inventory already getting dangerously close to a cluttered limit.

It was almost time. Tanya had left us with an idol—something similar to how Ren's healing charm worked—that would provide healing and Mana regeneration when activated. A second one lay beneath a rock in the middle of the square between houses that would do the opposite to those we intended to fight against.

The thought of them being switched was amusing, but at this point, it felt like I was begging for betrayal. Certainly, with both our newest members in the same house together, they could—

My train of thought fell off the cliff as I received a jab from the bow.

Show was about to start—it was time.

To begin—fireworks against the darkness. As a slimmer figure reached the front door, I fired the demonic cannon. Not only did the blast come as a surprise to them, dust washing through the windows as the door burst into splinters, but my Spear of Luck found a new home in the chest of the lucky audience member.

"Welcome," Ren yelled as she stood. "To the greatest show of your short lives."

Before they could get their bearings and turn to her, the bright stage lights illuminated center stage in the middle of the square—Quinn's light pulsing high in the air to reveal me standing there.

I gave them a bow as Ren's entangling arrow struck the one sporting my spear. The frogman leaped into the air to avoid it, so we'd have to play this a little differently. Beams of red energy shot out and exploded my dove into a cloud of feathers as I switched back to be beside the elf.

If our intro had been more effective, I'd have stayed to do a little more improvisational magic—but I didn't fancy my chances against a Knight. Other than the twice-impaled figure, only the Shadow on our side of the building was restrained by the vines. The two on the side hidden to us were free.

With a grin and the click of my fingers, the cannon fired again, a wave of confetti and wood chippings flooding out into the illuminated square. They had Dazzle icons. They had the crimson-hand icons. They had less than a minute to live.

The blast signaled the arrival of Wolf, our most extraordinary showman. *Show bear.* A red circle of light flashed up around the frogman and bleeding-out member as Tanya utilized her debuff idol. While the Knight glared for my position, partially blinded by dust, confetti, and feathers, the bear burst through the doorway of his house to bound straight into the melee.

Hidden audience members became less so as they got back onto the main stage to assist their fellows. Perhaps we set the trap too early—but this was work in progress. Learning by doing.

Purple card blazing with energy went straight for the entangled person. A shield came up in front of them—a small wall of rippling energy that caused my attack to dissipate. The vines burned away from their feet, freeing them. Their eyes glared out toward me, a hand grabbing for something as the other maintained the protective spell.

I gave them an exaggerated shrug just as a fireball from the roof pelted down and exploded on them. With the tip of my hat, I gave thanks to my Imp+ up there. In truth, we had agreed that I would not be the star of this show.

Heartbreaking in a way, but we were trying a new tactic with moving pieces. With the four of us obscured and with the advantage of range, we had decided that Wolf would take center stage on this occasion.

Quinn and Tanya sent down buffs and assistance from the top floor of the right-hand building, while Ren and I provided ranged support in the manner of pointed violence from our small mound just out in the wings.

And what a showman the bear had become. Back in his bowler hat and waistcoat for the occasion, he practically radiated with the number of Skills that had been cast on him. A spectacle in of itself. Health regeneration, Defense increase, attack increase, Crit Chance increase, debilitation resistance, stun resistance, elemental resistance. So many that I couldn't see the rest of the icons over his head—especially as he met the frog Knight and began battling.

His first swipe was blocked by the held sword, and the frogman slid back across the cobbled ground, the bear immediately back on him with a roar. Hopefully, he remembered that he wasn't supposed to eat that one. Well, I wouldn't blame him if he did—it was easy to get caught up in the act when the adrenaline was going.

My opponent had dropped the shield in an attempt to put out the flames that now licked at his armor. Unfortunately, burning might be preferable to the two cards now zipping toward him. He swung out at one, knocking it to the ground as his short staff flashed blue. The second one struck the weapon, cracking it in half before burying into his shoulder. Shame the first card was actually a Hellhound+ to replace the roof-bound Imp+, and the magic portal opened from the deflection to the ground.

Ren had whispered a word in Elfin and fired an arrow of water at the pair in the back before then firing one of ice. I'd have to get her to teach me Elfin sometime . . . Oh, that probably wouldn't work since the System translated almost everything. An arrow of white-blue beamed through the air, leaving a trail of icy specks in its wake. Where it struck, the water provided from the first strike also froze solid, pinning the two in place. A good audience stays still and watches quietly—this couldn't be denied.

The figure impaled by my cannoned spear must be their healer but was currently focused on keeping themselves from shuffling off this world into the unknown. This put the others at a disadvantage and—

One of our opponents at the back brought up an actual shield to block Ren's next follow-up, while their companion charged up an attack. I readied <Card Fan> to send out in front of either us or Wolf—but *no*, I was mistaken.

A foot-wide beam of crimson energy burst out from the pair at nearly a right angle to us, way above the bear . . . and straight into the windows where the other two were.

An explosion rocked the building as wooden planks and dust bloomed out of the openings.

"Fuck!" I seethed. The idol she had given us clicked and crumbled away, inert. She wasn't dead—we hadn't received any Party-based notification. Injured enough to need the regeneration Skill for herself, however.

Wolf was winning his fight against the Knight, but the frogman was remarkably resilient and had been buying time so that he could get assistance. This angered me. I *fucking* hated it when people were on stage and shouldn't be.

I gave Ren a quick glance. "I'm going to need to go steal some of the limelight."

"Break a leg or two, Max."

Now I was buzzing. Elated for a handful of reasons that bounced around in my head, unable to be tied down and crushed into descriptive words.

I shifted places with my Hellhound+. The man stumbled at the sudden change in force as he no longer had the canine pulling on him. It was enough for my card to find his heart. I stepped past him to circle around to the main stage, purple ears bursting from his skull before he even had a chance to hit the dirt.

A blast of confetti signaled my arrival. Illuminated by the flickering light of Quinn's glowing orb, I basked in the warmth, ready for the adoring cheers of the crowd. They had missed me—*I could tell.*

From behind me, against the house that held my fading cannon, I heard the projected voice of our fixer.

"Injured but alive. We'll help as soon as able."

Couldn't deny them a little break now and again. Union would have my head—and they'd done a bang-up job in getting Wolf up to spec for tonight's show. Even got the music right. I started humming along as I stepped up to my spear, which the audience member still held.

"Tricks over," I said, slurring the words slightly. "Return the prop, otherwise you'll be ejected by security."

Roger loomed up beside me, now holding the giant mace once more.

The pale face of the healer didn't really know how to respond to my request. Could be confusion at my tone or the fact we had switched the ambush up on them. In truth, my diagnosis was something much more dire and unforgivable.

Stage fright.

Their hand raised up to cast an Ability toward me. Roger's weapon came down and crushed their skull before they could finish the process. This was why you paid the muscle well. Couldn't have my fans manhandling me—certainly not in the middle of a performance. Unforgiveable. "Lifetime ban," I murmured to my pact demon before turning my eyes to the reprehensible pair who had destroyed some of the set pieces.

Their eyes turned to me. Saw the demon inhabiting their Party member. Glanced down at their healer—a mulched sack of bloodied meat. I drew the Blade of Shadow, and they recognized that as well. They'd been following my career with interest and wanted to ask for my autograph via a pound of flesh from my dazzling form.

An arrow whistled past my ear by a couple of inches, and they blocked it with their silly shield. I enjoyed it, however, as if my protégé was whispering sweet stage directions in my ear. My presence was undeniable—they couldn't keep their eyes off me even with the threat of arrows from the back.

One intended to use the shield to protect them both, while the second started charging up a red beam aimed for yours truly. Details were blurry now, as if I had stepped into a cartoon. A parody of my showmanship, the here and now becoming sketches in my planning notepad. I could no longer determine Classes, gender, or ancestry of those before me. They were mannequins of gray, with rough, dark outlines.

The course was plotted; we just had to go through the motions. Just as planned.

A large canvas covered view of me, a curtain that I flung at to the side, left to right. As soon as it ran out and I would become revealed, I did the same to a second one, pocketing the first and repeating the process to form a wall of billowing fabric.

They thought themselves not so easily fooled and fired their shot.

The beam of red pierced through the fabric, causing it to falter and drop to the ground, half in cinders. It had found a target, that was for certain, and the explosion in the backdrop was visible through the hole punctured through my torso. Oh, *sorry*—that's me being an unreliable narrator again—as what they had expected to be me was just the spent corpse that Roger had left before the strike.

I had turned invisible and strode up to them. A clap of my hands and I reappeared just two feet from their surprised eyes that I hastily sketched into my mental notepad. Even added some wiggly lines beside their heads to exaggerate the point.

<Finale>.

Max! Max! Max!

Applause and cheers from the audience. So kind! Frogman was preoccupied with the other part of the act so was unaffected—but the two before me were stunned. Even the icons agreed with me . . . although one of them was running out quicker than the other. A passive resistance, perhaps.

I drew an empowered card out, spun it like a saw. Into their neck. Not really a good trick, but their intention was to interrupt the flow of the performance, and security was currently on his break. Lines of gray scribbles shot out from the mannequin, zigzagging onto the ground to form a pool as the sketchy figure flopped over.

The second—and more patient—audience member had a couple more seconds before they'd be rejoining after the brief intermission. How rude of them not to sit and clap like everyone else. Almost soured the experience. But *no*. I was happy.

Into my hand, an apple. I placed it on their head and took two steps back.

A twang from offstage, and my smile widened.

Just as the figure came to and the adoration started to wane, I tilted my head to the side.

An arrow zipped past my cheek, almost grazing it, and buried itself in their neck. A moment later, a second arrow plunged downward at a steep angle to pierce through both the apple and the oddly round gray head of whatever the opponent truly was.

I turned and gave a brief bow to the elf before raising an eyebrow to the Knight.

Disarmed—literally. Sword strewn across the ground, one of his appendages in the bear's mouth as Wolf sat atop him, pinning the other arm to the ground.

Vertigo made the process of walking over to the pair slightly more awkward, when I was hoping for something more elegant. Late-night showings always took it out of me more.

I stopped and leaned over to look him in the face.

"Care to rate the show on a scale of one to five stars? Be honest . . ." My grin widened as purple electricity arced around my body. "We take criticism really well."

CHAPTER FORTY-FOUR

No Autographs

I sat on my chair in the middle of the illuminated square with a headache. Not uncommon at the end of a tense performance—especially one so late at night. It was more than that though. I felt like I was coming down off of some drug, experiencing withdrawal stronger than just the adrenaline and dopamine leaving my system.

Overall, it made me a little grouchy.

To my side, Ren walked over. "Everything okay, trickster?"

I raised an eyebrow but didn't have the heart to snap at her. "Feeling pretty rough."

"You . . . were something else tonight."

My other eyebrow raised to join the first as I tried to take in her expression. Intrigue and awe? Perhaps that was my hopeful mind filling in what I wanted to believe. No, we could read each other like books. She currently wanted to tear the pages out and chew on all the sordid words that comprised my being.

I wasn't even sure I understood the metaphor that I was trying to paint.

She averted her gaze toward the semidestroyed building to see the pair of Quinn and Tanya exit. The woman was limping, propped up by the fixer. Both were covered in small cuts that had recently healed, their clothes shredded in places and charred. Ren furrowed her brow and sent out a heal toward our new manager. *Manager?* I'd probably lost the plot somewhere along the way.

Tanya righted herself, testing her footing while giving Quinn a nod—she was now able to walk relatively normally.

"Thank you," she told the elf. "That's certainly a nicer heal than my slow one."

"More fool us for thinking we were safe," Quinn grumbled, rolling out his shoulders as he received a heal himself.

"Don't sell yourself short." Tanya shook her head. "It was coming directly for me. Without your intervention, I'd be dead."

He gave her a low bow, grunting from the effort and murmuring about duty or something, blah blah. My focus had already shifted back to our captive. Wolf still sat atop him. He wasn't keen to speak with me, partly due to the bear staring at him and slowly chewing the arm that had been ripped off.

I wasn't sure if I wanted to do good cop, bad cop—or even speak with him. Any questions answered would be suspect anyway. Eventually I came to the conclusion that I wasn't sure of much at present time, and the sooner I could get to a place I could sleep, the better.

Ren's hand pressed down on my shoulder. "Feeling okay, Max? Your hands didn't bleed."

She was right, and I lifted them up for inspection, mostly for the show of it. Whether it was because I was no longer holding back on the fully realized me or not, didn't really matter. With the buffs we had, there was no need for me to dip into <Bloodletting>.

I shrugged and stood up as her hand slunk away. It wasn't usually like me to shirk a connection with her, but I felt like I was at the end of a very thin rope. I took a step toward the frogman and stopped, looking back at her. "You were fantastic too. We'll talk more when we are safe."

The elf nodded, content enough that things were okay, before she went over to see if the other pair needed tending to. Moving myself adjacent to Wolf, the bear tilted his head to the side and regarded me. His waistcoat had been shredded, and his bowler hat had managed to stick atop his head despite being indented.

"Doesn't taste that good," the bear complained.

I nodded and crouched down beside our captive. He didn't look too happy, but then again, we *had* torn one of his arms off. It was a wonder he hadn't died of blood loss, maybe. A wide, frog-like face with bulbous yellow eyes. His skin was a pale green, but perhaps part of the paleness was due to the arm thing. Crimson handprint on his head, which tallied up the with icon showing that he had taken the blood. A few others showing the current near-death state he was in.

"Constantly besieged by those that seek ruin upon this world," I said as I tilted my head. "Yet the worst part is . . . you're all so *weak*. Children thinking they can rule the roost, with no consideration for any consequences or what it *truly* takes to survive."

"Fuck you, foolish man. I'll not talk to you or the traitor."

I cast a quick glance back at Tanya before shrugging at him. "Actually, I don't care if you talk or not. Keeping you alive was a moment of weakness and a mistake." A wry smile cracked at the side of my mouth. "But since you're here, I had something you might help with."

Into my hand, I drew Roger's card.

"Normally this only works on corpses," I began. "But I'm a huge fan of breaking the System, and you're a big lad. Perhaps there's room in there for both of you?"

Confusion had him silent, his tongue unsure how to address what I was actually saying.

Pressing the card against his metal armor gave him more of a clue, and he tried to writhe away—ineffective with the bear still upon him. There was an amount of force preventing my card from hitting its target, however. Like repelling magnets, the power was trying to push it away to deflect in a different direction. I clenched my jaw and sank more Mana into it. Gradually, it started to pierce through his plate . . . millimeters at a time.

I could override the System, bend reality to my will.

My brow furrowed, and I let the card vanish away. I stood back up to my feet and glared off into the dark of the night. "All yours, Wolf."

He wasted no time, going for the head first to silence the Shadow. The crunching noise almost prevented me from hearing the elf approach me from behind.

"Not to repeat myself again, but *is* everything okay?"

I turned to her, concern on both our faces but for different reasons. "It was like I was suddenly presented with two different futures. Like posters advertising the show." My eyes went back out to the pitch gloom. "In one, I was all-powerful. Someone without equal who would do whatever it took to stay at the top of the hill, wearing the bloodied crown of a tyrant."

A few moments of silence passed before she responded. "And the other?"

"Some amount of happiness." I turned back to her with tired eyes. "A Max accepting of the lot given to him here and making the best of it, enjoying living and loving."

"Second one sounds much nicer." Her hand came out and wrapped around mine. Hard to disagree with that statement when she made such a compelling argument.

Which was more likely? I was capable of both, but . . . there was a line. Designing the show to what I wanted it to be—or shaping it in a manner the audience was eager for. If anything, the showman flavor thickening the evening air had left a bad taste in my mouth, as well as left me hungry for some normality.

"Agreed," I eventually said. "You and the others ready to move out?"

"Loot first, trickster."

My right eye twitched. Of course.

"I'm a little slower than normal, but I'm good to walk," Tanya confirmed.

Quinn nodded. "Eager to get out of the darkness."

Weren't we all? Seemed to follow us around like an ugly duckling, however. I had arrived in this world, blood on my face and half dead, and fate had imprinted itself, repeating the same plot point over and over. That said, I hadn't almost died again since leaving the first area. Debilitated and restrained . . . slightly crazy— *sure*—but not at risk of death. I should count my blessings. Quick glance toward the elf, and then I went off to loot the dregs of society.

[5,638 Gold]
[Health Potions (6)]
[Power Tokens (2)]
[Bracers of the Trickster: +2 DEX, +3 INT]
[Intelligence Ring: +3 INT, +10% Mana]
[Fire-Circle Wand]
[Savage-Strike Wand]

A reasonable haul. I kept the unspent power tokens secret for now. Not to be deceitful, but we'd sit and deliberate somewhere safer—same with the wands. Ring and bracers went straight on, however. Now that we knew fifteen was the highest level we could achieve, it put a cap on the gear we'd be able to find. Nice of the Crimson Shadow to keep delivering us care packages of their acquired—or possibly also stolen—Equipment.

"I see how you have achieved everything now," Tanya said, drawing my attention from the last of the bodies. "You're remarkably proficient, despite appearances."

With a grunt, I stood to my feet and stretched out. She looked just as exhausted as the rest of us, but there was the light of excitement in her eyes. "I hope you were taking notes," I replied. "There are improvements we need to make."

"Of course." She huffed. "Now that I've seen you all in battle properly, I'm brimming with ideas. A conversation over breakfast tomorrow, however."

"We'll schedule in a team meeting once we've had some rest then." *There it was.* I could almost audibly hear the click as she filtered into the position we needed for the group. Ren and I were no slouches when it came to winning a battle and having some manner of plan . . . but Tanya's experience was more grounded in something other than our risk-laden mania.

I looked over at the elf currently helping the bear get his outfit back in good order, while Quinn was lost in his STAR planning our route. "You never mentioned your actual Class name."

"Fateweaver," she replied, following my gaze to the other members of the Party. "You were expecting Battle Manager or something, right?"

"Correct." I smiled. Casting buffs and debuffs was a way to change or weave fate, certainly. I'd allow that explanation. Made a lot more sense than Quinn actually being an Arcane Fixer. Then again, System might be translating that oddly.

Ren walked over to us, the bear in tow. "Best make a move. As much as I don't want to be traveling in the dark, I'd hate to be interrupted by another ambush during our sleep."

I nodded and gestured Quinn over. He dimmed his light and led from the front beside Tanya. Ren and I took up the middle, while Wolf watched our backs. It was mostly a path we had to follow, thankfully. No stumbling through the foliage to twist my ankle or crack my skull on something. We'd avoid all the Monster groups as well.

The elf sighed as she turned her blue eyes toward me. "Didn't want to say this earlier," she said in a low tone, "but during the battle . . . I could hear music."

"Same." I smiled. "What did it go like?"

Softly she hummed the beats of the tune to the best of her recollection. Interestingly enough, it was the same as the one I had heard. My nod caused her to wrinkle her face up.

"Now we have a shared delusion," she eventually whispered, looking out into the impenetrable darkness of night.

The moon was obscured, so we weren't even graced by a dim gray highlight on the trees and scenery surrounding us. Quinn and Tanya murmured the occasional thing to each other, but I couldn't overhear. He seemed to cool on her after knowing she was taken. While he appeared to fall for anyone remotely affable, he could at least accept no for an answer. I was glad to see them getting along.

Ren held my hand, this time our fingers interlocking. In some ways it felt almost juvenile, considering the death we had just wreaked with little remorse. Our relationship was still in the fledgling stages, however, and part of me craved this basic action. It would be safer to have our hands free and weapons out ready in case something untoward did happen upon us . . .

But the fear wasn't allowed to control our lives—we had decided that before. No sense living in the shadows when our flame could burn so brightly. It meant that others would want to extinguish us, but looking at the pair ahead . . . it also attracted *moths*. The show was on the road, moving from performance to performance.

I *loved* it. What more could a magician ask for?

Well, a demon to kill, for one. I had the feeling that Rolo's twin, grouped up with the necromancer, was going to be a bit of a linchpin to our efforts in this second area. Not the closest group to the Lady but trusted for keeping the starting third of the area under their thumb. Perhaps they were patting themselves on the back now that the camp was all but gone.

My eyes went up as my Chat received a message.

[Ruby: Hi, Max, I know this is late.]
[Ruby: Just wanted you to know things are going swell.]
[Ruby: Found a new Player that fits our group.]
[Ruby: We'll help them level, and then we'll come back.]
[Max: Glad to hear it.]
[Ruby: Fiona didn't want to tell you yet, but you know how she is.]
[Max: I do. Thanks for keeping me updated.]
[Ruby: Stay safe. And get some sleep—doctor's orders! {O>Ó}]

It was nice to have a reminder every so often that what we were doing had a positive effect on the world. Killing with little remorse had me looking at the crimson crown like it was almost an inevitability . . . but I couldn't go back and betray all those I had helped.

After all, it would be nice to have some fans once the dust settled. We could put on an actual show rather than the violent-combat version. In fact, the thought filled me with a hope and apprehension that tore down the grip of exhaustion like faded wallpaper.

"I hope the Dungeon has a little-bears' room," Wolf grumbled from behind.

My smile only wavering slightly, we continued to stride through the darkness. Victors and alive for at least one more day.

CHAPTER FORTY-FIVE

Waiting Room

I stood in infinite darkness. Cold and solitary. The deepest crimson shimmered across the horizon, barely visible against the void. Vertical waves that drew me in closer. From within them, something started to form.

A loose figure of red mist, becoming more detailed and defined by the second. Tall—impossibly so. Masculine and muscled, they dwarfed me by such a large magnitude despite being so far away. Twisted horns grew from their head as orbs of bright white burst from their bearded face.

I became lost within their gaze. As if tethered, I started to walk closer to them. An awkward gait and an insurmountable distance—yet I was making progress. Suddenly, a burst of warmth illuminated my back, and I broke my wide-eye attention to look behind.

A swirling vortex of radiant energy. The figure wanted me to come closer. Stand by his side—I was sure of it. But now, I could not. Every fiber of my being relaxed, and I allowed myself to fall into the golden light. Elation filled my core as the comfort enveloped me.

"Max?"

My eyes flickered open, and I was briefly disorientated. Stone walls, and I was on the floor. I turned my eyes to see the elf crouched down beside me.

"You were writhing about a lot. Bad dream?"

I deflated in my bedroll and tried to put the shattered parts of my brain back together. A few more hours of sleep would have been preferable . . . but now we were in the Dungeon. Not the most comfortable place to rest. We had lain in a rough star shape, five points against the walls, aside from Wolf, who blocked the door to farther in. Would have been nice to share some warmth with the elf, but . . .

"Nothing to worry about," I finally said, smiling as I placed my top hat over my face.

"Bullshitter," she replied before sighing. "Sorry to wake you, but the others are getting up, and we have another long day of hardship to get through."

I did nothing but groan in response. Even I had a little downtime before shows.

Hair tickled at my ear as I felt her lean in closer. "Come on, trickster. Survive the day and we'll find an inn . . . and I'll do that thing you like."

Who needed time off anyway? A true showman was always on the clock, and more hardship just meant more opportunities to work on my tricks and come up with new ideas. As soon as she moved away, I practically sprung up to my feet, almost knocking myself out on a stone shelf my head briefly grazed.

Ren picked my hat back up and handed it over, a tired look in her eyes. It was her own fault for promising we'd go over more real magic tricks together. At least, that's what I assumed she meant.

"Morning, Max," Tanya said from the other side of the room. She gave me a brief nod before sorting through some items.

"Morning." I smiled toward the gathering. It was nice that neither she nor Quinn had murdered us in our sleep. "Ready for another day fighting against the odds?"

Tanya grunted. "Make me a stiff coffee and I'll follow you into the depths of hell."

I pulled a face. "It's not a pleasant place." I raised an eyebrow toward the elf. As she was the bearer of the all-important coffee, I sought her approval for it to be distributed.

She nodded. "I think we could all use some. Some breakfast too?"

"Please." I gave her a low bow. "Anything you feel like making, I'll eat."

Her eyes lingered on me for a few moments before she turned to bring out her grill. I was starting to consider that I might be slightly off today. Either the extended murder day yesterday had my sensibilities left as scraps, or the uncomfortable dream was still lingering on my conscious thoughts like a wet blanket.

Chair out, and I sat so that my brain didn't have to worry about keeping me upright.

Quinn came up to sit nearby, his singular eye looking rather tired as well. Wolf appeared to be asleep by the door, but I could see his nose twitching as soon as the grill sparked up.

"Feeling sharp enough to cut through the Dungeon?" I asked the fixer.

His head tilted from side to side, his usual pomp and spark for life completely muted. "I'll admit I will be slower than intended, due to a couple of factors." He turned to raise an eyebrow at me—his missing eye clearly being one of said reasons. "But I trust you will do the heavy lifting when it comes to combat."

"Naturally." I narrowed my eyes at the chamber we were in.

Having arrived under the cover of night, I hadn't bothered to take much of it in—much preferring to hit my bedroll and never return to the waking day.

A rough hexagon shape, sun-bleached gray-stone brickwork despite it being fully covered from the daylight. Loose sand filled the edges and some of the splits between the stone. Relatively near the coast, it would probably be easy enough to guess at the theme.

"For Dungeon completion," he continued, "you just need to kill one of the main three bosses. But there's a secret reward for defeating all three—and that will be enough to level you up."

After giving me a literal cannon, I wondered how far the System would go to ensure I remained completely overpowered. Maybe it was running out of ideas for what a Demonic Magician should have . . . yet I was also apprehensive about it leaning into more of the evil side of things rather than the showman part. *Evil* being a bit of a tasteless word to use when I'd murdered nearly twenty people yesterday.

"Any messages from the Crimson?" I asked Tanya as she finished sorting something and came to sit with us. As we didn't wear backpacks traditionally, with the intangible Inventory we all had, it intrigued me that she had one.

"No. I'm sure it's not long before they start to suspect something is up, however."

Ren turned her head as she poured the first coffee. "Say, you don't have the contact details of the Lady, right?"

"Afraid not." Tanya gave us a glum smile. "Not something she gives out easily. Aside from those you've already killed . . . I can contact two of the roaming groups and one of her personal guards."

Part of me wanted to send out an open invitation. Come find us; be audience to the greatest and most fatal show the System had to offer. I knew these things shouldn't be rushed though. Unless they were heading toward some deadline, we'd take the time to grow more powerful and disassemble their different parts until none remained.

Clinical, which drew my gaze toward our newest member.

She lifted her mug up to blow away the steam, enamored by the hot liquid and seemingly relaxed and content enough to be around us.

"Did you have a Party before joining the Crimson?" I asked her.

Her eyes went up to me before back to her drink. "I did, yeah. We all declined the red."

There was a weight to the simple sentence that gave away what happened to them after the fact. *Dead.* I had enough sense to not prod further. If the rest of her Party had been killed in front of her, then I couldn't really blame her for joining the Crimson Shadow. It made some sense why her loyalty was easily replaced once she had found something strong and stable enough to take her away from those she probably reviled.

"In saying that," she continued after the heavy silence, "a good tank is worth their weight in gold, and Wolf is the best I've ever seen."

The bear perked up from his food at hearing the compliment.

"Truly, he has been the glue that held us together," Ren agreed.

I smiled. Couldn't really argue against that. While a human warrior or Paladin geared for front-row fighting would have to overcome the fear of being so close to death, Wolf had a more dissociated view. Added with his natural hardiness and whatever the System had filled him with, he was nigh unstoppable in a fair fight.

"Biggest weakness is spellcasting," I said. "Sleep and the like." Not that I wanted to throw a wet blanket over the praise, but there was a reason she switched to this conversation other than talking more about her prior Party.

"I thought as much." She smiled at the bear before looking back at me. "I am able to make a singular idol for each of us, and one with magical resistance and some Status immunity would be perfect for Wolf."

I tilted my head to the side. "Interesting how the System interpreted your Class."

"Half of it is these protective idols. The other half is . . . less savory. I hate to use it against other Players." She worked her jaw and thumbed at one of her inert idols.

Good to know she held some trauma locked away there, and I imagined it was something disease or biological warfare adjacent given her history. Sure, I killed people daily, but for the most part, we didn't let them suffer. Other than the fact that they had to endure the gaudy magician theme . . . if only briefly.

"For Ren, attack speed and lower threat. Threat seems like something rather abstract to protect against, but I'm not well-versed in arguing with the System." Tanya shrugged and handed over the idol to the elf, who stuck it in her belt.

"Quinn, you'll have the Health- and Mana-regeneration-aura idol as you'll be switching between front and midline in combat."

He nodded and gave her a low bow as he received his gray idol. Discussing tactics without me present made me feel a little left out . . . But then again, the point of having more bodies in the Party was to share some of the load. The less I had to think about, the more I could spend brainpower concentrating on my performance. My eyes went over to the elf as she packed away the grill. The per-formance *and Ren*, I corrected myself.

Tanya gave me a brief smile before addressing the group at large. "I've done this Dungeon myself, so between Quinn and me, we should have no problem navigating the traps and rooms before the bosses. Most enemies will be easily distracted by Wolf and put down between the Damage of Max and Ren." She stood and put away her chair. "Anything important to note we will bring up prior to moving between rooms."

I nodded, but inside I was probably pouting. Not exactly a worthy expression for such a prodigious showman as myself, but I wondered why she hadn't given me an idol. Perhaps I didn't need one? Sure, I was pushing the limits of what the

System should allow and carving up higher-level Players without breaking a sweat . . . but that didn't mean I didn't *want* one. I stood and waved away my chair. Decided I shouldn't be so childish and get on with the Dungeon.

"Let's get through this, nice and simple." I ignored the narrowed eyes from Ren. "After we get our level, we will stake out the blood couriers, and then see what the rest of the day brings us."

Nods and acknowledgments, even if Wolf's input was more of a grunt. I'd bribe him with more food at some point. Maybe see if he wanted anything else in life than being the wall between us and the sharp points of our foes. Couldn't only be food and sleep.

Quinn gestured for the bear to follow him. "I'll take the venerable Wolf with me down the first corridor to prepare for the first fight. And Ren, if you could kindly lend me your eyesight—I wouldn't want to miss the trap due to my condition."

"Of course."

It was nice to see them getting along better now. Life was already too stressful without everyone getting on one another's nerves. My eyes scanned around the room for anything we'd left behind before I clocked that Tanya had been waiting for me.

She stepped over, her arms crossed. "I just wanted to make sure I wasn't stepping on any toes."

I raised an eyebrow to consider this. "You're very pragmatic and headstrong. While we've done well playing things by ear, we could do with more order in our lives."

"Diplomatic response." She smiled and sighed. "I can be a hard-ass and a bitch at times. I just want you to know that you're still in charge here, and you can tell me to shut the fuck up if I'm getting too big for my boots."

"You have my word."

Her eyes narrowed like she didn't quite believe me—maybe able to see the dying part of me who had been a people pleaser. "You're an odd group but a tall glass of water. I'm sure you still don't trust me, especially with how I seem to want to join the winning side more than anything . . ."

"Correct."

"But I wouldn't trust *you* if you trusted *me* that easily." She smiled again. "We'll need to take risks and use what bullshit we can to beat the Lady. Trust me at least on that. Her bodyguard groups won't just keel over after some fireworks. But together, we can do it . . ."

She held out her hand, which had an idol in it. This one was different. Instead of the dull gray that resembled clay or stone, this was polished silver. A symbol was engraved into it, circular with rough points bisecting it. The indented area shimmered between red-and-purple light.

I took it in my hand as she gestured toward the door. "Let's catch the others up now."

My nod came out slower than my footsteps as I brought up the details of what she had given me.

[Magic Idol+: +30% Damage. Damage taken is doubled.]

Risk-taker. That's what she had deemed me, and she wasn't wrong.

I paused as we reached the doorway, and she stopped just in the corridor to see why.

"Who did it?" I asked, wanting to know whom we'd have to kill to avenge her old Party.

Her expression cooled as she rejoined the conversation we had avoided earlier. "The Lady herself."

With a nod and a chill in my core, I stepped in to see what the Dungeon had to offer.

CHAPTER FORTY-SIX

See, Food

As Wolf launched himself toward the next set of enemies, I stayed as far back as I was able. While I did not need an enabler to put myself in more danger, Tanya had filled that role pretty quickly. Of course, I could choose to not use the idol . . . but that seemed wasteful.

Indeed, as Wolf taunted and slowed the gathered crabmen, my cards illuminated the air with their glow. Cut through the ruddy chitinous shells of our foes with little issue. In truth, being a fully fledged Party solidified how powerful we were. For the most part, Quinn didn't even need to get his hands dirty aside from if a Monster tried to flank the bear.

The added buffs and utility gave us more breathing space to approach combat without it having to be life-and-death. Tanya would weaken and curse the enemies from afar or add resistances and healing to Wolf and Quinn, while Ren and I pelted any opponent from afar with our ranged attacks.

"You know . . ." I said to the elf as Wolf mopped up the last crustacean, "I don't think I've ever seen you miss a shot."

She raised a questioning eyebrow at me. "Why would I take a shot that was going to miss?"

I couldn't really fault her logic there. Why would I ever do a trick that I couldn't pull off? Few of our targets moved around a lot or were particularly agile, so with her old-world experience plus the bonus Skills given by the System, hitting what she intended to was probably very simple.

With the addition of Roger and the occasional Hellhound+ we were really blazing through the chambers of this place. Despite being underground, it was illuminated by odd plant life that shone just as bright as any lantern. The occasional small waterfall or lake ran through otherwise sandy rock rooms. Humanoid shrimp used giant seashells as shields. It was all very jarring, yet made sense at the same time.

"You alright, Max?" Tanya asked, weaving a spell into the air to poison the group we were fighting against. "Looking like you're expecting a knife in the back."

Part of me had considered that giving me this silver idol would be an amusing way to betray and kill me quicker, but that seemed so far behind us now. Our effectiveness in battle was the reward for giving our trust so freely.

"Last time we ran a Dungeon," Ren interjected, "we were ambushed outside and almost died."

"Ah, yes." Tanya gave a grim nod. "Were any of you Treants as well? That would have made it difficult."

My brow furrowed. "From the water? No, we didn't drink any."

"Smart. Two of my old Party did. It was a trying day or so before it wore off."

Ren and I exchanged glances but didn't want to pursue that conversation any further. If only Hadrian had explained that it was only a temporary curse, then perhaps his fate could have been averted. Well, no. We still would have killed him.

"First boss is coming up," Quinn said as he wiped the sweat from his brow. "Giant crab. Wolf just has to face him away from us, and it'll be simple."

This whole event so far had been simple—and I almost didn't like it. Not that I eagerly invited hardship, but the System had a way of seeing you were living life too easy. I was already inviting disaster by daring to love the Oathwarden. Ascending unopposed was not allowed.

"Don't worry, trickster." Ren prodded me with the end of her bow. "I can hear your thoughts from here. Perhaps enjoy a day off for a change? Trouble will find us when it's ready."

My expression softened, and I gave her a smile. Not that I could really call this a day off—we had plenty planned because the reality of the situation was . . .

We would soon become too much of a thorn to be ignored. The Lady had sent lackeys and left traps for us—and any others who tried to stop her—but we had overcome each in turn. Now we were turning the tables. Being proactive and aggressive instead of reactive and defensive.

Soon enough, the Lady would have to deal with us directly—either in person or by sending one of her more capable Parties our way. That's what I had been waiting for. Fighting Monsters was dull, and with a full group, it was also too simple. I craved the stakes of fighting against Players, impressing them with my magic and showmanship.

Between Tanya and Quinn, any trap or puzzle was a nonissue. Splitting the loot was a pain, and I had been spoiled by knocking over the Crimson Shadow piñatas that had better things than what had dropped so far. Sorting out gold didn't interest me, so we agreed that Tanya could collect both that and any tokens to distribute at the end of the Dungeon.

My share had fallen from 33 percent to 20 percent, but it didn't seem to matter. The greater distance from my own grave was worth the 13 percent. Money hadn't even meant that much in my old life; here it felt inconsequential. Power and adoration remained the key driving forces in my current existence. My eyes went over to the elf. *Especially* adoration.

Also revenge or something, to kill the Lady.

"Next room," Quinn confirmed, standing next to a roughly cut circular opening in the wall. "Wolf, go in first, face him toward the back wall. If he turns blue, then use your defensive Abilities."

"Second phase has additional Monsters that come in from the sides," Tanya added. "I'll take the right side. Max, take the left side. Ren, focus boss."

Wolf licked his lips. "Never eaten crab before."

Although I wanted to point out that some of the enemies had been humanoid crabs, perhaps there was more nuance to it. Something probably left to those of us that actually ate people, and Monsters, and not enough fruit and veg.

"What happens when it turns blue?" Ren asked as she thumbed at the grip of her bow.

Tanya adjusted her breastplate. "It's like a spray-of-water attack. Nothing Wolf can't weather with his current Abilities and my help. The danger is usually more in the force than the damage. Knocks people prone and interrupts, but that shouldn't be an issue with Wolf."

Our furred friend was definitely hard to shift. Other than leaving him rather wet, the attack didn't sound like too much of a problem.

With little else to discuss, we stepped into the next chamber and down a dozen or so rough stone steps. A wide area opened up at the bottom, where the floor was a lot thicker with sand than the rest of the Dungeon so far. Water ran around the edges to circle round in a curved arc at the end of the area and return on the other side. Across the sand, near the end of the room, was the boss in question.

Even though we had seen plenty of strange things in our short time here, there was some kind of odd dissociation about seeing the giant crab in person. A very cliché light-red to orange hue, with beady eyes of pitch-black. Two large pincers that could easily bisect me, even without the idol. I had never felt like a squishy spellcaster . . . up until now.

I flipped a card up into the air as circled it around my hand. "Ready check? Can we get a ranged volley off before Wolf goes in?"

Quinn and Tanya exchanged a glance before nodding.

"My taunt cannot be ignored," Wolf added, licking his lips again as he salivated at the sight before him.

A smile crossed my face. Then I could be allowed to be as insufferable as possible.

While they readied bolts or arrows, I hopped up into the air—landing atop the demonic cannon I had just summoned. I loaded it with my Spear of Luck and dropped an Imp+ to the ground. Into my hand a purple card that switched to bright crimson—a critical. All my remaining power went into it, and then I dipped into my own Health with <Bloodletting>. Amusingly, the idol caused my Health to drop twice as much, which only powered up my card more.

I could feel my eyes start to glow even despite—

"What the fuck, Max?"

My right eye twitched, and I looked down at Ren. She was scowling at me, some actual annoyance in her face this time. I didn't feel that it was fair that she could blame me for going all out. It was most pragmatic if we had the opportunity to—

"That's an uncomfortable amount of blood loss, considering we haven't begun." Quinn pulled a face that was more concern than ire.

I looked down at my hands. Oh, they were bleeding quite a bit—that had become such a rarity that it was unexpected. Didn't even feel it, but now with the heat of impending battle cooling off, I could hear the drips hitting the odd metal of my summoned weapon.

"Sorry." I gave them all a sheepish grin. "Got a little carried away. Can't talk for too long, otherwise this card might blow my hand off." Didn't think I could recover from that, unfortunately.

"On three then," Tanya said, raising up her hand to cast a spell. Green light illuminated her fingertips as she began the countdown.

I heard it as nothing but echoes. The pulsing adrenaline making this feel like a stage show once more. Ready for the curtain to raise. *She said three.*

The sound of my cannon reverberated throughout the wide chamber as it launched my spear. Closely followed by a bolt, a <Smite Shot>, a fireball, my critical card, and then whatever the weaver had cast.

Wolf burst with energy and leaped forward before taking a couple of steps and stopping.

Ahead of him, the crab slowly tilted down and landed face-first into the sand. The long chitinous legs kicked out briefly before curling up underneath the main body like a dead spider. Most likely because the boss was dead.

"*Fuck*, trickster. I'm not sure why that annoys me." She gave me a glare that had a little uncertainty behind it. "Saved us a lot of effort, so it's not *bad*."

I shrugged at her, a blank expression on my face. "You shot it too."

As she opened her mouth to reply, I fired a blast of confetti from the cannon, causing them all to wince.

"*Dickbag*." She clenched her teeth and walked off to join Wolf in approaching the crab.

She had a point there. I dropped down to the ground as I dismissed the cannon and gave a glum smile to my Imp+ as I sent him away. At least that was one of our three targets down. I turned around to see Tanya still back with me, while Quinn had gone to help loot and gawk at the large Monster.

"Would you like my advice?" The weaver crossed her arms.

I gestured for her to continue, my tongue no longer feeling like it should be part of current proceedings until it got itself in proper order.

"Ren clearly cares a lot about you. When you are reckless and hurt yourself, it hurts her too." She raised an eyebrow. "*Emotionally*, I mean."

"I'm not . . . Well, I *am* pretty dense." With a sigh, I looked over at the elf. "I was making light of her view on my condition."

"There's hope for you yet, magic man." She smiled and gestured toward the others. "Let's go make amends. You don't want the show falling apart, do you?"

I'd give Tanya one thing. She knew how to fit into a group. Whether this was pandering to maintain our trust or an earnest attempt to get along with us, I couldn't actually tell at this stage.

As I idly wiped the blood from my hands onto my suit jacket, I frowned.

Beyond the splash of running water and the murmurs of the group ahead, there was another sound I couldn't place.

A soft whisper. Something like a mournful song that struck me deep in my heart.

My eyes went to the water's edge, and my feet started to follow. Against my will.

CHAPTER FORTY-SEVEN

Dragged Down

The murmur of voices came from behind me, but they were muted against the melody that had increased in volume now. Close by . . . No—it was as if it was in my head. A solo rendition of something somber yet beautiful in such a sad way. It drew me toward the running water.

I *must* get closer to the source.

Perhaps the oddest thing about the way I so eagerly waded down into the stream was that part of me knew exactly what was happening. Not only did this scratch the itch of my folklore background, but there was also a type of demon that shared the same name.

Siren.

Yet even with this knowledge, even knowing the others were calling for me—coming to stop me . . . I could not resist. The cold water rose up to my chest, causing me to gasp in surprise. And then it was over.

I blinked away some ache from my eyes and took a breath of . . . air. Darkness surrounded me, but I was not submerged. In fact, with the couple of inches of water rippling away from my boots, this looked just like the weird dreamscape I'd met the other Max in. Slightly cooler tones to it, and a chill to the air that felt uncomfortable, but close.

A beep from my STAR told me that I wasn't unconscious or half dead—unless I was imagining this too.

[Tanya: Max? Where are you?]
[Ren: Better not be invisible]
[Wolf: pppp]

Quinn didn't seem to want to put his thoughts in just yet. As I went to reply, I caught the glimpse of something in the gloom.

It moved as I turned my eyes to it. Appearing again in my peripheral. Two orbs of bright blue—the eyes of my captor.

[Max: Continue without me. I'll catch you up.]
[Ren: But where are you?]
[Max: I'll let you know ASAP.]
[Wolf: oopp]

Better that I face whatever was currently stalking me in this odd plane rather than go back and forth with them. They'd be able to continue the Dungeon without me, and hopefully I wouldn't end up dead here.

"Why have you brought me here?" I asked out loud, not even trying to follow the avoidant gaze.

A whispered voice responded, circling around the area like a whirlpool. "I'm ever so lonely . . ."

It sounded female but ethereal. Probably the Siren that drew me here, although I didn't seem to be under the spell any longer. "Sorry, I'm not interested."

"I thought you might like to put on a show for me . . ."

I pursed my lips. They really knew how to dig their nails in. Still, I'd much rather be back with the others than doing a solo performance. That kind of thing was reserved for Ren only these days.

It would help to know who was asking. "Are you a Player or just a Monster?"

"*Just?*" The word repeated and vibrated around the space. "There are things beyond the killers and the pawns, trick wizard."

We had been in the Dungeon, so there was no chance a Player had snuck up on us and used a weird Skill to drag me away to this . . . Hmm. It was like a demonic Domain, but I couldn't sense any demons present. However, Monsters didn't have much capacity for going off script either—much less make demands of me.

"You were . . . born in this world and have more intelligence than most?" I turned, trying to locate the speaker, but the blue eyes remained out of view.

"Clever." The whispered voice felt closer now. "Ten were given such a life by the creator. Two have perished already."

My fingers twitched, ready to draw out a card. While they hadn't been aggressive yet, there was something malicious in their ghostly tone. Or . . . some kind of curiosity and I was their new plaything. "What are you called?"

"She with a Hundred Fingers. But you may call me Mistress."

Neither option was palatable. I found myself in an unknown space with an entity whom I was yet to fully understand, other than I was potentially at her mercy. Well, that's probably what she hoped. I ran my tongue across my lips—I could feel the performance coming, and the messages in my STAR beeping were doing nothing but putting me on edge.

"I refuse to engage you any further," I said. "Let me go back to the Dungeon."

There was a brief period of silence, as if my words had struck a nerve—or perhaps I had been wrong about her intelligence and she didn't know how to address the fact I declined whatever she had going on down here.

"Much too powerful. Full of wretched words and disgusting hubris." There was a sharper tone to her voice now.

She wasn't wrong, however.

"Show yourself, Siren," I said, my stage voice booming throughout the dim nothingness surrounding me. "If you truly want a show, you'll see no better." On account of being dead. Hopefully she could read between the lines.

"As . . . you wish."

A green dawn rose throughout the horizon, and the domed light illuminated my surroundings. It turned out I was not alone in here.

Humanoid figures stood silently, like mannequins. An apt description as they were faceless and androgenous—featureless heads of gray skin stared in my direction. They wore soft white togas and held a variety of obsidian-tipped melee weapons. As I slowly turned my head, there were countless of them.

No, if I were to take a gamble, I'd say there were a hundred of them.

"What will they call you if I kill all hundred of your fingers?" I asked as I flexed my hand out. It would be foolish to think I had a chance. Sitting here with the idol still, just asking to take extra Damage from every hit. Truth was . . . I didn't have a choice.

Ignoring the Party Chat for now, I took a brief moment to open up my messages with Ren.

[Max: I realize this is a worrying message.]
[Max: But I love you. You are the light of my life.]

No immediate reply. She could be in the middle of combat herself or unsure of how to respond to me. It wasn't a problem, really. I didn't need a response. I just couldn't leave her with our last interaction being me annoying her.

The whispered voice came back—softer, but it brought a chill that crept along the back of my neck. "If that comes to pass, I will be no more . . . and you would be more of a monster than me, killer."

A purple card of demonic energy appeared above my hand, spinning in place. "Then you have set yourself up for disappointment. Admission is steep, but the ticket office is now open."

Then it began.

One hundred enemies was quite the tall order to serve. Especially when they were all melee. I cleared my mind of every other thought, leaving only killing and surviving. Already, different tricks and potential uses of all my Inventory clutter cycled through my cool head. The nearest figures leaped toward me, eager to be first in line.

Card went straight through the head of the first, my old spear appearing in my left hand to block the second assailant's attack before the card zipped back and through their neck. Hmm, perhaps I should briefly name them by number?

Three stumbled as my Hellhound+ bit out at their legs. Behind me, I summoned my cannon horizontally to block the advance of those behind me. A little bit of cover that allowed me some stage control.

<Card Fan> went up on my left to block the jab of a spear, as my right controlled the magic card still in play. Four, Five, and Six all received fatal Damage as it zipped through. The cannon went off, pelting Seven to Twelve with a burst sack of potatoes that the System had allowed me to stuff in as ammunition in the side pop-up window.

Roger rose up from one of the corpses and, after some brief confusion, grabbed Jokkar's mace and entered the fray. There were enough corpses building up that he could switch out whenever in trouble. Which was quite often given the number of foes.

I dropped my card to bring out a crossbow, firing the bolt instantly. Letting it then fall into the shallow water, I repeated the process with four other crossbows I had ready and loaded. Fifteen. Sixteen. Seventeen was wounded but not dead yet. Metal sparks from my cannon as I turned to the side to avoid an axe—right in the way of the jab of another spear-wielding finger.

<Demonic Transposition> took me out of the way and into more danger as I became surrounded by the strange gray bodies of my assailants. Cannon blasted confetti throughout the crowd.

<Finale>.

No time to enjoy the adoration, but the warm glow it filled me with was appreciated. Dazzle icons were replaced by stun ones as the group around me were prevented from beating me to a bloody pulp just in time.

A card out. Split. Circling me, empowered with as much as I dared. Like a whirlwind, I cut at necks and featureless faces, drawing blood and causing Eighteen, Nineteen, and Twenty to fall to the floor—a handful of others only wounded before the stun wore off.

Already a fifth of my way through, but I was running out of Skills.

While the injured around me fell back for fresh fingers to work their way in, a swirl of fabric obscured me as I twirled two sheets of canvas up and around me like the bulb of a flower. When they fell down, I was no longer there. Invisibility allowing me to push through back to my demonic cannon. While most turned their attention to my demons, some saw the splashing in the water as I made my short trip back to cover.

Oh—but I didn't *want* cover. I was the star here.

I reappeared standing atop the siege weapon, a bright grin across my face and two cards in my hand.

"Hope you're enjoying the show," I announced as I released them into the air.

From atop my perch, I could see them all. So many impatient, yet having to wait for the early birds to die off. I'd not had such a large audience since arriving in this world, and it was . . . *joyous*. It threatened to burst me like a firework. Seeing all the faceless bodies enraptured by me . . . Watching them fall to the floor bleeding because they weren't worthy.

As I sent my cards out, things seemed to slow down. The mania threatening to overpower me took a back seat as my brain had time to consider things. Why was I here, and why did it have such similarity to when I had met other Max? I had allowed any explanation to slip away under the threat of the strange voice of the so-called Mistress.

In fact, why did all my opponents here look like they were fingers in white gloves?

My heartbeat thrummed in my chest, realizing there was something bigger going on than just a combat challenge. Ears started aching. Attacks started to falter as confusion welled up inside me. Maybe I just drowned, and this was another last fading memory?

"You seem lost." The voice returned, despite everything now going in slow motion. It was softer now and closer again.

"Who are you really?" I asked, my mouth dry.

"I am the weight of your past, something that still grips at you to this very day." Now the voice had a familiar sound to it. "Your own personal demon."

Of course.

It all made sense now. The Monster was using my own mental fortitude against me. Siren song to bring me down and bury me under the guilt of things I thought I had moved past. In a way, they were right. My mother hung heavy on my heart, even if I had accepted the show was my own choice now. I ached at the phrasing the Monster had used. Loneliness and wanting to see me put on a show. If I had clocked it earlier, then my emotions would have made the combat more difficult. Perhaps I *was* even more dense than I figured.

But . . .

There was something about the phrase *personal demon* that burned at my insides, past my heartache. A volcano erupting within me. Anger that I hadn't thought possible that quickly cooled into the biggest rush of dopamine and adrenaline I'd ever experienced. I felt fully awake, and everything was vibrant and lively. Apprehension and elation made me feel twenty feet tall—as if I suddenly realized something that put me above all others.

Eyes blazing bright purple and with a wide grin on my face, I held out my shaking hand, playing things by ear.

Domain: <The Grand Stage>.

CHAPTER FORTY-EIGHT

Demonic Domain

I stood upon a stage of varnished wooden planks. Tall curtains of vibrant purple sat on the wings, while a large row of bright lights arched above me on metal scaffolding. A darkened amphitheater stretched out before me, rows of plush red seats barely lit by the glow radiating across from the true star of the show—me.

A good sixty to seventy of the seats were filled with an enraptured audience. Faceless and dull—but then again, from this perspective, they usually were. I could see the icons on the closest . . . Dazzle but different. Red instead of the usual gray icon.

While the soft tunes of some harmony filled me with comfort, I started by giving them a bow. It was only natural. From my head, I removed my hat and made the show of proving that it was currently empty. Hand inside and I withdrew a ceramic vase, much larger than could fit inside the headwear. The counters on their icons rose by one, and they squirmed in appreciation.

Then, I flourished my cape to reveal a chair placed upon the stage. I placed the vase down on it with utmost care. From my sleeve, I withdrew a sheet of canvas—although it appeared as a deep-purple velvet. The show *must* go on. With a flourish, I unraveled it and obscured the set pieces from the audience. Gave them a wide grin and raised eyebrow.

It was hard to tell how much they were enjoying it, given that they had no facial features to gauge. A couple had passed out already, clearly the fanfare and performance a little too much for their sensibilities.

I flashed the held curtain away to reveal no chair—just the vase hanging in midair. Another distracting flash to obscure and then the vase had gone, but the chair returned. A few more audience members collapsed from their seating.

And now I had drawn the attention of a latecomer. From the gloom of the back of this faux auditorium, two bright-blue orbs revealed themselves. I shot a glance to the side to see Roger standing with his arms crossed. No longer inhabiting a corpse, I saw his true form for the first time.

For all intents and purposes, he was a large bipedal white rabbit. Eyes still pits of purple energy, but the rest of him was soft fur—although the scowl across his face dispelled any notion of calling him cute. With a potential heckler making themselves present, I might need security to step in to crack a few skulls.

But my show smile didn't waver, and I returned to my captive audience . . . as that's what they were—captive. Unable to do anything more than sit and observe or pass out, it seemed. Oh, now I understood it. Even as my active mind considered the next part of my act, at the back I started to piece together the underlying workings of whatever fresh hell I had wreaked upon my existence.

Dazzle now did Damage every time a new stack was added. Somehow, I had activated my own Domain, and this was the result.

I turned to face my back toward the audience, my cape briefly obscuring the view of the chair as I picked it up—only to turn around to find that it was gone and instead I held the vase again. Some fucking applause would be nice, but I'd make do.

As more figures dropped from their seating, the Siren came more into view. She was large, almost as wide as the building we were in . . . her face twenty feet across if I had the wits to guess. The bright-blue eyes sat in sunken pits of pale flesh, and she resembled a waterlogged corpse more than the false beauty I had been expecting. Sharp teeth as long as my arm extended from blackened gums. Giant hands clawed at the wall, dragging herself forward.

I'd need to wrap this up.

Vase placed on the ground. I reached in and drew out a long spear. Took a few strides away and stabbed the sharp end into the stage, splintering wood but keeping it steady. Maintenance crew would kill me. I clicked my fingers, and a hell dove flew out of the vase and came to perch at the top of the spear shaft. Confident strides took me around the stage, plucking up the vase along the way.

Tipped it and a dozen tomatoes fell out. Click of my fingers and the bird flew back inside. With one last smile toward the waning crowd, I tossed the vase high into the air.

It tumbled back to an empty stage and shattered—to reveal a figure that stretched out. The figure was me, of course. Invisible until the point of impact, where I switched places with the dove as the vase split apart. I stood tall and stretched my arms out wide, welcoming applause.

A dozen faceless figures fell down dead, barely a handful of skeptics left seated still. The Siren moved closer, a horrifying tongue stretching from her mouth like a thick tentacle, weaving through the rows of seating. Way too long for a tongue. Desire in her eyes to consume me and be rid of this odd place.

But this was *my* house.

Even without the bask of adoration, I felt content in this pose in front of my audience wowed to death. It had never really been about my mother, but I felt this *was* the show I needed to put on for her. One last send-off. A love that no longer pained me, knowing that I had grown into this. Still, I had one last trick to pull off to truly close that chapter.

From inside my jacket, I withdrew my magic deck of cards. The etched design shimmered in this lighting, and the white rabbit on it practically pulsed with power.

Chairs buckled and shifted away from the weight of the large Monster and probing tongue. I noted that she had no red Dazzle icons—able to resist the power of my Domain. Very rude.

"This was one of her favorites," I said with a smile. Quiet enough, but it carried through the building. From the pack, I withdrew the whole deck. Each card just as pristine and vibrant as the day I received them.

I held the whole deck in my right hand, only now realizing I had been wearing white gloves for this performance. Thumb at the bottom of the deck, index and middle on the top.

"Fifty-two-card pickup isn't much of a trick . . ." Purple lightning arced around my body, the glow of my power flickering across the reflective stage. "But I can think of no more perfect grand finale."

The words came from my mouth as if I was reciting from a script. All natural despite how abnormal this whole situation was. The cards flexed as I tightened my grip before bursting and spraying forth.

However, instead of fluttering to the floor in a mess, they flashed purple and zipped out into the air. Each card repeating the same action. Control was . . . difficult. They pelted the seating arrangements, taking out the remaining fingers of the Siren, shredding fabric, and splitting wood. I curved them around, circling and spinning them like a tornado of sharp demonic energy.

The Siren was perhaps even more surprised than I was. Eyes wide at my attack, she flinched away as dozens of cards started to cut and slice into her.

"Cursed shitling!" She growled, attempting to push through the torrent of energy but only receiving more cuts in the process.

Left hand gripped at my right wrist as my hand twitched and cramped. Crimson soaked through the white fabric of the glove as I maintained composure. It wasn't enough. My suit fabric frayed and peeled back from my hand, charring at the edges before the ashes dropped to the floor.

She was starting to panic now, no escape from my whirlwind of destruction. I felt cool despite the pain radiating through my arm. It was bare now, and I could see crimson lines running down it, my own flesh starting to strip away from the bone at the amount of power I could barely wield.

Still . . . this is what I was made for. As I watched the Monster slowly die, her tongue severing, eye bursting, blood streaming down her pale face, I had become the peak Max. Showman, demon hunter, and demon itself all together as one whole piece. Fully concentrated efforts. All to erase this living demigod.

The cards now went beyond piercing flesh as the Siren grew too exhausted to fight back. With one last push of energy, I drew all fifty-two cards back and then pushed forward with all I had. Bone split and cracked. Brain destroyed.

My vision flickered on and off. Cards vanished away. I collapsed on the stage into a pool of my own blood. Lights went off.

There were no dreams in this darkness, but after some time, light pricked at my aching eyes. Between the stage and wherever I was now, nothing occurred. It would almost disappoint me if I wasn't in so much pain. My face was pressed against rough sand. Not even warm and comforting. My body soaked through and cold. As I tried to right myself, I could not—but I coughed up a lungful of water instead.

I groaned and tried to blink away the blur in my eyes. Any notion that I had washed ashore somewhere with amnesia and would have to punch trees for survival was soon snapped away as my brain realized I was in the familiar Dungeon setting again. Not the crab room—not large enough. Couldn't really move my hands or head to see much other than the rocky wall ahead of me.

Soft footsteps pattered down a hallway, and a familiar figure in a soft blue suit slid across the light sand and into the doorway.

"Max!"

A pulse of healing washed through me, and I smiled. She rushed over me, dropping to her knees to lift me to rest against her. She gave my head a quick kiss before cradling me. I had gone through hell to grasp at this brief heaven. A mood quickly muted as her warm tears struck my face.

"I'm okay," I said, even my mouth feeling sore.

"The fuck you are." She squeezed me a little harder, although not all of me could feel the action.

My brow furrowed, and I looked down at my right arm. White-and-red ribbons covered it, obscuring it from . . . Oh, no. That was my flesh and blood. Another wave of her healing flooded my being, and some of the wounds started to close. The damage I had done to myself was . . . extensive. I wasn't sure I wanted to move it, even if I could.

More noises as the rest of them caught up.

"Sorry if I worried you," I managed, unable to see her face from this angle.

"You did, you asshole. Why do you keep doing this?"

A wide smile across my face, but my eyes started running with tears of my own. "I will always suffer twice as much if it means you are okay." The world didn't work that way, but I could pretend that it did. Pluck any malady intended for the elf and take it on myself.

"*Dickbag,*" she whispered, giving me a squeeze again.

My eyes went up to the Chat messages she had sent when I was busy being fucking ridiculous.

[Ren: Don't you fucking do this]
[Ren: Where are you?]
[Ren: I love you too]
[Ren: don't leave me]
[Ren: that's selfish but]
[Ren: I need you]

I shut it down and closed my eyes. Exhausted, but about as far from wanting a sleep as possible. Feeling started to come back to my arm, and with it the flare of constant pain.

"Fuck me," Tanya said, her shadowed figure blocking the light. "You look like you stuck your arm in an industrial grinder." Although her words were making light of the situation, her tone was dead serious.

"Is it recoverable?" Ren asked.

Tanya sucked at her teeth, something I'd usually hear when I was about to be overquoted for some repairs. "I'm no doctor, but we'll do everything we can. Can only do this once per day . . ."

I'd worked out how her idol Class Keystone worked. Five gray ones normally. She'd combined hers with mine to create a silver one. Extrapolating from that, three would make gold? Against my chest she pressed one that was made from radiant diamond. She moved my limp left hand over to keep the idol in place.

Ren's fingers ran through my hair. My hat must be somewhere else.

From behind her, the worried amber eyes of Wolf and the panicked expression of Quinn. That I had so many who cared for me was humbling.

"You're not afflicted with anything," Tanya said. She moved my aching legs around so I was in a more comfortable position, almost sitting up against the elf now. There was no hesitation in manhandling me as needed, but then I assumed that would be quite common for someone with her experience. "Other than the deep lacerations to your right arm, possibly nerve and tendon damage, you're mostly unharmed. System allowing, you should make a full recovery."

"Not in the next five minutes, I assume?" I gave her a glum smile.

"Healing will repair what it can. You'll be able to move soon enough, but as to making use of the arm . . ."

I nodded or at least twitched my head the best I could with my injuries and being restrained by Ren.

She rested her chin against my head. "Want to tell us what bullshit you got up to?"

"And then apologize for having us so worried, Max?" Quinn added.

My ruined arm was proof enough that what I had experienced was real. Part of my brain was still trying to catch up and fully process what I had been through. Maybe explaining it out loud would help me understand it—or at least share the burden of disbelief with the others.

"For starters," I said with a soft smile across my face, "you will be delighted to hear this injury is all self-inflicted."

A patch of my hair warmed as Ren exhaled deeply through her nose.

CHAPTER FORTY-NINE

Determination

After a period of recovery, we had affixed my right arm in a sling. Campfire out to dry me off. We each sat in chairs to hear my tall tale. Not usually one for public displays of affection other than the occasional hand-holding, Ren had given me a tight hug as soon as I was able to stand on my own two feet. Possibly the best hug I'd ever had. In sitting around the fire, she had placed her chair directly beside mine.

As much as it softened my insides to have someone so enraptured with my presence, it might be unwise for her to tether her happiness to my continued existence. Yet . . . I felt the same way about her, and I didn't want to be a hypocrite.

It was, as it turned out, not the most believable story I'd ever told. A mixture of disbelief and concern across their faces—especially at the mention of my own Domain somehow springing into existence, despite the System not giving me that as a Skill.

"Never heard of a *smart* Monster before," Quinn said, idly looking up at the cavern ceiling.

Tanya had her brow furrowed. "There was some . . . lore I remember reading. Can't think of where. Ten Guardians *were* mentioned."

"Oh?" I tilted my head, even as my neck protested the movement.

"Left to watch over this world in the creator's absence." The weaver pulled a face, still uncertain where she was drawing this from.

I went to rub my chin before remembering I couldn't move my arm. "She said two had already been killed. Possibly they are embodiments of certain facets of the System."

"Or something put in place to keep certain Players in check," Ren added.

It was neither here nor there. If I was targeted because I was powerful, I also won because I had all this unchecked strength. That said, I was self-aware enough to know an ass-pull when I saw one, and without my Domain suddenly appearing, I was sure to have fallen once the fingers had been able to lay a blow or two on me. I'd ignored the fact that I had a Domain up until now . . .

"So you *are* part demon then," Ren stated, reading through my inner monologue as if it were hanging out of my skull. Which wasn't that unlikely.

"I'm afraid so."

Tanya and Quinn looked more apprehensive about the prospect than Wolf and Ren. The elf looked more disappointed that she wasn't present and part of the process. Expectations had to be laid out on the table.

"It is a small part of me," I admitted, "and how I get my power. To forewarn you all, there may be an instance where you are drawn into my Domain."

Quinn grimaced. "What are we to do if that happens?"

With a smile, I raised an eyebrow. "Why, just help me put on a good show. Just as you do every day."

Well, every day was a stretch given how long I'd known each of them, but they'd already settled into the roles that they'd play onstage. If anything, the System was tying everything off into a nice package. The right people at the right time. An inevitability that we didn't have a say in yet suited us just as well.

"Can you make it happen again?" Ren asked.

I turned my gaze to see the amount of curiosity in her bright-blue eyes. Despite being holy adjacent and having means to apparently end me, she was constantly enamored by the demonic side of things. Or at least the me who had accepted my true being in this world.

"It's not . . . overtly accessible, like my other Skills." I shrugged and gave her a glum smile. It would be nice to think that I could just pop it out on occasion, even if it was limited to once a day or something. "Let me go through my System menus again."

She nodded before moving from her chair to go make coffee. Or that's what I assumed she was doing, as she had brought the kettle into her hands. The possibility that she was about to brain me danced about, but the likelihood that someone close wanted to off me was growing slimmer by the day. While a potential betrayer wouldn't want to deal with the rest of the Party, lying among the bloody sand was the second weakest and vulnerable I had ever been.

I furrowed my brow. Immediately something jumped out as wrong.

"Say, what color are your names in your STAR?"

They each checked, and even Wolf seemed to humor me. Silver-white came their agreed response.

"Strange, mine is gold. I don't think it was before."

The revelation was met with a mixture of blank confusion, except for Tanya, who had more of a scowl across her face.

Before I decided to prod her for her thoughts, I narrowed my eyes at what appeared to be a third bar beneath my name. It was empty, whereas the other two were mostly full and much more familiar. My glare revealed labels, as if they could hold no secrets under scrutiny. Red one at the top was Health, although the abstract gauge of how dead I was seemed rather moot in a world that still abided by real-life physics and injuries. Second was blue and labeled Mana. I had an even stranger relationship with this one.

Third now said Power, although it was written in Demonic rather than the common System language.

Tanya couldn't handle the silence any longer and filled it with her thoughts. "I knew someone else with a gold name, but I thought it was because she was a Guild leader or something . . ."

"The Lady." Ren shook her head, as if the answer couldn't be any more obvious.

I frowned. Not usually one to jump to conclusions, I found myself leaping to something that tied all the facts together. "*She* killed a Guardian, either on the starter island or in the first area."

More conflicted silence radiated through the group. While Tanya had taken to this like a duck to water, Quinn looked to be reconsidering tying his destiny to my own. I wasn't sure I even believed most of what I was saying. We *had* missed out on some important lore, perhaps.

My eyes went back through my menus to see if anything else had changed. The System didn't care to explain what my demonic Power did or represented—and there were no new Skills on my list. I had a feel for it though. The more bullshit I performed, the greater bullshit I could perform. In putting the cart before the horse, I had truly clicked my demonic nature into place and become something even worse.

For our enemies, at least.

"I used to know someone who is neck deep in the world's lore," Tanya began, filling the silence once more. "We aren't on speaking terms . . . due to the whole joining the Crimson Shadow thing, but I can see if he'll give us information?"

I nodded and went straight back to my STAR. Mostly everything was normal, except . . . I felt at my jacket pocket with my left hand. No card deck there, as I had moved it to my belt. Looking at my Equipment, the box that held my weapon still had the picture of the deck but was grayed out and had a padlock in the bottom corner. Did that mean I couldn't equip it anymore? No . . . It meant I couldn't get rid of it, surely.

Tanya sent messages out to her contact, and Ren poured the coffee while I held my left hand out. From the air above it, cards zipped from my belt holster to appear and drop into my grasp, one after another. Under the intrigued gazes of my Party, a pile filled up to fifty-two, and then I gripped it and the case appeared around them, switching from where it had been stored.

"Everything okay?" Ren asked, bringing a mug over to me last. She sat down, her eyes still tired from the tears shed over my trauma experienced.

That said—I didn't have the trauma Status, which was a miracle given the state of my arm. "Not *everything*, but the majority of things." I gave her a smile, but it seemed to just have the effect of bringing lethargy over me instead.

"You lost a lot of blood and used a lot of energy," she replied. "Take as long as you need."

Without two hands, I couldn't take my cup of coffee from her while holding my deck. I leaned forward, groaning against how my right arm flared with pain at being jostled. Placed the deck on the ground, standing up. As I sighed and sat back, I clicked my fingers together.

The top of the case holding the deck popped open, and the cards began spilling out like a reverse waterfall back into my open hand. As the last one settled into the perfect pile, I made a fist. Opened up to reveal an empty palm, the deck now visibly back in my belt.

"Are you going to take this or not?" Ren narrowed her eyes and tried to push the coffee toward me. Why she was sitting on my right side when I couldn't use that arm I wasn't sure.

"Sorry." I smiled and took the cup carefully. While my life as a magician had increased the dexterity of my hands, I was still a few shakes away from being ambidextrous.

"Looks like you have greater control of your deck, Max." Quinn tilted his head.

Almost spilled my hot drink over my legs as his accent made that sentence parse differently.

"Deck control is very important," Ren added.

"Seems so," I said through clenched teeth, avoiding looking at the elf.

Tanya took us away from the playground antics. "No reply yet. He's joined some group in the southwest, so if all else fails then we could find him there."

A date with destiny. "The Eternal Wardens." I raised an eyebrow. The group that had left me a note in the clearing with the scarecrows, their help offered if I could remove the necromancer from this world. I relayed this information to the weaver.

"Interesting." She rubbed at her face and sighed. "Are all your days this fucking exhausting?"

I exchanged a glance with the elf, then looked between the bear and the fixer, before returning to look at Tanya. "No," I lied.

Quinn shook his head. "So brazen."

Other than the vague notion that I had possibly killed some demigod or otherworldly beast that lurked within this world and apparently gained even further power to head the fight against Lady in Red, who had perhaps done the same . . .

Oh, I forgot where I was going with that thought.

I downed the last of the coffee, only the tinge of potential burning radiating through my throat. "Right, let's get back to the Dungeon. Day is still young."

They didn't seem to share my enthusiasm.

"You sure you're up for it, Max?" Ren stood beside me, putting her chair away but giving me a piercing glare. As if she could determine if I was about to crack and break in half.

"The show must go on." I smiled, but she was less enthused. "I will take it easy and let my summons do most of the work. If you think I'm doing myself some damage, I will cease at your command."

She cooled off as I relinquished some of my fate into her hands. We were both adults and didn't need the other to babysit our capabilities, but being in love muddied the water. It actually hurt her when I became injured, and unfortunately I was fated to brush with death on regular occasion. Allowing her to move me away from potential malady kept us both happier—or at least would attempt to.

With her nodding acceptance, it looked as though that was enough permission for the rest of the Party to be on board with the act continuing.

"I'll keep an eye on him," Tanya offered. "You need to focus on your shots for the next boss fight, and my Abilities have more downtime between uses."

"It's quite ranged focused," Quinn agreed. "I can brief you while we walk, Ren?"

The elf nodded again and gave me a quick glare before walking off. I much preferred it when she was undressing me with those eyes rather than putting me in my place . . . but perhaps I needed it.

Wolf stepped up beside me, my top hat in his mouth.

"Thanks, Wolf. I can always rely on you. How are you finding the Dungeon?"

"Not a great fan of seafood, but at least I get to eat." He huffed and turned to join the others, clearly unimpressed we had stopped for coffee but hadn't eaten.

I went to withdraw some food to hand him, and a pain shot down my right arm as I forgot that I couldn't use it still.

Tanya moved up beside me as we joined the group. "How is the arm?"

"An odd mix of numbness and agony."

She ran her tongue across her teeth. "Still too early to judge. Take Ren's insistence that you take it easy to heart. We do not need our headliner blunted."

I gave her a soft smile. "The lingo is appreciated but not necessary."

The weaver shrugged and looked ahead. "Been . . . years since I was in the service. Yet I still feel most comfortable when I can fit into a role or unit. Both at work and in my home life." She sighed. "Being organized into Parties of five here felt *right*. Allowed me to make do and accept some things."

"I'm only surviving because I am the mixture of two . . . maybe three people. The normal me would have cracked and broken long ago."

"You're resilient, Max." She raised an eyebrow at me. "It takes a lot to weather the amount of hits you have and still rise above it, and to lead others."

I grimaced. "I wouldn't consider myself a leader."

"A star has five points," she said. "Sometimes a leader is just the driving force to move throughout the sky. Even if your arm doesn't recover, I know that won't slow your momentum. Look at Quinn, for example."

She was right, of course. I trusted the System to give me a little wink and fix my arm back to full health, but it couldn't do everything. Dismemberment seemed to be permanent—at least at this stage. Losing an eye hadn't stopped Quinn from being his overt self or traveling the dangerous path we trod. The show would go on, whatever came our way.

I did note that her gaze lingered on the fixer for a few moments longer than expected before she snapped her eyes back to me. "If you want to soar as high as you can, you need to learn how to use those wings. Not just flap about wildly."

We were aiming for the pinnacle. I couldn't deny that. To stand atop a mountain of all our detractors and enemies, successful and safe.

As we reached the edge of the next boss chamber, I caught the brief smile of the elf before we looked at what lay before us.

Something to grind into dust.

My mood cooled as the magic deck of cards vibrated in my pocket.

CHAPTER FIFTY

No Rule Left Unbroken

It was hard to tell if my Abilities had changed due to my apparent ascension. Using my left hand to gradually shoot off purple cards one at a time without moving them or putting too much Mana into them was awkward enough compared to normal—so it was difficult to gauge if any difference was me taking it easy rather than that I was now a demonic lord or something.

The next boss was actually a group of four turtle people. My active brain checked out straight away, not wanting to draw any reference to anything—Tanya hadn't mentioned it either, so perhaps I had struck my head a few too many times. Wolf cycled his taunt and area slow to keep them all on him—assisted by my Hellhound+. It was a simple matter of attrition as Tanya delayed their actions and their self-healing gradually failed to keep up with our Damage.

Were I in top form then this might have taken less time . . . but we didn't appear to be struggling.

"Permission to summon Roger once one falls?" I asked my guardian angels.

"Granted," Ren replied, while Tanya gave me a stoic nod.

The weaver had done as she had told the elf and kept a frequent eye on me between her Skill uses. So far, I hadn't started bleeding from my eyes or grown horns—so I was sure that I was fine. Excluding my arm, which was still somewhat inert.

Tendrils of worry had started to worm around. I'd recovered from worse in less time, I felt, but then it was all down to how the System chose to see it. Life-threatening? It'd be patched up like nothing happened. Could survive it? It'd do the bare minimum. But it wasn't really losing the use of my arm that had me on edge . . . It was a different feeling that occasionally passed through it.

It had started once my Power meter had filled slightly. Ten percent or so—my current antics clearly not enough bullshit to really move it much further than that—but as soon as I reached the apparent threshold, a wave of energy went through me. Could have just been my imagination or a chill, so I didn't bring it up with the others. I considered opening my mouth about it when the pain level started to increase, but I noticed something else that kept me quiet.

The numbness was fading away.

Against better judgment, I saw this as a good thing. Felt like my nerves were being repaired if they could now feel the trauma wreaked to the rest of the arm. But what did that mean? Simple answers were preferred . . .

Roger's card went out and struck the first fallen turtle man.

. . . And the most straight forward answer would be that I had some kind of demonic regeneration.

The urge to raise my Power meter with a flourish of tricks grew, to see if more Power meant greater regeneration. I was liable to get more than some evil glares from the others if I started pushing myself, however. After the battle, I'd labor them with my findings and see what they'd let me do.

If anything, being stifled was almost more uncomfortable than how my arm felt. Well, no—I shouldn't exaggerate, despite it being in my nature to. Instead, I settled into being calm and allowed my brain some time to process my ordeal.

Using the threads of my past, where I wished my mother could have seen me put on my greatest show, the Siren had lured me into some pocket lair. *Like* a Domain, perhaps. Intending to bury me beneath a wave of . . . my own inept hands? The finger people were maybe a reference to my constant need to perform. I had some-how leaned into the ploy and actually put on a great show, using the Siren as a stand-in for the feelings I had that they'd had attempted to use against me.

Conquered those troubles with a deluge of attacks and emerged a more . . . whole person? It was hard to say. The System clearly held me in higher regard now, but I doubted this world was created as a means for me to get over my emotional issues. A glance at the company I kept determined there was something else behind the scenes that drove my destiny toward a particular point.

A card bloomed in my hand and then faded away as the last of the group fell to Wolf.

"Pretty painless," Tanya grunted. "Where were you guys when I first arrived?" Without waiting for an answer, she walked forward toward the fallen enemy.

Ren was beside me before I had even noticed.

"How's the arm?"

"Oddly enough . . ." I winced as I wiggled it about. "It feels better when you're close."

She rolled her eyes.

"That's not just a charming line to woo you. I mean it earnestly—perhaps radiant energy has some effect on it?" Or those beautiful blue eyes. I managed to not say that part out loud, lest I weaken the argument that I was being truthful—my arm did start feeling better when she was closer. And I was mostly sure it wasn't the eyes.

"I could imbue a bandage with radiant energy, but that's only once per day and lasts . . ." Her eyes unfocused to go through her menus. "Ten minutes."

My face screwed up, and I considered just asking her to stay beside me all the time instead. Before I could work up a less cheesy line, Roger approached from the side and went to one knee, bowing deeply.

"Boss," he said, purple ears flopping over the turtle face he was inhabiting.

"No need for that, Roger." I gestured for him to stand. "I trust you are still on the right path?"

"Yes, boss." He stood back up, shuffling in the odd puppet. "I'm honored to have been part of your grand show."

I nodded slowly. "That was really you then, and your true form?"

"Yes, boss," he repeated. "Next time I will post near the back to stop any late-comers from interrupting the performance."

"Thanks, Roger. I appreciate that." Curiosity got the better of me. "What did you think of it?"

He tilted his head from side to side. "Impressive. Scary as fuck. Pretty sure I shit myself when you pulled out all those cards." The pact demon attempted a whistle, but due to unfamiliarity with his puppet it just came out as a weird rasping sound. "Oh, that reminds me. Got you a gift, boss."

"A gift?" I raised my eyebrow toward the elf, who looked bemused at the reverence I now commanded. Possibly only slightly disappointed I wasn't giving the demon a verbal lashing.

"For helping me get my shit together. I was on a dark fuckin' path, and you unfucked it." Purple light swirled around his hands as he brought out something into his grasp.

I wasn't even sure how or why he could do that—so I just used the excuse of demon magic, as it seemed fitting at this point in my existence.

"Some of the gals helped out. It ain't much, but I'm going to leave now before I feel an emotion other than unbridled rage."

As he placed the item in my hands, the body slumped over, inert. That wasn't very fair—I didn't get the chance to thank him or pass on my regards to his wives. The thought of resummoning him into a different boss corpse slid away as I lifted up the gift to inspect it.

A belt. One side a dark leather that felt like it was made from something demonic rather than domestic. The other side was purple—bedazzled by small gems and sequins. It caught the light and warmed me with its brilliance. Affixed to the belt already was some kind of metal clasp . . . Oh, it was the perfect size to fit my card deck in.

"Seems I'm pretty good at unfucking things," I said with a grin, raising my eyebrows toward Ren as I went to put the belt on.

She opened her mouth to say something, then closed it. Gave me a blank stare for a couple of seconds, and then seemed to change subject in her head. "You said the real Roger was like a tall fluffy rabbit? Was he cute?"

Before answering, I double-checked that he had actually left this plane and wasn't faking his absence to see what I thought about the belt without having to interact with me. No, he was definitely gone.

"Imagine a six-foot-tall bipedal rabbit. Fluffy, bright-white fur. Long ears, purple eyes. Then make that rabbit middle-aged with three divorces, gambling debt, and a substance abuse problem. About that cute."

"Harsh." She crossed her arms. "I didn't know he had a gambling problem."

I grunted as I struggled to get the belt around me with one hand. "Yeah, he takes after me."

She sighed and stepped closer to help me out, kneeling in front of me to put the end of the belt through the hoops around my waist. "Thank you for going easy in the fight. I know that it was hard for you. Probably frustrating . . . I bet you're all pent up?"

I looked down at her perfectly blank expression staring back up at me. Despite my mouth opening to speak, my mind was completely empty. Devoid of any appropriate words to tumble forth.

"Nice belt!" Quinn stepped over, putting his hands on his hips.

Whatever spell had frozen the two of us ended, and Ren stood to circle around the back of me—lifting my jacket to find the rest of the hoops.

"Roger," I said, my mind still trying to get up to speed with reality.

"Indeed." He nodded toward me, not entirely sure what I was trying to convey. "Tanya says that we will be surprised with the token haul once we are finished."

"I can't wait." I managed a smile as I became grounded once more. System talk seemed to have a way of doing that. Putting one person in charge of loot acquisition and distribution was a novel concept, but it meant less thinking for my own brain. Put me at ease in some ways. At least until Ren moved her mouth close to the back of my neck.

"All the best things are worth waiting for, trickster."

Perhaps this was my penance for making her worry so much earlier. While I had become used to—and enamored with—the scowling grump that she had been in the first area, now that she was emerging from her shell . . . Well, I'd be lying if I didn't say I was a little scared. Now in love with danger, she had a firm grip on the part of me wholly unprepared for this step in our relationship.

She stepped back in front of me to do the buckle, and we locked eyes. Her hand moved onto the metal holder. "Where do you want it, Max?"

I narrowed my eyes. "Right in front of me."

Ren adjusted it slowly as we maintained eye contact.

With my left hand, I opened up my jacket to allow her access to my deck. "Could you put it in for me?"

As her mouth opened, Tanya cleared her throat loudly, and the haze around us blew away.

"For the next boss," the weaver began, "we need to travel underneath a waterfall. The water is probably cold, so perhaps that would be beneficial."

I nodded animatedly, hoping to move on from everything that was currently happening. Ren stood from me, the job done, giving me a last side-eye that said she enjoyed tormenting me all too clearly. She moved over to give the patient canine a pet before his time was up.

With a flourish of my fingers, three cards popped up from my holstered deck and circled around my left hand. I snatched them from the air into a loose fan and observed them. They weren't magic in the same way that my attack was. Concentrating, I turned two of them purple . . . but couldn't do the same for the third. Then, I returned one to normal and switched the <Pick a Card> energy onto the one previously inert. Interesting.

A quick flick and I dismissed them all, even the normal cards turning to brief ash before they were gone.

"Wonders never cease," Tanya said and sighed.

Quinn nodded along. "You truly are a spectacle, Max."

I grinned at this unintended compliment and watched them start to head out of the room. Ren shot me the least subtle wink as she passed, and I was pretty sure steam left my ears in trying to deal with everything going on.

Last in the pack, I turned my head toward the bear, my brow furrowing in seeing the look on his face.

He looked exhausted, breathing heavily with eyes glazed over.

CHAPTER FIFTY-ONE

Bear Minimum

I knelt down beside the bear and ran my left hand across the fur on his head. "You okay there, pal?"

He took a couple of heavy breaths before life came back to his eyes and he looked back at me. "Just indigestion."

With the best scowl I could muster, I waited for him to tell the truth.

It wasn't something easily given, and after he tried to squirm away from my glare, he eventually sighed. "I *suppose* eighteen is quite old for a bear," he said.

"Tell me what you need? We can take a break or call it quits for the day . . . If you need to leave us then—"

"Max."

I stopped my drivel and pulled a glum face at Wolf. Part of my heart aching in seeing the unstoppable force faltering. Maybe we have been pushing him too hard.

"My time is not yet, and I will let you know when it draws close." He huffed and shook his body. "This place dampens my spirit, and I seek to chew on mightier foes."

There wasn't much I could do other than nod and rise back to my feet. "You are my kin, Wolf. Do not hesitate to allow me to protect you, just as you do us."

He opened and closed his mouth before it upturned into a grin. "You talk too much. Let us continue, brother."

With a smile, I looked back toward the exit where Ren was waiting, arms crossed and concern on her brow. Should I talk to her about it? Perhaps not a good thing to worry her after she had just finished being panicked about *my* safety. Still, it wasn't a good idea to hide any truths from her either.

Looking at the bear as we walked over, I doubted he wanted to bring it up right now. Maybe not at all. He seemed fine and back to his usual self, but I'd need to keep an eye on him.

"At risk of this becoming a catchphrase," Ren said with a sigh. "Everything okay?"

"Too much seafood," I interjected before the bear could speak. "We were discussing shitting techniques."

"Max is surprisingly well-versed," Wolf agreed.

Whether Ren believed that or not . . . *Ah,* who was I kidding? Even as her neutral glare narrowed on me, I knew the game was up. She could read me like a flashing billboard. My name in lights. I'd always wanted that kind of fame.

I blinked a few times, my roving mind trying to settle me in the present. "I'm actually a little off too. Just needed an ear that had a less charged take on my current predicament."

Silence followed, as a few different emotions went on behind Ren's eyes. Wolf seemed content with my falsehoods and didn't add or dispute anything.

"Go ahead and catch the others up, Wolf." I nudged him. "Just tell them Ren and I are smooching, and we'll be there in a second."

He rolled his eyes, but with a grunt, he was off.

After waiting for him to move just beyond earshot, the elf turned back to me. "Max, I'm sorry that—"

I cut her off by pulling her in and kissing her, holding her tight against me despite my slung right arm complaining at being crushed.

"Oh," she said as we parted.

"Didn't want to tell a lie, did I?" I smiled and relaxed my hold on her, but she didn't move back away. Her eyes were hungry to eat me up, but I had to feed her something less palatable. "Wolf needs a rest soon."

"Oh?" This time some concern cooled her expression.

"Didn't want to put him on the spot, but he is tiring. We've been through a lot the last few days."

She nodded and now stepped a little farther away. "He weathers a lot during our storms. Is it injury? An illness?"

I shook my head. He had no other icons over him. Although, perhaps turning the one that made him constantly hungry off might help with his energy levels. "Just old and exhausted."

She gave me a glum pout and looked down the corridor to where his large shape was vanishing into the shadows. "Do I need to worry about *two* of you now?"

"No. I'm enough burden on your heart, and he'll be fine with a lighter schedule." I grimaced at the phrasing. "Let's get going before they think we're getting up to more than kissing."

"If only," she sighed before setting off in front of me. A nice trick to have the last word in a conversation and hide the emotion on her face—which I assumed to be a coy smile.

I hummed to myself, not even distracted by what she was insinuating. Strangely enough, the kiss had been enough to ground me. Focused the shards of my shattered mind so that they resembled something usable.

From my belt, two cards flipped out and into my left hand. "Say, Ren? I was thinking we should work out some kind of signal system using the cards for if ever we can't communicate or otherwise need to send a message discreetly."

"Yeah? I can see the use." She slowed now to walk beside me. "Do I get to be the queen of hearts?"

I grinned and rolled my eyes. "I was going to use the aces to represent us all. I was going to give you clubs."

"Is that because they look like little trees?" She narrowed her eyes at me.

"Wolf is diamonds because of how tough he is. Quinn is hearts because of his romantic nature, and Tanya has spades because . . . I don't know, a rebirth thing in joining us? She's killed people?" I shrugged.

"So that's a yes on the tree thing?"

The two cards in my hand faded to dust and three more flipped from my holster and into my left hand. Required a little more concentration in my nondominant hand, and my right twitched as the muscle memory wanted to kick in.

"If I showed you these three, what would you assume the message is?"

Ace of clubs, three of hearts, ace of hearts.

"You . . . want me to fight the three enemies attacking Quinn?"

I nodded and smiled. In truth, I didn't have a clue what they'd mean, but now that she told me, it had become the method we would use—easier to go along with whatever made the most sense to her with the least amount of explanation. "We'll go through more some other time."

We approached the sound of flowing water as a sheet of the stuff blocked our current passage. I was glad the elf had some clue as to where we were heading. "Ladies first." I gestured her forward and only partly enjoyed the grimace on her face. Not sure why, as I'd soon be suffering.

She went through, vanishing to the other side, and I stepped in after— immediately shivering as it *was* ice-cold. Certainly woke me up, and my hat did little to stop it going in my eyes. As I wiped them dry, Tanya was standing there with her arms crossed, the others close by, waiting for me.

"Not my place to tell you what to do." She looked between us. "But you need to focus on the task at hand."

I glanced between her, the bear, and then Ren. "I suppose I should be honest with you then. The reason I held Ren back was because my arm is affecting me worse than I am showing. It is both mentally and physically draining. I wanted to bend her ear, as I would like to have a rest day after knocking the blood courier down."

An expert lie, even if I did say so myself. Got Wolf the rest he needed without giving away that he was feeling weak. Showed I could be vulnerable and knew when to take a step back. Most importantly—stopped Ren and me looking like horny teenagers.

Tanya exhaled through her nose and unfocused to go through her STAR. "That can still work. There's a place we can rest to the west for a few hours, then we'd need to head northeast to cut off the courier—if their route hasn't changed. If we're still alive after that, we'll arrange somewhere to spend the night." Her gaze returned to me. "Separate accommodation if possible."

"Thank you." I gave her a bow and ignored the last part.

"If we are being honest," Quinn added, "I've also been struggling to keep up with the amount of conflict thrust upon us."

Tanya worked her jaw but nodded. "Alright, point taken. I'm not exactly in a position to dispute that, given I was one of the ones who attacked you recently." Tanya shrugged and gestured toward the boss's room. "We have some important gigs in our near future, and you all need to be in peak form. That said, I can't do shit if you don't tell me shit—so let's keep open comms on this sort of thing. Okay?"

We nodded and murmured our agreements. Seemed as though I had gotten away with not only a kiss but had also drawn up a healthier attitude toward our Party's health and readiness in the process.

"You talk more than Max." The bear yawned. "What do I have to get attacked by now?"

She certainly did, but that was kind of the point. Our two newer Party members weren't here because they had powerful Classes like us original trio. They were here to share the physical and emotional burden that our personal quest was labored with. If Tanya wanted to boss me about toward my goal in the most efficient way, then that saved me a lot of brain power. Less stress. Quinn had a handy utility Skill for every occasion, which made existing that bit easier. Other than our bumpy beginnings, he was affable and dependable.

They explained the boss. Some type of giant seahorse that would frequently lay eggs that could spawn smaller versions. There was the occasional environmental danger of waves of water from different sides of the chamber and sometimes whirlpools between egg waves.

It all seemed so . . . droll? Sounded like another ten minutes where I would stand at the back of the room casting the occasional single card with my left hand until we eventually clobbered it into mush. Almost something of a torture in itself for me.

"Hey, Ren. Could you do that bandage thing?"

She raised an eyebrow before clocking what I meant. "We'll try it and see, but go easy on the bullshit, okay?"

I wondered if she'd look back to get the weaver's approval, but she didn't. Good. For all the rambling internal monologues I'd had about Tanya being good for our

Party composition, I still felt that Ren had more weight in making decisions. Especially when it came to my personal safety. It wasn't even because of the romancing on the side—if we had retained the cool companionship from the starter area, then she'd have the same sway due to seniority and trust.

She unslung my arm, and I winced as gravity moved it downward. Pain meant it was getting better, surely? It was certainly better than when I'd emerged from the water with it all but shredded. That said, it could hardly get worse.

Ren held the bandage in her mouth as she raised my arm back up, then wrapped it. With a whispered Elfin word, a golden glow ran down the object. I'd need to fix my suit at some point—having only one arm on it wasn't exactly becoming of a great magician.

I furrowed my brow and lifted my arm. It was sluggish to respond—but it *did* respond. Pain was muted to a constant ache, but for the most part it was acting as expected. We'd need to get stuck into the fight right away to put this to good use.

A flurry of cards burst out from my holster, spinning around into a figure eight around my extended hands. With the click of my fingers, they turned to dust.

"Right," I said, beaming at my Party. "Let's see if I can last ten minutes."

For some reason, they didn't seem too enthusiastic with my chances of beating the boss in that amount of time or less. Well, Ren looked like she believed in me.

Maybe with a little too much confidence.

CHAPTER FIFTY-TWO

Disarmed

Despite the gloom the boss chamber tried to weigh down on me and the heartache that the group was starting to wear down from our traumatic lifestyles . . . I was enjoying this fight a lot more.

Mostly because I was being insufferable with my newly acquired ability to manipulate mundane cards. A circle of them spun around my outstretched hand as if I were wearing a gauntlet. Periodically, one would burst into purple light and shoot off to the giant Monster, the gap filled almost immediately by another normal card.

The interesting thing was that manipulating my deck this way didn't seem to use Mana—or if it did, it was a paltry amount to my total or current regeneration. Not that I bothered to check the bar usually. Having a feel for the amount I had left in the tank had suited me well enough for all the time I had been in this world.

Still, I had only two or three minutes left before the radiance constantly warming my arm would falter . . . And after that? Agony, most likely. Hopefully, some more progress on it healing fully. My main worry was being caught unawares by the Crimson while being disadvantaged. It made the group weaker.

Not that they'd see it that way. Ren had been a bit more proactive in keeping her heals and shields up on Wolf even when he looked fine. Other than once, when Quinn didn't catch the wave attack at the right time and almost knocked himself out into a pile of small Monsters, we had been mostly safe at the back. And he couldn't really be blamed with his eyesight, and he was in the middle of reloading his crossbow.

With a crunch and a wail that reverberated throughout this cavern causing drops of water to fall from the rocky ceiling, the boss was felled. Just in time.

"Could you sling me up, Ren?"

She turned to me and gave a brief nod. Put her bow away and withdrew the fabric we had used. All business. Removed the bandage as my wounds needed room to breathe and started to hoist it up into the sling once more.

And then it began.

I clenched my teeth together, as all the damage felt as though it was being done unto me once more. Cold and warm flashes ran through me as sweat began to bead and roll down my face. Blue eyes looked up at me in panic.

"Shit, hold tight." She put a radiant heal through me.

Didn't help much with the sudden feeling, but the pain tapered off to something more manageable. Only felt like I had popping candy mixed in with my damaged muscles.

Then Tanya was there. Took my hat off with one hand and put the back of her other against my forehead. "This temperature isn't normal, right? Because of how you've changed?"

Ren shook her head and placed her own hand on my forehead just as soon as the weaver moved hers away.

"Changed?" I asked, feeling too nauseous to care that I was being manhandled. I might draw the line if Quinn or Wolf wanted a turn, however.

"Fuck, trickster. You're burning up bad."

"Yeah, *changed*." Tanya started digging around in her Inventory for something. "You might come from Earth, but your irises are bright purple."

"Oh, yeah. A recent development." I clenched my teeth together, and vertigo had me stumbling away from them. A cushion of soft fur caught me, and I slunk to the floor under the concerned looks of the two women.

"Rest easy, brother." Wolf's voice reverberated through the back of my head, comforting me.

Tanya sighed and shook her head in exasperation. "I'm not sure what I really have for this. It's not an injury so much as . . . You might have an infection, or it's just the trauma from the wounds. You still have my idol."

I exhaled and closed my eyes. "I have a potion of gradual healing and a greater antidote."

"Take them," she ordered me.

Ren crouched down beside me. "I'm too full of worry to chastise you for pushing too hard again. Maybe the rest is what we all need."

"Perhaps." As much as I wanted to give a more elaborate response to her statement, I was currently trying to arrange a phone consultation with my regular doctor. Not that staring at the keyboard was making me feel any better.

[Max: Hey, Rubes]
[Max: Can you diagnose without touch?]
[Ruby: Maybe? Are you okay? I'll need symptoms at the least.]

[Ruby: {o>o}?]
[Max: Deep lacerations, fever, agony, delirium, and nausea]
[Max: vertigo, nerve pain, numbness, agony]
[Ruby: . . . What have you done?]
[Max: Right forearm, overwhelming power, agony]
[Ruby: Fuck. Let me think {->-};]

"Max?" Ren jostled me. "Stay awake."

"I've fine, had worse by . . ." I stopped before my tongue could throw out a sentence even more incorrect that what had already transpired. Instead, I went through my Inventory to draw out the two potions. Under Ren's supervision, I downed them one after another. They both tasted like bile, which didn't seem correct.

How many times had I ended up sitting on the ground up against the bear, feeling useless and under the weather? Something about this Dungeon had thrown a gloomy cloud over me, and it wasn't just the abduction by something I didn't understand. The fact that this was partially self-inflicted just made me feel worse. A hindrance. A liability. A fraud.

[Ruby: Not much I can do without seeing it.]
[Ruby: Sounds like it needs some goop.]
[Ruby: Time and rest. I'm sure you've tried most other sources of healing?]
[Ruby: Sorry.]
[Ruby: Keep me updated? {u>u}]
[Max: I will, thank you.]

My eyes switched back to the present situation. Ren was hoping that staring at me intently could cure me. Tanya was briefly frozen with indecision. Quinn looked all out of place. Wolf was content enough to be my place of safety.

While my thoughts were nothing but wriggling eels in my jellied skull, I grabbed hold of them tightly and took charge. The System wasn't giving me any clues, but I felt it in my bones. Almost literally. Poisoned by the blood of the Siren or something of the sort. Washed together in the whirlpool of my eager self-injury and overwhelming power. Something of her had . . . seeped within. Nevertheless—I *had* to take control.

"Tanya, go finish up the looting. Quinn, get the location from her and start planning our exit route. I'll probably need you to keep me steady, Wolf."

Ren leaned in a little closer. "What do you need me to do, Max?"

I looked up into her worried face. She really *was* beautiful. I'm sure she would deny it, complain about the dirt and grime of battle, the grease and smells accumulated from the turmoil endured, and the uncomfortable and stifling outfits we forced ourselves to wear . . . but none of that mattered. It wasn't even the shape of her nose, her soft skin, pointed ears, or radiant hair that drew me in.

I was just powerless under the spell of her eyes. An unnatural light blue that seemed to glow and pierce straight through me. Always giving away her true feelings, whatever her facial expression was.

"Just . . . don't ever break my heart, okay?"

She frowned and pouted, unsure whether to laugh or burst into tears at the ridiculous ask. Eventually, despite it being the daytime still, she settled for something else entirely.

"I can't promise we'll have a happy ending, trickster. But I will be by your side wherever life or death takes us."

Now it was my turn to pout. Maybe that sort of thing was already implied when we had declared our love and been through so much already. I had no idea how relationships worked past awkwardly going to cafés or movie theaters and failing at not being full-on insufferable with my magician side. If anything, going through that portal—or those two portals, as the case may be—was probably the best thing that ever happened to me.

Especially since one of me had been about to be either clobbered to death or eaten alive by pigmen demons. Plus, they also copulated with corpses, which was neither here nor there, and now I wished I had a better grasp of where my delirium was taking me.

"If I start saying anything about necrophilia, it might be best to knock me out."

Ren stared back at me with a blank expression. Perhaps whiplash from the subject change. "*Okay.*"

"Everything's looted," Tanya confirmed.

"Route is added. Twenty minutes average pace," Quinn added.

Wolf grumbled and shifted. "Let's get brother someplace healthier, sister."

The elf nodded and lent down both hands to help pull me to my feet. Having Wolf consider us his family sounded nice at first, but referring to us as brother and sister made things weird for our copulation. Oh, I should definitely stop using that word. *Copulate.*

Quinn led the Party forward, back to the waterfall. Ren and Wolf were either side of me to hopefully catch me if I tried to enact a knock-knock joke on the stone floor with my soft skull. The punch line would be . . . Hmm, maybe it *would* actually fix these thoughts I couldn't control. I eyed up the damp rocks jutting from the cavern walls to find something suitable for such a purpose.

System had determined this to be my fate, but I just kept fighting it. I just had to be the winner and persist. Stupid fucking rock walls could fuck off. Survival was my middle name. *Maximum Survival Dickbag.* Sweat dripped from my head.

"The cold water might help with your temperature, *or* it might give you an infection." Tanya shook her head. "We should have been more careful when you received the injury. I'm sorry."

"Don't be," I managed. My eyes ached though. Perhaps she had planned this. A slow way to kill me off that didn't draw suspicion to her. The betrayal clear as day, I watched as she stepped through the curtain of falling water. Her intent was out here for all to see. I would die, drowned, and full of nasty bacteria and whatever gunk the System filled the water with.

Despite my brain trying to push for conflict, I stepped through the waterfall calmly and at a decent pace, so I was only briefly chilled. I shivered off, rather unhappy that my suit was now soaked once more. Tanya was waiting for us, and I smiled up at her. *My savior.* I was sure she could lead the Party to seal the deal against the Lady in my stead, should I fall.

"Stop one second," I requested. They did so. "If you could all step over to Tanya, apart from Wolf." Curious, but they did so. I gave him a pat and asked him to turn sideward. Now, with him blocking most of the view of me—I set my outfit to be fixed, the System dropping me to my underwear only.

"Max," Ren complained. "You'll catch a cold standing there like that."

Of course, they could at least see the back of my shoulders as I stood and faced the waterfall. Maybe I should jump in it. Cool off—or no, maybe it would be warm this time? I ran my tongue across my lips, tasting the errant drops that had wet my face. Once my suit came back, it would cover my wounded arm again, which sounded painful.

In my Inventory, I switched some things around. Top layers unequipped and wouldn't repair now, I instead changed to some spares. Whatever the medieval version of a tank top was called, in a deep muted gray. Black shorts, which had little armor but seemed more comfortable than some of my other options. Sandals because *fuck* this world.

I turned back to them and tipped the invisible hat I wore, the real one someplace safe, I hoped. Belt and sling remained present, which was nice. Wolf moved back to my side to reveal my outfit change.

"Weird," Tanya surmised. "It's like seeing a tortoise without its shell."

"Odd," Ren partially agreed, "but kind of cute as well."

My scowl turned to Quinn now to see what the third judge thought. Briefly awkward at being put on the spot, he eventually shrugged. "I agree more with Ren, although it is slightly—"

"Yeah, yeah," I interrupted. "I'll take cute. Let's keep going."

A compliment that wasn't related to my performance acts? I'd cherish that forever. Especially coming from Ren. The change of clothing helped my body temperature regulate better, although made me feel off being so weirdly dressed compared to what I was used to.

I flexed my fingers as we continued toward the exit, almost giddy at seeing the open air and sunshine once more. Oh? I *could* move my fingers with . . . little pain at all.

In fact, my arm was feeling a lot better all of a sudden. A beat thrummed in my ears that at first I dismissed as a fever-bound heartbeat gone awry. But no, it kept on going and . . . was drawing me. A thread leading to the left. Another whisper? Friendly and familiar, but different . . .

"Max?" Wolf asked, drawing the attention of everyone else.

I took a couple of steps toward a wall and stopped before it. "I need to go in *here.*"

"We need to get out, trickster." Ren sighed. "Have your manic break under the clear sky instead."

No. I shook my head and gestured Quinn over. "Did you know there's a room here?"

"There is? I did not." He raised an eyebrow back at Tanya, who returned a shrug. "I can have a look."

I wavered as I took a couple of steps back to allow him access. Seemed so clear to me, as if it were written there. *Max,* the secret room called out. *Your presence is requested. I was here, secret room,* please be patient.

"Oh! There is? How strange." Crouching down by the wall, the fixer had his brow furrowed. He moved his finger to press against something, and a click signaled my words were nothing but truth.

Stale air washed through the passageway as the stone moved to the side—a sliding door that crunched and wore across the damp rock surrounding it. And inside? A blue light illuminated a small room that I was already stepping toward.

Ren was beside me before I had noticed, eager to ensure I wasn't about to do anything stupid. But how could I when I felt so right?

By the back wall of this dozen-foot-deep space was something akin to a fountain—some metal font made of tarnished copper. It was an altar; I knew this fact somehow. Patterns and designs spun out around the walls as if the engravings had sprayed forth from the centerpiece. Each of them told me the same tale.

It was related to the Guardian here.

My left hand went up and undid my sling. Right arm came out with no pain. Still looked terrible, but I moved it around to show the elf. Perhaps this was my reward? I had defeated the Siren; now it was solely up to me to reap what I deserved. And I *was* so deserving.

Slowly, I stepped toward it, feeling better and better every inch. Fever cleared, and my mind sharpened.

With a wide grin across my face, I reached out and placed my hand on the cool metal edge of the fountain. All was right with the world.

Oh, and then my entire forearm exploded off of the bone, painting the room and elf in bright-red gore.

CHAPTER FIFTY-THREE

Return to Sender

It took me a good few seconds to really understand what had happened. The Party was a chorus of confused or shocked screams and yells. I liked to think the most high-pitched yelp was Quinn.

Between my elbow and my wrist, only bone remained. Glistening and wet. I was so disassociated that I felt nothing, other than the surprise at being pelted by the burst fragments of my own body. None of this seemed real.

Of course, that was when things started to get really strange.

While the ringing persisted in my ears and I was frozen at the sight of my meatless arm, purple energy started to flow out, enveloping the altar and my body. Ren tried to pull me away, but a crack of static lightning prevented her. By then, it was too late anyway.

Tendrils of this power circled my arm, obscuring it in bright light. Smoke billowed around, pouring from the fountain. A mauve mist that felt cool and comforting. It covered my vision and pooled behind me, filtering through to the passageway where the others stood.

A grin crossed my face. There was an unspoken understanding that flowed from this energy to part of my subconscious brain. Wasn't even words, really, just the knowledge. A feeling that I had enacted something both terrible and magnificent in this Dungeon. This was my punishment *and* my reward. Impurities had been exorcised, but was that all?

I turned and stepped back out of the room. Smoke blew away from me to reveal my sparkling purple suit. I removed my hat with my right hand and gave them a bow.

"Your arm?" Ren managed to say, worried confusion overriding any disdain for my entrance.

As I stood back straight, I held it out. Eyes went out to my Inventory to swap my jacket off, and then shirt and waistcoat. My bare arm—and the rest of my torso—awaited their judgment.

It looked fine.

No pain. No damage. No otherworldly runes or illness to say that I'd been possessed or cursed. Nothing so overt, at least.

She reached out and touched it. Her fingertips gingerly ran down my flesh made anew.

"You have an explanation for this that *isn't* bullshit?" Tanya asked, looking uncharacteristically out of sorts.

I shook my head, still trying to understand it myself. "Something to do with killing the Siren, but I don't know what it really did to me." Everything else aside, I was pretty sure that it wasn't just a healing font. Something had been purged from me and built back different . . . although I didn't *feel* different. Nothing in my STAR gave a hint to whatever new malady I had ungraciously accepted. It would be more comforting if I could place whether the new power was demonic in nature or not.

"You good to walk, trickster?" Ren watched as I put my clothing back on. "We should leave." Simple words, but my speckled blood that covered most of her gave them weight.

"A little lightheaded, but I'm feeling much better." I nodded and smiled down at Wolf. The only one who didn't look traumatized from the brief violence I had endured.

In fact, I was pretty sure I was only remarkably calm about it due to dissociating still. I *was* awake, right? This wasn't a fever dream where I was imagining everything was okay? It was equally likely I had passed out or been drawn into another dream world or Domain for further agony to be labored on my tired shoulders.

I stopped briefly and turned to the elf. She paused too and tilted her head in expectation. Instead of saying anything, I just raised my hand up and cupped her face. Ran my thumb along her soft cheek. Some apprehension and concern lingered in her eyes.

"Sorry," I said with a brief smile. "I just wanted to make sure that this was real."

She returned the smile—which melted my heart—and rolled her eyes. "Unfortunately so. Now keep walking."

I did so but gave one last glance back to the chamber, now devoid of smoke and no longer pulling me toward it. This didn't feel like the end to a chapter, however. It felt like a window we had left open—fine while the weather was pleasant, but as soon as something more turbulent and chilling came our way, the true nature of my mistake would come to rain upon us.

Or maybe I just got a new free arm, the same as we received gold for defeating Monsters.

[Max: I touched an eldritch fountain and now am fully healed.]
[Ruby: . . .]
[Ruby: I don't know whether to be more or less concerned.]
[Ruby: fucker]
[Max: I'll let you know when it comes back to bite me.]
[Ruby: {->-};;]

My eyes went back to my Party. Like me, they all now had the trauma Status, something I was loath to accept . . . but the System didn't lie. Even Wolf, despite his impassive glare. I had thought the Status was something only personally gained through hardship, but apparently seeing parts of my body explode into bloody mist was enough to do it for them.

I knew it wasn't the right take, but it was nice to know they cared enough to be distraught about my personal injury. Especially considering the amount of violence we already endured every day.

Ren was stuck beside me as we walked. I could see her jaw working, plenty of things she wanted to say or do—but getting out of here was our priority. Wolf was behind us, while the other two led. Through all the emptied rooms and chambers we had fought previously. I was tired of the smell of damp stone and dead sea monsters. It had become oppressive, and I longed for fresh air.

[Dungeon complete]
[Experience gained]

"Oh." I wrinkled my face up and lifted my left arm to see my STAR shining a bright gold. "Almost forgot what we were here for."

"I'm saving mine for when we're somewhere nicer. My eyes are tired." Ren looked more exhausted than I'd ever seen her. While she seemed immune to my Dazzle attempts, seeing her with the trauma Status wrenched at my heart.

Tanya gave a glum smile. "We may need more rest than we first anticipated."

"I can see buff and debuff icons, by the way." I wiggled a finger above their heads. "Can't remember if I'd said that before. We *all* have it."

She relaxed slightly, knowing that it wasn't just her that had to soldier on. We could push through it, I was sure . . . but we'd pay a price. When the stakes meant death was more likely, it wasn't worth the risk.

"I have something that can help us, but we'd still need downtime."

I nodded. I'd save my level up for when we were settled too. It sounded like it wasn't too far away, and I'd literally kill for a moment of peace. We were almost back at the starting room now. I was excited for this to be done, but a brief bit of paranoia rose up—what if we would get ambushed again?

Ren held my hand. "Lightning doesn't strike the same place twice, trickster."

I wondered if lightning knew that. "Let me go first, invisible, to check that the coast is clear?"

As we entered the staging room where we had slept the previous night. A healthy amount of concern was painted on their faces at my idea. As if I had been at all out of my usual mind lately or didn't spend half this Dungeon dancing with an apparent demigod that may have been a delusion. If it weren't for my arm at least . . . Although, perhaps that was part of it.

Ren sighed. "Fine. Straight back in if there's any trouble. Wolf is coming out in ten seconds. Okay?"

I nodded. "Understood."

We arranged ourselves near the exit, a portal that would take us back out to the daylight. I rolled my shoulders out and stepped through, exhaling through my nose as I activated <Vanishing Act> on myself.

The light of day burned at my eyes despite it being rather gloomy and overcast. Perhaps it had rained, and we were emerging into the end stages of a brief shower. My eyes went over to the figure idly standing by the entrance. Lightly armored. Not only had the young man not noticed me, but his gaze looked vacant. I dropped my invisibility.

"Max," he said. "A delivery for you."

Into his hand, an envelope. I took it, my brow furrowed, and put it away in my Inventory. As if his purpose had been fulfilled, he turned from me—taking a handful of steps before vanishing into nothing. I blinked, and then Wolf came and pushed me out of the way, emerging from the portal expecting some danger but finding me alone.

"Feels like it's been days since I've had fresh air," I said as I stepped over to the side so there was room for the others.

The bear sniffed around the damp grass but didn't seem to have anything to note.

A sea breeze hit me and washed away all the stress. I almost felt calm. My eyes closed as I allowed nature to absorb me once more. The sounds of the rest of the Party appearing distant as I tried to focus on the movement of leaves, a shoreline buffeted by the tide, and muted birdsong.

Some manner of warmth pressed against me, and I opened my eyes to see Ren wrap her arms around me, her head to the side, ear to my chest. Past her, I saw the drab group before me. The Dungeon itself hadn't really been that difficult or draining, but whatever I had dragged them into had worn them out.

"I apologize. Whatever curse follows me went a bit far today." I gave them a glum smile.

"We'll deal with that and your miraculously healed arm when we're at our destination." Tanya gave me a tired scowl. "Apology accepted."

As much as I had been expecting a curse word or new moniker to add to my collection, she didn't seem to directly blame me. With a nod, we set off in silence.

Ren was . . . clingy, in a way that felt unlike her. She not only held my hand but tried to walk as close to me as she could without tripping me. An ache in my chest stuck with me during our journey, in seeing that she did not deal with the trauma Status well. Other than being knocked out during the Jokkar fight, she had managed to avoid most calamity, as I was a magnet for it.

As a group, we had become crestfallen. Sick of what we had endured despite the necessity to continue. I wondered how a little body horror had them gaining the Status when we had maimed our way through the opposition to this point. Did they hold me in such high regard that my downfall had such an effect? They were my biggest fans, sure, but . . .

No, it was unfair to paint them in that light.

Before I knew it, we had arrived. We stopped, and Ren used the opportunity to put her arms around me from the side again.

A crescent-shaped rocky hill sat before us, and at the bottom was a small cottage. The stone steep enough that it would be nigh impossible to climb—making the building only assailable from the singular direction we were approaching from.

"It's empty," Tanya said. "Make yourselves at home."

Home. If only.

But I could pretend. Delude myself into thinking this was the true end of the road. That this could be a comforting place of rest and safety. There weren't vultures waiting high overhead for us to make any mistakes. We could just exist.

My exploits were growing wilder by the day, but such a trick might be one of my best yet.

CHAPTER FIFTY-FOUR

Rest for the Wicked

The sun had come out and blessed us with warmth and light. Any dew and damp left over from the rain that we had avoided had evaporated away, leaving us with . . . bliss.

I sat in a swing seat outside the front of the cottage, among patches of flowers, idly rocking back and forth. Ren was sleeping on me, her head against my chest. Her hat had fallen away, leaving her radiant hair at the forefront of my peripheral.

In the thicker grass, Wolf lay almost on his back. Smile on his face and tongue lolling out as Tanya rubbed through his belly fur. To the side, Quinn was fast asleep in his chair, head hanging low. The occasional snore made its way to my ears.

I shed some silent tears at the whole picture of it. Not really sadness or elation . . . It was just the relief, perhaps. We were hardened to the conflict we had to partake in, but we weren't unbreakable. Time off was needed, lest we burn out. Show business was tough.

That said, I couldn't sleep. As much as my body yearned to relax and drift off with the elf . . . I was still on edge. Violence never let us sit idle for too long, and I couldn't shake the paranoia that something would want to come and burst this bubble we existed in. However, other than the chirping of birds and occasional butterfly, it felt as though we were the only ones left in the world.

Instead, I prodded open my STAR, to see what the System cared to grant me now.

[Level up—<12>]
[Stats increased]
[New Ability: <Shuffle>]
[New Passive: <Strong Entrance>]
[New Passive: <Elemental Imp>]

I raised my eyebrow as I read through the text descriptions of each. <Strong Entrance> made my first attack on a target increase Damage for further attacks against the same target by 10 percent. So one person per fight would receive slightly more ire from me. Sounded like something good for bosses that would pair well with <Shatter>.

<Elemental Imp> wasn't a new summon but changed which spell my small demonic friends could cast. The default had now become fire, whereas I could instead summon an ice, lightning, or stone variant now. Helpful if we went up against Monsters with elemental weaknesses—I'd have to see what their spells did before knowing how useful against Players they'd be.

My jaw worked as I took in the active Ability. It made sense—the language used was plain enough. I could see how thematically it fit into my persona and what kind of Class the System thought I should be . . . It was just all too convenient. Or perhaps I was taking every coincidence as a plot against me. Or *for* me.

<Shuffle> allowed me to change Dazzle icons on a target to a different, random debuff. Not entirely useful on the surface—Dazzle played into a lot of my other Skills aside from being a damaging bonus for me and my demons. The problem was the wording of the Skill . . . in that although it was clearly intended for Dazzle icons, they hadn't accounted for the fact that I could now see and interact with most other icon types.

Would it let me push the rules out of the way a little with its ambiguity?

I brought up my Status window and looked at the trauma icon sitting there. Amusing that it was only mild, considering I had borne the brunt of the damage. For a moment, I hesitated, but then—the System *wouldn't allow it*, surely?

The Skill activated, and I watched the icon change.

Immediately I leaned forward. Pushing the elf away from me I dropped to my knees among the soft grass. Projectile vomited. Even as my body fought against it, my eyes were going into my Inventory. A brief pause in the spasms, and I brought the other greater antidote out and glugged it down, my throat contesting the action—but I survived it.

I then saw the icon vanish. Cured whatever terrible poison it was, and the trauma icon had gone. Despite my bleary eyes, I grinned wildly.

Ren's hand was on my back. "Max? Are you okay?"

Wolf had righted, and Tanya was moving over in front of me. "Something to do with your arm?" she asked.

I shook my head and gathered my thoughts. "Sorry again. Was just a little overexcited to level up."

Before I could stand, the elf moved her mouth to my ear. "Five seconds to explain or else."

For some reason, the ambiguous *else* was more threatening than if she'd already had something in mind like actual bodily harm. "It isn't exactly safe," I began as the love of my life allowed me to stand. "But I have rid myself of the trauma Status."

Ren crossed her arms. Clearly unimpressed to be woken from a nap to find me throwing up. Tanya had some tired curiosity, and Wolf wasn't too keen to engage unless food was involved. Quinn was still fast asleep, which was somewhat remarkable.

"I'd ask, but I'm guessing the answer is System bullshit?" The elf rolled her eyes. "Can you do it on me next?"

"Ah." I tilted my head from side to side—feeling pretty great despite the circumstances. "It changes your trauma into a random debuff. I drew up some poison, I believe."

She shrugged. "I can't think of much worse than trauma—and if we can all get cured of it, it won't set us back for the rest of the day."

Tanya put her hands on her hips. "I'm afraid there is *much* worse than trauma, unless there was a short list or any other indication?"

I shook my head. "Like I said—it's risky. I only used it on myself to test. It would be too dangerous to use for everything." After all, it wasn't intended to be used on allies.

"Agreed," the weaver said. "Imagine one of us were accumulating stacks of a slow in battle, and you tried to switch it—and instead it gave hemorrhage or stun. *Rot poison* or many other countless high-level debuffs. Some of those are fatal at a certain number of stacks. It could be a death sentence."

She was correct. It had some use cases against enemies but was too dangerous to throw it around in my normal rotation.

"That said . . ." she continued. "Use it on me, please."

Ren turned a scowl toward the woman. "Pretty sure I had dibs."

Tanya smiled. "I am immune to a certain amount of conditions, due to my Class Keystone, and can provide you all with moderate resistances. There's a good chance the changed debuff won't affect me—and then I will assist you."

The elf clicked her tongue. "Acceptable."

I wasn't entirely convinced either way, now that she had named some things that I didn't like the sound of. As much as I had quickly cooled on the idea this could be an easy out for our trauma Statuses, I was not a gambling man. Other than with my own safety, of course.

"Alright." I sighed. "Have a heal and antidote ready, just in case." I held my hand out, looking at the icon above her. <Shuffle> activated, and the box vanished, to be replaced by a ghostly skull that I could barely see, which quickly faded away. Had I just killed her?

"See?" She smiled. "Immune. Good thing too, as that was a nasty one."

I deflated. "That doesn't make me feel any better about this." I turned my head as Ren was pulling at my jacket sleeve.

"*Please*, trickster?"

How could I say no to those eyes? "No." Oh, just like that.

Rather than scowling at my refusal, she instead gave an exaggerated pout, sadness filling her eyes. Alright, she won there. I *was* only human.

"Fine." I rubbed at my eye sockets. Perhaps I did need a nap after all.

"You can't be the only one to put your life on the line all the time, Max." Her tone was soft, easily breaking down the barriers I was trying to put up.

No point telling her I didn't want to see her hurt—she could easily turn that back around about my own lax attitude to my mortality. Plus, I *actually* got hurt. Badly and regularly.

Tanya stepped over and held out a golden idol for the elf to hold. Something with resistances, I presumed, based on her earlier declaration. I took a step back from the pair to have a better view of both Ren and her icon. She really did look tired and miserable, and I felt guilty for waking her up. This cottage must have a bath . . .

She gave me a nod, and I raised my hand.

Trauma vanished and was replaced by . . . armor weakness. My eyes quickly brought up the information in an unnecessary panic. Twenty percent less armor on equipped gear. Two-minute duration.

We both sighed in relief.

"This has no right being so stressful." I shook my head and turned my gaze to Quinn. Still asleep. Should probably get his consent for this, however.

"Let me get him awake and up to date," Tanya said, taking the idol back with a smile.

I nodded my thanks. "Go start up a bath, Ren. I'll join you soon."

The elf pulled a face at how brazen and open I was about the request but left all the same. I watched her go, more energy in her step now that trauma was gone. At least, that's what I assumed it could be.

"You're a cute couple," Tanya said, drawing my gaze away from the elf as she entered the cottage. "It's wonderful, really, given the System."

My eyes went back out to the woods that blocked the horizon. Another slice of paradise that we were fighting for, something to come back to once violence wasn't so baked into our day-to-day.

"I certainly wasn't expecting love." I shrugged and gave her a smile. "On Earth, I was a loner and workaholic. I'm rather out of my depth beyond that."

She returned the smile, albeit with a bit more sadness to it. "Well, you've done well, Max. Ren is tough and competent, and clearly besotted with you."

"Yeah. Having all of that is difficult sometimes." We stepped closer to the sleeping fixer. "Feels like it is just building a case for calamity to take it away."

"Hon." Tanya stopped and tilted her head. "Love is about fighting as hard as you can to keep it. Always. Doesn't matter if you have a dragon at your door or the mundane existence of a decade of marriage tiring you out—you always strive to keep the candle alight."

I nodded.

"Some days it burns bright by itself, and others it threatens to die out under the constant rain. But you don't let it. Will I see my husband and child again? I *want* it more than anything in the world . . ." She turned her gaze away, looking out at the scenery. "Is it likely? Probably not. But I will fight and claw my way to find any remote chance because that is what love is."

"Thank you, Tanya."

"No. If anything, I should be thanking you, Max." She shook her head. "You had every right to kill me. To not trust me. Now I live longer to continue fighting for love."

In truth, I was rather at a loss for words. Originally, I had kept her alive because she had useful information, and part of me wanted to believe that evil was a choice and she deserved a second chance. Even gifted my life in her hands to see her true intentions.

I withdrew an orange into my hand and lobbed it underhand to the sleeping man. He caught it and blinked his one eye rapidly, coming to. In following my lead, Tanya chucked the idol to him, which he caught in his other hand.

Confusion spread across his brow. "Everything okay?"

"Max can remove your trauma, at the risk of either giving you something worse or something inconsequential."

His eye looked between the two of us. "A gamble then? Freedom or suffering?"

A pretty apt way of putting it. Nerves were creeping up within me. I felt as though I were flipping a coin and we'd gotten heads three times in a row. Tails meant doom, and we were due one—despite probability not working that way. Still, it was his choice, and I told him so.

He took a moment to think about it, brow furrowed as his eye darted aimlessly alongside his thoughts. "Alright." He looked back at me. "I accept, and any malady that befalls me will be my own doing. No blame on you, Max."

I nodded and held my hand out as he gripped the idol and an antidote potion.

Trauma vanished . . . and was replaced by . . . sleep.

Quinn dozed off immediately, and I sighed in relief. A glance behind me, and Wolf had also drifted off—looking rather content with himself. For some reason his trauma Status had already gone. I didn't care to question it—thankful at least that I didn't have to flip another coin for the bear who needed a break from conflict.

"Mission accomplished?"

I turned back to Tanya and grinned. "*Sleep*. Guess I'm rolling well today."

She nodded and gestured toward the house. "Go spend some time with her. I'll use the peace out here to come up with a plan for later. Oh, I have dibs on the bath once you're done though."

With a smile, I tipped my hat. "You have my word."

I still had that envelope burning a hole in my Inventory, but having my arm restored, beating the odds against trauma, and with a beautiful bathing elf waiting for me . . . I'd put it off just a few minutes longer.

It wasn't often I received fan mail, so I'd savor it.

CHAPTER FIFTY-FIVE

Something Written

The room was steamy, condensation from the hot bath clinging to the deep-brown tiles and wooden-plank walls. Sparsely furnished with a few empty shelves and potted plants that somehow lived despite the cottage being seemingly abandoned.

I pulled a face as Ren put her foot on my chest and wiggled her toes at me.

"Not my fault the bath is so small, trickster."

While most of the tubs we had graced during our travels were wide and circular, this small, slim one was very much not designed for duos. Since we insisted that we sit opposite each other, it had become an awkward game of where we could fit all our legs. The blissful hot water and comfort far outweighed the minor issue of space.

"I have some fragrant oil," I said. "If you're good for the rest of the day, I'll give you a foot rub tonight."

Her brow furrowed. "You'd do that? Promise?"

"You have my word." I was slightly curious why that seemed like a big deal to her. After she'd given me a few shoulder rubs—and considering we spent so much time walking—it seemed like a fair enough deal.

"I hope so. I'll be excited all day now." Ren removed the offending foot from me and tried to move around up to her knees, threatening to spill water out onto the floor. She propped herself up near the side, giving me the chance to watch the water run from her body—before she caught my glance and gestured with narrowed eyes. *"Arm."*

I extended my right arm across the edge of the bath, and she shuffled in front of it—a struggle with how little room there was. She placed one hand at my wrist and the other near my inner elbow.

"Looks normal," she said. "Feel any different?"

"Feels like nothing ever happened."

She brushed wet hair behind her long ears and moved her face closer, inspecting my arm carefully. "Can't be. Normal healing can't do that."

"It was definitely unusual—that I can't deny."

"*Unusual*," she repeated. As if we hadn't watched my injured arm completely burst into red mist and then reform with purple energy.

Her face even closer now, she pressed her lips just below my wrist and kissed it gently.

"No pain, odd sensations, awkwardness?"

"No."

Now in the middle of my forearm, she repeated the same soft kiss.

"Your plans in this world haven't changed unexpectedly?"

"No."

Another kiss near my inner elbow.

"You don't want to betray your feelings, lash out at your friends? Grab me right now and drown me?"

"No, of course not."

I raised an eyebrow as she turned to face me, putting her arm across to hold the other side of the tub. The clumped ends of her wet hair tickled at my chest.

"No? Then what *do* you want to do with me, Max?"

The bathtub gurgled as our dirt and sins swirled around and emptied down the drain. Dried, we now got ourselves dressed. It took me a little longer, as I was constantly distracted by the elf. No idea why.

She caught my glances as she buttoned up her waistcoat. "I'm sorry for how I've been lately."

I raised an eyebrow, not understanding her train of thought immediately.

"Being so needy and full-on. I'm . . . It takes a lot to get me out of my shell, and I swung a bit too far the other way."

My mind went back to the recent conversation I had with Tanya. "Ren, we could die tomorrow or live for a hundred years together. Both would not be enough time to fully share our love, so don't waste your time on *sorry*. Squeeze as much as you can from life."

She pouted and stepped over to me, pulling on my shirt to draw me in for a kiss. "Charmer," she said as she moved away, her eyes staring deep into mine. "You like it when I'm clingy and soft, don't you?"

"Just as much as you like it when I'm firm and commanding, I'm sure."

"Got me." She smiled, illuminating us both.

"Oh." My brow furrowed, as the sensible me tried to drag us from the otherwise perpetual cycle of affection. "I received a letter by courier."

Her expression cooled, and an eyebrow went up. "Really? When?"

"Let's relieve Tanya, and we'll go through it."

I'm sure we had taken a lot longer than she had perhaps expected—although in saying that, she seemed pretty wise and understanding about what we had going on. Ren and I had come a long way since awkwardly sharing a muddy hole in the ground. Hardly recognized her, almost—and I was sure to be a lot different from the *always fine* showman just trying to get by.

We stepped through the hallway into the open-plan living room and approached the door, some slight surprise on both of our faces to hear the murmur of conversation and light chuckles from outside. I opened up the door back into the fresh air, which felt fantastic on my clean skin.

Tanya and Quinn were sitting around a small campfire, smiles on their faces over whatever their conversation had entailed. Wolf had moved closer to the fire but was fast asleep once more.

Before I could apologize for taking so long, the weaver was already up on her feet. "You two look about ready to go onstage. A good scrub was clearly what you both needed."

My tongue caught in my mouth, but I managed a nod. Ren had a wry grin but didn't seem keen to add her confirmation to the statement.

"My turn for a soak." She sighed and stretched out. "All of you share your Equipment screens with me. While I bathe, I will go through and assign loot and get your gold and token shares sorted."

I did as she asked, if only so that she'd go into the cottage and I could feel less awkward about whatever was happening.

"Sorting Equipment distribution is relaxing for you?" Ren asked her as she sent over her screen.

"In a way. Part of my role here is to take some of the unnecessary pressure off you, right? You only need the gear that will be an improvement, so consider me a filter for that." She smiled and gave us a nod. "Plus, I like to feel there is some order in this world, even if I have to force it myself." She turned and strode off toward the building.

Turned out I respected Tanya quite a bit. Not only because she was putting effort into making my life easier, but she was doing that even after the bullshit of the last few days.

Ren went to sit by the campfire, while I stopped and knelt down beside the bear. I ran my hand around the fur on his head, and he opened a sleepy eye.

"Hey, big guy. You hungry?" I noted that he didn't have his usual debuff—he'd made the decision to toggle off his attack buff for the first time since I had met him.

"Please," he grumbled, closing the eye again. "Nothing too heavy though."

I gave him a pat on the head and moved over to the campfire.

"Would you like me to cook, Max?" Quinn tilted his head to the side.

"Hmm. I was thinking of doing like a . . . vegetable stir-fry? The only oil I have is scented, however."

"Oh." He rubbed at his eye patch. "Does that make it a better weapon?"

I nodded slowly, while the elf squirmed in my peripheral. "Maybe just a stew up some veg or something then. If you could?"

"It would be a pleasure." He stood from his chair and gave me a brief bow.

Ren had an impatient look on her face that said *sit and open the letter.*

With a smile, I pulled out my favorite chair close to hers and withdrew the envelope. I wondered if it was worth checking for any dangerous foreign substances or curses. Holding it up to the light . . . it looked pretty mundane. I'd take the chance. Splitting the plain wax seal, I withdrew the contents.

Dear Magician. I understand I am to welcome you into the fold as one of the few who have defeated a Guardian. It makes more sense now how you've been such a thorn in my side. You are soon to know the burden your victory brings—but I offer out an olive branch. I can hone and protect you as your bud blooms. Either way, our fates are now intertwined. Everyone has a breaking point. Do you think you are closer to yours than I am to mine? Gamblers always pay the steepest costs.

Yours unfavorably, Lady in Red

I folded the paper back up and put it away in my Inventory. Brow furrowed, I stared off at the horizon in thought.

"*Max*," Ren whined.

"Oh, sorry." I shook away the shadow covering me and gave her a sheepish grin. "It's from you-know-who. An offer to join her, or otherwise a warning that killing a Guardian is bad news."

She pulled a face. "That means she is scared and hurting, right? If she thinks that you should join her, she'd rather not face you."

I didn't verbally answer but nodded. What she had said about the Guardians was more concerning than anything else. She couldn't afford to fully commit to stopping us without overextending the power she needed to consolidate for Candlekeep. That didn't mean we were safe—but we weren't at all-out war yet.

She knew something about the Guardians that I did not, however, and was twisting that knife into sowing doubt in my mind. Other than my new Power bar and ability to manipulate mundane cards, I didn't feel any different. My Domain was probably the reward for a full meter. My arm was . . . I frowned at it before catching that Ren had been patiently watching me for further conversation.

"We are resting," I said. "I will not ruin that with my dour thoughts. Instead, I will eat well, enjoy the pleasant company that surrounds me, and dream of basking in the lights and applause of a show well performed."

Ren attempted to roll her eyes but didn't have the heart to. Instead, she exhaled and accepted the inevitable. "I'll toast to that."

"Yeah, I'd love a coffee, thanks." I gave her a shit-eating grin that *did* earn me a bit more exasperation.

"*Dickbag*," she murmured, giving me a pat on the leg as she went over to the campfire.

I went into my Inventory and sent a copy of the letter over to Tanya. Was rude of me to interrupt her bath, but I figured she deserved to be clued in as soon as possible in case she had any knowledge to bless us with.

While I waited for a response, I watched the elf set up the kettle and have a conversation about the stew with Quinn. Offered him some ingredients and a coffee. Despite part of me feeling like I was harboring a potential nuke in my arm, I felt relaxed again. Wolf seemed content, if still overly tired.

A slice of heaven, interrupted by the gentle beep of the Chat.

[Tanya: We'll need to be wary.]
[Tanya: This reeks of desperation.]
[Max: Agreed. Any thoughts on the Guardian stuff?]
[Tanya: No. Mind if I fwd this to my contact? Might prompt him to talk?]
[Max: Alright. If he is with the Wardens then they know me already.]
[Tanya: Fantastic.]
[Tanya: Oh. You willing to drop some DEX to go with a more
INT-heavy build?]
[Max: Sure. Card damage is INT based.]

I closed the Chat, feeling . . . I wasn't sure what. Like I was haunted by a ghost. The shadow of something clouded me, but I didn't know what or why. Was I just supposed to die to the Siren? Seemed unfair to put me in an unwinnable situation and then curse me when I beat out all odds. But . . . *was* I cursed? Not in the traditional way, and if it wasn't for the odd nature of my renewal or the venom dripped by the Lady, I wouldn't think twice about it.

My eyes rose up to see Ren standing there with the steaming coffee.

No, the Lady was wrong. Any power I had stolen from the Guardians was not a curse but a blessing. Another tool in my arsenal that would eventually be her undoing. I lived in illusion and falsehoods—her words were flimsy and transparent.

I was the panacea to rid this world of her blight, and tonight I would carve out her supply lines and watch her bought followers starve out.

Perhaps after a nap though. I'd certainly earned it.

CHAPTER FIFTY-SIX

Token Gift

We lived. *Were* living.

Using the bear as a backrest, Ren and I sat next to each other on the ground and relaxed. Some odd nostalgia in the action, despite it only being a few weeks that this was commonplace. The warm fur of the bear was comforting—I hadn't even seen when he had cleaned himself. But as he slept, all our worries washed away.

Tanya exited the cottage and sent Quinn in for his own turn in the bath. She stopped beside us and smiled, crossing her arms over the comfortable black clothes she had changed into. "It amuses me that you still choose to relax in your outfits."

I glanced down at us to realize she was correct. "Old habits die hard," I replied with a sheepish grin.

She brought her chair over a little closer and sat, deflating with a long sigh. Rubbing her eyes, she then looked out toward the woods. "Came across this place by accident. I think it was supposed to be the staging area for something, but haven't seen it used. Monsters and the like stay clear. There's nothing here for Players other than to be a place to rest."

"I think it saved our lives," Ren offered. "After what we've been through, this allows us to stay sane. And clean."

"You're telling me." The weaver smiled. "Amenities are few and far between. After a month or two, I'd given up trying to shave or get my hair looking as good as it used to. I'm content feeling like a yeti."

Ren wrinkled up her nose. "I lucked out there in a way. My ancestry doesn't grow body hair."

Tanya raised an eyebrow. "No beards either?"

The elf shook her head. "My aunt used to tell tale of a certain elfin ancestry that grew hair all over, but I'm not sure if that was true."

I nodded my head sagely, not really sure where my place in this conversation was.

"Are you sure Max isn't an elf then, or has he found the secret to shaving here?" The twinkle in Tanya's eye clued me in to it being a jab, but I took the bait anyway.

"Hey." I furrowed my brow. "I'm starting to grow in a five-o'clock shadow, you know. And the baby-faced look polls better for performances."

"*Baby face*?" Ren snorted.

I deflated and allowed myself to be the target of their humor. We needed the levity. Not only to soothe our souls, but this was team bonding. It was also good for my ego to pretend that I was *letting* them prod fun at me.

"That aside," Tanya said, a content sigh sinking from her. "Before we embarrass our starlet any further, I have loot to distribute if you're both ready?"

We nodded eagerly, the results of our time spent in the Dungeon finally coming to fruition. In fact, I hadn't even asked Ren what her level up had given her. We'd been enjoying the departure from the usual System rubbish.

"Here you are, Max. Everything is twenty percent share, aside from Equipment, which I'm giving to whoever could best use the upgrades."

"Where were you when we started?" Ren murmured.

[4,200 Gold]
[Power Tokens (12)]
[Health Potions (3)]
[Mana Potions (5)]
[Spellbound Belt: +5 INT, +10% Mana]
[Boots of Intelligence: +4 INT]
[Arcanist's Badge: +3 INT, +10% spell-casting speed]
[Ring of Choices: For every 5 INT, +1 Luck]

I equipped the gear immediately, dropping some Dexterity and percentage Damage for greater Intelligence, as we had discussed. My eyes were wide, however, at the amount of power tokens we had accumulated throughout the Dungeon.

She caught the look on my face. "Usually you'd only do one boss, so the numbers wouldn't be that high. I also rounded the gold down a little—I hope you don't mind if I start a shared rainy-day pool with the extra?"

I shook my head and glanced at Ren, who had no complaints either. So far, gold had seemed to be the most useless commodity we had been accumulating. Until we found a sweet-cake vendor anyway.

That aside, I now had more tokens than ever. I could upgrade a dozen of my baseline Abilities . . . or upgrade something already advanced to the next level. That seemed like the smarter option, so I would probably—

"Hey, trickster." Ren nudged me in the side with her elbow. "Can I give you a couple of my tokens?"

"What?" I turned my eyes away from my STAR menus to frown at her. "Why? And no."

She pouted. "You have better System bullshit. It'd be better for you to get those to expert quicker."

I shook my head. "I don't like the pity when everything is shared equally. You deserve to power up from your fair share."

"It's not pity; it's investing in our star attraction."

The sharpness in her blue eyes had me struggling to come up with further reasons why I shouldn't give up and accept her offer. Loot distribution was something I was resolute about, and as keen as I was to be the spectacle and main performer of our troupe—I didn't want special treatment for it.

"I'm in for that as well," Tanya said. "I'm sure you'll earn me back two tokens in no time, Max."

I turned to pull a face at her.

"Can't have two of mine," Wolf murmured, apparently listening in despite his eyes being closed. "Used them all already."

I still had two that I had held back from previously that I had forgotten to tell them about. As much as I itched and squirmed, I felt as though this was a losing battle. "I already have two extra. You all really shouldn't."

Ren pressed up against me, unnecessarily close to my ear. "What if we have a say in what you pick?"

Tanya nodded. "Yes, that way it is more of an investment, something less of a gift. I do not know what Skills you have, so I will defer to Ren on what . . . makes you tick."

The weather hadn't changed, but I was feeling a lot warmer all of a sudden. Perhaps being pinned between the elf and the bear while the weaver controlled the flow of discussion had me feeling a little out of place. I exhaled through my nose. "Fine, I relent to the democratic vote, I suppose."

Back behind us, the cottage door opened.

"Quinn," Tanya said immediately. "I have your Dungeon rewards ready now. We are giving two tokens to Max to—"

"Of course." He paused his journey over to us to give a deep bow. "Max may have all my—"

"Just *two*." The weaver sighed and shook her head.

Seeing as the fixer had pledged to give his life up for me since I saved him— giving up all the worldly possessions he had just earned was not a big deal at all. I begrudgingly accepted the trades offered from each of them, and now had twenty of the things. Able to advance two Skills to the next level.

"What do you ask of me, then?" I raised an eyebrow at the elf.

She leaned closer and whispered in my ear.

"That's . . ." I sighed. "That's not one of my Skills."

With a brief grin, she moved away. "Well, I'm not sure I'd say *that*. How about your Inventory-management bullshit? That and your magic cards are most important, and I assume you've already decided on that."

Read me like a book as usual. "It was under consideration. I'm not sure how much faster I could even—"

"*Do it.* It is my choice."

I held her gaze for a moment, wondering if there was an ulterior motive for wanting me to upgrade <Sleight of Hand>. Perhaps it was just the simple fact that it was one of my key features. Although not specifically what the System envisioned a Demonic Magician should be, it made sense that my Class was apparently unique. It wasn't even part of the Skill as written but an unintended bonus.

"Alright, a compelling enough argument. But I will repay you all in kind as soon as possible."

[<Sleight of Hand> is now expert: Your Deception success chance increases greatly with both INT and DEX]

Other than the addition of the word *greatly*, the description hadn't changed from previous versions. Now it was called <Sleight of Hand>, and the grayed-out upgrade required something called a power sphere to get to this next level. I looked away from the screens to see that everyone had their eyes on me.

"Expecting a show? Don't you have your own Skills to pick?" I narrowed my eyes. It would be nice to have a little space to fully get into the new changes before being expected to put on a performance.

I repeated the same process, waving goodbye to the stack of tokens as I upgraded my main card attack. <Pick a Card> now let me summon three active cards, with 10 percent more Damage and 10 percent less Mana cost per card. With the legendary headband I had not replaced that turned Mana spent into Damage and <Mana Manipulation> allowing me to empower my cards, this was just stacks of extra Damage upon extra Damage.

"It is done," I announced. "Sixty tokens from that one Dungeon though?"

Tanya sighed and rolled her eyes. "Can never let sleeping dogs lie, can you? Fine, I put some of my own stash in the pile. Happy now?"

"No." I grinned. "But thank you. You don't have to explain why. I'm very perceptive." My eyes turned to the elf, who was busy making her own Skill choice. For example, I still remembered how Ren told me she had a demon-killing arrow but didn't use it against Rolo.

Part of me almost blurted that out—but I realized how much of an asshole that would make me sound, especially in front of everyone. If she had just frozen or didn't get the chance, then it'd make her sound weak. It wasn't that though; I could tell. The truth would come out eventually. I was sure of it. When she was ready.

I was hungry for something more important anyway. *Power.* Two expert skills were nice, but I wanted to get my cannon and everything else to advanced. I stood from my place of safety and comfort and stretched out.

"If we're successful tonight, then I would like to farm out another level and more tokens tomorrow."

Tanya nodded. "There are several decent spots locally with repeatable Quests. It would be smart to be as prepared as possible for cutting the core out of the Shadow in defeating Tyler and his ilk."

"Being level fifteen before taking on the Lady would be nice too, although I'm not sure either of us has the patience for that."

She gave me a shrug, knowing that these sorts of things couldn't be planned to fine detail without more time and information.

Into my hand, an orange. I held it up in front of me and then lowered my hand, leaving the fruit to hang in the air, perfectly still. There was still a soft ache in my eyes from the process, but it was almost a flawless act of my mind alone—the System menus barely illuminating my vision as I repeatedly pocketed and replaced the orange in the exact same position at an unnoticeable speed.

"Name a fruit," I asked the weaver as the others started to pay attention to the new bullshit I had been allowed.

"Apple."

As soon as the word was uttered, the orange was replaced by an apple.

"Pear."

Again, a near-instantaneous switch.

"Tomato."

My eyes narrowed and went up to her, the motionless pear wavering in the air slightly. I was all out of tomatoes, so instead, my cards burst out of my holster. A spray that condensed into a stream that enveloped the hanging fruit, spiraling around it constantly. I illuminated three of them purple, activating my Skill, before switching which cards held the charge. Repeated the process, causing it to look like a spinning disco ball.

Faster. The lights flickered wildly. I was half dazzled myself, lost within the colors. Lightning arced around the ball of circling cards until my fingers snapped. All of them vanished, washed away in a brief burst of ash to reveal the pear once more. Unceremoniously, it dropped down onto the grass.

"Oh," Tanya said. "I *was* actually expecting a tomato. Way to subvert expectations."

I grinned and gestured the group to look to the side. "You're just not looking hard enough."

To my right, a good two dozen feet away, sheared branches and leaves lay strewn across the ground, as a formerly rough and wild bush was now carefully trimmed into a smooth rounded shape.

CHAPTER FIFTY-SEVEN

Stewing Away

I lay against the bear, who appeared to be asleep still, somehow. He clearly needed the rest, if not only to take a breather from the conflict we kept getting into, but he also probably needed to catch up on his digestion from everything he had been eating.

Ren and Quinn had gone back into the cottage, intending on using the cooker to make us all some food rather than us sticking to the campfire. Tanya remained outside beside the fire, nursing a steaming cup of coffee.

"You told Ren, didn't you?" Wolf murmured, his voice vibrating through the back of my head.

"Yeah."

He grunted but didn't seem annoyed by the fact. It was only fair she was kept in the loop with regards to his health. The trio of us were family now. Whether it was just exhaustion or he really was getting old, the elf deserved to know as much as I did—hence my simple, unapologetic answer. He didn't press the issue.

Leaving him to his nap, I stood and went to sit near Tanya. "Doing okay?"

Her eyes went up to me briefly before back out to the woods. The distracted look melted away, and her hands grasped at her mug a little tighter. "I just wish I understood this place a little better . . ."

"The System?"

"Yeah." She looked down at the hot drink. "At first I thought this was some sort of purgatory or punishment, but occasionally we get these little slices of . . . *bliss*, and it doesn't feel right. Undeserved, almost."

"*Punishment*," I repeated. Most people we had met here were some shade of asshole, but I didn't think it likely we were here just for the sins of our pasts. That she should bring it up though . . .

Tanya looked over at the sleeping bear, then the cottage, before looking at me. "You can keep a secret, Max?"

"Of course." I nodded.

"I wasn't exactly the best person in my old life. Had my share of demons." She shook her head at the humor of saying that to *me*, of all people. "Bad childhood, full of chaos. Joined the military and the . . . order of it soothed me. Became accomplished when I left, but the real world has a lot of chaos that I struggled to adjust to, no matter how much order I tried to build up around me. A lot of the last year is a hazy blur, yet strangely, I remember the day I came to this world with such clarity."

I remained silent as she gazed off toward the horizon.

"I was in a diner for breakfast, reading the newspaper. Something I usually avoided. The biggest story on the front page was how a diner out west had exploded. Gas leak or something. Two dozen dead, including three young adults. It . . . crushed me, despite being so detached from it." Tanya furrowed her brow, as if she still struggled to understand it.

"How life could just be *taken*. All those futures, and it could just as easily happen to *me*, in *that* diner, right *then*. The sheer chaos and how everything could be changed, and I'd have no control at all over my safety." Tanya paused for a moment, as if those feelings had started to tug at her anew. "And you know what I did? You think I went home to my husband and daughter, enjoyed living and not taking things for granted?" She turned back to me now, pain wracking at her eyes.

All I could do was raise an eyebrow and wait for the crescendo.

"No. I did not." She shook her head and looked at her coffee. "Skipped out on work and hit the liquor. A little self-destructive escapism to try to feel *okay*. That my choices were my own. Got into an argument with Paul. Left in my car. Drove drunk . . . Went off the road and hit a tree. Out of the windshield, and then I remember the bright pink washing over me." She bit her top lip. "Thought I died. I . . . should have died."

"You received a second chance," I said.

Tanya shrugged. "Since being here, I've quit smoking and drinking. Best physical shape that I've been in almost a decade. Mentally, I'm calm, less anxious. In some ways, this *has* been a miracle."

"But you can't let go of those left behind?"

"The last words exchanged with my husband were ones of anger, and the last memory my daughter has of me is me being in a deranged state. For the two things I love most in life, that is unacceptable." She sighed deeply. "But . . . they probably think I died, and maybe that's for the best?"

"Tanya, if we find a way back, then—"

"It's okay, Max." She gave me the saddest smile I'd ever seen. Her normally stoic confidence totally absent from her face. "*They* deserve better. Maybe I'm not meant for that world."

It had been easy for me to move on from what few connections I had back on Earth, and I was selfish enough to not consider Reggie or the show as soon as I'd landed in Othea. Ren had lost Flynn on arrival here and seemed distant enough from her parents and the responsibility she was supposed to inherit. There were similar tones to it though.

"Ren would be the best one to talk to in regard to loss and moving on." I removed my hat and placed it on my lap. "But it's not my place to tell her story. You're the one who told me to always fight for love, remember?" I sighed, ill-equipped for this sort of conversation. "For what it's worth, the Tanya sitting before me isn't an irredeemable asshole."

"Thanks, Max. Fighting is often easier said than done, it seems." She smiled and wiped at her eyes with the back of her forearm. "Hadn't even told my old Party all of that. Something about you guys just makes an old gal soft. Perhaps this can be like my rehab. Iron out those flaws, whether or not I can go back."

I grinned and leaned back in my chair. "We're all odd and flawed. Whatever we were previously, I feel like the System has forged us into something new. We're willing to take you as you are now and will support you in your growth."

Tanya closed her eyes as she took a sip of coffee. "I was worried at first that you trusted me because you were too gullible or desperate. But it quickly became apparent that you were clued in to the stakes and would take on the risks required to get ahead."

With a nod, I turned my eyes over to the cottage just as the door opened up to reveal Ren carrying a large pot of something. "Likewise, I wanted to onboard you as quickly as possible. We don't have the luxury of not knowing if you are trustworthy and doing a long vetting process."

"Confident enough to put your life on the line as well?"

"Now, now, Tanya." I shot her a wry grin. "We both know I was in no real danger there."

She narrowed her eyes and sighed. "Of course, a magician wouldn't leave something to chance?"

I raised my eye back up to Ren as she stood beside us and lowered the large pot onto an empty chair. "Well, I don't know about that," I said. "I'm open to *some* surprises."

The elf looked at me and put her hands on her hips. "Well, don't get excited. It's a *stew*. Didn't *start* as one, but that's how it turned out."

My amusement at how she had only clocked the tail end of my statement without context was only strengthened by how exasperated she looked over the results of the cooking. I looked back at the house. "No Quinn?" Maybe she had cooked him. I should be concerned that was one of my first thoughts.

"He is taking five minutes, as I called him some bad names." She gave us a shrug. "Some people just don't cook well together."

Although she hadn't seemed like much of a commanding chef in our time spent together, it was quite possible that in making something more than a simple grilled meal she had a clearer vision of what she wanted to do, and the fixer was stepping on her figurative toes.

"Also, he stepped on my feet *twice*." Ren lifted the lid from the ceramic stew pot and allowed a billowing cloud of steam to escape. "Once is forgivable, but I only have so much patience."

It worried me how often the narrative followed what I suspected it to be. Perhaps my ability to read people and plot out eventualities and viable outcomes had saturated my being so much that I was now believing myself to be prophetic. Being two and a half beings squashed together certainly did something for the brainpower . . . *and ego*, that was for sure.

I turned to see Wolf beside us, waiting patiently for the hot meal. Hadn't even heard him move.

He caught my eye and grinned at me. "My new Skill improves my stealth in woodland terrain."

"Nice. Oh, Ren, what did you get when you leveled?"

She turned from the pot, ladle in hand and awaiting Tanya's bowl. "Oh. Nothing impressive."

"Bullshit."

Her eyes narrowed at my skepticism. "Fine. It's like a single-target curse that causes additional radiant damage when they're attacked."

I nodded eagerly. "A target? Does it have to be a Player or Monster?" With my hand, I gestured to the nearest object, which happened to be Quinn's chair.

Relenting to my request, she turned and opened up her free palm toward the wooden seat. With a small flash, it became illuminated with a faint golden sheen. "It also prevents invisibility, I guess."

From my belt, a fan of mundane cards came out and hovered beside me. I flicked one out, striking the chair. Another flash, this one brighter, emanated from the aura and sent small sparks into the air. It was delightful. I sent three more normal cards in succession against the glow, each providing a bloom of light and dazzling sparkles.

And then the chair fell apart, broken at each joint as if it had taken enough damage to destroy its very spirit of existence.

We turned as Quinn now stepped out of the cottage, looking a little forlorn but apparently recovered from the verbal lashing Ren had dealt out. The elf started ladling stew into provided bowls as we sat in silence.

With a sheepish grin, he reached our seating arrangement and withdrew his own bowl before noticing the state of his chair.

"Wolf sat on it," I offered.

"That's beneath me," the bear grumbled.

I gave him a grin. "Sure was. Don't worry though, Quinn. If you're in the market for a new chair, I have the greatest variety in the area."

While he stood—slightly bewildered—and Ren filled up his bowl, I emerged from my chair and waved my cape across. Three chairs of varying designs appeared in its wake. A good chair was *always* needed, and I never missed the chance to abscond with as many as I could take. Within reason—I needed room for all the other random assortment of things.

In the time he took deliberating, I realized two things. The first was how quickly I put down the three items—and while normally it was little effort, I had reached a slightly higher step where time between object manipulation had decreased. Not by a long shot, but enough to make the process easier on my eyes and brain.

The second thing was that I had used my mundane cards as an attack. While they would do no damage to a real target, they seemed to cause Ren's new Skill to pulse with the radiant Damage, nonetheless. I'd need to pick her brains on the exact wording of the Ability, as I may be able to shock the entirety of the stored Damage at once with a flurry of cards.

"Bowl, trickster."

Ren's prodding took me out of my idle thoughts, and I held it out. I received three generous scoops of the stew before she started to sort her own out. As I couldn't let a good deed go unpunished, I dropped my bowl. Tanya and Quinn weren't expecting it, but it piqued Wolf's interest. Ren had already seen too much of my nature to be bothered by it.

The bowl didn't hit the ground, however—it simply vanished. I turned and stepped back over to my own chair and picked up my hat to reveal the steaming stew beneath.

"Didn't anyone teach you not to play with your food?" Tanya scowled at me.

I clicked my fingers as I grinned at her. "Speaking of which, let's talk about knocking over that blood courier."

CHAPTER FIFTY-EIGHT

Bait

Full of warm stew and thoroughly rested, we made the decision to force our-selves to have an amount of downtime every so often. We needed to maintain some softness so that our hearts didn't harden too far and crack. And . . . I *adored* it. Mostly because I now felt as though I had a social life. Not the expected peers I'd perhaps have in the real world, but I had started to believe that what I had now was more real than anything my prior lives once knew.

We had been lucky with my ability to erase trauma, allowing Tanya to detail us on the best place to make our assault. If we had needed to wait until the next day, it would have been a struggle to catch them up or head them off at certain points—not without putting ourselves in danger.

Being able to go this evening meant that a few groups would be waking up to no blood, while we'd be resting easy. At least, until we went to farm Quests to level up. The cottage retreat had been good for the group, and it was sad to see it go. Remaining in the same place for too long was asking for trouble, however. We could be tracked or just happened upon. I'd already had enough ambushes to last me a lifetime. Two lifetimes.

"Don't think too hard, trickster."

Ren's voice took me out of my thoughts as we continued walking. It was early evening now. Somehow, the day had melted away quicker than the grime we had washed away in that hot bath. I blinked away those thoughts as well.

"I'll try not to. Something about the courier doesn't sit right with me." I gave a glance out at the woods around us, as if the darkened recesses beneath the can-opy had any answers for me.

She nodded and furrowed her brow. At least more than it already was. "The Wizard said that it was three people on a coach, right?"

That was it. "But the Lady requires all groups to be five. Yeah. Hey, Tanya?" I turned to the woman who was farther back with Quinn. "Have you seen the couriers before?"

"Twice. Relatively small enclosed carriage. Two horses pulling it."

I grimaced. "Riders?"

"Three that I saw." She shrugged. "One up front, one inside, one clinging to the back."

Ren jostled me with her elbow. "You know what that means?"

All I could do was give her a glare. What would be the chances of there being two more Player horses, and them both being utilized to draw the blood around? That said, if they were just normal horses, I didn't feel comfortable just killing them or have them be collateral in the ensuing battle.

We had already discussed some tactics on the way over. There were one hundred and one ways in which we could stop or destroy the coach—the key was deciding on the most likely to succeed. They weren't likely to try to engage us in a fair fight, so killing the horses had been brought up as a potential starting point. Wolf seemed to be the only one keen on that.

It wasn't beyond us to find a way to sever the animals from the carriage. The issue there was Tanya was sure the main structure of the vehicle would be guarded with spells and auras. A direct assault was just as likely to flare off a shield and engage an emergency speed boost as to destroy it outright.

Still, with the five of us, there was no way they could truly evade our reach. I wasn't even sure why I was so adamant that we didn't harm the System-created horses. Part of it was wanting to avoid the cruelty often displayed by the Crimson Shadow . . . but we tore through dozens of Monsters with little thought. These were animal shaped but no different, surely?

I was getting tired of morally gray scenarios. Gone were the simple days where there was a separation between things to keep safe and things to destroy. Then again, I didn't think I had made any terrible calls so far. *No*, I'd stay the course with the original plan. The point wasn't about morals. It was about ability. We weren't a blunt instrument, but something finely crafted. We'd split apart what needed to be erased from whatever wasn't important to us.

And look damn fine doing it.

I turned my head back to the weaver again. "Elephant in the room, Tanya, but do you know what happens when they don't get their blood?"

She shook her head slowly. "As far as I know, it's never been allowed to happen."

"Interesting." Or more accurately, I should have said *intriguing.* We'd be finding out in the near future, but I could see that Ren already had some ideas of her own.

"I think they lose their belief in her bull, and thus she loses power."

That seemed a reasonable guess and would be something the Lady would be keen to avoid. "But what of them after? Are they now deranged from the withdrawal, or do they revert to how they were before?"

The elf wrinkled up her face as she considered this.

Another sea of gray that dampened our normally cutthroat way of life. Show business was like that. If we were to find out that depriving the Crimson of the blood would have them slowly become whatever normal asshole they used to be . . . it put into question our methods. Well, that was unfair. As much as we tired of being ambushed, it gave us the out that we were only acting in self-defense.

"For what it's worth," Tanya spoke up, "most of them weren't the best of people even before taking the red. It's not . . . brainwashing or anything. More like alcohol, maybe." She bit her lip. "Brings out something that's already there."

The good people refused and were killed, so it made sense that we had only met the dregs who remained. Not exactly a comforting thought that so many were so easily talked into wanton violence. There was something uncomfortable about the whole thing that I couldn't quite process yet, my mind still reeling from our rest period and not wanting to grab hold of the stark reality we were about to face.

Wolf was the first to push through the next clump of bushes to reveal a dirt road running through this wooded part of the area. While I was getting somewhat tired of trees, it seemed to suit Ren and the bear just fine, so I wasn't about to complain. Plus, any built-up areas had been an excuse for the bad guys to come and kick us in the knees.

Ren knelt down and ran her finger through a groove in the dirt. "Wheel tracks, but not recent."

Tanya nodded. "Good, that means we haven't missed them. I estimate between twenty and thirty-five minutes until contact."

"Right," I said. "Gather around and let's tighten up the plan."

Part of me wished I had arranged things so that I would be waiting for the stagecoach beside Ren. Something rather selfish, but I understood that to perform some tricks, the right angle was everything. No reason for her to be at ground level— and I'd sooner fall out of the tree she was currently in and smash my head open.

I did need to arrange some one-on-one time with her though. As our Party had grown, our attentions were now shared a couple of extra ways. Not that I could complain, with both Tanya and Quinn getting on well with both her and each other. Our alone time being spent bathing was pure bliss, but often conversation melted away into silent contentedness or unbuttoned passions.

So as I lay among uncomfortable twigs and vegetative lumps, I penciled in a date night for the both of us. Tanya had earmarked a small town where we might find safe rest for this evening. Not the closest accommodation, but we didn't want to be too obvious in case revenge was hot on the heels of the wagon we were about to upturn.

Being the team leader was a heavier weight than I had anticipated, even if I tried to delegate to democracy as much as possible. As a trio, it had been simple to prod one of my two companions and make sure they were doing fine. Extract their thoughts on how miserable life currently was. Now, with Tanya and Quinn, there didn't seem to be enough time in the day to make sure all their personal demons were being quelled.

Ah. Was that the people-pleasing side coming out again?

I smiled. Even as much as I wanted us to all grow as one, it was nice to have this space to myself. Really dig around in my thoughts and contextualize everything that had been wreaked upon us lately without the soft love of Ren or the odd humor or violence that otherwise filled the space.

It wasn't a lie that I wanted to make us all happy, but now it wasn't at the cost of my own well-being. I required them to be in peak form so that I could trust them when the true danger hit the fan. For the most part, I had been managing fine.

Certainly, with Tanya opening up so much to me, it showed that she trusted us and our purpose. It was like . . . Hmm. In some ways, we were all driven by love. Her for her family left behind. Wolf for food and rest—living a good life. Quinn for anything that moved. Ren and I for each other and a future without so much bloodshed. The Lady and her ilk were driven by a hatred for this System and its rules.

That sort of thinking at least allowed me to paint our actions as more heroic than us being coldhearted mercenaries.

We had spent a quick ten minutes getting the stage ready for the show, and another five or so had passed as we waited in position. It wasn't often we had the opportunity to prepare a performance in advance—and I was excited about the process. The couriers were in for a real treat. Assuming they didn't immediately keel over in surprise.

It was hard to imagine that this would be such a pivotal fight in our war against the Lady. While we had a lot pinned on removing the necromancer from his position, starving them of the necessary blood was something they'd be foolish not to anticipate. Tanya had mentioned that she had been made kill on sight and blocked by anyone associated with the Crimson Shadow.

I fidgeted on the uncomfortable ground. The green fabric covering most of me would at least obscure most of my garish suit and—

[Ren: Movement.]
[Tanya: Prepare for contact.]
[Wolf: opppp]
[Quinn: Ready^]
[Max: Nice and clean. Stay safe.]

The elf had better hearing than any of us, and even as I strained mine, I couldn't quite hear anything past my heartbeat and the ambient noise of the woods. I knew better than to doubt her, however. In fact . . . Yes, *there* it was. Faint but approaching quickly.

Soft thuds of horseshoes against dirt, which caused me to shiver involuntarily. Thundering of wheels trying to stay in the loose ruts of prior journeys. It was like an approaching storm, and I had tingles of anticipation running down my arms. Mostly my right arm, which was worrying—but then again, it was relatively newer to this sort of thing.

Despite nothing having happened, my Power meter was already at 10 percent.

In my wand holster, the group had somehow cobbled together three fully charged zap wands. Not very damaging, but that's not what they were for. My spell holster had dispel, arcane-evasion, and flame-shield scrolls. Mostly provided by Tanya, who had a modest stock of a variety of things. She had also given me a specific gray idol, engraved with a cloud symbol embossed with emerald.

Ren was in position in the trees. Wolf was down the road from me and farther into the tree line. Quinn and Tanya were together on the opposite side of the road, low and among the bushes. I continued to lie among the cool leaves of my hiding place, the preshow nerves making me antsy. I couldn't wait.

But I did.

Closer and louder now. I narrowed my eyes as the stagecoach rocked past my position. The flash of two horses, deep brown in color, followed by the ivory of the coach itself, large wheels spinning past.

"Whoa! A tree has fallen across the road," the voice from the front shouted out.

I was grinning widely now. *So close.*

"Careful," a second man grunted from the back. "Could be a trap."

It was!

"We'll circle and go back around," the first again.

And that was the cue. Curtain was set to rise, the audience not knowing what they were about to get themselves into.

I took one last deep breath and stepped out on stage.

CHAPTER FIFTY-NINE

Rolling With It

First part of the performance was the pyrotechnics. Something to let the audience know that they should buckle themselves in. *The show had started*. Before the stagecoach had a chance to move, a wall of fire burst up behind them, causing them to be stranded between the felled tree and the impassable flame.

"Ambush!" the one at the front yelled, far too excited for the act to begin.

Bright light illuminated the area, blinding them briefly as Quinn set his light center stage. With soft footsteps, the main attraction—yours truly—stepped down on top of the roof of the wagon. A wide cover of fabric shot out from me on either side. One toward the man sitting at the front, trying to stand with one arm across his face to shield his eyes. A weapon drawn into his hand. The second over the man at the back—a large fellow who didn't seem to be fully human. He had a better idea that I was here but hadn't been able to react.

I drew a trio of cards into my hand. Pointing down toward the roof between my feet, I arranged them in the shape of a triangle and punched through, creating a hole into the interior. Just as soon as they had left my hand, the idol and two bottles of oil dropped in succession, landing within.

My brow furrowed. While everything appeared to be moving in slow motion, it allowed me to pick up the hint of something odd. Something unexpected— yet, as soon as I clocked what it was, I knew *exactly* what it was.

I had found the fourth Player in their group—the stagecoach itself. Unless they had also packed the wood with blood for *fun*.

The brief amount of confusion it elicited in me was enough to have a knock-on effect on my timing, and I missed the short window to swap positions with my dove. We rolled with the punches, however, and the show *would* go on. It would just make the next few parts of the act a little more awkward.

"Pain. Intruders on roof," a voice bellowed out that could only be said stagecoach that was now unhappy. I had cored a new entrance into its . . . flesh?

With the thrum of energy, a spherical shield of blue energy encircled the living vehicle, and Ren's first arrow bounced off harmlessly. A faux attack, in the grand scheme of things—planned in advance to see what they were capable of.

Seeing the tendrils of magical energy tether my left arm to the glowing protection magic, I activated the dispel scroll. Their shield vanished in a puff of spent ash. The door on the right side flung open as another humanoid stepped out. Perhaps the fifth would be in there too?

Currently, my position was a wet blanket on our original plan. I'd *have* to—I dodged to the side as the large figure at the back of the wagon swung a sword toward me. My legs wavered as I neared the edge, but I kept my cool. Flung a handful of flowers in his face as he attempted to climb up on top with me. As he was temporarily blinded, I clicked the trigger of my best crossbow and put a bolt in his face.

I spun in place as the weapon vanished and then leaped down upon the audience member who had just made an appearance. He hadn't the foresight to catch me properly and only just turned in time to avoid getting my dagger in his neck. Instead, a shoulder would do. We fell to the ground from the impact and as I rolled away, I dropped the rest of my furniture wares across him. Only chairs—a varied display that did little damage but tied him in place for a few extra seconds.

The horses had remained unnaturally stoic during this whole process. Not budged an inch. Using the crackling power that now arced around me, I sent a direct message to Wolf in a split second, my eyes hitting the necessary keys with a practiced precision that was almost beyond human capabilities.

[Max: Dig in.]

Ren had struck the front man with an arrow, but he now had a shield to protect against further impacts. From the back of the stagecoach, the larger Shadow had risen back up, the bolt still protruding from his forehead. The one by me was recovering from the ground.

The show had become something of a mess. I raised an eyebrow at the Imp+ beside me. It could *still* be saved. This gentleman had made the rude mistake of leaving the door wide open. Before the sentient coach could consider closing it, things were in motion.

I broke the rules.

Threw one of the chairs up into the air and hit it with the card for my <Demonic Cannon>, which dropped from the air to land on the crawling figure, crushing his legs and the spare chairs alike. My demon threw out his fireball, the eyes of the Crimson turning to it in shock but too slow to change its course.

Straight into the stagecoach, it exploded, setting off both bottles of oil. Among the flame a pulse of green, as a cloud of gas began filling the interior.

Two noises pierced the air.

The first a howl of intense pain from the living vehicle. Something very inhuman, and yet . . . it almost sounded like music to my ears. Like an orchestra of violins in agony. I *adored* it.

Second was a roar as Wolf clattered into the front of the stagecoach, folding both horses as if they were made of paper. Even in death, they showed no fear—nor any expected movement. The coach itself writhed and creaked as it tried to shake off the inferno burning it from within. More shattered glass sounds. The Lady's blood, I was sure.

Large Shadow was on me before I knew it, some Skill having him warp fifteen feet to me. I looked at him with cold purple eyes as <Card Fan> blocked his first swing. I vanished and drew two loaded crossbows. There was a fury in his eyes that erased any confusion, and he drew back his sword to swing wildly in the space I had been.

Almost got me too. Forty percent on the Power meter. Two clicked triggers and two more bolts in his head. He stumbled and dropped just as a wave of crackling power washed over me. Pain that had me clenching my teeth. The pinned Player had cast a spell on me. As he readied a second attack, the growl of my Hellhound+ drew his eyes to the side, wide with sudden panic.

I shook the buzzing from my head and stepped back toward the road. The screaming of the vehicle was subsiding, just as I watched Wolf throw the driver an easy dozen feet away with his jaws. Forty-five percent—I was running out of audience to impress. The smell of burning wood and blood filled the woodland, overwriting the pleasant evening air. Flame would eventually take over the rest of the stagecoach. Perhaps there wasn't even much of the performance left . . .

No, a shadow caused me to flinch, but it was too late.

I had heard the rustle of leaves and felt the displacement of air slightly too slowly to react. The *fifth* member of the group had found me. The half-naked woman with feathered wings grinned at me with razor-sharp teeth. In her hand, the barbed spear had found a warm home through my chest. A *harpy*, my strangely calm brain told me.

Couldn't help but grin.

"Something funny, worm?" She twisted the spear, tearing up some of my internal organs.

"There's something behind my ear," I whispered, managing not to choke on the blood coming up through places it shouldn't.

Her angered glare turned into a scowl, although nothing as cute as what I was used to. She tilted her head to the side to see what I meant, and Ren whispered a sweet arrow to me. A line of blood just above my ear and a killing blow to the stunned harpy, now full of radiant light.

I switched places with my Hellhound+, leaving the spear behind to fall inertly to the floor with the rest of her corpse.

Popped the cork of a healing potion and put it to my lips. The pain was burning away at my chest, but I soldiered through it. Fifty percent, and interestingly I seemed to be wearing white gloves now. <Card Fan> went up as I drank, as the man with three bolts in his head tried to strike me again.

An arrow hit him in the neck, but he only wavered before raising his blade once more. I smashed the potion bottle into his face, lacerating his pained expression. With the stem shard in my hand, I stabbed him again in the face, then chest, then arm. His grip released his sword, and I looted it from the air. As his other hand came up, I placed the nullification cuff on it. He was blinded and reeling.

A swift kick, and he tripped over another summoned chair, landing in a seated position on the muddy ground.

My hand up, I fired a faux gun with clenched fingers and cast <Shuffle>.

Dazzle icons shifted and faded away, replaced by something with a red cross on a black background. The large man took one last gasp of air before freezing, his skin suddenly shriveling and drying up, rapidly falling off of his bones in thick clumps. In just three short seconds, he had devolved into a skeleton surrounded by the mulch of his previous form.

I put my gloved hand up to my chest, fresh blood soaking through. Why *white* gloves? They'd only get ruined immediately, even from my own actions. Harpy had hit me on the wrong side of the chest and missed my heart. The warmth of Ren's heal came through to me, but I couldn't see her within the darkened canopy. Surprising considering what she was wearing.

Wolf had eaten the driver, and my Hellhound+ had finished the cannon-bound man off. The stagecoach was . . .

My brow furrowed as a deep groan vibrated through the woods. From beneath the burning vehicle, shadows had started to form. I stepped over to my cannon, my legs feeling shaky and weak for some reason. Needed to load it with something—we hadn't reached the grand finale, clearly.

Thick legs of darkened chitin cracked and moved out from the underside of the coach. Dragging the spent forms of the faux horses, it now rose up onto six of such sharp legs. Something like a crab or spider. I didn't sign up for eldritch horrors and wouldn't let this dampen our parade.

I stepped out closer to it and raised my hand up. "Abomination. *No more.*"

My mundane deck flickered out of the holster, each card flitting up into the underside of my palm. With my fingers outstretched to the Monster, I stood and watched it turn toward me. A sharp leg went up into the air, ready to crush me, but I was still waiting for my cue.

A radiant flash illuminated the area, as the stagecoach became aglow with Ren's new Ability.

Time for the fireworks.

In tandem, I sent the full deck of mundane cards in a stream toward the coach alongside firing all three zap wands in succession. As the first of both struck my opponent and caused the flare of radiant damage, it bathed the area in bright golden light. The stagecoach shuddered and recoiled from the pain, so I hit the big red button.

My cannon fired the 354 ball bearings I had accumulated on my journey. Buckshot that blinded the woodlands, causing a deafening silence to vibrate through my body, before I heard the final screech and resulting explosion.

Just in time, my eyes adjusted and saw what remained of the creature shatter into thousands of parts. Cracked like a mirror, it collapsed down into rough shards of whatever foul being it truly was.

I summoned my fire Imp+ once more and ordered him to repeatedly strike the debris.

We would leave nothing to chance. I held up my hands to see they were no longer gloved. Just covered in blood.

Even as my Party came out of their positions and tried talking to me, I couldn't help but just stare at my hands, and the *blood*.

"Max? *Max*."

I snapped out of it as Ren stood before me, a scowl on her face. "Yeah?"

"How injured are you? Feeling okay?"

Felt tired, that was for sure. "Still some internal bleeding. Minor organ damage. Some other small lacerations probably."

She healed me again, muttering something under her breath.

I looked past her at Quinn, Wolf, and Tanya, who had all gathered and were watching my Imp+ torch the remains of the vehicle. "Sorry," I told them. "I feel like I cocked up the show there."

Met with grumbled disagreements; they seemed a little out of it too. Expecting a handful of Bandit-adjacent Players we had instead gone against something monstrous, alongside a chap who just refused to die. At least until I forced the issue.

"A lot of unknowns came up," Tanya offered. "We had to change some parts up, but we reached the same ending."

Didn't get to use <Finale>, however, which left me a little glum. Blue balled the showman in me who wanted that dopamine fix. I raised my hand and watched the shards of glass fall out.

Quinn rubbed at his eye patch. "Your planning certainly saved us a lot of headache."

I exhaled through my nose as another heal went through me. Perhaps they were right—it wasn't so bad. We'd destroyed the courier and the blood. Lived to tell the tale. Although . . .

With tired eyes, I cycled up through my own icons. The look on Ren's face as she tried to heal me didn't fill me with much confidence. It was no normal

wound—the internal bleeding continued. Ah, there it was. Persistent bleeding—a debuff that worked like a curse to . . . Hmm, that was pretty overpowered
against Players. Deadly, even.

Eyes narrowed at the terrible icon, I hit <Shuffle> again.

I didn't get to see what it changed to, as there was nothing but darkness after.

CHAPTER SIXTY

Role Call

H ey, asshole?"

I furrowed my brow and opened my eyes. Confused, I was completely disoriented. Dim light gave no clue as to my whereabouts. Maybe dead.

The elf moved over my vision, blocking out the drab shapes around me. Perhaps not dead then.

"Blerf," I managed. Just as my consciousness had returned, the ascending throb of a headache made its introduction.

"About time." She sighed and moved away. "If you tell me which part of you controls your reckless attitude toward your own life, I'll reach in and pull it out of you."

The past moments of my waking existence were being slotted back into place, and I remembered what had occurred. To avoid bleeding to death, I had shuffled away the debuff and replaced it with something that . . . did something else. Didn't kill me—although I wasn't entirely convinced this was reality yet.

With a groan, I writhed on aching muscles and tried to push myself up. I was on something soft and covered with a thin sheet. A bed. In just my underwear—which seemed like a strange curse to have. The surrounding space now coalesced into a small room, sparsely furnished with basic furniture.

"What happened?" I asked, turning to the elf in her nightshirt, as if I couldn't put two and two together.

She tilted her head, and some of the ire melted away. "Some sort of temporary coma. We made sure the blood was destroyed and bundled you up on Wolf. Went to the safe village, as previously discussed."

I nodded slowly. Mostly because my head might burst from the change in pressure. Swapping an internal rupture for a forced nap wasn't the worst thing, but I could have easily killed myself with being so careless.

"Sorry for making you worry, Ren."

The elf sighed and brought up a hand to grasp at my face. "Final warning, put yourself in unnecessary danger again and . . . we'll have problems. *Forgiven*, dickbag. Before you ask—Wolf is downstairs in the living room. Quinn and Tanya are in a different house. And no, it's not like *that*. They both assured me."

I smiled and shuffled myself a little closer to her. A soft kiss before I slowly collapsed back onto the bed. "Feeling low energy. Aches across most of my body. Headache. Emotionally fragmented."

Ren smiled and lay down beside me, putting an arm across my chest. "I appreciate the full disclosure, trickster. Tanya left an idol. It's an active one rather than passive but will help with the pain."

"And for my fragile heart?"

"That's why you have me, isn't it?" She sat back up to retrieve the gray idol from the side table.

In some ways, *it was*. Over time, she had worked me into something that she wanted. Decisive leader, pragmatic and assertive. In return, I had the adoration and companionship that my previous lives were near devoid of. I oft repeated the phrase that we had come to meet in the middle, just as we had agreed all that time ago, but a lot of it had come naturally.

"Sometimes I feel as though we spend the whole day together, yet it is still not enough."

She turned back to me and handed over the idol, a soft smile on her face. "That's love, Max. We haven't had the most conventional courtship, but . . . I honestly couldn't see myself being apart from you."

It didn't take the dimly lit lanterns and soft darkness beyond the windows to know that it was nighttime, that was for certain. Although, the fact that the sun wasn't out made the time of day obvious even before Ren was open with me.

"Can I tell you a secret?" I activated the idol, and a warmth ran through me, softening the aches.

"Of course."

I looked up at her and raised my hand, softly running my thumb across her eyebrow. "Sometimes I miss your grumpy scowl."

She smiled, and her hand came up to hold mine there. With a sigh, she nuzzled her face into my palm. "You like it when I'm a hard-assed bitch, huh?"

"If I wrote upon each star something that I adored about you, I would still be bereft of space before finishing."

Her eyes closed, and the smile widened. "Fucking poetic asshole. I love you."

"And I you, moonflower. Now lie beside me once more and let's discuss how we're going to take over the world together."

Generally speaking, we had shied away from being too overt with our feelings, just in case the System found a narrative way to split us apart. I cared no longer, even if it made it that much more likely to happen. Tanya had told me to fight for love, and that's what we'd do. Any assailants or obstacles in our way, we would overcome with overwhelming force. Our hearts may be vulnerable, but in being out in the open it caused them to be stronger.

After all, we had allowed the two new Party members into our collection of oddities. It was hard to deny that we had enough drive and competency to try to bring a fix to the System. We'd turn the world into somewhere a love like ours could bloom in total safety, and the looming trauma of being mass murderers was something unthinkable.

"Let's talk Wolf first," I began as she pulled the cover up and shuffled herself beside me.

"It hurts to think that he could be getting old already."

"Agreed. He assures me he has plenty of life in him, but our current schedule has been draining on our dear brother. Earlier he even turned his hunger debuff off."

Ren sighed. "I thought the eating and sleeping was just a fun bear thing. But we've just been running him ragged."

That wasn't *entirely* correct. It was hard to judge, as the bear himself would assure us he was fine if questioned—and being a sentient animal, he might not have the same kind of handle on how much stress and hardship he could really take. "I think it's the same as his diet. He doesn't know any better so will rush headlong into whatever is required of him. We'll need to manage him better to ensure he has proper rest."

She nodded. "Unless we are tracked, it should be an easy day of farming Monsters tomorrow."

Good. We needed a little break. Well, in saying that—the time at the cottage was our break. Fighting System-created was more of a . . . low-stakes work environment. With the five of us now, I had no doubt we could chew through any group with little issue. Another level and a few more tokens, and I'd feel ready for the true test of our accomplishments.

The necromancer's group.

"Quinn next," I prompted. "He seems to have calmed a little now that we are a full Party. While combat isn't his strong suit, I feel he greases the wheels of our overall existence."

"I was a bit of a shit to him when we were cooking today. He tries to help, but I feel he is like a lost puppy at times." Ren pouted. "That said, he means well. Compared to the first day we met him, I actually trust him now."

"You think he is up to the trials ahead of us?"

She was quiet for a moment as she considered this. "Hmm. He said he will jump on the sword for you, and I fully believe he would. It's stupid, but for that reason alone, he would follow us into hell."

My thoughts exactly. Even if he wasn't the powerhouse in battle that Ren and I were, as long as he held things together behind the scenes, then I would allow him to take the back seat. We needed him to keep us . . . stable. Or at least I felt like less of a mercenary hit squad with him around.

"So the new girl then, Tanya?"

"She spoke to me earlier, while you were *out*." Ren turned to me, moving onto her side. "Told me about the chat you had and what caused her to join with the Lady."

"I feel for her. She's conflicted that she wants nothing more than to be back with her family but also doesn't believe she deserves them back. That she is uncomfortable with how much happier part of her is in this world."

The elf grunted. "In her heart, she wants to go back. Whatever you told her, she's made some peace with being here."

I furrowed my brow. "Really?"

"At least . . . she wants to fix the world to be somewhere safe. She told me she will worry about going back not only when the world is better, but when she is too."

A silence filled the room as I contemplated this. I was pretty sure that I had just allowed her to speak her mind and open up about herself. There wasn't any guidance intended; even from the start I told her that her destiny was her own to decide on. I raised my eyebrow to see that Ren was watching me intently, as if trying to read the thoughts straight from my brain.

"What are you thinking?" I asked.

She shook her head lightly. "Sometimes I just like looking at you. Seeing all the different angles and shapes that make *Max*. Trying to . . . pick out what makes you different from everyone else."

I smiled. "And the verdict?"

"Beats me." She leaned forward and gave me a kiss on the forehead. "You're just stuck with my grumpy ass until some bullshit kills us, I'm afraid."

"An acceptable fate." I closed my eyes. There were certainly worse death penalties. "But Tanya has a personal stake in fighting the Lady and is kind of a lightning rod for the rest of us. As a full Party, we need a clearer path than whatever mania you can dissuade me from."

"I'm surprised, really, that she fits in so well." Ren returned to lying back down. "Not suspicious, just . . . We aren't the most normal group. I'm tired of thinking up ways in which we can be betrayed, however. I trust her because the alternative is exhausting."

Grunted my agreement, and we fell into another comfortable silence. It was nice to get all of this out into the open with her. Between kissing and violence, we were in danger of losing sight of the reins. That we were on the same page on near everything was expected and soothed my soul. Still, ripples always remained in the calmest of ponds.

"Your demon killer arrow doesn't really do *that*, does it?"

The bed shifted slightly as she tensed up. "No . . . not really."

I ran my tongue across dry lips. Probably too late in the night for coffee now. Instead, I just took a deep breath in. "Something I should worry about?"

"I . . ." She shuffled back up to an elbow to look down at me, and I met her gaze. "This is a judgment-free zone, right?"

Although I nodded, my breath was still held. Ready for . . . Well, I wasn't even sure what.

The elf deflated and looked off to the side. "The culture I come from, and my family especially . . . They're all very xenophobic. Especially with humans." Her eyes came back to me. "Part of the reason Flynn and I wanted to do a run from it was we didn't believe in the old ways."

"Oh?" I wasn't too sure what more I could add at this stage, but I allowed myself to exhale.

"There was a human merchant that used to come by at the start of spring every year. My parents would turn up their noses and bite their tongues to do the trading . . . but once he left, they were horrid. He probably knew. One of the nicest people I met in my old world." She shook her head. "Never let the drama change how friendly he was with us as kids."

I wasn't too sure what the difference between an elf and a human actually was, aside from a couple of cosmetic changes. Out of all the odd humanoids we had come across in our travels, she was probably the closest to being mistaken for a human. Assuming you hid her ears and didn't think about her radiant hair or piercing light-blue eyes anyway. More fool me because I thought about them all the time.

"So . . ." I drew my brain back to the matter at hand. "The arrow doesn't kill *demons*."

"It's for killing humans, yes."

"Can't most of your arrows do that?"

She gave me a dull glare. "I haven't used it on prior occasions because it feels . . . gross. It's not a part of my heritage I care to bring into this world."

"Understandable. No further questions." I gave her a smile that seemed to relax her once more.

"I figured you'd be accepting. I'm sorry I didn't bring it up before." She moved over and rested across my chest.

My fingers went up, and I ran them through her hair. Either the action prompted her to sigh and deflate, or perhaps she had let some weight off her shoulders by laying bare that murky part of something she held in her past. Maybe both. I enjoyed the process too, and as I played with her hair, she made the outlines of shapes or letters on my torso with her fingertips.

I preferred to think it was some kind of unsaid love letter she was writing to me, but it could also be some kind of curse. Willing to accept the worst-case scenario, my eyes went back out to the window to see that it was still night. A decent chat about our Party and some living with the love we shared, and I was ready to turn in for the day.

"Shall we sleep, moonflower?"

She moved up to look me in the face. Her eyes were tired, but some spark bloomed within them. "I wanted to try something first, if that's okay?"

"Oh?" My eyebrow practically rocketed off my face with how quickly it rose.

"How many oranges do you have?"

CHAPTER SIXTY-ONE

On the Back Foot

As much as I yearned for the sweet release of another good sleep in a soft bed, I couldn't help but sit in an enamored fascination with the elf. Standing on the floor in her nightgown, a scowl of concentration on her face and a pair of oranges in her hands—it was as bizarre as it was cute. She'd picked up juggling relatively quickly. Two oranges, not a problem once she got the movements correct. Three was slightly more effort, but her natural dexterity helped the process along.

The soft thud of the fruit on the floor was accompanied by a murmured curse, and she knelt down to retrieve it. She stood back up and pushed her radiant blonde hair from her face. "Well, I think that's enough extracurricular activities for tonight."

I smiled. Odd to hear someone use that phrase without intending it as a double entendre. "Come to bed then. Let me hold and protect you."

"Ah." She gave me a soft smile and tilted her head. "You certainly know the way to my heart, trickster."

"Not that you *need* protecting, of course," I added as she moved to the bed and got under the covers. "But I will anyway."

The lantern was dimmed as she shuffled up to me so that I could put my arm around her. "We all need protecting," she said. "Just as we all need to protect you."

Just because I had been kidnapped by a demigod, had my arm explode off, and nearly killed myself trying to save myself from a potentially fatal strike from a harpy, it didn't mean that I . . . Actually, I forgot where I was going with that train of thought.

"You ever get the feeling that things are getting weirder? More dire?"

Ren sighed in comfort and held on to my arm. "Of course. Knowing that the final act against the necromancer is coming up, the stakes have to be higher. Keeps the show more entertaining. The audience stays . . . engaged."

Her voice trailed off as sleep took her. It had been a long day for all of us, and she would have been worried after I had put myself out of action with my own carelessness. Why I had to constantly gamble with my own well-being I wasn't sure. It wasn't even that I thought myself invincible or beyond fate. I had just grown confident in my ability to rise above the odds.

While her comment on how the show was progressing sounded like a little pandering on my behalf, perhaps there was some truth to it. Not that there was a greater narrative pushing things into neat arcs that could be resolved. But . . . the harder we pushed against our greater foe, the greater they'd have to push back.

With that in mind, I was cautious about tomorrow. Or today, depending on how late it was. Killing System-created Monsters to grind out another level sounded simple in prospect, but we had large targets on our backs. Larger targets. In a way, we had accepted that as a fact when we took Tanya in. Or at least when I had made that decision for us.

Being leader was a lot harder a job than I envisioned, even if not explicitly taking up that position. I felt that I had done my due diligence in speaking with Tanya today and ensuring Wolf stayed safe. Ren and I had traded thoughts on everything so far. Perhaps Quinn was due a wellness check. We were taking a risk in splitting the Party between two houses, but the weaver had mentioned she had alarm idols or something earlier in the day. Sleep *was* important.

I checked through my Stats, only really putting my tired eyes over the three figures that made a difference to my fighting ability.

[Stats]
[Dexterity—30 (22 + 8)]
[Intelligence—55 (22+ 33)]
[Luck—17]

[Other—+25% Mana, +20% magic Damage, +5% spell-casting speed]

My Intelligence had taken a leap of twenty points since I last checked at the campground. Something only days away, yet it seemed like weeks ago. Dexterity up by three, even though I had fallen out of favor with that Stat. Luck increase from fourteen to twenty-four. A decent jump and something I would use to explain how I got away with murder. And from it.

I didn't really think about the meta progression too deeply, as long as I was getting more powerful per level. It was clear this world wasn't designed with PvP in mind, and I wondered why someone had enabled it at this stage. I could work on stacking solely Intelligence, magic Damage, and Mana—then my cards would be without equal.

As my brain tried to pick apart ways in which my gear could influence my performance, I fell into a deep sleep.

An odd dream came to me. A reflection of my fight against the Siren, but it wasn't against her this time. Instead, a faceless being of deep crimson sat patiently at the back of the audience, twisted horns like gnarled trees curved from the sides of their head.

Clearly a demon.

Much like a cliché running-in-a-dream scenario, none of my tricks seemed to land or work. I stood there, floundering as countless eyes stared at me—although there was nobody actually present aside from the large demon. No Ren or Wolf at my side to assist, nor the others. Even Roger was absent. A panic unlike anything I'd ever felt before rocked me to my core as my movements became even more sloppy and awkward. Melting under my own failure. If there was any metaphor or lesson to be learned from the experience, it faded away as my body rocked.

Eyes open, I blinked away the confusion.

"Max? Bad dream?"

I looked up to see the elf sitting beside me as I lay in bed. Still in her nightgown, but now long swaths of our reality were painted by bright morning light entering through the window. In contrast to the picture-perfect vision in front of me, I had been sweating heavily during my sleep, and the side of my face was gummed up with drool.

"Terrible," I managed. "Perhaps even criminal."

"We kill people and avoid taxes, trickster." She left the bed, flinging back the covers to obscure my vision. "Can't be any more criminal than that."

I groaned and pushed the sheet away from my face, sitting myself up. She had used the brief moment of being out of my line of sight to switch into her normal outfit. The disappointment on my face must have been obvious, as she rolled her eyes.

"Don't give me that." She stretched her back out. "If you want a show, you'll have to make it up to me first. You're down a few points for almost killing yourself again."

"Then let me get a head start." I grinned and went into the Party Chat.

[Max: Team meeting in half an hour.]
[Tanya: Understood.]

[Wolf: oooO]

I looked back up at the elf to see her with a raised eyebrow and little hope I was about to suggest something she'd be up for. Instead of the obvious, I skirted to a mislaid promise. "Time for that foot rub."

Any disdain she held washed away to be replaced with surprise. "*Oh?* Are . . . you sure?"

Her apparent caution over the act was again an interesting oddity. I'd seen her feet before, and there was nothing untoward about them. Surprisingly unblemished given the amount of walking we did, but it wasn't really anything notable.

"I *am* sure." With the flourish of covers, I exited the bed—although I completely misjudged how close the edge I actually was. As half of me slipped, I twisted and struck my soft skull on the edge of my bedside table, collapsing to the floor. Not wanting to waste an opportunity, I then popped up from my temporary abode and flourish my hands—now dressed in my own outfit.

The thin trickle of blood running from the graze across my forehead only dampened the reveal a tiny amount.

"Oh, for fuck's . . . That's another point you need to make up, dickhead."

As the brief rush of adrenaline from my injury swirled out of the drain, I gestured for her to lie on the bed, totally ignoring her annoyance at yet another clumsy wound I had afflicted myself with. Better I did the deed than my enemy, I considered.

She relented to my offer and sat on the bed to remove her boots and socks, eventually lying down atop the covers—shuffling down a little farther so that I could sit at the end of the bed. With my chair produced, I did just that. From my Inventory, the flask of oil. Wasn't even too sure where I had picked it up, as scented oil was something a little strange to have in this kind of world. Possibly the campground?

I put a healthy amount in the palm of my hand and placed the bottle on the floor beside my chair. Not only should this earn me a point back, but it seemed useful in keeping my hands busy while giving my brain a chance to think about the day ahead. She seemed tense now. Perhaps she was ticklish and afraid to reveal such weakness?

As the scent of raspberry filled the air, I took her right foot into my hands and began plying my thumbs into her sole. Almost immediately, I was on autopilot as my fingers performed practiced movements, allowing my mind to wander. First port of call was to check with Tanya and see if there was any loot among the wreckage of the coach we had all but burned to cinders. It was nice to have someone do all the looting for me now and not have—

"*Oh,* oh my god."

I paused and tilted my head to look at the elf. She had an odd look on her face, like I had been torturing her. "Are you okay? I'm not hurting you, am—"

"*Don't you fucking stop,*" she hissed, furrowing her brow.

Not wanting to argue, I continued massaging her foot once more. She squirmed and writhed, gripping at the pillows.

"You've done this before, haven't you, asshole?"

"I, uh, had a girlfriend who used to run." A brief relationship amounting to about three months, just after I had left school . . . before I let my desire to weave illusion encompass most of my waking time.

"Lucky bitch," the elf murmured.

At this stage, I had no idea what was going on. Despite her body language and occasional groan or gasp, she didn't seem to be enjoying it. It left me in an odd position where I couldn't focus on my thoughts.

"Just a . . . little more!" She closed her eyes and bit her lip as I continued to knead into her soft sole. Her toes curled tight, and she exhaled deeply. "Fuck! Do the other one, asshole. Quick!"

I did so without question. Mostly because I wasn't even sure what I'd ask given the chance. Hopefully, by finding the same release in her left foot, Ren would then labor me with some answers to what was going on.

"We should have been doing this shit since day one. Fuck."

My head nodded along, despite knowing that if I had suggested such a thing, then that little underground hiding place probably would have been my grave. After she had stabbed me to death. I allowed my mind to be blank as I performed the necessary motions, applying more oil as quickly as my dexterity allowed to not invoke her ire from pausing the ritual.

After another agonizing five minutes, and constantly wiggling and expletives, she found the same release with the other foot. I sat back in my chair, unsure of what to even do, as the elf deflated like a balloon into the bed.

I ran my tongue around my teeth. "That was . . . *unexpected.*"

"Really?" She sighed deeply and covered her eyes with her forearm. "That's not a normal reaction?"

"No . . . *No.*" I pocketed the oil into my Inventory and withdrew some cloth to wipe my hands. "Usually it's relaxing or even sensual. I wasn't really sure what it was doing for you."

Ren sat up, her hair a tangled mess and hat long discarded. Before answering me, she wiggled her toes energetically. "It's more like . . . Well, it's hard to explain." She didn't seem to want to extrapolate on this.

"Could you try?"

She shook her head and swung around to hop off the bed and onto the floorboards of whatever house they had dragged me into. "Holy fuck—quick, with me."

Before I had a chance to interject, she was off. Door open, her freshly oiled feet padding out of the room and down the landing. I scooped up her footwear and hat into my Inventory before following suit, emerging into an open space just as she was going down the stairs. How she managed to keep balance throughout all of this was more surprising than the sudden burst of energy.

Down into the open living room, the large form of Wolf sat with his amber eyes narrowed at me. Only getting the audio from the given massage probably gave him the wrong idea about what we were getting up to. No time to explain, as following the elf took me out of the building and into the warm daylight.

She had stopped just off of the path on a grassy area. Head up and eyes closed, the sunlight illuminating her radiant hair. As I walked over, I could see that she was clenching her toes against the ground. On her face, the widest smile I had possibly seen—on anyone, ever.

"I have sensitive feet," she said unprompted. "It's a trait of my elfin lineage. Helps us have a natural feel for the woodland or something. That said, it's also looked down upon to touch other people's feet. It's unbecoming, apparently."

"Like sticking your fingers up someone else's nose."

". . . Yeah." She turned her head to me and opened her eyes. "Like cleaning out your sinuses, it was more of a relief for me than something pleasurable. But I feel *anew*. My untapped potential has been unlocked."

"For humans, it's not that much different from any other muscle massage. Like when you do my shoulders."

She reached out and grabbed my arm to pull me closer to her. "Well, I owe you one, Max. This makes up for yesterday."

"Anytime you need your feet unlocked, Ren, my hands are yours."

The elf bit her lip. "It's not something I can endure often, but . . . I will take you up on that."

Her bright-blue eyes bore into mine, and her face came gradually closer. Our first morning kiss was on the horizon and labored with some new—*and kind of strange*—connection we had made together. My hand went up to hold her cheek and—

"Morning, you two!" The voice of Quinn was an ice cube that slithered down the collar of our simmering romance.

We turned to see the fixer, followed by Tanya, who seemed to know better when to not interrupt something good happening. Relaxing into more casual positioning, I raised my hand up to wave at them before plopping Ren's hat back onto her head.

"Want your boots back yet?" I asked from the side of my mouth.

She pouted. "The longer we can stand here on the grass, the better your reward later."

Shame about the Lady, I guess. She had won, but at least we could eke out an existence living here right on this exact spot. Although, now I imagined the elf slowly turning into a tree. Not a fitting existence for my protégé.

"Glad to see you have recovered," the weaver said as the pair reached us.

"Thanks for the idol." I gave her a nod, but my mind was still trying to think of excuses why we wouldn't leave the area. "Either of you eaten yet?"

They shook their heads. "Honestly, it was just so nice having a soft bed and some safety." Tanya looked back at the building they had stayed in. "Almost wanted another couple of hours."

From behind us, the house groaned as Wolf pushed himself through. "Someone say food?"

With a grin, I raised an eyebrow to Ren. "Well, here in the lovely sun seems like the perfect place to warm up the grill!"

She mouthed a thank-you at me before she withdrew her cooking appliance and the others brought out chairs. With mine appearing as I sat, I leaned over and took off my own boots and socks.

"Want to sort out loot and debrief from last night?" Tanya raised an eyebrow as she looked between Ren's bare feet and mine.

"Soon," I replied, a soft smile on my face.

The grass was cool, still laden with a little dew that the sun had yet to evaporate away. Beneath it, the dirt was soft. Not quite comforting, and I clearly didn't have the visceral connection to nature that Ren felt. As I watched the weaver remove her own boots, with Quinn shortly following her, I couldn't help but feel contented.

I took this moment to enjoy living, for I could read between the lines of our script. We were in the eye of the storm. A slight calm before the biggest test to date.

While our harshest critics lay in wait, I was mentally sharpening my blade. Even beneath the smile and jovial attitude, the demon within me was preparing to do the worst so that our best days could survive just that little longer.

The seats were filling, and I could hear the impatient murmurs rising.

Soon, my audience. *Soon.*

CHAPTER SIXTY-TWO

Stepping Stones

We all sat with our bare feet in the grass and ate a good breakfast. Slightly toasted bread with fried tomato and bacon on top. I even convinced Ren to let me put the garlic I had on the grill to fashion up some garlic butter. A comforting silence followed. Enjoying the moment, knowing what I knew, even though we didn't need to say it. Bad things were on the way.

"Bad news, Max." Tanya wiped her mouth on a produced napkin. "None of the loot from last night is any good for you."

"Really? I guess none of them were casters as such." I pulled a face, clearly too used to getting a worthwhile bounty from Players.

"There's three potions, however. Ten percent increase in Intelligence for an hour."

I held my hands out eagerly. "And yet I will still continue to make poor decisions." Better to get in there first before anyone else could get a jab in.

My eyes turned to the bear as I looted up the trio of drinkable boosts. He was exceptionally bright-eyed this morning. Normally, food and sleep were his default nonfighting states of being. Yet since leaving the building, he seemed alert and ready for the day. Clearly, he got the rest he needed. I could only hope that it was something more permanent.

"Some stuff for Ren, however." Tanya transferred something across to the elf.

Ren herself had also retained a brighter outlook for the day. Not quite smiling but as relaxed and content as I'd ever seen her—certainly among company. A little hardship and our newest members had found some comfort in being a part of the jigsaw.

"Sixty-five Dexterity now," the elf nodded to herself. "Not terrible."

I raised my eyebrow. "And I thought I was doing well with my fifty-one Intelligence."

"What's the Damage formula on your card attack, though? My attacks usually only do seventy or eighty percent of my Dexterity bonus." She swung around in her chair and placed her feet up on my lap.

Having recently run through the house while they were still slightly oiled up, she now just had mud and blades of grass stuck to her. I knew better than to touch them—she was just airing them out after soaking in nature. "Oh, my cards are a full hundred percent Intelligence damage."

"Balls to that." She wrinkled her nose up. "Why's the System always kissing *your* ass?"

I shrugged. "Even better than that, when I get my Power meter high enough, I get some free white gloves."

She didn't seem convinced. "Where are they now?"

"Well, they vanished after—"

"Not *free* gloves then, were they?" Her eyes narrowed, but I could see that playful spark within them.

Tanya turned to the fixer, who was being quieter than normal. "Quinn, I have a sword with evasion increase and threat reduction. Interested?"

"Please, that would be appreciated." He placed his coffee mug down to receive the weapon, holding it up to catch the light as he observed it with his one eye. "Delightful. I feel I haven't been pulling my weight in combat lately, so—"

"Ah, *ah*." I held my hand up and waved a finger. "You've been doing enough. Not everything has to be an all-out brawl."

He smiled and gave me a nod. "Diplomatic as always, Max. I will continue to do my best."

Although he could have nailed the stagecoach with his explosive boomerang, I preferred we kept that as an emergency option.

"Hey, Max." Tanya tilted her head toward me. "What does Quinn's accent remind you of?"

I furrowed my brow. "I've struggled to place it. The extra difficulty lies in not being able to remember the names of places back on Earth."

"Right? He has like a musketeer look to him, don't you think?"

"Yeah." I rubbed my chin and narrowed my eyes at the bemused fixer. "But it's not a *baguette* or *pasta* accent."

"Oh, clever!" She nodded. "It's more like a . . . *kangaroo* accent?"

"Yes." I clicked my fingers. "Definitely *kangaroo* adjacent."

Ren pulled a face. "Kangaroo?"

"They're like a bipedal marsupial . . . You know, a mammal with a pouch," Tanya offered. "Long feet that they hop around on like a rabbit."

"Oh." The elf nodded slowly. "We have something similar, but they are called kangaroos."

I winced.

"I don't sound like a *kangaroo*," Quinn murmured.

"You're saying kangaroo . . . Well, we're hearing *kangaroo*," I began, "but the System must be translating it in some way."

"I am *not* saying kangaroo." Ren pouted.

It took a while for the group to try to decide who was really saying what. Any annoyance didn't take hold with how completely silly the whole conversation truly was. With little else left to do, we packed everything away and set off to where we'd be farming for the day. An hour or so walk, Tanya informed us. Judging by her Map, we shouldn't be close to any known Crimson Shadow— unless they had moved.

Ren sidled up to me and gave me puppy dog eyes. "My feet feel so constrained and stifled in these boots now."

I returned a dull glare. "You can walk barefoot, but if you hurt yourself or step in anything icky, then you'll get no sympathy from me."

She pouted and looked forward. "*Mean.*"

While I loved this woman more than breath itself, if the day started to revolve around her feet, then I'd start to . . . Oh. Was this how people thought about *me* and my tricks? My expression relaxed, and I nudged her. "You can feel it too, right?"

Her coy act melted away, and she gave a serious nod. "Something is happening today. Probably an ambush, knowing our fucking luck."

I nodded. Glad we were on the same page. Not that I wanted to paint the courier attack as an easy win, but things had been calm since leaving the Dungeon. Now we'd forced their hand in denying them the blood—they'd have to act. I had already made some contingency plans for the inevitable interruption to our leveling today. But still . . . there was something else.

A tingle that ran around my right arm. Placebo or coincidence? Or a portent of something even worse? My money was on the latter, and I had a lot of it. The looming possibility that there might be something more to my arm than just the ability to manifest gloves and cast my Domain was still on the horizon. The fact that the Crimson had worse and weirder than grubby assholes with swords was both surprising and worrying.

They had a Player that could manipulate System-created, so the choices for what could be sent our way were varied and uncountable. That wasn't it, still. Something close to the tip of my tongue, but I couldn't chew on it just yet.

Tanya and Quinn were ahead of us in animated conversation. I'd even heard them laugh over something, which caused Ren and me to exchange glances. They'd been clear that nothing was going on between them, and for the most part, I trusted that. Certainly I didn't see a reason Tanya wouldn't be frank with me about it, unless she felt guilty. They could just be friends, and I wasn't about to ship them until they came out with the truth themselves.

Wolf was behind us and still seemed as energetic as earlier. I widened the space between me and the elf so he could move up between us.

"How you feeling today, big brother?" I shot him a wide smile.

He looked about ready to dispute me being the less senior of the two of us but let it slide. "I feel unburdened. A weight has been lifted, and I feel five years younger."

"That's great!" Gently, I gave him a few pats on the shoulder.

Ren leaned forward so that she was a little closer to his large head. "Any reason for the change, *big brother*?"

He grunted. "I think the addition of fruit and vegetables to my diet played a key role."

I wasn't about to dispute that or delve into any further details. As long as he was happy and healthy, I was content. "I want you to keep me updated when we're fighting. We'll take breaks whenever you need."

"I will probably eat fewer of our foes," he admitted. "I'm learning self-control."

He no longer had the hungry debuff, so that probably helped with his endeavors. While we had taken his appetite at face value, it turned out he was overengorging himself regularly. Exhausted from trying to process an overabundance of food while still being constantly ravenous. I felt guilty that we had been so blind to his well-being.

"We're about here," Tanya called from up front.

Time flew when you were eager to enact violence and hopeful to avoid a different violence.

We rounded a corner through a group of trees and were met by a village. Small stone and wooden huts, surrounded by humanoids going about their System-designated business. I had to stop and glare at them for a moment to make sure they weren't real . . . as they were all human.

"Why are they hostile to Players?" I screwed up my face as I rolled out my shoulders. A little preshow warm-up so that I didn't pull anything. Like my own spine out.

"Some bullshit *lore* thing." Tanya yawned and began preparing idols for us all.

Quinn pointed out at the building farther into the village. Slightly larger and more ornamental. "Leader resides in there and is trying to secede from the Crown. For as well as that will do them."

For several reasons, I was sure. "Well, as long as we can massacre them and steal their belongings without the Crown being mad at us, I'm fine."

"Not shying away from a little regicide, are you, trickster?"

I turned my head back to the elf as she drew her bow and prepared her quiver. "I have enough enemies at present. Plus, wouldn't you rather *perform* for royalty?"

The face she pulled told me that perhaps not.

We prepared ourselves to engage in combat. The Villagers were a mixture of melee, ranged, and casters. Wolf would tie up as many as he could while Ren and I picked off the more dangerous System-created at the back. Quinn would flexibly switch between sword to help the bear not get flanked and moving back to use his crossbow and pull farther opponents. Tanya would set up dead zones that would poison our enemies when not debuffing the ones in combat with Wolf.

A sound plan that would *surely* go without a hitch. We had come to the agreement that I would not use <Shuffle> on a Party member—which included me—after they witnessed that Shadow melt away to ashes. I had underestimated the risk that it carried, and knowing it could cause such destruction, we probably wouldn't have used it for our trauma previously.

I dropped down an Imp+ card—this one the ice version. Instead of the reddish skin I was used to, he had a pale-blue coloration with specks of frost in his beard. I'd get Roger up as soon as possible and have him support Wolf and act as a decoy, so we three at the back weren't an easy target.

"Make sure you accept the repeatable Quest," Tanya prompted, watching me pretend to kill our enemies with my glare alone.

"Oh, of course."

[Progress: 0/20 Dissenters killed]

It was almost a shame this kind of fighting required no pizzazz. Simpleminded enough that we could just pelt them with Damage and pick their corpses clean, repeating ad infinitum.

"Ready check?" I asked.

They each nodded or grunted their acceptance. Each tense and ready to fight. I wasn't though.

At first, I tried to ignore it. Maybe just nerves or adrenaline. Perhaps even the anticipation was having a physical effect on my body? Pins and needles had started to prick at my right arm. A numb sensation that felt awkward.

"Max?" Ren stepped up closer to try to read my face.

"Oh? Sorry. No, my arm is just fuzzy. I'm sure it's nothing."

They were all watching me. Expecting it to explode again? Not really. Their glances were something more of a normal concern. I grasped at it, hoping some touch would shuffle the feeling away. Closed my eyes and leaned forward. Was holding my breath for some reason.

Ren's arm went around me, and Tanya was already crouched down in front of me, hand against my forehead as if looking me in the eye could expel a diagnosis. Vision was spotty and their voices distant. Heartbeat pounded in my ears.

And then a voice, a simple sentence that scratched its way across my brain.

I gasped for air, my senses flooding back to me in a sudden rush. Despite the pair clamoring around me, I stood up straight and risked passing out from the burst of oxygen and elevation.

"Speak to us, Max, what's wrong?" Ren's face was a picture of panic.

My finger rose up. I needed a second to compose myself as my breathing returned to normal. The fuzzy feeling in my arm faded away over a few short seconds, leaving me feeling . . . normal. Just a little out of sorts.

The message reverberated around the back of my skull. A language I didn't understand, but something instinctual knew it as clear as day.

"*Well*." I took a deep breath and sighed. "Someone has just killed the fourth Guardian."

CHAPTER SIXTY-THREE

Dizzying Heights

My odd outburst had been a wet blanket over the energetic fervor that had taken us right up to the precipice of murdering our way through the village. Seemed as though the Guardians were connected in a way. Explained how the Lady knew I had killed the Siren.

But what did it really mean?

No reactions from the rest of the Party, so the thought that one of them might be harboring one of the other Guardian kills in secret faded away. Ren and Wolf were both proficient enough that I had kept an eye on them, just in case. Not that I felt either would hold such a thing from me, but you never knew.

The second point that boggled my mind was—*who* had killed this fourth Guardian? Odds on it being someone in the Crimson Shadow? Near guaranteed, I reckoned. As nice as it would be to assume it could be one of our few allies—or a character from the unmet neutral parties . . . it just didn't work that way.

We had taken to fighting the System-created in near silence. Wolf was a pulsing ball of buff effects, carving bloody swaths through any foolish to get close enough to him. As they were just Monsters, that was most of them. The occasional Ranger, healer, or magician were quickly dealt with by Ren or me.

I started sending out three mundane cards alongside my three magical ones. They had less range of control, but as soon as the <Pick a Card> attacks had dealt Damage, I switched the power to the basic cards, meaning I was able to strike another three times straight after. I'm sure there was even more bullshit I could wrangle from such tricks, but I didn't have the stomach for it right now. Power bar hadn't peaked over 12 percent, my performance scoring low with critics.

[Quest complete]
[Progress: 20/20 Dissenters killed]
[Reward received]

[200 Gold]
[Supply Crates (3)]
[Materials (2)]

[Progress: 0/20 Dissenters killed]

My eyes went through the motions, and I accepted the repeat Quest. Autopilot, as I saw nothing but boxes to move and shapes that needed dropping to the floor. The others needed to pause to go through the menus, but I was already killing it. A familiar sensation where I became a conductor just weaving through the gestures.

My ice Imp+ sent out a bolt of frost, striking a warrior charging toward Wolf. Other than Damage, it also slowed the target and those close by. A nice crowd-control option compared to the more destructive fire Imp+. I gave him a nod as his time was up and he faded away back to Hell. Roger clobbered the delayed Monster with his large mace, leaving the bear to focus on the two he was already fighting.

"No hounds, trickster?" Ren pouted from a few feet away.

"Hmm? Oh." I raised an eyebrow but didn't turn to her fully in case I messed up the trajectory of my cards. "Not right now."

"A lot on your mind." A statement rather than a question. She let loose an arrow that pierced through the extended palm of a spellcaster, embedding through into their forearm.

Tanya rubbed at her wrist. "I've told the guy in the Eternal Wardens you believe another Guardian has been killed. He is still being a little shit and ignoring me."

I nodded. Didn't particularly care for the extra lore right now anyway. The Wardens were hiding out, sniveling in the southwest. Away from the necromancer. If they wouldn't meet us here or talk over Chat, then they could get *fucked*.

"My mood has soured. Rotten," I announced as my cards continuously carved up the face of an opponent that was long finished. "Just a forewarning."

Ren put a heal through me by instinct, but it did nothing to move the needle. Ever since I had accepted that I was partly a demon, I no longer shirked away from her radiant energy. Didn't really make sense on the face of it, but I didn't have the heart to work out why. Lots of things weren't exactly sensible as of late.

I turned to the elf. "Thank you. Unfortunately, the only thing that will clear the dark clouds is a thunderstorm."

She gave me a stoic nod, understanding the subtext. A show had been booked; we just weren't sure of the venue or participants. Knocked over the courier, and now a Guardian had been slain. That meant someone had received a power boost. Didn't take a genius to start making the connections.

I had turned the page and taken a glimpse of the script. Maybe the Siren was just the god of being cocksure over vague foreshadowing. *Of course*, conflict *was* in our near future. Didn't need the supposed power I had been granted to take a stab at that revelation.

Then why did it make me feel so dour?

Couldn't avoid the inevitable. Even as I thought this and ran cards through the next set of dissenters, I was still working my jaw. It just wasn't . . . engaging enough. Born to rise up over the normal rules of the System, even with the ease that we chewed through these Monsters, I didn't feel satisfied.

"Requesting a break," Wolf called from the front.

Cards dropped, and I gave Tanya a nod. She called it. We'd back away and drop aggro, take a breather. Well, even as they did so . . . That wasn't my plan. At the risk of annoying everyone . . .

I had to create my own thunderstorm.

As they stepped off closer to the woods, I vanished. Appeared atop one of the small houses. Lightning Imp+ summoned to my side as I dismissed the hell bird. Full deck of mundane cards burst from my belt holster and swirled around me in a torrent.

And then I drowned the unworthy. I cast my basic cards like a breaking wave, and they washed throughout the street. Every time one would strike one of the confused Villagers, it flashed purple, turning into one of my magic ones to slice through them just in time. Turning slowly, I swept around in a circle. With the crackle of energy, my Imp+ shot a beam of white light that arced between opponents.

He was a light-gray color, like the clouds I had purported to be. An odd bliss warmed me as I increased the pace, maiming the targets before they were shocked by my demon. Roger had joined the fray, not wanting to be left out. He acted like a conduit, drawing in enemies from afar into the range of my rolling tide.

It was rude and selfish of me to act the fool and bask in the glory of my own ego. Something about it grounded me, however. A warm-up for something on the horizon. Dizzying grandeur. Above all others.

Quest completed. Quest accepted. A show tune hummed between my ears as I felt at peace. Power meter said 20 percent. No tricks being performed, but part of it was due to my need to be a spectacle, as if I was rewarded for taking risks and being insufferable. I couldn't be any other way.

Made even more appalling as I clocked the expressions of my Party waiting on the sidelines. Mostly displeasure at me putting myself at risk, but there were the hints of awe within their eyes. I *was* a spectacle.

Spawns exhausted in the area, I turned and hopped straight off the roof. Landed on the open end of my cannon that I somehow summoned completely vertical. A blast of confetti rose up from between my legs as the siege weapon slowly tilted to a horizontal position. I jumped from the end before it crashed to the ground, rolling across the cobblestone road and back up to my feet. Took a deep bow as a second shot of confetti washed over me.

"*Fuck you!*" Ren called from their resting place.

I couldn't help but smile. Twenty-four percent and some of the gloom had shifted from my brain. Hands in my pockets, I unsummoned the cannon as Roger and the Imp+ both fell away back to hell.

"I'm *not* sorry," I announced with a shrug.

"Yeah, I can tell by the smile, dickbag." Ren shook her head, but she wasn't even mad despite the scowl.

"Didn't realize we were holding you back so much," Quinn said, his arms crossed but a smile among his beard.

"That's not it." I wiggled my finger. "I have a compulsion to be the star of the show—*a curse*, if you will."

They weren't buying it . . . but they at least begrudgingly accepted that it was just part of me. We had snacks and water while Wolf stretched out and caught his breath. Still had that spark of energy in his eyes, so he was being more conservative with his Abilities. Perhaps I could learn from him.

I looked out at the village. Some near the start had started to respawn now, so we should be able to cycle back around once we hit the end. It seemed as though I had been a bit too forceful with my metaphors, as there were now dark clouds coming in from the east, blanketing out the blue skies.

"I'm just destined to have to keep worrying about your dumb ass, aren't I?" Ren stepped beside me and leaned her head onto my shoulder.

"You are." I put my arm around her and gave her a squeeze. "And the only time I'd owe you an apology is when I wouldn't be able to give you one."

"Melodramatic ass. Plenty of things you could apologize for while still breathing." She sighed and moved away to look me in the face. "I love seeing you be extra and enjoy yourself. Just don't push it *too* far. If there's something worse coming our way, then . . ."

I placed a finger on her lips. "Then they will fall to the ground, split in twain."

She screwed her face up. "You're going to lose that finger one of these days, motherfucker." Her bright-blue eyes rolled, and then she gave me a smile.

"I'm ready," Wolf grunted and stood back up, stretching his back out.

Tanya clapped her hands. "Alright, troupe, back into formation and we'll take it from the top. No alterations to the performance. Oh, and Max?"

I turned my head away from the elf and raised an eyebrow at our manag—At the *Fateweaver*.

She flipped something through the air, which I caught deftly. A power token.

"A little bonus for putting in the extra effort and completing the Quest ahead of schedule." She gave me a wink and then set about corralling the others, who now looked a little put out at my preferential treatment.

"Kiss ass," Ren murmured. "Two can play that game." She adjusted her quiver and worked out her shoulders.

Tanya hadn't been with us long enough to know that I shouldn't be encouraged. Now that we knew there may be rewards for putting on a show, what had started as a boring-but-safe level grind was now an all-out brawl to impress the woman. A dangerous game to play, and one I was sure to win.

Holding the token tight in my grip, I cycled through the Abilities and Passives that were still at basic level. Too many to count . . . Perhaps instead of getting two Skills to the third level, I should have spread things around. No, I already disagreed with that thought.

I had made my decision.

My cannon had been a mainstay in most of my performances since receiving it. Upgrading it to advanced increased the amount of Dazzle icons it would stack on targets and allowed me to load up each of the three payloads all at once rather than having to do one after every shot. Delicious.

"Alright then." I grinned and nodded that I was ready.

As Wolf began to glow from his several buffs, each of us stood ready to launch forward and see what manner of ridiculous combat we could get into. I licked my lips, almost able to taste the applause. Power had dropped back to 14 percent, but I didn't need to push it all the way for System-created.

Cards circled both my hands as I stood poised for bullshit, just waiting for the bear to initiate combat.

Ren lowered her bow, a sudden scowl across her face as she looked toward the east.

Maybe the bad weather was coming in quicker than expected. More fool her for being distracted—that would just give me a head start.

Instead of bursting forward, Wolf tilted his head and then raised his nose into the air. Also toward the east.

I turned my head in that direction. Knowing what I would see. A picture painted so clearly it should have been obvious from the height of my ego. We all knew what was to the east, but we'd expected it to stay there. The threads I was so eager to join were tied together, the pages of the script unable to tell me lies even if I didn't want to believe it.

Ren cursed under her breath as the first drops of rain started to patter from the sky.

I saw the uncountable shadows move among the tree line on the other side of the village, and my body temperature dropped.

CHAPTER SIXTY-FOUR

Greatest Burden

A roving horde of the undead might not mean anything. Even if it meant what I thought it did, it didn't change our current predicament. As my jaw clenched, cards of bright purple bloomed in my hand, spiraling around, ready to be flung forth. Similar to the ones that assailed us at the camp, they looked like generic System-created.

No prizes for guessing whom they had come from.

Something like this wasn't natural . . . No chance the System would give this sort of power to a normal Player. I didn't want to think it out loud, just in case it drove the final nail of truth down into the coffin of my disbelief . . . but I was pretty certain we had found out who killed the latest Guardian.

"Shit me." Tanya took a step back, her eyes trying to count the number of potential assailants. "I have something for this, but I need to know *now*. All in or fall back?"

"Retreat would just be delaying the inevitable," I said through clenched teeth. "I will *not* be bullied around." We weren't afraid to fight, and I had enough power to shred dozens of the shuffling corpses with ease.

"Fine. I'll stand with you. Here . . . This is the best I can do." In her hands, she created two idols. Both were made of silver with thin bands of opal around the circumference. "It will allow you to resist the diseases the zombies can spread, but there's a limitation."

Ren already had an arrow ready to fire. "Which is?"

"They are *small* area of effect auras, and I can only have two of them at once. I would suggest Ren and I stay as a pair, and Wolf and Quinn as another. Max, you'll have to decide which group you want to fight with."

I nodded. "Got it. If it's just zombies, I will take the high ground and get a better view of the situation. If we aren't alone, I will return to one of you."

"You turn into a zombie, and we're over," the elf said, her eyes narrowed. Raindrops bounced from the rim of her top hat as she glared at me.

Well, that certainly worked as a better motivator than any other warning they could have leveled at me. Then again, I was assuming she meant us as a couple rather than us as a greater Party. Same difference. It was hard to see how many undead there were, but I had no intention of getting close enough to be bitten. They weren't even interested in most of my tricks. A waste of time, if they weren't so eager to take a bite out of me.

I drew out a glass flask of water. "If you could do the honors." Although not much of a movie buff, I had seen enough zombie flicks to know about the tropes and clichés. "I'll need your eyes around us to ensure we aren't surrounded . . . This may be a trap." Or we could easily be overrun.

Ren whispered the Elfin word to imbue it with radiant energy before giving me a nod of acknowledgment. "If there's too many . . ."

"Plan B is a fighting retreat." I cooled my temperature, knowing the stakes. "We have the advantage of speed as long as we have a route to escape. Kill as many as you can and we'll keep falling back."

Tanya nodded. "That's more sensible than us making a last stand."

"Good." I grinned. "I'm glad you came up with it."

Before they could respond, I was away. Back up to the house I had been using to kill all the . . . My heart immediately sank down to my stomach. Past the edge of the village where the zombies had started to crest into the open, they did not stop at the visible tree line but continued on down through the woods. Hundreds upon hundreds, like a sickening wave of decay.

"Plan B," I called back to the Party. "Fire at will." I wondered if they could see the look on my face. No doubt Ren could read how dire the situation was . . . because suddenly I certainly felt like a fish out of water.

Beside me, I summoned the cannon. Loaded it with three things. Dropped my fire Imp+ next and told him to light up what he could. Slightly to the left, the first cannon blast fired out a lit lantern, which struck a tree and spread the oil around the area. Second to the right, a similar payload and effect. Third to the middle, and it was the holy water Ren had prepared. Bursting against the thick bark of a tall tree just outside the village, it sprayed the contents down on a group of undead, melting away at their flesh. The flames struggled to catch as the downpour continued, only a few zombies laden with the thick liquid catching aflame.

Entangling arrow followed by <Smite Shot> pinned and blew through zombies down below. Crossbow bolts and minor spells from the rest of them peppered among the unending horde. My Imp+ threw a fireball down, exploding with amber flame and scorching the cobblestones. I summoned Roger into one of the dead Dissenters and commanded him to go wild. Cooldown was up and I used <Demonic Transposition> again to go back to the group.

"How many, Max?" Tanya's eyes were wild, some panic within. Of course, if it wasn't that many, I would have danced a little dance while throwing my cards out.

"Far too many. Looked like from the east only, but things could change." I was at somewhat of a loss. Dozens we could work through; scores—sure. Hundreds was risky.

"Only zombies?" Ren asked, firing off another arrow. There was worry in her eyes too, as much as she was trying to hide it.

"From what I could see." I shrugged. That didn't make sense though. How quickly we could go from feeling on top of the world to suffering on the back foot. Some manner of joke about how that was show business fizzled before I could even grasp at it. Any lingering humor had been scrubbed away by how serious I found our situation. No easy out.

Even with the idols, it was too dangerous to jump into melee. Wolf could pulp them like soggy newspaper, but he would eventually tire from the sheer amount. We'd be putting his health in jeopardy and committing to being knee-deep in an enemy that could easily swarm around him and cut the bear off from the rest of us.

Something like fear gripped at me. An odd sensation when I had been so filled with gusto during my time in this world. Even if some of it was false confidence, at present I was now full of dread. But why? The answer was as clear and immutable as the growing throng ahead of us.

I was about to lose them all; I knew it. A vision of my Party torn asunder by the countless living corpses. Me powerless to save them. Enveloping darkness that I couldn't fight against. I had found my match and brought death to those I held closest. One by one, they would be taken from me.

Was this just paranoia? An effect of the Siren, or perhaps something our enemy was using to cause me this odd feeling? No, it was part of the script. A magician alone and angry, suffering because . . . he needed to be the star of the show. They would be gone, and I would wreak terrible vengeance until my body couldn't withstand the power. Until I fell heavier than any final curtain.

"Max, you alright?" Ren shot me a concerned glance.

I looked into those blue eyes, and I couldn't tell her a lie. Couldn't pretend that we were fine and that I hadn't just envisioned her death if we stood around here. I shook my head. "Bad vibes."

Not the most informative response, but she knew me well enough. "Should we fall back?"

"We . . . need to get *very* far away," I said, a shakiness in my voice. "There are hundreds of them. Too many for us to put on brave faces and suffer through."

She swore under her breath. The undead were halfway through the village now, slowly shambling toward us and taking out some of the respawning Dissenters.

Our attacks had made a dent . . . but it was paltry compared to how many were left. We weren't well equipped for doing large-area damage.

Wolf looked ready to go if asked but otherwise not keen to get stuck in. He knew as well as I did what could go wrong, even if he was used to powering through such problems. Beside him, Quinn looked even less enthused about fighting. He seemed tired already, as if just seeing the horde had exhausted his will to live.

Ren's expression had hardened. Ready to do whatever I decided was best. A terrible burden to put on me when I couldn't see the light at the end of the tunnel. My breathing felt stifled—was this a panic attack? Power was at 0 percent, as if I couldn't feel any further away from being myself. I tried probing around for other Max or my internal demon, but there was nobody home. It didn't work like that anymore.

This *was* me, but I'd never felt so unlike myself.

Tanya put her hand on my shoulder. "Max. I've been keeping something secret from you. I'll apologize later, but I have a teleportation scroll."

"Oh? To where?" I felt clammy now, my heartbeat pounding through my ears but none of the usual adrenaline to accompany it.

"I have it set for the cottage. I . . . was keeping it for an emergency or to save my own skin if things between us didn't work out."

I shook my head. "Fine. Fuck if I care. Just get it ready. We'll go. This *is* an emergency." I had to save them at any cost.

With a nod, she brought it up and stood closer to the rest of us. "Hands all on the scroll, three-second cast, and then we're gone. It's not that far away but gives us time."

But how much time? My mind was reeling. I was closer to believing I was under some kind of spell, but my Status screen was giving me the all clear. Normally, I was more levelheaded than this. Where was the bravado? The cunning? Any sliver of willpower that I could bullshit my way through this obstacle?

Absent and sorely missed. I felt ever more like it had been stolen from me.

Still clutching at the idols, we each hurried around her, Wolf putting his paw on the unraveled scroll before the rest of us joined him. Had to make sure there was enough room for the five of us. The blue arcane runes on the page lit up as Tanya started to cast the spell. I took a deep breath, still trying to guess the next step we should take. This was only a brief delay to something bigger.

Three. My right eye twitched as a shrill sound rang out in my inner ear.

Two. A whisper growing louder, a language I didn't understand but the voice so familiar.

One.

I removed my hand from the scroll and watched the Party vanish in a flash of blue light.

CHAPTER SIXTY-FIVE

Twin Peaks

He was here.

Abandoning my Party had not been a foolish self-sacrifice or an attempt for bravado to lead me to an early grave. It was just the knowledge that someone was close and what I was about to do should bear no witnesses.

Even as my STAR lit up with messages, I chose to ignore them. Didn't have the heart to explain, nor the time. A flash of air surrounded me as I switched back up to the roof of the central house.

The horde had truly swarmed in now. Among the pattering rain, their glowing yellow eyes sought me out. Soon enough, the entire village would be drowned in walking dead, with little chance of escape. It would take them a while to destroy the building to get at me—or less time if they could climb, but for now, this was a sensible enough place to gather my thoughts.

My tired eyes looked down to see Roger in constant conflict. Every time his puppet became overwhelmed, he would switch to another, grabbing up whatever was closest to renew his onslaught. His dedication was admirable, but it didn't hit any emotional marker within me. He would find a lack of applicable hosts soon enough and wasn't gaining any ground against the endless sea of corpses.

My mood had cooled, as if the persistent precipitation had melted away the blind panic I had not a minute ago. The truth wasn't so simple. Now, without the weight of love clouding my mind, things had become clearer. I knew what I was and what purpose I had to fulfill at this stage of the show.

I turned slowly.

Across the village street, atop the roof of the building opposite mine. There he was.

A singular eye of bright white glared at me. Deep-red skin and ivory horns. Muted leathers, the handprint of the Lady on his forehead as well as on his chest plate.

I blinked, and his mouth upturned into a sharp grin.

"The trouble with my Domain," he crooned, "is that it allows people to escape, in exchange for a wider area and specific effect."

Cogs in my head clicked around. My brief mania, the fear instilled in my mind, was part of his Domain. A reason why it didn't show up as a Status, perhaps. Something to learn.

He tilted his head. "You must have strong willpower. Most would be reduced to a blubbering wreck by now."

That must mean I was still in it. Odd, considering I didn't have the lashing of paranoia keeping me cowering any longer. In saying that, I had a lot more cards up my sleeve that he wasn't privy to. My own Domain. My demonic side. My hunter past life that sought to erase beings like him.

He'd know soon enough.

I rolled my head around on my neck and stood to face him fully. "Last I heard, Rolo is feeling pretty lonely. So eager to join him?"

"*Human fuck!*" He seethed in response. "You sealed your fate when you killed my twin."

A thrum of energy vibrated through my ears. Part of my psyche was fighting against his power. Pushing through the weight he was trying to smother me with. And I was *winning*.

I grinned. "Do you want to know how I did it?"

"Just die!" A sword of red energy burst out into his grip, and he surged toward me, zipping across the open air with a streak of crimson blur.

He struck the empty air as I appeared on the roof he had just left, leaving us in switched places. My foot slid slightly on the tiles that had become slick from the rain. The gnashing crowd below looked up with eager eyes. Stage diving wasn't really a done thing in the magic world, so I'd leave them hungry.

My head turned back to the demon, a smile still on my face. "You didn't come alone, surely? I'd hate to think you are as foolish as Rolo?"

Confidence was seeping back through my body quicker than the rain dampened my suit. In fact . . . I ran my tongue across my teeth. Purple lightning crackled around my body, and the rain abated, falling around me but no longer striking me. A bubble of dry air, rejecting the inclement weather. Part of his Domain that I no longer allowed.

His eye narrowed at seeing my shirking of his Ability. "I fight my own battles. Here I stand before you to take vengeance."

Foolish. Even more so than I was. "Idiot," I scoffed. "You have an army of zombies as a backup for when you realize you are too weak."

"I had not expected to catch you on your own." He flourished his blade and tensed for the next attack.

So the original plan was to separate or distract my team while he got in a cheap shot and finished me off. I suppose I should be more flattered that an assassination attempt took so much effort, but he had made a fatal flaw.

All demons must die.

I raised up my hand, and a trio of purple cards bloomed around it, spinning as he prepared his next attack. "Come closer so that I may reunite you with your twin."

He growled and burst across the gap between rooftops again. Instead of moving, I summoned my cannon right in front of me. The demon slammed into it but twisted and rolled across the top as my Spear of Luck jettisoned out into the horde below. My cards went out toward him, and he vanished.

<Card Fan> went up as he reappeared behind me and swung out. Damage negated, but the force sent me stumbling forward into the cannon. My eyes darted back over to the other roof, and my hand went up. I vanished, and he burst out to cut me off—another streak of crimson power behind him as he landed deftly.

I had only used my invisibility, a little misdirection with my body language, causing him to make mistakes. Of course, now he had jumped himself right into where I had adjusted the cannon to aim as he flew across. A blast caused a bag of nails to split and pelt the area with shrapnel.

Windows shattered, wood was splintered, and tiles cracked. A wavering shield of red flashed over the demon, but as it faded, there were telltale streaks of a handful of fresh cuts and shredded armor. He was enraged and his off hand went up, power running through it.

I moved too late. Long spikes of demonic energy burst up from where I stood. Several feet long and bright-red in color. Couldn't help but add my own shade of crimson to them, as several pierced through my legs. Eyes up into the air as he had leaped at a greater height to swing down on me with his sword, avoiding the range of my cannon. Cooldowns were still ticking away.

The several planks of wood I summoned just above me shattered into splinters, and I was knocked down prone. With the spikes vanished away, I slid down the roof, only stopping a foot away from dropping into the salivating mouths below. I spun out a trio of cards with half a dozen mundane ones, circling them like a tornado just before me to stop him from getting closer.

As I rolled to my front to push myself back up, into one hand, I quickly downed several potions in a row. Healing. Intelligence boost. Action speed. My legs screamed out in pain as I put my weight back on them, but they were just about able to hold me up. It'd do.

"You're a slippery shit," he growled. "No wonder you've been such a problem for the Lady. It will be my pleasure to—"

I started laughing. Even as purple energy sparked and ran over my body, the pain just brought me greater elation. It was all the same at the end of the day. Bullies spouting out bullshit before I kicked their shit in.

"You're a pitiful excuse for a fucking demon, pal." My eyes were burning up now, the first time they had held the glow since accepting what I was. Forty-five percent Power and rising.

"And you are a feckless human with no sense—"

"A-*ha*. No." I raised up a bleeding finger and wagged it at him. "You want to know my secret before I kill you?"

He growled, and a circle of white light pulsed up and down his blade. "That you can summon demons? Big deal. A weak tether to my kind won't save you."

"*Our* kind."

I launched myself forward, sending my circling cards out in a burst. His sword came up to deflect them, but I switched which were powered just before they got to him. Still, one his shield caught. Second deflected by his quick blade. Third cut through his left arm, severing into muscle.

And then I was upon him. Dagger spun up into my hand as I lashed down at him. As he blocked my strike, I changed it into the raspberry-scented oil, bursting over his weapon and splashing down his front. My left hand jabbed upward with an empowered card, missing as he vanished to appear three feet back. Catching me off guard, he lunged forward and struck my extended left arm just below the STAR.

Blood burst from the wound and continued to trickle down, soaking my sleeve. Might have hit something important there. I held my right hand up, now wearing a white glove, as another trio of cards bloomed.

He paused to gauge how I was about to attack. Fucked him there. It was just another distraction.

Cannon went off. It had taken some time to turn it all the way around, so the melee suited that purpose. Not aimed straight for him directly, however. Pointed down against the roof, tiles burst into a mist of blue as the paint can rocketed through the supports. With a groan, the footing around us shattered, and we dropped down into the room below.

I bounced slightly, landing on the single bed, while the demon crashed onto the wooden floorboards. Amid the cloud of dust dampened by the constant rain, I hopped down, bringing the Blade of Shadow into the recovering figure. Pierced him straight through the chest, burying through the gap in his rib cage into his stupid fucking demon internal organs.

He groaned as he slunk over before I vanished, switching places with my ice Imp+ back up on the roof at the edge of the wreaked hole.

The real demon missed his swing, crimson blade crackling through the air just above the Imp's head, before my pal blasted him point blank with an ice bolt. Singular eye turned up to me, confusion and anger near blinding him.

"I'm more of a demon than you are." I smiled. "You are but a wriggling worm, not even fit to devour the corpse of your brother."

"Cursed shit, you know nothing. Those true to the Lady will pick the flesh from the bodies of you and that pretty elf you hold so dear."

Oh, and I thought we could get away with keeping it all fun and games. This murder attempt just something casual between demons. Bringing in the Party just ruined my mood. Then again, I wasn't even treating this as a show. That part of me had taken the back seat.

"What is your name, demon?"

He spat on the floor before attempting to swipe at my Imp+ as I sent it away. "Syther. The last you'll ever hear."

Seventy percent.

"Why don't you put your little Domain away? Let's fight as equals. You . . . wouldn't want me to get mine out, would you?"

"You're . . . bluffing."

He turned as the bedroom door burst open. Roger staggered through, his own eyes aglow with fury as he strode toward Syther. "Fucked the door, boss."

I leaped down from the edge, two-handed axe in my hands as my opponent was distracted. Cooldowns were being a pain once more, so I had some time to kill before this building needed to be evacuated. Roger had let the tide in, and we were about to be flooded by my hungry audience. Ah, *there* it was. Time to meet in the middle once more.

Syther stepped to the side as my weapon buried into the wooden floorboards, his shield flaring up as my pact demon lashed out with a mace. As he tried to take advantage of my stuck axe, I instead switched it out with my knife once more. Slashed across his collarbone and shoulder, narrowly missing his neck as his attack went wide. Mace struck him in the side of the head, and he stumbled back into the wall, knocking a shelf of books down.

I was already back upon him. The falling books looted and flung back into the air one after the other, like a fountain of dusty tomes. As I added in a wave of mundane cards, even Syther's large eye couldn't see where my true attack was coming from. Another lunge with my dagger that was mostly absorbed by his armor. I ducked as Roger swung in a wide arc, pulping some of the wall as Syther vanished.

Spun in place and shot out three powered cards right behind us. A reasonable guess, with one slashing through his leg. Eighty-four percent. Adrenaline and hatred had all but erased any pain or aches I should be feeling. I shouldn't play with my food, but he kept squirming. A demon that must be erased. I turned my head to see the first of the zombies that had made it up the stairs. Time for a change of set.

"I'll buy time, boss." Roger immediately sprinted out toward the landing.

Syther pulsed with energy as he blurred up back out onto the roof. A glare back toward me and he repeated the process, probably onto the next building.

Running from me. I grinned and wavered. Felt warm. Blood still poured from my left wrist, while both white gloves were now soaked crimson. Ninety-six percent. My suit sparkled as if a cloud of glitter hung around me. Wasn't even performing that many tricks, but he was a *demon*, and that was fuel enough.

I closed my eyes. It was time.

A rush of air and I stood before him. His eye widened in surprise as I grabbed him by the collar, appearing out of invisibility. "I told you to turn off your bullshit. Now you will learn the hard way."

One hundred percent.

Before he had the chance to raise his sword, I cast my Domain, cracking his in half like a bad egg. The dark clouds parted from the split, and a ray of sunshine bore down, illuminating me.

Showtime.

CHAPTER SIXTY-SIX

Held to Account

I'd never seen anything like it. Certainly not for a while.

I stood upon the stage, illuminated by the overhead lights. A warmth and familiarity energizing me. Before me, the largest crowd I had the pleasure of performing for. At least since joining this world. A packed venue—I was growing in notoriety. This couldn't be denied.

Sure . . . the glowing yellow eyes didn't seem too excited for what they *should* be expecting, but perhaps in time they would grow to enjoy the proceedings. Actually, that was unlikely.

My eyes fell on the special guest sitting dead center in the front row. I smiled at my choice of phrasing there. Syther looked awestruck, and I hadn't even begun. He knew as well as I did . . . The power of my Domain. The spectacle of a grand show.

But . . . I wasn't here to make friends. The demonic power within me had granted me early access to the stage, and it was that part of me that was running the performance. Still, old habits die hard.

I removed my hat and threw it across the stage. It landed and slid across the varnished wood before popping up into the air atop my cannon.

Three blasts of confetti, one after the other. Knowing the mechanics took some of the luster out of the gig, but the audience didn't deserve my best.

The hundreds of captive faces twisted and groaned as painful Dazzle icons erupted upon them. Damage for everyone—and the upgraded cannon was merciless. Scores of the audience burst, their heads like gore-laden fireworks. The aisles ran with a thick river of viscous blood and liquified internal organs to pool down close to the stage.

The VIP struggled and squirmed, unable to escape the show.

"Please remain seated, sir," Roger said, my pact demon stepping through the gathering muck to chastise Syther.

It was amusing to see him in his proper rabbit form. Nice to know I wasn't alone in this show—I could always rely on him.

Still. My opponent was insufferable and unworthy of a decent showing.

"Allow me to end you, just like I did your brother." My smile widened, and I held my gloved hands up into the air.

This was *my* Domain. Not even the System knew what I was supposed to be capable of. In some ways, it was a captive of my power, just as I was under it. White gloves soaked through with crimson. Purple electricity arced around my body as I drew forth on my demonic power. Mana reserves totally tanked, and I dipped into what Health I still had. It . . . didn't stop at the usual percentage. I could go beyond it, as my body began to twitch and split.

A crawling feeling inside my skull waved a warning flag. Pressure built up on my scalp, as if two horns wanted to burst through my skin. I tempered the power to prevent that from happening. The whole Domain shook as the timer started to run out on Syther's restraints.

But it *was* too late for him.

Dust and debris started to fall from the shadowed ceiling. A few zombies were crushed by falling stone and wooden beams. All eyes went upward before being blinded by the bright-red light that bathed the scene. Painted a hellish picture.

A single magic card, easily fifty feet wide and close to double that tall, cracked through whatever passed as a roof of this faux hall. My hands trembled, the amount of force in trying to control it almost snapping my fingers clean off. Health slowly trickled down; exhaustion started to hit.

The demon was frozen in fear.

"Become ashes," I growled, pushing the card down on those present.

There was a flash, and the air was knocked from my lungs. Some feeling of vertigo but little else. Darkness. Something of a close friend at this point. Pain . . . Another awkward companion that I had little choice but to go along with.

The patter of rain on my back, and I gasped for air.

Eyes blurry, I tried to push myself up from the hard stone road, immediately vomiting. Beneath my hands, thick mud or . . . No, it was the mulched undead. My grip tensed against the thick sludge of the long deceased. Blinking away whatever clouded my eyes was difficult, but I could clearly hear the approach of footsteps against the slick cobblestone.

Eyes of glowing purple leaned down in front of me. Bright-white fur that looked so soft and cozy.

"You've fucked your left leg, boss."

"Is . . . he . . . ?" I found it a struggle to get enough air into my lungs.

"Yeah. Dead as shit. Here, we need to get out of this place. Where's the elf?"

My heart did a leap, which was painful given how fragile my insides felt. With little ability to object, I was lifted to my good foot. Roger held me up.

"Go west." I felt his fur brush against my face as he looked back and forth. Made me feel like it was time for a nap.

"I'm . . . shit at directions, boss."

"Roger . . . You're a demon. Just use . . . our natural overconfidence . . ."

With a grunt, he set off, assisting me through the slippery path that I could still barely see. I should probably let the others know that I was not dead . . . or at least at present I could state as much. The blue of the STAR menus hurt my eyes and shifted around as if I were on a rollercoaster.

[Max: ren demonm dead]
[Max: sorryy, injurs]
[Fiona: What are you on about?]
[Max: rgr help s hel]
[Fiona: Are you okay? Max?]

A job well done. I allowed myself a smile, which also hurt. Darkened shapes passed, and then we stumbled across softer ground. Greenery brushed across me, and I assumed we had headed out of the village and into the woods. Although Roger was pact bound to me, I was humbled by his actual care for my well-being. Could just let me die and he'd be free . . . or stop existing—it wasn't clear how it really worked.

We both knew that this was a temporary thing. He'd never been in his full form out in the real world before, and he had a time limit. The goal was to get me far enough away from the scene of the crime that any lurking Crimson didn't find me and finish me off.

"Here . . . Stop a second," I requested my demon.

He did. It took three tries, but I withdrew a healing potion out of my Inventory to hover in the air in front of my face. Cork out and tilted toward me. Most of it missed my open mouth, but a slight amount of warmth went through me. Ren's healing charm was already broken. Perhaps in my . . . fall? Some of the pieces slotted together with the help of the potion. We had been on one of the buildings before my Domain cropped up. After it went away, I must have dropped and landed poorly.

Any further deliberation faded away as darkness enveloped me once more.

A familiar dream, but different. Ahead of me, the demon of crimson, now split in half and fading away. The thrum of energy from his substantial wound reverberating my name. Behind me, the radiance was . . . distant. Fading too, but a sliver of it snaked through the abyss and connected to me like a tether.

I willed it to be stronger, but it wasn't improving. Everything was becoming pitch-black, threatening to leave me alone with nothing. I had to hold on. Necromancer and the Lady weren't dead yet. I needed the strength.

Slowly, everything ceased to be.

Footsteps. My eyes cracked open, and the dim light burned at my eyes despite my current grave being shadowed. Waving green shapes surrounded me as the pace of the soft beats of whomever approached increased.

The rustle of leaves and someone grabbed at the collar of my shirt and lifted me up slightly. Roger hadn't taken me far enough, and Syther's group had tracked me down. Oh well, at least he tried his—

Soft lips pressed against mine, an act that resonated with frustrated desperation. They parted away.

"*Fuck you.* I am this close to breaking your neck myself, dickbag."

Another intense lock of our lips.

My brain cycled through all the people I had met in my life. Chances were this was slightly more likely to be Ren rather than any of the Crimson Shadow.

The pulse of warm healing through me helped that conclusion bear fruit. My eyesight was still blurry, but I blinked away enough gunk to see radiant hair and soft blue clothing.

"Ren?" I croaked.

"Who else, dumb shit?" She ran her hand along the side of my face and tried to help me sit up. "Unless you wanted Fiona to come rescue you?"

"Fiona?" My brow furrowed. "Where's everyone?"

"About a minute behind because apparently cardio is a sin." She brought me in for a hug, and her hair covered my aching face. "I'm still *so* mad at you, Max. You *can't* do that to me. You want to break my heart?"

"No." I closed my eyes and sighed. "I'm . . . I'm really sorry, Ren. I'll make no excuses."

"You hurt me," she said quietly. "And you'll need to earn that trust back. But . . ." The elf leaned away from me so that she could look me in the face. "I love you, and we'll get through this. Understand?"

Pain radiated through my heart, remembering the messages she had sent me when the Siren had snatched me away. *Don't leave me. I need you.* Guilt was a new thing that my gusto didn't seem to be able to wash away.

I nodded. After all that she had lost, I was her rock. Protection and guide. I had abandoned her and flaunted a potential death over her own aching heart. Our flame flickered from the gust I had invited but wouldn't go out. Time and time again, risking it all . . . and for what?

"Good. Let's get you healed up and then you can explain to the others why you're such an asshole."

"We have that much time?"

She sighed and held my chin gently. "You look like you've been beaten to death by an ox. Even your eyes have been bleeding. Yet *still* you persist with the humor."

"Coping mechanism maybe. Or mental illness." She was clearer now to my improving vision. Obvious that she had spent the last . . . however long completely stressed. My heart continued to ache. "How did you find me?"

Her bright-blue eyes relaxed. "I will *always* find you, trickster."

I chose to take that romantically rather than as a threat. The simple answer would be her Oathwarden Ability. She knew when I was in trouble, and so knowing where I was in trouble wasn't that big of a leap.

"How did you get out this far with *this* leg?" She prodded my broken limb, causing a flare of pain to snap up my body. Deserved. "You're a little way from the village."

"Roger helped." I glanced around at my surroundings. It seemed as though he'd dumped me in a bush when his time was up, maybe hoping it would hide me. Before the elf could reply, a gathering of footsteps came from behind her.

She gave me one quick peck before standing, holding her hand down to me. "Let's get you out of the shrubbery and into a chair, dickbag."

I took the extended hand and groaned as I righted myself onto my good leg—or at least the best of the two. A short hop from the grasp of the bush branches and I sank back into a summoned chair. Ren crossed her arms and gave me a tired glare, as the rest of the Party crested through the grouping of nearby trees to find me.

Relief washed over their faces immediately. Wolf bounded up to me ahead of the others, pushing up beside me before giving me a worried glare.

"Reckless, brother."

Tanya looked almost as tired as the elf and immediately stepped in front of me to put her hand on my forehead. "High temperature. Report other injuries."

"Fever. Fractured left leg. Lacerations. Broken ribs. Moderate blood loss. Exhaustion. Trauma." I read the laundry list of things from my Status menus, skipping over the minor cuts and bruises.

She handed me an idol. "If I see you use <Shuffle> on *any* of those maladies, I will break your other leg personally."

"I'll help," Ren offered.

Quinn just shook his head and crossed his arms. "How am I meant to die in your stead when you leave us like that?"

I was humbled, in a way. The fact that this group of strange people cared this much for me. Never wanted to be a leader, but I fit the role because I was a trailblazer. Told Roger about the overconfidence of demons, and perhaps that's where I got it from as well. Just fated to see how close to the edge I could get and always believe I could win.

"Firstly," I began, sighing and looking down at the ground. "My apologies to you all for the worry and betrayal of not teleporting to safety with you."

I was met with murmured acceptance. They hated it and would hold it against me, I was sure. But we needed to continue what we'd started, and they'd soon have bigger problems than how much of a jerk I could be. Still . . . I *had* won. The edge was farther away than I'd thought.

"Put on some coffee." I raised an eyebrow up toward the elf. "And let me tell you all the tale of the most disappointing show I have ever put on."

CHAPTER SIXTY-SEVEN

Only Natural

We sat in a circle, steaming coffee mugs in our hands, as I explained why I had abandoned them. The voices, the demon, and the Domain causing me to act differently. Not really excusing the act but giving them the full picture. And then it was the duel with Syther, the emergence of my own Domain once again, and finally the erasure of all enemies.

"Still a shitty storyteller," Ren murmured.

Tanya tilted her head. "So you're saying you killed all those zombies?"

I was hesitant to give the nod, despite knowing that I had. "As far as I am aware. I wasn't attacked when my Domain faded, but I also couldn't really *see*."

"That's going to be a huge setback for them?" Quinn rubbed his eye patch. "Even with the power of a Guardian, I doubt they could bring up such a sizable force in short order again."

"Oh." Tanya sat forward. "That reminds me—the Eternal Wardens douche got in touch finally. Says we have to go see him if we want answers."

I groaned. They were too far out of the way. That would set back our plans by a few days—and all for some useless lore? "I'd hate to leave this central area without usurping the necromancer first. Otherwise, he will bring about another large force of undead."

"I know," she agreed. "He asked which Guardian you killed, but I didn't give him any information. It might be important, like there's a difference in their powers? Although he tipped his hand, I couldn't see the cards."

As always, she was keen to impress by continuing the lingo. The Guardians granting different boons seemed . . . reasonable? There were still a huge amount of things I did not understand. In part because we didn't read up on any of the world's legend along the way—but also I felt as though we were pinned in. With a barrier preventing us access to the wider world, we had been quarantined from the bigger picture.

Ren had decided to sit close by, even though she was still mad at me. The times we had been apart were few and far between, and although I managed to get by whatever the cost, she still had that worry. For the day that I didn't come back.

My leg had clicked back together, in a way that made most of those present wince. I barely registered it and wondered if I was disassociating still. Tanya had made mention of the gash alongside my head—which I don't remember receiving. Couldn't really call it a battle without damaging my skull in some way, however. The most worrying part of that injury was I no longer had my hat. Lost in the village somewhere.

"Is it worth going back to loot the demon? You didn't get experience from the undead, did you?" Ren furrowed her brow.

I shook my head. "No experience. It would be dangerous to return. They'll either be on the hunt for us or they'll be on the move to consolidate near Candlekeep."

Her head tilted. "So sure of their plans?"

"Without access to blood and with their groups being cut down by the day, it would make the most sense for them to hedge their losses and combine into one unit to assault the city."

Tanya nodded along with my thoughts. "That's the most pragmatic thing to do. Otherwise, she'll be losing most of her power through attrition."

"Which is what *we* want," Ren surmised.

We each murmured our agreements, but there seemed to be little else we could do at present. Most of my wounds could be healed away, leaving me with the exhaustion and trauma. They wouldn't allow me to whisk it away to something else, and . . . I supposed I agreed with them. Trouble was they might not want me to adventure at all today, and we didn't have the time to sit around.

I was gradually working up the courage to tell them I would soldier on when Ren placed her hand on my knee. My eyes went up to meet hers, and although she looked emotionally drained, some of the ire had worn away.

"Look . . . I won't keep going on at you over this. All I will say is you need to stop suffering alone. Not everything is your sole burden. If we did the show together and I was sitting beside you right now with a broken leg and bloodied suit, I would still be ten times happier than I am being *fine* but left out."

My tongue caught in my mouth. It wasn't just about her being worried for my safety, but my constant need to try to keep her safe by absorbing danger like a magnet. I kept saying we were a partnership, but I was too scared myself to allow her to be an equal in everything.

"You don't have to say anything." She gave me a soft smile. "I can read your eyes like a book, trickster." The hand on my knee gave it a squeeze.

If anything, I was glad I had given her that foot massage earlier—otherwise she would be a few levels more annoyed at me. I was mentally making light of the situation because the weight of what I wanted to say felt oddly prophetic despite how simple the arranged words were.

"I won't leave you behind again."

Her eyes brightened and read my expression. A tentative couple of seconds before she nodded. "I believe you."

Wolf shifted his weight into my chair and turned his head up to glare at me. "What about me?"

I smiled and looked around the group who had just been audience to the elf and me hashing out our emotional fragility. "Of course. Next time, you'll all be up onstage with me."

Tanya rolled her eyes. "Perhaps then one of us could stop you from half killing yourself performing tricks."

"It does seem as though your Domain just causes you injury," Quinn agreed.

I shrugged but maintained my smile. Some truth to their statements. What would have happened if I had gone back with them? No doubt the zombie horde would have continued to pursue us until we were found. Syther was intent on getting his revenge, after all. Perhaps we could have prepared the cottage area to expect such an assault? It would be putting us in a last-stand scenario again, which we were keen to avoid.

At the end of the day—or whatever time it currently was—there was no use debating over the what-ifs. The demon's Domain had pushed me into making the selfish decision. My unfettered power turned the tables on him, but it could have easily gone the other way. Even worse if we had all stayed.

"We need to go level," I eventually announced. "As I have trauma, I will have to sit back and just leech your efforts. Tanya, any repeatable Quests down toward the southeast?"

"Back that way?" Her brow furrowed. "Let me check the Map."

"Ren." I turned to the elf. "I'll need you to be our eyes while we travel. If we are being tracked, then I want an arrow through their neck before the rest of us even see them."

She gave me a nod. "Your fragile skull is safe with me, baby bird."

As much as I tried to ignore the new pet name, I couldn't help but pull a face in response—much to her amusement. "Wolf and Quinn, follow whatever direction Tanya gives you. We need to hit level thirteen today. No excuses."

It was a bit much for me to be bossing them about after what I had done, but in some ways they needed to see I was still in peak form. Persistent injuries and missing hat aside, *I was.*

We packed up our chairs, and Tanya sent a location over. Hour and a half of travel. My left leg was aching and sore, but she passed me the painkilling idol, and it soothed away the worst of it. Wolf led from the front. Ren stuck like glue to me in the middle, her bow out and ready as soon as we started off. Quinn and Tanya held the rear.

"Sure you don't want to go back for your hat, trickster?" She raised an eyebrow at me.

Couldn't deny that I had considered it. "No. I have all that is important to me right here."

"Mushy shit won't get you back in my good books." She tutted. "But . . . it smooths over the process. You *still* owe me for the <Shuffle> bullshit, and you pulled *this* off? Dickbag." She nudged me with her elbow, her eyes not showing the disdain that her furrowed brow signaled.

"I should have saved the foot rub for now, huh?"

She rolled her eyes and looked away.

I still had much to learn about . . . well, everything, really. I'm not sure where the break between normal human, Slime-killing adventurer, and demonic charmer had come about. Perhaps I shouldn't give myself too many props on the last one until I'd patched things over with Ren.

When they say history has a habit of repeating itself, I didn't think it would be on such a regular basis. My head injuries. Being humbled when my Party cared for my well-being. Hurting myself gaining new power to the ire of those closest to me.

"For all that the System does to try to get me alone, I have realized one thing." I squinted as the afternoon daylight ground away at my tired eyes. "I do not do well on my own."

Ren turned back to me. "I'm pretty sure you could bullshit and solo anything at this point."

I shook my head. "Maybe, but every time it happens, I fall a little further. Injure myself in becoming more of a monster."

"You're not a *monster*, Max." She sighed. "Just an asshole who thinks he can win. Mostly, you *can* and *do*."

Perhaps if they had been present during my Domain uses, she might have a different opinion. I always felt . . . uncontested within them. As if the System itself hadn't considered that it might have demons with such power. Was it making do with what it thought I should be allowed, or was I creating my own power unchallenged?

I brought up my Chat as messages beeped in.

[**Ruby: <{o>o}>?]**
[**Ruby: Are you okay?**]
[**Max: I still live.**]
[**Ruby: Something to do with your arm?**]
[**Max: Rolo's twin.**]

[Ruby: Ah, shit! I guess you won.]
[Ruby: Don't tell her I told you this . . .]
[Ruby: But Fiona was pretty worried about you!]

I spent a second cycling back, realizing that I had messaged the fighter instead of Ren or my Party in my injured haze.

[Max: I roughed myself up pretty bad—how's things there?]
[Ruby: Peachy~]
[Ruby: Taking it slow. Most people here are *not* chucklefucks.]
[Ruby: Maybe coming back there in a few days?]
[Max: Oh! I'll keep you updated if anything big happens.]
[Ruby: Thanks, Max! <{^>^}>]

I didn't have the stomach to go back through the log of messages the Party had sent me after the scroll incident. Instead, I sighed and closed it down. Took to looking at the scenery.

There was a silence between the elf and me that was a little uncomfortable. I had thrown an ice cube into our love nest, and now we were both trying to squirm away from it to avoid the chill. I hadn't even clocked that my suit was half tatters— the other half soaked with blood or zombie mulch.

With a furrowed brow at the state of my outfit, I switched to my underwear so that my suit could repair. There must be some way of getting a spare . . .

"Max!"

My eyebrow raised as I turned away from the screen to Ren. "What?"

"Seriously? In the middle of the day?" She had gone a little flush but was mostly concerned that I might have hit my head harder than it looked.

I checked downstairs to make sure I was actually wearing some form of undergarments—which I was. So I shrugged. "You've seen it all. I'm sure Wolf does not care. Tanya has certainly seen a lot worse, and Quinn needs to know what he is going to die for, surely?"

"Something worthy," the fixer murmured from the back.

Ren shot them a glare, but I was correct on all accounts. "It's not just that. What if we are attacked?"

"Technically, I am still in my equipped gear, so I still have my Stats." My armor value was in a ditch at the best of days, being a caster. Seminudity was only a short step down. "Plus, I have trauma, so I'm not allowed to get involved."

Her eyes narrowed. "You're really going to sit out while we farm System-created?"

"I won't lift a finger. Not even to summon a hound."

It was unlike me to sit out and not be the star of the show. Perhaps a hard sell, but given that we had just recovered from my rocky and selfish decision-making, I was willing to make the sacrifice. We could have a moment of almost recovery where I didn't put myself at risk for a change.

There were surely darker skies ahead and further ways in which I could absorb harm like some manner of sponge. For now, all that mattered was being accepted by my peers. Step one was getting them to believe that I could be trustworthy and sensible for an hour or two. I glanced at Ren to see how much she was buying my promise.

At first, she looked as though she might make an exception and even allow me to participate. Eventually she shrugged the notion away, her shoulder cold for a little longer. "Words are one thing, trickster. Let's see it first." Her eyes went back out to keeping watch.

I smiled and accepted her partial acceptance. It was almost enough for me to feel optimistic about the rest of the day. I would give her exactly the show she needed.

After all, seeing *was* believing.

About the Author

Kleggt is the author of the Death of the Party and Demonic Magician series, originally released on Royal Road. Upon clawing his way out of the depths of Scheduling Hell as a Forever DM, he began writing web novels, channeling his love of world-building and oddball characters into his own LitRPG and progression fantasy stories.

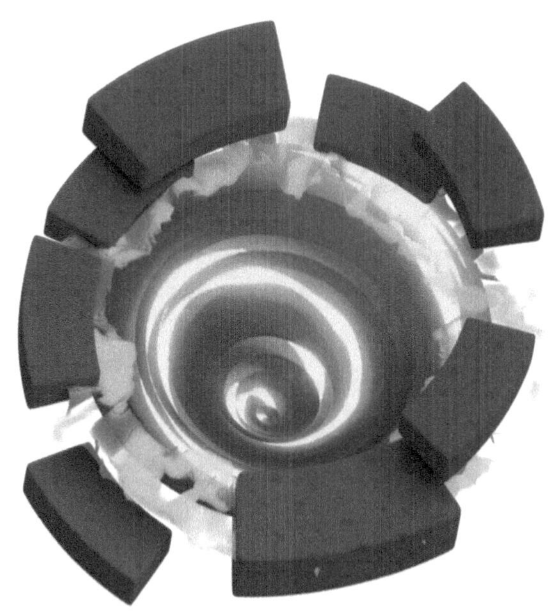

RESPAWN YOUR CURIOSITY

follow us on our socials

 podiumentertainment.com

 @podiumentertainment

 /podiumentertainment

 @podium_ent

 @podiumentertainment